ALSO BY ALICE HANOV

The Spare Who Became the Heir and Other Stories
The Head, the Heart, and the Heir
The Heir Rises
The Last True Heirs

BROKEN SONS

BROKEN SONS

ALICE HANOV

Gryphon
Press

Gryphon Press

Published by Gryphon Press
Waterloo, Ontario

Second Edition

Paperback: 978-1-7780476-7-1
Hardcover: 978-1-7780476-9-5
Hardcover Special Edition: 978-1-998835-00-3
KDP: 978-1-7780476-8-8

Edited by Intrepid Literary
Cover design by The Book Designers

This book is for my sister, Denise.
My own Daniel who's by my side every day, even if I can't see her.

Dear Reader,

Please be aware that this book deals with sensitive subject matters including mental health struggles, trauma, severe bodily harm, and abuse of various kinds. I handle them in a way that helps the characters learn and grow, similar to my journey, but I understand that many of these topics are troubling for readers.

If you'd like a list of what exactly this book will touch on, please see my website, AliceHanov.com, or scan the code below with your phone.

Happy reading, and take care of yourself.

Alice

CHAPTER I
ALEX

"Whatever deal you made isn't worth it!"

The desperation in Aaron's voice made Alex's heart break. She swallowed hard. "A week with you, even for decades of servitude, was worth more to me than centuries of freedom without you. You'll be a great king, Aaron. Have the faith in yourself that I do."

Please understand. I love you too much to let you die because I made a mistake. I can't live in a world that doesn't have you in it.

Alex turned and took her uncle Moorloc's hand. Wind sent Alex's chestnut hair swirling around her pale face as Aaron, her father's garden, and Warren's castle disappeared and the cracking sound echoed in a strange, massive hall.

Despite the late hour, Moorloc's castle hall was as bright as daytime without a single candle in sight. The scent of fire hit Alex before she heard the crackling. She glanced up and gasped, bringing her hand to her mouth. The entire hall was illuminated by flames dancing across the ceiling. Somehow, the room was still ice-cold, and she shivered. She was about to pull water from the air when a hand squeezed her shoulder.

"That won't do any good. I've enchanted the hall ceilings to burn all night to provide light. You can't douse it with water, and it creates no heat." Flickers of flames lit up Moorloc's ashen face as he released her.

How is that even possible? Pulling Aaron's cloak tighter, Alex carefully examined the room. The hall looked older than her mother's castle, and it was in nearly the same state of disrepair. Pieces were missing from the walls, floors, and ceilings. The weathered stones looked as if they'd stood here for centuries. The wall opposite the door had an intricately carved throne with two smaller thrones on either side. Alex stepped toward it but froze and clutched her satchel strap as she looked back at her uncle.

Moorloc nodded and motioned for her to go look. He crossed his arms and stoically watched her.

The throne was larger than the ones in Warren and Datten and featured more elaborate carvings. The cushion was the same violet color Moorloc's cloak had been at the tournament. On the spindle was the same infinity symbol that was on both her uncles' necks.

The mark of Merlin for the Titan of Merlin.

Along the sides and the arms were smaller shapes. Looking carefully, Alex realized they were the other line symbols that Merlock had taught her—an ax for Ares, a leaf for Celtics, a grave for Hades, the Mire mountain, the clouded moon for the Mystics, waves of Poseidon, flames of Salem, and the Tiere fox head. Two smaller thrones flanked Moorloc's. On the right stood a simple throne with the Merlin mark and on the left ... Alex's blood ran cold. The second throne was identical to the first, but the mark carved into the spindle was that of Cassandra.

Alex bent toward the gold cushion sitting on the seat. *The same gold as Datten.* She moved her fingers across the fabric. It was softer than any material in Warren. Holding her breath, Alex moved her fingers to trace her symbol on the chair.

"Had Datten not interfered, we would have brought you here as soon as your mother died," Moorloc said.

Alex jumped back. She hadn't heard him come up behind her. "What do you mean?"

"This seat was your mother's. Anytime she visited, she sat beside me. In the place of honor."

Alex looked up at Moorloc's face. "What about Lygari?" *Do you not see how much you mistreat your son? It's no wonder he's so terrible.*

"I moved him to sit with the men."

"Wouldn't that upset him?"

"Nonsense. He realizes that the place at my side has always been for the most powerful sorcerer, and that, my little prophetess, is the daughter of Cassandra. The *Titan* of Cassandra. First, it was your mother. Now it's you."

"What exactly makes someone a titan?"

"A titan is the most powerful living sorcerer of their line. They each embody the entirety of their line's specific powers and wield them with a depth and precision others could only dream of. It's why our eyes shift to our line's color. When we harness that immense power, our eyes change because we become the living embodiment of those powers. Some even glow, depending on the situation and the sorcerer."

"How long is a sorcerer a titan?"

"Until death. Or another surpasses them in skill and power. It is possible for them to surrender the title, but it's rarely done."

"How can I be a titan already? I'm barely of age."

"More important is the level of power. By winter solstice, you'll have all of yours. So even though you're young, your powers are beyond your years."

You forced my remaining powers on me without ever asking. What should have taken decades to arrive will now take months.

Moorloc's smirk sent a chill down her spine. Turning away from him, Alex spotted the only two portraits in the entire room. They covered nearly the entire back wall. The first was identical to the one in her mother's castle and depicted Moorloc with a young Lygari. Their matching gold eyes and black hair against the gray stones around them made their skin look sickly pale. Beside it was a painting of Merlock, Moorloc, and Victoria. Alex looked identical to her mother, from the waves in her hair to the pale pinkish hue of her skin. Her cousin Megesti resembled Alex and her mother, with the same chestnut brown hair and emerald eyes. Megesti's father, Merlock, was the combination of the siblings with black hair and green eyes, but here it was impossible to see since Merlock's face had been burned away. The sight of Merlock's burned face made Alex swallow a terrified scream. She stumbled back and slammed into her uncle.

"Understand that he's the reason she's dead, and had you not chosen correctly, he'd have caused your demise too. Victoria served Datten for decades, but they abandoned her the moment she needed them. My brother is as guilty as they are. If it wouldn't strip me of my power, I'd have murdered him years ago," Moorloc said.

Goosebumps erupted along Alex's arms as a shiver ran through her core at Moorloc's icy tone. Even Aaron's soft cloak was no match for the chill that suddenly filled the room.

Alex glanced at the ceiling. *How can it burn when the ground feels like ice? Wait ...*

"Strip you of your power? Is that the consequence of hurting your own kin?" Alex asked. *Does that mean you can't hurt me?*

"Not kin—*twin*. Sorcerer twins cannot seriously wound

each other without suffering the consequences themselves. Enough questions. It's late, and you're tired. Follow me and pay attention. I'll provide you with a rundown of the castle once, so pay attention. You'll need to know where you will be expected to be at what time. Then I'll show you to your sleeping arrangements. I've procured everything you could need and left it in your room," Moorloc said.

Alex pulled Aaron's cloak tightly around herself when she realized Moorloc was watching her. *He must expect an answer.*

"A tour would be helpful."

Moorloc motioned for her to follow him. Terror burned in her chest as she swallowed the lump in her throat and obeyed. The only sound Alex heard was the crackle of the fire above and their boots on the stones as they entered the hallway.

The flames followed them down the ceiling of the deserted hallways as they made their way around the entire first floor.

Alex noticed the bare stone walls as they passed. *Is the lack of decor because the fire would destroy it, or does he prefer it this way?*

The castle was mundane and not the magical structure she'd been expecting. Other than the fire lighting the ceiling, everything was ordinary. It was square, and the main hallway looped around the castle perimeter. Each corner had a simple square guard tower with a fifth in the middle of the castle. It required one to enter through the central courtyard. The outer hallway led to the various rooms, including the first hall they'd appeared in, guards' quarters, armory, kitchen, library, and two large bedrooms.

"This bedroom," Moorloc explained, pointing at a massive black wooden door, "is mine. Lygari's room is on the opposite side of the building. You'll be staying there while you are with us."

"In Lygari's room?" Alex asked. Her palms went clammy, worrying about how little she trusted her cousin.

"Yes. I need to ensure your safety while you adjust to life here. He's been moved to another room."

"But why—"

He raised his hand to show this conversation was over. "As I was saying, while you live here, you'll have access to most of the castle and the grounds, but a few areas are off-limits. My bedroom is one of them. As trusting as I am with you, I'm old enough to know that we all have our secrets. The Prince of Datten is finally aware of how good you are at keeping secrets."

At the mention of Aaron, Alex's pounding heart froze in her chest. Moorloc stared at her as she fought to push back the heartache desperate to escape her.

Please forgive me, Aaron. I had to.

"I'll respect your privacy, within reason, as you find your footing here. And you will respect ours."

Silently, Alex nodded. Moorloc broke his stare and motioned for her to follow him down the hallway again. As they rounded the corner to the back of the castle, Alex looked longingly at the library Moorloc had shown her.

"The library is yours to visit whenever you desire. There are books that will help you with your studies and some for pleasure too. I'll assign you specific books and readings to go with whatever it is we are working on at that moment."

"Whenever I wish?"

"Naturally. Your mother kept odd hours when she was studying. Some days she'd be up at dawn, and some days she'd never sleep. I assume you take after her in that regard. Sorcerers are controlled by their mental curiosity and less by their primal need for sleep or food."

Alex exhaled loudly. Moorloc looked down at her as she tried to hide her face.

"You are my niece; you don't need to hide your feelings from me. Unlike my brother, I am the titan of our line, meaning I have the additional powers for our kin. I can sense when you have powerful feelings about something. For example, at this moment, you are feeling relief, guilt, and sadness."

Her arms twitched. *How? How does he know exactly what I'm feeling? I'm going to have to go back to hiding my emotions.*

Moorloc looked smug. "I presume you feel sadness at leaving the boy you believe you're in love with, but you'll learn you could never be happy with someone as simple as him. You feel relief at knowing that you are not alone in your strange behaviors. Lastly, you feel guilty about that relief because it tells you that your decision to come here was correct."

Alex avoided looking at him. *Aaron isn't just some boy I think I love. I gave up my freedom to save him and Stefan, even if my adopted brother will be furious I put his life above mine after everything he sacrificed to keep me safe. You may sense what I feel, but you don't understand the reasons behind it.* Wanting to end that train of thought, she spun around and scurried down the hall.

Moorloc cleared his throat, standing before another door.

Alex stopped and glanced over her shoulder. Without a word, he opened it and stepped inside. There were no other doors for the entire stretch of hallway at the back of the castle.

This room must be immense.

Alex followed him and gasped. The lab was as large as Warren's main hall and dining hall combined. Mesmerized, Alex wandered around the room, desperate to take it all in.

It smelled the same as Merlock's lab: fire and strange herbs. Yet here the stench in the lab was potent despite the massive size. Moorloc had covered the wall closest to the door in a gigantic bookcase. Alex traced her fingers along the stiff spines of the journals, modern reference books, and ancient texts. Moorloc's footsteps moved away from her. A quick scan of the shelves revealed that none of the books were from her line. She crept to the next corner and saw another monstrous set of shelves covered in jars and tins filled with bizarre plants, herbs, and all manner of things. Despite being curious, Alex avoided getting too close. A jar had jumped at her once when she tapped it in Merlock's lab.

A giant white bear rug lay in the middle of the room. Alex stopped and bent over to examine it. Despite being on the floor, the fur was as pristine and smooth as the silk lining of Aaron's cloak around her shoulders. She'd never seen a white bear. The rest of the room had a large table and a fireplace with a pile of cooking pots stacked next to it, a wooden chest, and a giant wall of weapons and tools.

These would have fascinated Stefan.

She carefully examined the various lengths and styles of whips, daggers, swords, bows, and staves.

"I'll bring you back in here tomorrow when we go over the rules," Moorloc said from behind her. "Afterward, you'll have unlimited access so long as you follow those rules."

Rules? Alex exhaled to control her retort and slowly turned to look at her uncle. She kept her features stoic to not allow him to see her fear.

"Of *course* there are rules, Alexandria. Discipline is critical to the successful training of any young sorcerer. You, however, will need additional rules."

"Why? Because I'm a girl?" Despite her fear, Alex frowned at her uncle, making the flames on the ceiling crackle and light up more. She swallowed hard, worried her temper was about to get her into serious trouble.

"Yes, but not for the reason you think. Daughters of Cassandra hold the power of that line. It means that you carry more power than Lygari."

"More than *you?*" Alex gulped. The words came out, and she instantly regretted it.

Moorloc's eyes narrowed, and his lips scowled for an instant. Had she not been watching him, she'd have missed it.

He stepped directly in front of her. Icy cold spread across Alex's chin as he tilted her face to look at him and smiled. "That, my little prophetess, remains to be seen and is precisely why you will have more rules. Are you ready to see the rest?"

Alex nodded and followed Moorloc out of the lab. At the door, she paused, looking back. Her mother had been in this room. *Maybe some small part of her is still here. Something that can help me get through this.*

Moorloc led her down a corridor, past more guard rooms and the armory. The entire second floor was just hallway after hallway of rooms for the mercenaries. The basement was damp and filled with old storage rooms.

"Now to your room." Moorloc led her back to the main floor.

"Where is the kitchen again?"

"Beside the hall. You are not to go there. The servants have too much work to do to entertain you. Meals are served twice a day at breakfast and dinner."

Once in the east hallway, they stopped at a large black door that matched Moorloc's bedroom. He turned the handle and pushed it open for Alex. Inside, the fire on the ceiling sprang to life. Cautiously, Alex entered, and Moorloc sent the fireplace roaring to life.

"The wardrobe is full of simple clothes—the ones you were so fond of while training in Warren. I had the servants sew them in gold and violet in honor of our lines."

Alex unfastened her cloak and hung it on the hooks next to the wardrobe. She removed her satchel and, after looking around, hung it up on another hook. The inside of the wardrobe was similar to Aaron's in Warren except it was all gold and violet. Something sparkled and caught Alex's eye.

"Gold thread to embroider your line mark," Moorloc explained before she could ask. He scratched his impeccably trimmed beard as he watched her.

"Is Lygari angry that I'm in here? I could have taken the other room. It wasn't necessary to move him." Alex closed the wardrobe and crossed toward him but stopped when she spotted a massive rug on the floor in the middle of the room. She crouched to examine it as Moorloc continued.

"This room has always been occupied by the second most powerful sorcerer in the castle. When your mother visited, she stayed here. Lygari has had it for decades, but he's aware you are more powerful than him, even if you lack focus and control."

Alex glanced up from the rug but couldn't read Moorloc's face. Merlock had never looked at her like that, so she had no basis to go on.

"It's a lynx," Moorloc said.

"I thought so. I've never seen one this large."

"It's from the Forbidden Lands. They grow larger there. I used this one to send a message."

"How? Why?"

"No more questions. It's early in the morning, and there will be enough time for all your questions in the months to come."

Alex's knees buckled as she stood. *Months or years.*

"Until you get your bearings on how this place runs, remain in the castle and courtyard, but I expect the library will keep you busy for a while."

Alex looked up at her uncle, clenching her hands hard enough to hurt. The pain held back the sadness that threatened to engulf her.

"Welcome to your new home, little Harbinger. I'll send Lygari to fetch you tomorrow for dinner. Breakfast is early, and I expect you'll sleep through it." He turned to leave but paused. "I don't think I need to remind you that any attempt to escape or even leave the grounds without permission will forfeit the lives of both the lout and whelp."

I'm well aware Stefan and Aaron's lives depend on me behaving according to your archaic rules. Any slipup and you could undo the healing that saved them after I lost my temper and gutted them.

Alex nodded and looked down at the lynx pelt. When the door banged shut, all of her resolve drained from her. Droplets hit her legs as the tears ran freely. Hours ago, she'd been with Aaron in his bed. Parts of her skin were still on fire and tingled from his touch, and the soreness between her legs meant it hadn't been a beautiful dream. She held her face in her hands and cried.

When she was drained of tears, Alex wrapped her arms around herself and struggled to stand. After her third try, she managed it and trudged to the hook where she'd hung her satchel. She pulled out a worn gold Datten tunic. As she carried it back to the bed, her tears started again. The wood was dark and the quilt was gold with her line mark on it, but the style was identical to those in Warren. She threw back the quilt and crawled onto the giant bed. The fabric was even softer than what she'd slept on back home.

Will I ever see Warren again?

After she pulled up the gold bedding, Alex curled up in a tight ball. Clutching Aaron's shirt, she breathed in deeply, smelling him, and cried, filling her chest with a burning pain until she fell into a restless sleep.

CHAPTER 2
AARON

The town bells in Warren rang four times as Prince Aaron marched down the hallway away from the room of his godfather, King Edward. Despite Aaron's protests, the generals and kings decided they'd wait until after breakfast to summon the Warren knights Aaron had selected. They would embark for Datten on horseback and recover long enough to collect the chosen Datten knights. They'd remain in Datten until Aaron's father, King Emmerich, and General Jerome Wafner deemed them ready; then they'd begin the ride through the Ogre Mountains toward the kingdom of Betruger. If everything went according to plan, they'd be there in a month. Then all Aaron would have to do is convince King Harold to help him—or die trying.

It was early in the morning, and Aaron turned down the deserted side hallway and climbed the stairs that led to his room. Without thinking, he turned left and froze when he opened his door. He'd forgotten this wasn't his room anymore. One last time, Aaron crossed the threshold into his old room.

An hour before, Alex had been in here with him; she'd shared his bed.

I was such a fool. What if she gave herself to me because she knew she was leaving? Does she even want to marry me, or did she say yes knowing she'd get out of it? Why did I let her do this to herself?

"No. She said yes *before* the accident. She loves me, and I'm going to get her back," Aaron said out loud, surveying the damage of his room. "Please want me to find you. I need your love for me to be as strong as mine is for you."

Stepping over the shelf debris, Aaron could see someone had turned his dresser over and emptied it. The scattered books were missing, and so were Alex's crown and letter. *Did Megesti take them?* With a final breath, Aaron left his room and crossed the hallway to the room that belonged to his dead brother, Daniel—his new room. Until he had Alex back, he couldn't face the room they'd made love in. The taste of her still clung to his lips, and her scent would still be in that bed.

His new room was larger and had a balcony. He'd refused to use it after Daniel died. But with his room in shambles, it was this or a proper royal suite, and he intended to move his things one last time—when Alex returned and they were married. He'd move into her suite and never move again, especially knowing how she despised the idea of a king and queen sleeping in separate rooms. Aaron opened his wardrobe and realized that his gold cloak was missing along with his favorite training shirt. She'd loved his cloak when he'd given it to her all those months ago, and he'd insisted she keep it. But it had been ruined in that unfortunate training accident where she'd set herself and her father on fire. He smiled. *I hope you took them as reminders of me.*

He saw their matching gold crowns sitting on the side

table. Aaron remembered how badly Alex wanted him to tell her how he could tell them apart.

Daniel threw mine at our father's head once. The royal goldsmith never could get that one prong perfectly straight again.

The servants had moved both crowns since only he and his parents could tell them apart. Alex's crown would stay here, but his would travel with him. Nestled between them was his great-grandmother's ring, which he'd used to propose. Inside his crown was her letter. Exhaling, Aaron picked up the letter and sat down on his bed.

My dearest Aaron,

I love you. I love you more than I could ever tell you in this lifetime, and I need you to know that everything I said and did this past week was true. I meant all of it.

Please don't be angry with me. I know if you aren't yet, you'll be later when you wonder why I didn't tell you what I'd done. When I hurt you, Merlock took you away so quickly. I realized I couldn't live in a world without you, couldn't fathom a life that didn't have you in it, so I made a deal with Moorloc. He saved you and Stefan, and for that the price was giving myself over to be taught by him until he thinks I'm ready to return, however long that may be. But at least I was allowed a week with you.

Don't torture yourself wondering why I didn't ask for your help. I couldn't risk Moorloc learning that I'd told you. It would have broken my oath and undone your healing. I feel responsible for Datten losing Daniel. I couldn't let them lose you too.

I need you to know this: I trust you.

I trust you to become the man your father expects of you, to take care of Michael and Stefan now that I'm gone, to be strong and brave for my father, but most of all, I trust you to come for me. This entire week when we were planning how to get my family's journals, every hint and suggestion I gave you was to help you find me. Your strategies are always as sound as your father's.

Use that Datten piece of you and put everything together.

Be the crown prince you were born to be. Earn the loyalty of your men, discover your Edward, and convince him to join your side. Then come for me, and with my blood, you'll be able to find me. I'll learn all I can while I wait, so it'll be safer for us all when I come home.

I'm not afraid of Moorloc or of my powers. The only thing I'm truly afraid of is a world without you. I took so much from you, and all I could leave behind for you was my heart. Guard it well.

Forever yours,

Alex

Tears streamed down his face as he read the letter over and over again. Finally, when he'd cried out everything he had in him, Aaron stood and tossed his crown in the pile on his bed. He fastened his sword to his belt and began gathering things for the journey. He picked up a gold chain from his wardrobe, slipped Alex's ring onto it, and placed it around his neck. The second he got her back, the ring would be back on her finger and never leave it again as long as he lived.

He ran his hand through his golden hair as he moved to his wardrobe and took the old copy of *The Iliad* he'd stolen from her, his other favorite shirt, and a few necessities. As he moved to close the wardrobe, he paused. In the drawer, he spotted the green handkerchief Alex had given him at the start of the tournament. The stitching was so terrible he couldn't help but laugh.

Jessica needs to give up on teaching you needlework. Alex's lady's maid had her hands full with that task.

He'd accepted her favor and planned to bring it to the joust, but after all the misunderstandings with Stefan and

Cameron about the suitor business, he'd left it behind. More than anything, he needed to find Alex to make that right. Even a lifetime might not be enough to truly earn her forgiveness for not hearing her out when she needed him to.

No wonder she didn't tell me about making a deal.

Bringing it to his lips, Aaron kissed the handkerchief and placed it on the pile.

The bells rang five times, and Aaron sighed. The kitchens would start breakfast, but he wouldn't wait. Dropping his plain shirt on the bed, he put on his formal Datten-crested shirt and crown. Then he grabbed his list of knights and hurried down to the stables.

Aaron pushed Thunder harder than he should have without a proper warm-up, but he didn't care. Even though he knew Cameron would help, part of him worried. *He might not do it for me, but for his king and princess ... he'll do it for Alex. He has to.*

When he arrived at the Strobel estate, he tied Thunder to a post and pounded on the door until Reginald, an elderly man in a long, tailored coat, answered it. The man gasped when he realized it was Aaron.

"Your Highness." He bowed to Aaron as he opened the door, and Aaron strode past him toward his uncle's office.

"I need to see my uncle and Cameron immediately. Don't even let them get dressed. And Thunder is tied outside."

"Yes, Your Highness." Reginald dashed upstairs after closing the door.

Bernhard Strobel's office looked like a small library. He'd covered the walls in bookcases except for the one with the fireplace. A massive carved desk stood in the far corner, and two large comfortable brown leather chairs faced the fireplace. Above the hearth were a pair of swords and a shield with the Warren crest.

Aaron stood staring at the shield when the door opened and Cameron trudged in dressed in his sleeping clothes. He snorted at Aaron's formal attire and crown.

"So it isn't my cousin who dragged us out of bed but the *Crown Prince* of Datten. What do you *want,* Aaron?" Cameron bumped Aaron with his shoulder as he pushed past him to sit in his favorite chair. His blond hair sparkled in the glow from the fire, making his light bronze skin look almost as golden as Aaron's hair.

Aaron opened his mouth to say something when his uncle Bernhard arrived. At night, the man looked even more like an older version of Cameron, except his coloring was pinkish like Aaron's. Cameron's complexion came from his mother. Aaron hoped his uncle wouldn't be as upset. At least Bernhard had quickly changed and was wearing his less formal attire of black pants and a sea-blue tunic, the clothes he wore whenever Aaron came for dinner as his nephew and not crown prince.

"Aaron, what's happened?" Bernhard motioned to Aaron to sit at the desk, but Aaron held up his hand, lifted the empty chair beside Cameron with ease, and brought it to the desk. Bernhard gave Cameron a reproachful look before taking his seat behind his desk. Cameron groaned and moved the other chair next to Aaron.

"I need your help," Aaron said before Cameron even sat down.

"Aww, did Alex finally realize you're *annoying* and leave you?" Cameron crossed his arms and smirked as he leaned back in his seat.

"Cameron, behave," Bernhard said as Reginald arrived with the tea. "Thank you, Reginald. That will be all."

"Yes, sir." He bowed and slipped out of the room silently.

"All right, Aaron, let's hear what's so urgent that it couldn't wait for a civilized hour," Bernhard said as he poured each of them a cup. Cameron's blue eyes glared at Aaron.

"We need your help," Aaron said. He wiped his palms against his knees, trying desperately to stop their shaking.

"With what?" Cameron snapped.

"With horses." Aaron held his list out to Cameron, who snatched it. As soon as he glanced at it, his eyes widened and his body tensed.

"Why do you need fresh horses for fifty men?"

Aaron looked from Cameron to Bernhard. "Bernhard, within the hour, you're going to be summoned to an emergency council meeting where Edward and my father will explain that we're going to war with Moorloc. I'm going to Betruger with the men on that list."

"*I'm* on this list," Cameron said, looking from his father to Aaron.

"What happened, Aaron?" Bernhard asked.

"Moorloc took Alex. I'm going to get her back."

"What do you mean *took*?" Cameron was on the edge of his seat, suddenly interested in what Aaron had to say.

Aaron explained what had happened earlier that night, leaving out certain personal details. As he talked about the meeting between the generals and the kings, Bernhard listened intently while Cameron kept rereading the list of men.

"So I'm here to ask for your help. I'll even *beg* because I'm not asking as the cousin you're furious with or as the Crown Prince of Datten. I'm asking as the man in love with your future queen because if I could give up my crown and get her back *right now,* I would."

"What do you need from us?" Bernhard asked.

Aaron stared at Cameron, begging him to look at him.

"From you, Uncle Bernhard, I need horses. A lot of horses.

Strong and fast enough to carry our men to Datten and then through the Ogre Mountains."

"And me?" Cameron asked as he looked up at him.

"I need your skills. I'm taking a cavalry of men to the Ogre Mountains to try to speak to the King of Betruger and need someone who can help with the horses. There's no one better than you—no one I *trust* more than you."

Cameron turned to face his father. Without a word, he leaned forward and picked up the tea his father had poured for him.

"The decision of whether to go is yours, Cameron. You're old enough. But if you're looking for my permission, you have it," Bernhard said.

Cameron took a long sip of his tea before he looked back at Aaron. "I'll go, but not for you. You and I are far from being all right. I'll go for Edward, for Warren, and for *her*. We lived twelve years without our princess, and if I can help make sure we don't go another unnecessary day, I'll do it."

"Cameron, you're welcome to hate me for the rest of our lives if you help me get her back." Aaron finally allowed himself to breathe deeply. Leaning forward, he grabbed his tea.

"Which horses are you thinking, Cameron?" Bernhard asked.

Taking a long drink of tea, Aaron listened to Cameron and Bernhard debate back and forth about which horses to take. When his cup was empty, there was a knock on the office door.

"Enter," Bernhard said.

"Beg your pardon, sirs," Reginald said. "The younger Sir Bishop was at the door with a summons from the king. I informed him of His Highness's presence and sent him off to the next estate with assurances that I would pass on his message."

"Thank you, Reginald. As soon as my son is presentable, we'll head to the castle."

"I'll prepare the horses," Aaron said as they all stood and got ready to go.

ARRIVING AT THE CASTLE, Aaron, Bernhard, and Cameron headed straight to the throne room.

"Seems you beat us to the Strobels," General Matthew Bishop said when they arrived in the hall. His loose onyx hair fell against his rich brown skin when he nodded to Aaron.

"I did," Aaron said. "I wanted to ask for their help personally."

"We're happy to help however we can," Bernhard said. Aaron watched him strut over to Edward and Emmerich; they whispered together. Edward wore a simple Warren tunic like Bernhard, but it looked better on him. His dark brown complexion made the blue and silver stand out. His own father wore a gold tunic even though it washed out his pale complexion and was almost the same golden color as his hair.

"If I'm not needed here," Cameron said, "I'll head down to the stables. Gregory and I'll need to see what they have before we send knights to get supplies from our estate or the shops."

"Cameron," Edward called, leaving Emmerich and Bernhard to join them. "Thank you. I know you and Aaron aren't in a great place, and I'm sure you're not thrilled with my daughter either about how things turned out, but I want you to know I won't forget this."

"Of course, Your Royal Highness. I don't blame her. You gave her the choice, and she made it. Regardless of how I feel about Aaron's actions, she's still my princess, and I couldn't live with myself if I didn't do everything I could to help get her back." Cameron bowed to Edward and hurried out of the room.

Edward crossed his arms and turned to Aaron. "You're going to have to find some way to make things right with him, Aaron. He clearly cares for Alexandria."

"She's always had that effect on people," Michael said, arriving in the room with Stefan.

"We're ready to help. What can we do?" Stefan asked.

Emmerich arrived at Edward's side. Aaron noticed the color on his father's pale cheeks. *Hitting the ale harder than usual?*

"Michael, find Randal and see who's missing from Aaron's list. Once they arrive, let us know so Aaron can address the men and see who volunteers," Edward said.

Emmerich said, "Stefan, as the son of Datten's general and the captain of the princess's guard, we'll need your help to convince the council this is what's best for the kingdom. Your link to both kingdoms will come in handy. Aaron, you'll need to convince a group of our best men to follow you on a mission without ever having been in battle—sorry, an *actual battle*, as opposed to the recent skirmishes."

Aaron smiled mischievously at the kings before looking at Stefan. "And last, Michael needs to ask Jerome for Lady Jessica's hand before we leave."

Edward's blue eyes lit up as he turned to Michael with a wide grin. "Is this true, Michael? I can confidently say I approve of the match."

"As do I," Emmerich said.

"You know Alex and I do," Stefan said, fixing his brown eyes on Michael.

"I'll make a deal with you," Michael said, pushing his shoulders back and glaring at Aaron and Stefan. The candle-light set off his light copper skin, making his blue eyes seem brighter. "If you two can get every man on Aaron's list to come with us, I'll ask Jerome."

"Done," Aaron and Stefan answered in unison before Michael swallowed and left to find Randal.

"Stefan, would you go keep the council members company? We need to speak to Aaron," Edward said.

Stefan nodded and ambled toward the other council members.

"It's alarming how quickly he became good at that," Aaron said, watching Stefan speaking to the council members who had already arrived.

"He's Jerome's son. Same fiery red hair, build, pale complexion, rationality, and military might. The Wafner name commands respect. I think being around Alexandria made him constantly have to fight to be in charge because she tried to take over. Since *you* took all of her attention, he's found his footing," Edward said.

"You said you wanted to speak with me? I assume it wasn't about the Wafners," Aaron said.

"Indeed." Edward grabbed Aaron's arm and pulled him closer. "I'm giving you the pearl to take with you."

"Why?"

"You're going to Betruger. We've been fighting them for six hundred years, and I doubt they'll trust you. It's likely they'll want to imprison or even kill you. I believe the pearl will be a tempting enough gift to get you an audience with the king."

"You're giving Betruger your pearl?"

"Aaron, I would give Betruger my kingdom if it got us Alexandria back."

"That's an empty offer," Emmerich said. "They'd never be able to defend it, and Datten would take it back in a month. But I agree. The pearl goes with Aaron."

"Why would they want it?"

"It's not about the gift itself. It's what it'll provide for you," Edward said.

Aaron looked at his father, and it suddenly made sense. "The pearl's my *proof*—proof that I am who I say I am, that Alex means to me what I say she does. If the king uses it and sees his own past truths, he'll know mine are real too."

"Now you're thinking like a king," Emmerich said.

Aaron looked at the two men before him and couldn't help remembering Alex's words.

Find your Edward.

CHAPTER 3
ALEX

Alex slept until noon. When she awoke, the room was dim. A sliver of a window faced the courtyard. She remained in bed for most of the day, alternating between crying and sleeping until her body refused to allow her to do either anymore.

The room smelled musty and stale with a faint hint of burned wood. Alex shook her head and tried to push it out of her mind. She forced herself up and took in the room in the daylight. Alex wandered around but found no paintings, no treasures, and nothing of any emotional value. Glancing at the books on the sparse shelf, she found reference books and nothing to read for fun.

I never thought I'd feel pity for Lygari. But what kind of life must he have? Even at the camp where we were poor, we all had some personal things. She grabbed Aaron's tunic from the bed and took a deep breath, taking in his scent before tucking it away on the top shelf of the wardrobe. Then she unpacked the few meager things from her satchel she'd managed to grab before she left Warren. Her sparring clothes went into the wardrobe. When she saw Aaron's cloak, she swallowed hard to keep herself from crying again. She'd stolen this cloak to replace the first one.

I remember the look he gave me at the camp when he put his cloak on me to keep me warm. So thoughtful, so kind.

Along with the clothes, she pulled out her mother's favorite necklace, slipped it over her neck, and tucked it into her shirt. The jagged black stone chilled her skin but still comforted her. The strange stone wasn't obsidian, and despite asking a dozen masons and sculptors in Warren, Alex had never figured out what it was.

Maybe there are books about stones in the library.

Finally, she took out her books: the copy of *The Iliad* Aaron had left her when he stole her old one, the journal her mother had written to her, the old healing ledger, and two blank journals. One was to keep track of the lessons, skills, or powers she got here, and the other was to write to Aaron. Part of her hoped she'd manage to complete her training and be released in a year before anyone was hurt trying to save her. Then the journal would give Aaron a glimpse into her time here. But another part of her feared it would be a long time before Moorloc let her leave.

Looking toward the window, her curiosity got the better of her. Alex dropped the journals back into her satchel, slipped the bag over her shoulder, and crept out into the hallway and to the courtyard. The castle's fifth tower stood between her room and Moorloc's and was accessible through the courtyard. Alex was surprised to find the yard empty as she crept to the tower.

What in the Forbidden Lands ...?

The base of the tower was a bedroom. The floor was dirt, so everything smelled musty. There was a wardrobe missing a leg, so it leaned to one side, and the bed was small and broken.

Unease filled her, as if something horrible had happened here. She opened the wardrobe and found a few simple dresses and pants. When she moved to touch them, an icy wind tore through the room, slamming the wardrobe door shut. Alex jumped back. Her heart pounded as she rushed to the stairs in the corner and scanned the room. Confident no one was there, Alex ascended the stairs. The gentle thud of her footsteps echoed as she climbed. The slit windows provided little light, and there was no railing, so Alex trailed her fingers along the uneven stones as she climbed to the tower's viewing area. This was the tallest of the five towers, and the top was open all the way around to allow a view of the entire castle and surrounding area.

The view is incredible up here. I can see for miles.

To the north, the Oreean Sea beckoned. Alex hadn't realized how close they were to it. She closed her eyes and focused, and the lapping icy waves chilled her legs. The cries of the gulls found her as the salty air swirled into her lungs. Being this high up would take her out of the noise and stench of castle life. Opening her eyes set off a fluttering deep inside her as the sea sparkled like jewels, almost close enough to touch. Turning to the other three sides, Alex sighed. Despite the time she'd spent studying Torian terrain, she'd never grasped how massive the Ogre Mountains were.

The mountains imprison the castle the same way the castle imprisons me.

As far as her eyes could see, there was nothing but rocks and ever-growing mountains. Even if Aaron and her father wanted to come for her and Aaron could see the castle with her blood, it would be impossible for them to find their way through the mountains, especially with an army the size they'd need to take on Moorloc.

She set her satchel on the ground and walked back to the

north side to watch the water. As the waves crashed into the sea, she sniffed back tears. Even with the sea in the distance, the surrounding silence was overwhelming. She'd never been so alone in her entire life. There wasn't a soul here who cared about her.

What are my friends doing right now? Are Michael and Stefan angry too? Will Aaron ever forgive me, or does he think I betrayed him for not telling him? He has to believe I didn't want to leave. That I had to.

A bell rang in the castle. She took one last longing look at the sea to settle herself and then hurried down the stairs. When she reached her room and turned the doorknob, it flew from her hand, the open door revealing Lygari.

He sneered at her. "Snooping around already? He won't be pleased. Now move or you'll be late for dinner. No one is waiting for you to eat here, *princess*," he said.

Lygari loped ahead of her, forcing her to run to keep up.

The hall was set up with four long tables, and over two hundred mercenary men sat eating and shouting over each other. Mugs struck mugs, and silverware banged on the tables as they shouted at the servants to bring more. It was worse than a tavern. The smell of fish and bread made Alex's mouth water and stomach grumble, but mixed with the body odor of all those men, the smell made her queasy. She followed Lygari to the main table. Every man stopped eating and looked up at her. A few smirked and snickered; some scoffed while others stared. Their eyes were cold and cruel.

Warren knights had honor and showed respect, but it was clear these mercenaries didn't care for any of that. Alex's chest tightened, and her hands grew slick as she caught up with Lygari.

I may not like him, but at least he doesn't look at me like they do. They make me feel insignificant.

Individually, the men acted like any other she'd met except they were taller and many of them had strange colored eyes— all different shades of purple. She'd read that Betruger men were much taller than Warren men and even more so than Datten men.

Moorloc motioned for Alex and Lygari to take their seats. Lygari started to go left but caught himself and went right. Alex sat on Moorloc's left. She tried to get comfortable on her throne as a pale older woman dressed in plain clothes placed food in front of them. She moved so fast Alex didn't get to thank her, but when Alex looked at the food, she wrinkled her nose. She felt nauseated from her nerves and lack of sleep, and the violet-colored fish smelled sour. Swallowing the lump in her throat, she took a bite and realized how famished she was. Despite the unappetizing appearance, Alex finished her plate and mug of ale quickly.

Afraid to ask to be excused, she studied the room. As each table finished eating, another set of men replaced them. Their varied height, mismatched leather clothing, and shades of brown skin tones made it feel as if Alex were watching a living forest move around. Alex lost count after three full switches from the four massive tables. Soon after, men and women dressed in shabby clothes came to clean up, but when Alex tried to thank them, they fled from her. Alex wanted to know why but was too tired to ask. It could wait for another day.

"Shall we?" Moorloc rose from his chair and extended his hand to Alex. When she stood, he motioned for her to go ahead of him while Lygari followed. As they reached the hallway, Lygari headed off in the opposite direction.

"Where's he going?" Alex asked.

"To check the spells on your room."

"Why?"

"The mercenaries who came with us believe men were

meant to lead—never women. So a powerful sorceress who is also crown princess is more than most of them would tolerate. You'll need to learn your *place* quickly if you want to avoid drawing unwanted attention."

"My place?" Alex snarled.

"Yes, little titaness. It's a pity you didn't bring that lovely green pendant your idiot uncle stole for you."

"Stole for me?"

"It belonged to our mother. Merlin made it for her."

Alex wanted to know more but was reluctant to push.

"I didn't realize how many people lived here," she said as they arrived at the lab. Moorloc leaned in front of her and opened the door, and she followed him inside. Alex paused before the weapon wall again while Moorloc began the fire.

"You assumed I'd be powerful enough to protect myself? I'm flattered, but no. You're truly exceptional in your powers, Alexandria. Few sorcerers can wield the power you have growing inside you. Already you're more powerful than most sorcerers of Lygari's age—a fact that has enraged him since he met you at your welcome home celebration."

Alex thought back to first meeting Lygari. *He was so angry with me, and I didn't know why. But I lost control of my wind powers ... he must have realized how strong I was compared to him. No wonder he hates me.*

"I didn't ask for this power, and I don't want it," she said.

"True as that might be, do not let my son hear you saying that. It would not make him kinder to you. The indignation of so much power going to someone who didn't even want it would make him more resentful of you."

Alex groaned and took a seat at the table. She poked the bear rug with her foot as Moorloc moved to the chest and came back with a violet velvet bag. It made a thump on the table as he dropped it in front of Alex.

30

"That is for you."

Alex lifted the bag, and a wide gold bracelet spilled out onto the table. Alex immediately identified the marks carved into it as the ten line marks of the Forbidden Lands. At the top was an eleventh symbol, a ten-sided star.

"What is it?"

"It's a training tool used for young sorcerers with potentially dangerous powers. Once I place it on you, it'll be impossible for you to take it off until *I* decide you're ready. As you learn your powers, the marks of the lines corresponding to your skills will turn black. That way, we'll see where your talents lie. Inside the band is red steel."

Alex pushed it away. "What's red steel?"

"I see my brother hasn't taught you anything. They made red steel from ore that is soaked in dragon blood. Specifically, a dragon slayed violently. This releases toxins into the dragon's blood, and when it soaks into the ore, the steel becomes poisonous to sorcerers. Your bracelet has a spell around the steel to prevent it from hurting you. The ten-sided star allows me to remove a portion of the protection to drain your powers if needed. If you're losing control of a power, I can stop you using it, protecting you and us."

Moorloc held out his hand. His beard made his expression hard to read.

Alex sighed and placed her arm into his hand. A shiver ran up her arm and down her spine.

Grabbing the bracelet, he spoke the words so quickly Alex missed most of them, and the bracelet split apart at the star. When he placed it on her wrist, the bracelet glowed white, snapped shut, and shrank to fit her wrist perfectly.

"So what else does it do?"

"Pardon me?" Moorloc asked. He interlocked his fingers

and placed them on the table. As he stared at her, a smirk spread across his face.

"You'll have to forgive my suspicion, but I don't believe you told me everything. I suspect you told me what you believed would get me to put the bracelet on—but *you* would be incorrect. I agreed to come here to save Aaron and Stefan's lives. If I have any chance of going home, I need to learn to use these powers. So tell me."

"What I said was true. I can take away your powers while you wear it, but I can also track you. If you leave the grounds to go see your prince or anyone else, I'll know you broke your oath."

"Considering I can't crack when I want to, that wasn't ever an option," Alex said. *I wish I could crack. Then I would at least be able to move around the castle however I wanted without having to risk running into Lygari in the hallway.*

"Not today, but one day, and I need you to understand the rules."

"I'll follow your rules so long as they're explained to me."

"Fair enough. We'll begin now."

Wind rushed past Alex, and they were on the beach she'd been admiring before dinner.

"Rule one. You have free rein of any unlocked room on the castle grounds. If I have locked it, you stay out. Your room, the lab, and the library are enchanted against everyone except sorcerers and a few select servants. That is what Lygari was doing after dinner. None of the men can get into those rooms."

"How can you be sure he performed the spell properly?"

"You'll have to trust us. Letting harm come to you will slow your lessons, which will displease me. Lygari knows what happens when someone disappoints me."

Alex nodded. Her eyes moved to the sea as the evening sun

danced on top of the dark water, making the waves look like shooting stars.

"Rule two. As we begin, you'll focus on the line powers *I* choose. Tomorrow, we'll test your powers to see which lines you've discovered. You're not to practice powers from lines that I have not yet assigned to you."

"Why?" Alex asked, looking back at him.

"Your powers will need to be managed, and it's safer for you *and* us if we know what we're working with. I'm aware accidents will happen, especially while we wait for any remaining lines to come in, but you're not to use those lines unless told to. Especially your healing magic."

"What's wrong with me learning to heal? It certainly isn't dangerous."

"I'm not a simpleton, princess. You know that if it weren't for my spell—which I am keeping as part of our bargain—the whelp's mortal injuries from when you *gutted* him at my sister's castle would immediately return. If you could, you'd betray me. You'd run back to your love and heal him the moment I removed that spell. Healing will be the last skill we work on."

Clenching her fists in frustration, Alex held back her temper as she spoke. "Anything else?"

"Rule three. You'll do exactly as you're told without hesitation, complaint, or argument."

"I don't know if I can do that one. I'm known for speaking my mind and asking questions, and I've also been told I have a temper and a stubborn streak in me," Alex said.

"If you want to learn to manage your powers, you'll have to. I wasn't as patient with Lygari when he was learning as I should have been. I intend to correct that mistake with you, but only if you behave."

Alex shifted uncomfortably in her seat and tugged at the bracelet that suddenly felt heavy and constricting.

"I will tolerate you wandering around my castle and the grounds because that bracelet will tell me if you wander too far or work on magic I forbade. You will be memorizing books for a long while before you are ready for my tutelage. Those full lessons won't begin until you have all your powers. But until then, if you break my rules, you'll learn how ruthless sorcerers can be. Understood?"

Alex gulped and nodded.

"Very good. It's getting late, so I'll escort you to the library. If you have any of your mother in you, you'll make good use of it. Then you can spend the evening making yourself at home. Tomorrow morning, we'll begin testing your Celtic and Poseidon powers."

"Why those powers?"

"They're safe to start with, and I've seen you use them."

Alex tugged her shirt hem, and Moorloc cracked them back to the library. It was smaller than the Warren one, but it had the familiar smell of dust and old books. Every surface of the wall was lined with bookcases bowing under the weight, and in the middle of the room was a large table with stools around it. In this library, two shelves seemed wrong to Alex, the same way the shelf at her mother's castle had. Carefully, Alex moved toward one of them and placed her hand on it.

"You're correct."

Alex jumped, having forgotten Moorloc was in the room.

"They're doors," he said. He pointed to the one near her. "That one leads to the lab while the other leads to my room."

Alex made a mental note of it and watched Moorloc move to a bookcase in the middle of the room. There, he tapped the spines of a few larger books.

"I had Lygari pull these before you arrived. These are the

Poseidon and Celtic history books. You'll want to start here." He turned to leave but paused. "If there's nothing else, I'll leave you for the night."

Sweat trickled down her back. *Ask him. He probably knows what you're thinking.* Alex sighed loudly as she shuffled toward Moorloc. "When you teach me about the powers and the sorcerer world, will you also tell me about my mother? I've heard little about her, and I'd like to know what she was really like."

Moorloc stilled. For a moment, sadness crossed his usually indifferent face. "If you wish. But I won't tolerate it detracting from your studies."

"Understood," Alex said as Moorloc strode from the room. She waited for the door to close behind him and looked around the empty library.

"Alone again. Are you gone too, Daniel?" she asked. After a few minutes of no reply from her ghostly guardian and friend, she tucked her loose hair behind her ear the way Aaron would and moved toward the books Moorloc had pointed out to her.

CHAPTER 4

AARON

Aaron marched to the jousting field with Cameron and Stefan in tow. Michael, Randal, and Jerome had gathered all the knights from Aaron's list who were in Warren since a handful were stationed in Datten. Someone had set a platform up for Aaron, but he strode past it and stood before the men at their level.

"I called you all here by request of the Kings of Warren and Datten. Some of you have heard that last night, my betrothed, the Princess of Warren, was taken." Aaron allowed a moment of chatter and disbelief.

"Her uncle and cousin coerced her into leaving. These same men have twice now attacked us and lost. I've come up with a plan and will head to Datten and then the kingdom of Betruger. I'll be asking for their help to bring her back."

The men all started at once.

"Enough!" Michael shouted.

Aaron took a deep breath. "I understand your fear. I'm asking you to go into the mountains—the heart of Betruger territory. We haven't tried it in over a hundred years. But we will learn from my ancestors, and we *will* be successful. I won't force any knight to take this mission, but I beg you to consider this: What if it was your daughter or sister? I've never been in command of an army, but you've worked with me, and you know what I'm capable of. I *won't* take this mission lightly. I trust in myself and in our plan. If I didn't, I wouldn't have brought Cameron or Michael. So whoever wishes to bring honor to themselves by helping me return the future Queen of Warren and Datten, gather your things and return here. Those who wish to stay and return to your wives and children, I commend you for your dedication to your families."

Cameron addressed the crowd. "If you intend to come, pack lightly and see General Nial or General Bishop at the armory to be fitted with Warren armor. Our shields and weapons will come from Datten. My father and I will provide appropriate war horses for anyone who needs one."

"We will leave at noon," Aaron said and then dismissed the men with a wave of his hand. He turned and headed back into the castle flanked by Michael and Cameron.

"Are you nervous?" Michael asked.

"Terrified. What if no one comes?"

"Then it's up to us and Merlock," Cameron said. "At least then we could crack there and it would be over faster."

I respect Merlock so much, but why does he have to be the sorcerer who can only crack a handful of people when his brother and nephew can crack an army? It's frustrating.

Back inside the castle, Aaron went to his room to finish packing. Adding the pearl required some careful adjustments, but when he finished, everything fit, including Alex's letter and handkerchief. Aaron took his bag and headed down to the stables.

Cameron was out front with an enormous pile of horse blankets.

"Do you have everything we need?" Aaron asked.

Cameron scanned the list he'd nailed to the board in his hand. "I think we do. If we're missing something, we'll manage until we get to Datten."

"Good. Do you have your things?"

Cameron pointed toward the saddle bag leaning against the stable door. "Do you think we'll get to talk to the king, or are you taking us on a suicide mission that only you'll return from?"

Aaron groaned. "Do you honestly think I'm capable of that?"

"A month ago, I would have said no, but now ... I don't know what you're capable of."

Aaron scoffed and dropped his arms at his side. "Just say what you feel, Cameron. Get it out. I can't have you bad-mouthing me around the men."

"I wouldn't do that. So don't lose your crown over it, Your Highness."

Don't bring up what he said to Alex. It won't help, and it's her pain to handle.

"Cameron ... I didn't ask you to come because I want your expertise with the horses. I trust your opinion. *I trust you.*"

"How can you trust me if you don't respect me?" Cameron asked.

"The decision was hers. I had no right to ask you to back off, no matter how much I wanted to, because she genuinely had feelings for you."

"How can you be sure?"

"Because when we planned the tournament, she smiled at you the way she smiled at me."

"So what happened? You're the better kisser? Or you took liberties, knowing Edward won't do anything? Look me in the eye and tell me that crown on your head isn't why she picked you," Cameron said.

Aaron sighed and ran his hand through his hair. "It isn't. And do not disrespect Alex because you're angry with me. She didn't have to use you to get close to me because I was already in love with her. I was just too stubborn to admit it."

Cameron scoffed and went back to his list.

"You were the easier option. A connection to Datten and no crown. Instead, she picked me, the only cowardly prince ever born in Datten."

Cameron looked up. "You aren't a coward. Considering what happened to Daniel, you hate senseless death. We watched your parents suffer through the loss of your brother. Why would *you* want to cause that pain to another parent?"

Aaron stared at Cameron. "No one has ever put it like that."

"Then the Datten council your father has is full of idiots because my father has been saying it to Edward for years."

"Will we be okay ... one day?" Aaron asked.

"I hope we can get there—eventually." Cameron waved, and Aaron turned around to see Michael coming over with his bag. He held his hand out to Aaron and, taking Aaron's bag, sat theirs next to Cameron's.

"Do I have to separate you two, or are you going to play nice?" Michael asked.

"I will if he does," Cameron said, walking back into the stable.

Aaron grumbled.

"He'll come around," Michael said. "Remember, she picked you. *You* get her. That hurts."

"Is it impossible to hope I could get the girl *and* keep my friend? Cameron is family."

"Which is why he'll eventually come around. You two

snuck around behind his back, and he lost someone amazing. Neither of us have had to give Alex up."

"You gave her up to me," Aaron said.

"Not yet I haven't. You'd better smarten up, or I'll join Stefan's side and talk her out of marrying you."

"It's sad that you're the funny one," Aaron said.

"What are you talking about? I'm hilarious," Michael said, elbowing Aaron. "She told me if anything ever happened to her, I should take care of you and make sure you find someone worthy of you."

"Michael—" Aaron said.

"It felt so out of place then. I'm worried she's not confident she'll come back—at least not in our lifetime. She was making backup plans in case we fail."

"That's not an option I'm willing to accept. I'm getting her back, or I'll die trying. Now let's go see if anyone else believes I can." Aaron marched toward the jousting field.

When they turned the corner, he froze. Before him, the field was covered in red and blue tunics as the knights he'd invited stood at attention, waiting for him. Every man he had picked was there, and at the front stood Julius Bishop and Caleb Reinhart, the sons of two of the most distinguished military families in Datten and Warren.

"We're all with you, Your Highness," Caleb said. His pale skin was flush with excitement, and his blond hair sparkled in the sun.

"Twelve years without the princess in Warren was too long. We're going to get her back. For you, for us, and for His Royal Highness," Julius added. With his warm umber complexion and striking brown eyes, he was the spitting image of his father, General Bishop, even down to the same serious expression.

Aaron breathed easier. Having Julius along would be great

41

for morale. Like Cameron, he was smart, brave, and hard-working—everything the noble families of Warren expected of their sons.

"All right. Let's saddle up," Aaron said, a smile spreading across his face. "It's a long ride to Datten."

CHAPTER 5
ALEX

A lone in the lab, Alex moved toward the weapons wall. *What would a sorcerer need these for?*

Whips of different materials and sizes featured prominently. A shiver ran through her. One in particular stood out. Something was different about it. She looked closer, but it was a normal brown leather whip. As Alex stepped back, a familiar icy chill engulfed her, and she sighed.

"Hello, Daniel," Alex whispered. Twisting her head to look at him, she realized he, too, was staring at the whip. "Is Aaron angry with me?" Her voice cracked as she spoke.

Daniel's attention snapped in her direction before he shook his head.

"How bad is he hurting?"

Daniel pressed his lips together and scrunched up his nose.

"He's not doing anything really stupid, is he?"

A smile spread across Daniel's face, and he leaned forward and kissed Alex's forehead. Goosebumps spread across her entire body as Daniel stepped back.

"Datten men. Did he figure out the hints I left?"

The handsome blond ghost stared at her for a long while before he nodded and faded away, leaving the ice-cold air in his place.

He's coming for me. That means I need to find those books and figure out how to get out of this oath. And that means breaking his rules.

Alex walked into the library and found Lygari at the table.

"What are you reading?" Alex asked, hoping she'd get a proper conversation out of him. *Talking to someone would be nice.*

"Some dull book about the Hades line."

"Do you have Hades powers?" Alex asked, sitting across the table from Lygari and pulling a Poseidon book toward her.

"No, but I find them entertaining. Everyone looks down on them, but Hades is the only line where the titan's biggest job comes after death." His voice dropped to a whisper. "They control the entrance to the human underworld."

"So they're responsible for the ghosts I see?"

Lygari raised an eyebrow at her. "You see ghosts?"

"Yes."

"Can you talk to them?"

"They understand me, but I can't understand them."

He slammed the book shut and stood. "Basic powers then. Yes, Hades decides who can come and go from both the good and bad parts of the underworld. They also keep the monsters in check."

"Monsters?" Alex's eyes widened.

"Hellhounds, three-headed dogs, gryphons. The rotting corpses of former mortals. All manner of beasts to rip you apart. They live in a mist around the underworld and torment the souls of the damned. If you want some actual nightmares, try this book." Lygari pulled a small Hades book from his stack and held it out to her, but Alex shook her head.

"No. I have enough nightmares already."

"Suit yourself. But ghosts have been known to talk people to death if you ignore them."

"I'll keep that in mind."

Lygari left, and Alex spent the evening in the library looking over a few Poseidon books and wondering how the books didn't catch on fire when flames grazed the tops of the shelves. When she read so much that her eyes hurt, she got up to leave.

It was late, and the hall was deserted except for the fire above her head. At night, a smell like a campfire overpowered everything in the hallway. Alex crept toward her bedroom, but as she reached her door, she heard footsteps. After she slammed and locked the door behind her, she pressed her back into the door and listened, but all she heard was the pounding of her heart. Forcing herself to take deep breaths, she slowed her heart and tried again. Silence.

So I'm hearing things now? Alex removed her clothes, put on Aaron's shirt, and crawled into bed. Tomorrow she'd start her training. She hoped she'd have time to write in her journal. As she tried to sleep, she made a list of things she wanted to ask about her mother until her eyes grew heavy and the fire on the ceiling slowly extinguished itself.

☙ ❧

ALEX BOLTED UPRIGHT IN BED. She couldn't breathe. It was as if someone had been pressing on her ribs, trying to crush them. She'd drenched her shirt in sweat, and it clung to her chest and back. It took her a moment to remember where she was as she forced air into her seized lungs.

"Moorloc's castle ... you're in Moorloc's castle. You saved

Aaron and Stefan's lives. The price was worth it," she repeated over and over as her heart pounded.

She wouldn't be able to get back to sleep, so she left her bed and opened the wardrobe. Staring at the hideous clothes, she couldn't decide if she should wear the new gold ones or stick to her old garments. She peeled her wet nightshirt off and hung it on a hook. Alex sighed and grabbed the gold tunic and black pants. She needed Moorloc happy with her. After she'd dressed, Alex tucked her mother's necklace securely into her shirt and pulled her hair out from under the fabric. She started rummaging through the wardrobe for a brush to tame her tangled hair.

"Jessica would be appalled with me," Alex said as she looked at her messily braided hair and glanced back at her unmade bed. Thinking of Jessica made her miss Stefan and Aaron. Sucking in her breath to fight back the sob threatening to leave her, Alex made her bed. It wasn't great, but it made her smile to think of how both of them would have teased her terrible job.

"It'll get easier and will hurt less," she said before pulling open the door and walking back to the library.

Alex had scanned a few books and made a stack of notes by the time the door opened.

"Here you are. Didn't you hear the breakfast bells?" Moorloc asked.

"No. Why can Poseidon control the weather *and* the sea?" Alex asked without looking up from her book.

"It's because the elements that make up the weather all come from the sea," Moorloc said.

"What about wind?" Alex asked, finally looking up. "I understand water coming from the sea, but wind?"

A smile spread across Moorloc's face. "In all his years of studying, Lygari never once asked that question." He took a few steps and pointed to one of the massive bookshelves. "Check the blue book on the third shelf. It was written by the Titan Triton. He talks about how water funnels create the wind needed for tornadoes and such, thus tying the sea to the wind."

Alex pulled the book off the shelf and skimmed the first few pages. Her eyes widened. "Interesting. I wonder how he figured that out when no one else could."

Moorloc was watching her intently. "You are your mother's daughter in mind as well. She asked that same question when her Poseidon powers came in."

"How did my mother and Merlock get Poseidon powers if we're Merlin and Cassandra? Was a grandparent Poseidon? I thought you inherited one power from each parent."

"We'll walk to the sea, and I'll explain on the way." Moorloc held open the door.

She glanced sadly at the books but followed him anyway, remembering the rule about listening. *The first day probably isn't the best time to ignore the rules.*

"Remember, the library is enchanted, the same as your room. Only sorcerers can enter, and Lygari doesn't have Poseidon, so he'll leave your books alone."

He led her to the northwest tower; there, they exited the castle to head toward the water.

"Merlin is a special line," he said. "There used to be nine lines—then Merlin was born. He was born to mortal parents in a faraway world with sorcerer power beyond that of a normal sorcerer. He wasn't a Head or a Heart, but he held his own against every titan of the time, including the Titan of Ares."

"Why is Ares significant?" Alex asked.

"Ares is arguably the strongest of the ten lines. They control chaos, and they can ignite unimaginable violence in themselves and others. They're brutal, treacherous, and never to be trusted."

47

"Merlock told me they were strong but had calmed down in recent generations."

Moorloc stopped and turned to face her. Alex swallowed hard as Moorloc's eyes flashed violet for a second before turning gold. "I warned you about discussing him. My brother is a fool, and his incompetence as a sorcerer will be his downfall. Ares is stronger now than ever before. If you ever meet one, *run*."

"Run? That doesn't sound like something my parents would do."

"How would you know?" Moorloc snapped. "Your mother's been dead most of your life, and your father picked his murdering father over you."

Alex opened her mouth to reply but closed it when he stepped into her space and grabbed her shoulder, squeezing it hard enough to hurt as he looked down at her.

"Enough about your ineffectual parents. We've gotten off-topic. When Merlin arrived in the Forbidden Lands, it soon became apparent that he didn't fit into any of the existing lines. He was so powerful in his own right that he needed his own line, something that hadn't happened in over a millennium."

"So there were nine lines until then?"

Smiling at her question, Moorloc released her, and they headed toward the beach again. "Yes. The nine founding titans all arrived in the same century. The Merlin line is defined by its ability to possess skills from different lines. For example, my father, Hermes, could control fire like Salem but not explosions. He could do weather but not water, and he could kill plants, not grow them. He had one skill from multiple lines."

"I think I understand. If we listed every power held by every line on a separate page in a book, Merlin sorcerers would get a certain number of pages scattered throughout the book rather than the powers in the chapter for their line."

"That's exactly correct, little titaness."

"Is there a set number? What did you get? What did Lygari get? What about my mother?"

"There aren't enough of us to know how many skills we should get. I have a variety of skills. Victoria was gifted predominantly in Celtic, Cassandra, and Poseidon, with a few bits from the Mystics and Salem."

Alex's mind was racing by the time they reached the sea.

"All right," Moorloc said. "Show me what powers you have. We'll start with Poseidon."

Alex looked at the sea and breathed deeply. Concentrating hard, she pulled some water from it and made a puddle in front of Moorloc.

He scowled at her and crossed his arms. "You sent a river to douse the fire at the tournament, and now you give me a puddle."

"I can't control when they get powerful," Alex said. "They come when I have potent feelings. When you sent the mercenaries to attack us, I was afraid. The powers took over from there. I did little."

Moorloc sighed. "It's clear my simpleton brother taught you nothing. How they expected you to learn with his help, I'll never understand. Try something else."

A cold sweat ran down Alex's back at the idea of failing, and, still facing away from the sea, she tried to focus on the puddle before her. After a moment with nothing happening, she looked up at Moorloc, but his eyes were wide as he watched behind her. Turning around, Alex saw the same roaring seas she'd conjured for Merlock. In the distance, she could see a boat being tossed around. As fear for the vessel hit her, the waves grew, and the sea became more tumultuous.

"So there is power in you, but you aren't connecting with it; your feelings are. You'll need to learn to control it. Show me your Celtic powers next."

Looking around the rocky shore, she found a small patch of dirt. She aimed her palms at the ground and held out her hands. Alex closed her eyes and pictured Aaron's face. His blond hair sparkled in the sun, and he smiled at her. Next, she heard Michael's laughter, Edith's giggles, and Jessica's sigh and felt the courage Stefan had taught her rush through her.

"Impressive," Moorloc said.

Alex opened her eyes. She'd covered the entire rocky area in grass and flowers up to the sand on the beach.

"What did you think of?" Moorloc asked, bringing her attention back to him.

"My friends," Alex admitted. "When I'm happy, things grow."

"Your mother was talented in Celtics too. Her friend Birch helped her a great deal with it."

"Birch?"

"The Celtic and Tiere lines have a history of naming their children after things from their lines. Tiere sorcerers name their children after animals and Celtics after plants."

Alex stepped toward him, feeling a rush of excitement. "I had a doll named Birch. Did my mother's friend have raven-black hair, beautiful acorn-brown skin, and wear green?"

"We will not speak about her. She betrayed your mother as much as Merlock did. They're both dead to you now."

Moorloc's tone made it clear this wasn't a request. Alex rubbed her hand along her arm and something caught her eye. "My bracelet. The leaf and waves are black."

"That means it's working. Good. Now, for the rest of today, I want you to continue your research into Poseidon and Celtic powers. You came up with some insightful questions after yesterday's reading. Figure out how many specific powers from each line you've exhibited. Tomorrow, we'll start testing the more challenging spells. We'll find out what's hiding in you, though it's clear you'll need significant time to study before I can begin proper lessons with you. I hope you read quickly."

Moorloc turned to head back to the castle, but Alex looked back at the raging sea. She could see the strange-looking ship still being tossed around by her waves. Alex's hands glided before her, and when she opened them, the sea was as smooth as glass. She smiled to herself and rushed after him.

Alex spent the rest of the day in the library reading about Poseidon and Celtic line powers. She left long enough to grab some bread for dinner and then hurried back to the library. In one day at Moorloc's castle, she knew more about both lines than Merlock had taught her in two months. She hated to admit it, but Moorloc seemed better suited to teaching her than Merlock.

In no time, the ceiling fires started again. Alex grabbed her book on plants of the Dark Forest and headed to her bedroom.

Nights were the hardest for her. At home, she'd struggled to sleep even when surrounded by people who loved her.

I'll learn a lot here, but this unending silence is already weighing on me. I wish I had someone to talk to.

She knew the loneliness would grow the longer she was here. So, since she'd been told she was allowed, Alex went exploring. She hoped to get a feel for the castle without Moorloc influencing her senses. The lab and library were open to her all the time, so she skipped them. The guardrooms were not something she wanted to explore, and the hall, while unusual, was plain, and she spent enough time in it during meals. Alex made her way along the hallway and paused at the southwest tower. One side was the unguarded tower that would let her explore the basement or second floor, but behind her was the kitchen. The growl that came from her stomach made her creep across the hall to the door and twist the door latch.

Moorloc said I was free to go into any unlocked part of the castle. Though he also said the kitchen was off-limits. But the cooks aren't working now. Alex pushed open the kitchen door.

The ceiling fire followed her into the kitchen and illuminated the room. Alex was shocked at the small size. The kitchen at the inn in Kirsh was larger. Alex remembered helping Irma in the kitchen when she was too young to work in the stables. The memories of Irma and Ian made her heart hurt as her stomach rumbled.

What I wouldn't give for a hug and a bowl of rabbit stew.

Surveying the space for something she could take that wouldn't be noticed, Alex couldn't believe this kitchen fed hundreds each meal. There were two large worktables and three fireplaces. Beyond that, there was barely any space to move around, yet somehow they made enough food for everyone. Alex stood at the larger worktable. No pots, spoons, or baskets of vegetables. Under the bench was empty too, but Alex noticed the floor was worn in a narrow path. The path took her toward the fireplaces and then forked right into a wall.

The wall gave her the same feeling as the bookcase in the Verlassen Castle. Alex smirked as she held her hand out in front of her and stepped toward the wall. Her fingers reached to touch it but passed through the wall. Her arm and body followed, and she found herself at the top of a dark stairwell. The fire didn't follow her into the narrow space; she was grateful for that. The bottom of the stairs was lit faintly. Finding her courage, she nimbly hurried down the stairs, but when she arrived at the bottom, there was nothing but a dirt floor in a large circular alcove. She couldn't believe there would be stairs that led to nothing.

"There *has* to be a door."

She ran her hands along the walls but couldn't find or feel anything. About to give up, she remembered Megesti's book and tried the magical unlocking spell. Before she uttered the last word, four doors appeared in the alcove.

Alex eagerly opened the first door. It was full of pots, pans, and many cooking supplies.

"That explains the empty kitchen."

She closed the door and moved to the next, a root cellar filled with barrels of fruit and vegetables. She stepped inside the dry but musty room. Finding a bushel of apples, she grabbed one and closed the door behind her. She paused in front of the remaining doors and then decided on the closer one. It was a room full of snow and every manner of meat imaginable. Taking a big bite of her apple, she let the door swing shut with a thunk while she wiped the juice off her chin. As she reached for the last door, she heard movement behind it.

Alex stood still and listened. *More movement.*

Finally, she pressed the handle and pulled it open. Standing before her was the old servant woman who had served her dinner the first night. Startled, Alex dropped her apple on the ground.

Wrinkles and age spots covered the woman's nearly translucent hands and face, but her hazel eyes sparkled with a youthful fire. Alex froze in the doorway and looked her up and down. Her clothes were worn and stained. They reminded Alex of the ones she grew up in. The woman's silver hair was done up in a tight bun. Behind her were at least thirty other people of varying ages in equally shabby clothes. From watching their mannerisms during meals, Alex knew these men and women of every age were from all over Torian.

The old woman crossed her arms, stepping toward Alex and forcing her to move back. "You shouldn't be down here."

"Who are you? Why are you living down here?"

"I'm Reinhilde Vinur. I'm one of the castle servants. Now go back to your room and don't ask questions that aren't your concern, princess."

Alex sucked her breath and stepped back. "How did you know—"

"I come from Warren. I knew your mother."

"If you knew her, then why are you here?" Alex asked. Her heart pounded in her chest at the idea of someone else here who knew her mother.

Reinhilde turned her head and shushed someone behind her.

"How many of you are there? How did you get here? Why are you all in that room?" Alex tried to look behind Reinhilde, but the woman now held Alex in place. She was incredibly strong for an old woman.

"This is where all the servants live." For a moment, Alex could see lines of small cots on a dirt floor, but then Reinhilde pushed Alex away from the door, letting it close behind them.

"Is that how you live?"

"Yes."

"That's horrible. I have to do something about it. You can't live like this."

The old woman chuckled, and Alex looked at her, confused.

"His boy tried to help us when he was younger. All it got him was a severe beating. He learned to accept it. You will too."

"The boy? Do you mean Lygari?" *How long have you been here?* "Why are you here?"

"Because my son got sick and your mother was dead."

54

"What?"

"After your mother died, we had no one left to help us if someone got sick. I sought the dark sorcerer, and he saved my son in exchange for my servitude."

Alex's throat went bone-dry. *He's made this deal before. How many people has Moorloc tricked into this?* "For how long?" Alex asked.

"My life. A life for a life, a price I'd pay again to save my son."

Alex gasped and stumbled backward. She couldn't believe what she was hearing. Bringing her hand to her mouth, she shook her head. Then footsteps thundered on the stairs behind her. Spinning around, Alex was face-to-face with Kruft Rassgat.

His brown eyes stared as fear rushed through her, sending a wind rushing around them in the small area. Alex's instinct was to protect the old woman, but Reinhilde turned to Kruft.

"I told her to get out and mind her business, but she's stubborn as a mule."

Alex took advantage of Kruft's distraction with Reinhilde and the dirt her wind had kicked up. Alex tore up the stairs and raced out of the kitchen. She didn't stop running until she was back in her room with the door safely closed.

Unable to calm her heart pounding in her chest, Alex lay on her bed, still in her clothes, and wrapped Aaron's cloak into a ball and clung to it. She'd forgotten about Kruft and how well he knew her after guarding her for a month with Stefan and Michael.

He betrayed Emmerich and helped my grandfather kill my mother. How could I have forgotten about him?

Adrenaline still pulsing through her, Alex stared at the wall, trembling until she passed out from terror and sheer exhaustion.

CHAPTER 6
ALEX

Alex tried to block the sun from her face. Somehow, she'd slept through the night without nightmares, but her body ached as if she'd been up all night. The terror of being caught by Kruft in the kitchen had been enough to make her sick. That, or seeing the conditions the servants were living in. In Warren, everyone who worked in the castle was paid well, had nice accommodations, and had time off when they needed it. Her father was kind to all his people, but Moorloc was … something else. Alex rolled over to find Lygari scowling at her from beside her bed. She screamed so loud he covered his ears.

"Why are you screaming?"

"Because it's terrifying to wake up to someone staring at you! What are you doing in my room?"

"So it's *your* room now?"

"Temporarily, it is."

"*Temporarily* being the important word there, princess."

"What do you want, cousin?"

Lygari opened the wardrobe and scoffed. Alex slipped out

of bed and followed him. She'd slept in her clothes from the day before, but she didn't care about her appearance in front of him.

"Such lovely uniforms," he said. "I think the gold is the right color for you, seeing as it's the ideal line for a sorcer*ess*. Leave Merlin to the sorcerers."

Alex pushed the door shut and glared at him. "Stay out of my things." Alex remembered her journals she'd hidden for safekeeping in the top of the central tower. *What if he finds them? Then again, I can't really see him wanting to go watch the sea.*

"Apparently, you were snooping last night—it displeased my father. He's summoned you to the lab immediately. Get dressed."

Lygari wrenched open the wardrobe doors and threw a clean training outfit at Alex. Snorting, he turned toward the door.

"Hurry up. He can't stand it when mortals waste his time, and I took the long way here."

Breathing deeply to calm her shaking, Alex changed as fast as she could, leaving her old clothes in a small pile at the end of her bed. After running a brush through her hair, she braided it on the way to the lab.

Lygari grimaced at her when she arrived. He opened the door to the lab and walked in. Alex caught the door before it hit her and followed him inside. Lygari leaned on the bookcase, and she turned from him to her uncle. Moorloc had taken a spot in front of the weapon wall. Her stomach dropped as though it were full of rocks when he looked down at her.

"Sit," Moorloc commanded, and she obeyed.

Alex's throat went dry as she finally noticed Kruft and Reinhilde were in the room too. They were standing in the corner opposite of the door next to the unlit fireplace. The smirk on Kruft's face told her all she needed to know, but Reinhilde wouldn't look at her.

You were an unwilling accomplice, weren't you?

Alex's eyes darted around the room. Moorloc was breathing deeply, hopefully calming himself before punishing her. She looked carefully at Kruft, examining the long red scar that ran along the entire left side of his pale face. It hadn't been there the last time she saw him in Warren, and she hadn't stayed long enough to look last night. His nostrils flared when he noticed her looking at it.

"I have the younger Wafner to thank for my new appearance, *princess*," he said, snarling. "Maybe I'll give you a matching one as payback."

Alex tried to shrink back onto the stool. A wind blew through the room, sending ash from the fireplace all over the floor and Kruft's legs. He took a step toward her when a voice boomed through the room.

"Kruft! You and your men will not lay a finger on our guest. As titan of her line, sorcerers will treasure Alexandria in the Forbidden Lands, as all true daughters of Cassandra should be. But as our Heart, they'll fear her exceptional power. In this ... *indiscretion*, she is merely my disobedient niece."

What does he mean I'll be treasured in the Forbidden Lands?

Lygari chuckled in the corner, diverting her attention. He was watching his father. Slowly, Alex turned back to her uncle.

"I didn't think I was breaking the rules since I couldn't sleep and got hungry. You said not to go into the kitchen because I'd be in the way. In the middle of the night, I wouldn't be in anyone's way. Please don't punish Reinhilde. She told me to leave. I didn't listen."

"I've already dealt with her. Besides her, the servants won't acknowledge you. If you need anything, Reinhilde will provide it. If you continue to talk to the others, I'll punish *them* for it.

They're here to work off debts, not be your friends," Moorloc said.

"Debts for what?" Alex asked.

"Most came to me looking for help for their family. Powerful magic costs us a lot in this land, and so the price is steep."

"Magic has a cost?" Alex asked, standing up from her stool and looking at Moorloc.

"Everything has a cost," Moorloc said. "Without being in the Forbidden Lands to refill our power stores, we have to collect it from the elements we have power over. As a water sorceress, you have an effortless task of it. Simply being in the sea will strengthen you. It's why you're drawn to water. Lygari and I are fire."

"Does that mean you can go into fire?" Alex smirked, picturing Lygari in a bonfire.

"No, which is why my magic costs more. Anyone who wants help from me pays dearly for the privilege."

"So they're slaves?"

"Call them what you will, but they are here of their own free will because they gave up their lives to serve me in order to save someone they loved from a horrible end."

Alex bit her lip to stop the horrified cry from escaping her. *He's done this so many times. I wasn't the first. How many of their illnesses did he cause, just as he caused my accident?*

Kruft cleared his throat. "The punishment, Lord Moorloc."

Moorloc's eyes flashed violet at Kruft before he turned back to Alex.

"It isn't going into the kitchen that is the issue, titaness. Discovering the wall was fake and going through it was bordering on breaking the rules. But it was unlocking the doors in the basement that brought you here."

"I did that?" Alex hoped playing innocent would save her.

"Unlocking spells are not accidentally performed," Lygari said. "It seems you have more skills than you're letting on."

"Indeed. It seems I'll be able to push you harder than I expected," Moorloc said. "If you want me to trust you, niece, you'll need to earn that trust. This behavior is not how you go about that. There will, of course, be consequences for your actions."

Alex swallowed hard. "What consequences?"

"No need to be frightened. We are civilized, after all. The punishment will fit the crime. A sparring match, since you have more power than we realized. Anytime you break a rule I have given you, you will spar with Lygari. It will help sharpen *both* your skills. Help you hone the idea of magic as a weapon, and since he's obviously more skilled than you, it will teach you a lesson. At the minimum, you'll spar at least once monthly, even if you obey."

"When?"

Moorloc snapped his fingers and cracked them to the courtyard. Kruft called over a bunch of his men while Lygari rolled up his sleeves. He wore a cream tunic made in the same style as Alex's. She looked at Moorloc, completely lost. Moorloc crossed the yard and placed his hands on her shoulders, leading her to a bare patch on the grass.

"You'll stand here, and he'll be over there. Being chivalrous as he is, he'll allow you to go first. Do your best, and remember we can heal almost anything he does to you." Moorloc patted her back before he turned to stroll away.

Almost?

Ice rushed through her veins, sending a wind across the yard strong enough to toss her braided hair. She glanced at Lygari. His stance reminded her of Aaron at the tournament. He pushed his shoulders back and stuck his chest out. But it was the smirk on his face that infuriated her, especially since there wasn't anything she could do about it.

I'm going to lose badly. I hope the damage isn't permanent.

"You first, princess," Lygari said, sauntering to his position in the courtyard. He kicked the ground for a moment and then stood on the balls of his feet.

"Why do you call me 'princess'?" Alex asked.

"Because that's all you're ever going to be. A silly little mortal princess." The smirk on Lygari's face was getting tiring.

Alex dug her feet into the ground, adopting the fighting stance that Stefan had drilled into her.

"I'm waiting, *princess*. We don't have all day." Lygari brought his hands in front of him.

Grunting in frustration, Alex breathed slowly and worked to summon the water from around her, but she was struggling.

"I think we could teach the dead Betruger king to do this faster. I'm rather good at disposing of royalty, princess. Should I head to Warren next, or would you prefer I go back to Datten and finish the job?"

Rage exploded through Alex's veins. Immediately, all the water she worked so hard to pull evaporated as her fire power came out. Lygari chuckled.

"My turn." With his eyes fixed on Alex, he ground the ball of his foot into the ground and then clapped his hands together. Flames erupted from thin air between his palms, and when he pulled them apart, there was a fireball in each hand.

Alex swallowed hard and braced herself.

Lygari threw the first fireball. Alex ducked, but the heat singed her ear. The second one came fast. Alex only had enough time to get her arms up to shield her face. Water burst from her hands, extinguishing the fire. Struggling to get her footing on the slick grass and mud, she watched in horror as

Lygari created a larger fireball. She regained her balance, but he'd already thrown it.

The fireball struck her right shoulder so hard her lungs emptied of air as she hit the solid ground. The smell of burned cloth and flesh hit her an instant before the excruciating pain. The moment the first pained whimper came from her, thunder cracked above their heads. Storm clouds appeared out of nowhere, and a torrential downpour soaked them all in seconds. Immediately the fire went out, but the pain spread everywhere. Her head and back throbbed while her shoulder burned as if it were still on fire.

Lygari shouted obscenities at her as he ran into the castle. Moorloc walked over and looked down at her. "Once you've calmed the storm, get dressed and meet me in the lab. I'll teach you how to make an ointment for your burn. Hopefully, this brief lesson will deter any future late-night explorations of locked areas."

CHAPTER 7
ALEX

Black spots flooded Alex's vision, and she clenched her teeth so hard she worried they might break as she struggled to walk to her bedroom. Safely inside, she started to remove her charred and soaking wet tunic. In seconds, the pain became so unbearable she fought to not throw up. Dropping to her knees, she swallowed back the bile that was trying to burst out of her. Her sobs broke free as the pain worsened. She wondered if she could heal the wound. She'd always healed quickly, but this was an ugly mass of black, burned flesh. She heard the door close behind her, and when she glanced back, Reinhilde was standing there with a basin and cloth.

"How—" Alex couldn't form any more words and cried out.

The old woman moved with lightning speed toward Alex and dropped to her knees in front of her. "That was brave and incredibly stupid," she said.

"Which part?"

"The nighttime exploring. Letting him see you have more power than he realized. Now hold still—this *will* hurt."

Alex watched Reinhilde dip the cloth into the water. After wringing it out, the old woman looked into Alex's eyes and waited until Alex nodded she was ready. Reinhilde gently pushed the cloth to the burn. She ignored Alex's shriek of pain, and pulling out a small knife, she cut what was left of Alex's shirt from her body. In a flash, she'd moved to the wardrobe and returned with the Warren tunic and helped Alex slip it over her head. She left the string at the front loose so Alex's shoulder would remain exposed and then helped her put on dry pants.

Alex knew she had to hurry to the lab. She didn't want to make Moorloc wait in case it made him angrier, but she needed answers.

"Why are you helping me? I know he ordered you to, but that can't be the reason."

"I told you last night. I knew your mother."

Alex glared at her, and Reinhilde sighed. "I was born in Warren. It would be my honor to assist you, as much as *any* Warren royal."

Alex sighed and flinched from the pain in her lungs. She still wasn't used to people wanting to help her because of who she was.

"Go. He doesn't like to be kept waiting. I'll tidy up here."

"I'm sorry for the mess."

"You're much cleaner than any of the men here."

Not sure how to thank the old woman, Alex nodded and hurried as best she could to the lab. Carefully, she opened the door when her knocks went unanswered. The room was deserted. She let out a sigh of relief and stepped inside to wait for Moorloc.

She moved to the shelf of plants and herbs, being careful not to dirty the white bear rug. "I'm going to call you the minotaur since we're both trapped in here," she said.

Alex tried to remember the plant types to distract herself from the pain. "*Mint*—used for digestion and gout. *Hyssops*—soaked in wine to keep away chest colds. *Yarrow*—for inflammation, pain, and to stop bleeding."

"Correct," Moorloc said, walking into the room. "I see that at least something sank in yesterday." A smile spread across his face.

He's impressed with me—and happy. Now is my chance.

"I'm sorry for wandering around at night. In Warren, they allowed me to go anywhere I wanted when I couldn't sleep, and I didn't think looking for the food stores would be a problem when I couldn't find them in the kitchen. I'm truly sorry."

Moorloc stepped up to her.

If I show fear, you'll know the truth.

She fixed her gaze on Moorloc's gold eyes as he stared down at her for a long time before he moved again.

He gently took her chin between his thumb and index finger. "I know you are, which is why I'll forgive you this time. But next time, I won't be so gentle with your punishment."

That was gentle? Alex bit the inside of her cheek to avoid reacting as he released her.

"We'll begin with the aloe and lavandula to help combat the pain," Moorloc said as he strolled back to the bookcase and pulled out a book with a golden cover. "We'll want beeswax for the balm, so fetch that too."

Alex turned to the plants and used her good arm to gather the ingredients he requested. When her tunic shifted, pain flooded her, sending black spots swimming through her vision. She caught herself but dropped the beeswax. A hand gripped her shoulder. Pain worse than any she'd ever experienced filled her body and soul and then heat. Not like the fire that had burned her, but soothing, like a mother's embrace. When she looked at her shoulder, she saw Moorloc's hand was glowing gold. The color was brighter than anything Alex had ever seen, but it didn't hurt her eyes. Moorloc released her shoulder, and the pain became manageable.

"Thank you." Her voice wavered and was barely audible.

He shook his head. "I wanted to punish you—not maim you. Your mother would be furious with me."

Alex hurried to gather the beeswax and brought everything to the table, setting it before Moorloc. He asked for the mortar and pestle, but Alex was already bringing it over.

After he explained the process of grinding up the herbs and melting the beeswax and the best way to mix them into a uniform texture, he had Alex try it. Soon, she was following the book's instructions on her own.

"Your mother was exceptional with potions too," he said.

Alex stopped grinding the leaves and looked at him. "She was?"

Moorloc nodded. "It's common with Celtic powers, and, not surprisingly, she was exceptionally good with spells of a healing nature. When someone comes to me for help, it requires much of my healing magic since my Cassandra power isn't as strong."

Alex's eyes widened as she turned to her shoulder.

"*I* didn't heal you," he said. "You healed yourself. I summoned your healing powers to the surface so they could do what was needed. I assume you usually heal quickly."

Alex nodded. "Unnervingly so, according to Stefan."

"The lout's opinion is irrelevant. In time, you'll learn to forget him and the others and move on to become what you were meant to be."

"But I care about them." Alex clutched the ointment they'd made tightly to her stomach. The sharp metal container nearly cut her hand as she gripped it.

"You're a true daughter of Cassandra, and you have the strongest healing concentration of any sorcerer in our world. You're beyond *all* of them."

Alex looked down and watched Moorloc's boots enter her line of vision. She swallowed and turned her attention back to him.

"Why were you snooping around the castle last night?" he asked.

Alex opened her mouth to speak but closed it again. *Even if I tell you the truth, you won't believe me or you won't think it's good enough.*

"When I ask a question, I *expect* an answer. I do not speak to hear my own voice."

She sighed. "I don't sleep much, and I'm often hungry at odd times."

"Then you should make a habit of bringing books with you to your room at night when you finish in the library and eat more at dinner. In this castle, we eat at breakfast and dinner and not at other times. Understood?"

Alex nodded.

"Leave everything where it is. The servants will clean it. It's time to begin your lessons." Moorloc crossed the lab and opened the door to the library. Alex begrudgingly left her ointment and walked through the door.

"I thought the lab was protected so only we could enter."

"I said sorcerers *and* servants. Certain servants have been granted approval by myself or Lygari to enter each room."

"What about Kruft?"

"He's allowed in any room that I am in with no enchantment. It saves time. But he cannot get into your room even if I'm there." He motioned for Alex to sit at the table in the library. "This is going to be your routine from now on, little titaness. Breakfast followed by research in the library and then hands-on work in the lab with potions. Then you'll practice your skills. You can try whatever you learned about in your research. Afterward, there will be dinner and more research before bed. It won't be exciting, but consistency is important. That's how you'll learn to manage your powers quickly. Once you have reached an appropriate level, I will begin teaching you more regularly."

"Do we start today?"

"Should unacceptable behavior limit your learning?" Moorloc asked, glaring at her.

"No." Alex shook her head and rubbed her shoulder.

"Then we'll continue testing your abilities. I'll even let you choose between Celtic or Poseidon."

"Celtic," Alex said.

He frowned, and Alex expected him to pick Poseidon to spite her.

"Celtic it is." He snapped his fingers, and they were outside of the castle on a large and rocky dirt field.

Alex precariously stepped around the jagged rocks and foot-sized holes that appeared before her. She hadn't seen the outside of the castle before. It appeared to be in ruins. The towers looked as if they were crumbling, the walls missing, including the tower Alex had climbed and knew was whole. Time had lined the walls with moss and dead ivy while the surrounding land was barren and the little vegetation was withered.

"I think this place could use a princess's touch. What do you think?" Moorloc asked.

Alex closed her eyes to stop herself from rolling them. "Not a princess—a *sorceress*."

She kneeled down on the ground and scratched the hard, dry earth. *Growing anything here will be a challenge.* She reached for a section of dead ivy on the castle wall and affectionately stroked it. Slowly, a green spot appeared in the brown. She pressed her palm into the vine, shut her eyes tightly and concentrated. She thought of her friends, of the fun they'd had together, and how loved and safe they made her feel. The memory of Aaron's kiss sent a surge of power through her, and when she opened her eyes, the green crept along the entire length of vine until every shoot and leaf was flush with life.

"Not terrible," Moorloc said. "Can you grow more?"

Alex began again. Soon the entire wall was adorned with vines of all kinds, some leafed and some flowered. They snaked their way across the inside and outside walls. Alex smiled and sent the flowering vines growing up to the top of the tower, above her favorite spot to watch the sea. Moorloc seemed satisfied with her work, but she suddenly became dizzy and weak. It was as if her arms were made of stone, and her legs weren't any better.

"Should I feel so tired?" she asked.

"You're feeling drained of magic, not tired. You're young and lack the ability to control how much magic you take. As you study and practice, you'll get better at controlling how much you use, and that will make it easier for you. If you've drained yourself, we'll end here today. At your age, taking too much of your power is dangerous, and it'll be dinner soon. After you've eaten, you can spend as much time in the library as you please before bed."

Moorloc cracked them back into the hallway outside of the dining hall, making servants swiftly dodge them. The dinner bells began the moment Moorloc entered the hall, as if they were waiting for him. She followed Moorloc in and took her seat beside him. She ran her fingers along the side of her gold cushion as she watched the room.

The men all dressed strangely; their worn-out clothes were a mix of different colors and styles. She'd read about the

Betruger people in her father's library books. They were supposed to be stronger and taller than the people of Datten and Warren, and while that was true, their skin and hair weren't out of place—those with purple eyes were. They colored their clothing to match the local forest and rocks for camouflage. The idea of all of them hidden in the jagged rock hills around the castle was terrifying. They were shouting at one another over their food and banging on the tables with enough force that the sound made Alex flinch. Despite having grown up with loud boys, Alex wasn't sure if she'd ever get used to that.

"Your meal." Reinhilde brought Alex's attention back to her table. Reinhilde nodded and placed the plate in front of Alex before leaving.

Alex avoided looking at Lygari or the men and focused on her food. Again, it was the strange-smelling violet fish. Alex poked it with her fork and managed a few bites before the color and smell were too much for her. She could sense Moorloc watching her. Smiling weakly, she picked at the boiled potatoes and root vegetables even though they were bland and mushy. She glanced at the men long enough to watch the tables change over and lost count again. Alex's eyes darted to the slaves bringing food and drink to all the tables. All hair colors and skin tones were present. It seemed no kingdom had been spared or favored in Moorloc's collection of forced labor.

Near the end of the meal, Kruft came over to Moorloc and spoke in hushed tones. He jerked his head in her direction, but Moorloc shook his head in reply. Kruft glanced at Alex. He snarled at her, but she narrowed her eyes back at him. A wind tore through the hall, sending the dust all over, and Kruft sneezed on the table. Alex's hand shot to her mouth in disgust, and she barely kept her food down as she looked at the snot he'd left on the table. Kruft laughed and turned to head out of the dining hall.

Moorloc leisurely finished eating before excusing her. Alex jumped up and skirted between the men to get into the hallway before the mercenaries left the dining hall. She'd reached the library door when Kruft appeared. Alex swallowed her scream and tried to control her powers as Kruft blocked her way. The long scar on his face was hideous.

Why didn't Moorloc heal that for you? Aren't important enough to bother with, are you?

Before she could say anything or try to flee, he grabbed her and slammed her into the wall so hard it made her teeth rattle.

"Little princess. *Witch*," he snarled at her. "Didn't your witch mother teach you it's rude to stare? Oh, that's right. She's dead."

Alex scratched at the hand around her neck, but it tightened, cutting off her air. She wheezed and struggled against Kruft's grip as footsteps sounded down the hallway. Moorloc appeared with Reinhilde behind him.

"Kruft, release her!" Moorloc's violet eyes glared at the guard. "My niece is our guest, not someone for you to torment. Remove your hands from her!"

Kruft nodded at Moorloc before he growled. "We aren't done, little witch."

Alex stumbled as she hit the ground, gasping for breath. Reinhilde rushed to her side to help her straighten herself. When Alex looked around, she saw Kruft had vanished.

"He shouldn't bother you again," Moorloc said as he waved his hand and went back on his way down the hallway as though nothing had happened.

Alex bolted through the library door as fast as she could, slamming it behind her. She couldn't stop the shaking as she slid down to the floor. Heart pounding and sweat drenching her back, she curled her legs up to her chin to calm herself.

After what felt like an eternity, she stood and shakily made her way to the table. Taking a deep breath, she sat down and read, desperate to take her mind off what might have happened.

"I need to learn to crack," she said to herself.

"Mystics." Lygari pulled a book off the shelf and dropped it in front of her.

How long have you been in here? I never heard you come in.

"Like levitation, cracking is a basic skill all sorcerers possess, but the Mystics are the most gifted in it. The rest of us need to know where we're going anytime we crack, but they have a longer range and other ways of getting there. This book will give you the basics."

"Thank you."

Lygari grabbed another book Alex couldn't make out and cracked away before she could say anything else.

When she couldn't read another word, Alex picked up the Mystics book and two other books from the table to take back to her room and stacked the rest neatly for the morning. Clutching the books, she opened the library door and peered down the hallway. The flames crackled, moving out into the deserted hall. Soundlessly, Alex slipped out of the library with her books and crept down the hallway to her room.

The ointment was waiting for her on her pillow. She stripped off her dirty clothes, moved her necklace chain, and rubbed a generous amount of the ointment on her shoulder. Moorloc had used her magic to close the wound, but it was still red and tender to the touch. From the size of it, she knew it would scar.

What would Jessica think about this hideous scar showing with my formal dresses? The ointment relieved the pain, and she put on Aaron's shirt. *I wish I could go to the tower to watch the sea, but with how much trouble I'm in, it probably isn't the best idea.*

Instead, she walked over to the small window and breathed in the cool night air. A faint hint of moonflowers hit her. Alex cocked her head and looked up at the tower to see her work from earlier in the day. She closed her eyes and wished she could see the sea. A familiar rush of wind hit her.

Opening her eyes, she found she was at the top of the enormous tower, looking straight ahead to the Oreean Sea.

I cracked.

The moon was just rising, illuminating an eerie golden-white path from the beach all the way across the sea. Alex thought of Warren and wondered what Aaron was doing at that moment. The night air chilled her face as tears poured from her as she thought of him. When she had nothing left, Alex picked up her journals and wrote down the magic she'd managed that day. After all that, she picked up the last journal and wrote a letter to Aaron about the day and her experiences at the castle.

THE NEXT FEW days bled into each other. Despite Moorloc's assurances about her room being safe and protected, Alex could never sleep deeply enough to feel rested. The constant threat from the guards and the endless silence was getting to her. She grew more anxious each day as isolation and sadness began to take root, especially when she didn't talk to anyone all day. On the few nights she slept, new and disturbing nightmares tormented her—sparring with Lygari, having a sword fight with the mercenaries, her friends and family growing old without her, and being trapped here forever.

After a week, the mercenaries began to harass her. She

learned that the new King of Betruger was young and forward-thinking, like her father and Aaron. These men left because they had no interest in that life. They believed women should be seen, not heard, and obey the men in their lives. The idea that a girl could be a powerful sorceress was unacceptable, but the fact she was also a crown princess who would rule Warren disgusted them.

They enjoyed scaring and harassing her, especially liking to remind her that women should be silent around men. Whenever they ran into her, most would push her aside as if she was insignificant to them, but a handful were more vicious. Tristan and Doyle were Kruft's second- and third-in-command and were the worst offenders. Even seeing one of the three terrified Alex enough that she'd flee if she wasn't with Moorloc.

In a week, the confident, feisty princess who had held her head up high and gone against the King of Datten was gone, and in her place returned the cowardly, broken girl who'd hidden behind Stefan when they first arrived in the woods—a girl Alex thought she'd left behind for good in the forest.

Moorloc had not exaggerated that each day would be the same. Breakfast was *always* the horrible gray gruel that smelled like old shoes and tasted like dirt. Her days were spent in the library studying spells; working on potions in the lab; avoiding the mercenaries; working on Celtic or Poseidon powers in the courtyard, woods, or on the beach; avoiding Kruft and Lygari; eating the same disgusting violet fish with mushy vegetables for dinner; and then reading in the library until she was too tired to think. Finally, it was back to her room or the tower for journal writing followed by a restless, nightmare-filled sleep.

Soon, the stress caused Alex to struggle in her lessons. She was learning much more than she had in Warren, but she couldn't achieve what she knew she was capable of and wasn't keeping up with her power growth. Every day, she woke up with more power pulsing through her than the night before, and though Moorloc's methods were helping, it wasn't enough.

Where is he hiding the family books? I need to figure out a way to find them. Those journals are the one thing that might help me get out of this oath and finally manage my powers.

Anytime Alex couldn't sleep, she thought of going to hunt for the books but knew she needed Moorloc to trust her so she wouldn't be punished again. Even though she'd freely taken the oath, she'd done it to save Stefan and Aaron. Like the slaves, she'd sacrificed her life for those she loved. She was Moorloc's prisoner. Every day, she fought to hold her powers in check and only use the approved ones. But now, barely eating, sleeping little, and living in constant terror, her body began to fail her. After Daniel's arrival, Alex saw more ghosts in the castle. Just as in Warren, all of them ignored her except Daniel, who stayed with her more than he ever had before.

CHAPTER 8

AARON

We arrived in record time, cutting off two days, but we've been in Datten five days. I'm losing my patience with my father and his council refusing to let us leave. We have the additional men and are rested. I can't imagine what is so important that we need to keep postponing.

"Have you asked him what the holdup is?" Michael asked.

They were standing on a small hill at the edge of Datten's sword training field, supervising the men. The crisp morning air was better for it than the hot afternoon sun. The sounds of fifty knights practicing were louder than the sword match at the tournament, but Aaron barely noticed.

"No. He's busy with his council. Even Mother and Jerome won't speak to me about it." Aaron crossed his arms and focused his gaze on the men.

The elder Sir Reinhart arrived to summon Aaron to the throne room. With a nod from Aaron, Michael took over the drills while Aaron followed Sir Reinhart back to the castle.

The Reinharts were as much a staple in Datten as the Nials

were in Warren. When Jerome was busy with the knights, Sir Reinhart handled the archers. He also handled the castle guards when Jerome was away.

Aaron followed Sir Reinhart toward the castle. It contrasted with that of Warren. Warren's castle was built for activity and life, allowing the ingenuity of its citizens to flourish within its walls. Datten's was a fortress. The centuries' old monumental walls surrounding it were still as solid as when they were first built. A third larger wall ran around the town to keep the citizens safe from anything that might hide in the Dark Forest. Both the inner and outer walls were thick enough to withstand any battle and had stood unconquered for over a millennium. In the center of both sides stood one tall spiral tower. Victoria had put protection spells on them long before Aaron's time, and everyone knew they'd last forever.

Aaron followed behind Sir Reinhart as they crossed the moat on the monstrous wooden drawbridge and headed through the castle's double wall. As his feet left the old wooden bridge, Aaron remembered Alex's laughter when they'd snuck out of the castle through the emergency tunnels beneath the moat. The day they'd spent together in Datten rushed through his mind—visiting the burned-out stable; joking at the tavern with Lucas, Hunter, and Caleb; and her kissing him outside the tavern.

I was such a coward. I should have told her how I felt. If I'd done it that day after she kissed me, it would have saved us all a lot of grief, especially Cameron.

They crossed the small entrance courtyard and headed up the large stone stairs into the castle. The throne room was directly across from the main stairs, and Sir Reinhart nodded to Aaron before he took his place at the door outside of the room.

Aaron exhaled and pushed open the ancient wooden doors

and entered the throne room, letting the doors slam shut behind him. He looked down at the worn but impeccably polished marble floor. *What could my father possibly want? It's not as if we're in a rush to save our princess from mortal danger or anything.* Aaron stalked to the front of the room.

When he looked up, he gasped. They weren't alone. His parents were joined by Merlock, Megesti, Jerome, his father's entire council, and Wesley. Guinevere sat on the edge of her throne on the left side of the massive obsidian stone dais, which had been a gift from an ancient King of Warren when they'd made peace. She nodded at him without anyone noticing her golden hair move. Emmerich stood stone-faced at the base of the dais, flanked by Jerome and Merlock. Off to the side stood the council—his father's advisers and the patriarchs of the oldest families in Datten. Behind them were Wesley and Megesti.

"Apologies. Sir Reinhart informed me you wished to see me, but he didn't say it was an official summons. Had I known, I certainly would have changed." Aaron took a knee before his father. "What can I do for you, my king?"

Aaron never failed to notice the smirks on the council members' faces as he genuflected before his father. *I hope your horses bite you.*

Emmerich motioned for him to rise.

"Your father has made his choice, Your Highness," Jerome said stoically. Aaron recognized the glint in his brown eyes— Jerome was excited.

"What decision specifically? As king, you make so many," Aaron said.

His mother stood. She moved as if she floated down the stairs from her throne and grabbed his hand. "Your father has chosen the successor—who will take the throne of Datten upon his passing."

ALICE HANOV

Aaron's eyes darted to Wesley, who glared back at him. The look of disgust on Wesley's face was unmistakable. Beside him, Megesti's face revealed little, but his emerald eyes sparkled like Alex's, and for a moment, he smiled.

"It would seem your actions of late have impressed your father, young prince," one of the older men said.

"That betrothal to the Princess of Warren certainly didn't hurt," Wesley's father, Nathaniel, said. "Imagine a crown going to the man simply because he got the right girl into bed."

Aaron left his mother's side and was in Nathaniel's face in the blink of an eye. "I'd suggest you keep your opinions of Crown Princess Alexandria's personal life to yourself."

"My opinion, Prince Aaron, became of consequence when *you* declared war on the sorcerer who took your betrothed without consulting your father or us. You're risking sons of Datten—our sons—to get her back. It might only be fifty men, but why should we risk even one of our sons for your *whore*?"

Before anyone had time to blink, Aaron backed Nathaniel against a wall without touching him. *You're lucky there are witnesses here. I know better than to strike a council member in front of my father.*

"The men I'm taking are honorable—a quality the Rassgats know little about. And before you try to accuse me of slander, remember your son was sent home in disgrace and your brother has been charged with treason. Every man going with me willingly volunteered when I asked them to join my cavalry. They believe in getting back the Crown Princess of Warren not for me, but for her father and her people. Twelve years without her was enough. I may not have the promise of my father's crown, but you better make arrangements for your family."

"Why's that?" Nathaniel snarled at Aaron, but his ashen face gave away his fear.

82

"After your and Wesley's recent behavior toward my betrothed, I intend to defend her honor. Regardless of what my father decides, I *will* be King of Warren one day, and after Edward passes and I take *that* throne, I'll see to it we remove the Rassgat family from Datten. Because getting Alexandria back is not a mission for my fifty men. I'd have taken the entire army of Datten to Moorloc's door if I could and had them tear that place apart stone by stone to get her back."

"Aaron." His mother's voice snapped the spell his temper had on him. Her pinkish hue was now pale, but she held her hand out to him. Aaron left Nathaniel to join her.

"His betrothal to Alexandria had nothing to do with my choice," Emmerich said. "His actions in trying to save her did." He walked toward Aaron and Guinevere with a familiar sword in his hand. "Kneel."

Aaron looked up at his father. Emmerich's face was stoic, but his blue eyes gave him away as they beamed at Aaron. His mother had tears in her eyes. Aaron took a knee before his father.

Emmerich drew his sword and tapped Aaron's shoulders. "Today, before my queen, my general, and my council, I, King Emmerich of Datten, proclaim that following my death, it shall be my second son, Prince Aaron, who shall have my throne. No successor and no other relatives can make a claim. It's his by birthright and through his honorable actions that he shall follow me as King of Datten. Arise, my son."

Aaron swallowed hard as he rose and gazed at his father. Emmerich stepped toward him and held out the sword he'd used to bestow the title of future king on Aaron.

"You're giving me Daniel's blade?" Aaron asked.

You wouldn't even let me touch this sword, and now it's mine?

"This is not merely your brother's sword. It's the heir to the throne's sword, and it's high time you had it."

Aaron shook his head, not believing it. "And you're giving me the crown?"

"I can't allow my goddaughter to marry anyone less than a future king."

Aaron looked down at his brother's sword. Slowly, his hands closed around the blade and handle. Memories of it being on Daniel's hip in all their adventures threatened to overwhelm him. He looked up at the paintings behind the throne. The Warren family painting from twelve years ago was gone. In its place hung a new painting of Alex.

Aaron smiled. *How did anyone manage to get her to sit still long enough to have an updated royal portrait made?*

Emmerich placed his hand on Aaron's shoulder. Aaron glanced at his father and saw him looking at Daniel's painting. The wall held Alex's portrait, then Aaron's, and then his brother's final painting. Looking made Aaron realize his had been updated to the painting from his twentieth birthday.

His father had tears in his eyes as he looked along the three paintings and squeezed Aaron's shoulder. "You don't have to say anything, Aaron. But know that I couldn't be prouder of you."

"Are your men ready?" Jerome asked.

"They are." Aaron nodded.

"Then you'll leave at dawn," Emmerich said, straightening back up. The King of Datten's mask was moving back into place.

"Dawn? We could leave today," Aaron said. *Why are you so determined to delay us from leaving?*

Emmerich paused and looked Aaron over for a moment. Aaron struggled to read his father's face. When Emmerich patted him on the back, something he'd done so rarely, Aaron flinched.

"You'd rather leave to go to Betruger than stay one more day and celebrate being given my crown?"

Aaron swallowed. "I don't mean to appear disrespectful, but I've been sitting here for five days already. I need to *do* something—not wait."

Emmerich leaned down to Aaron. "Celebrating with your men *is* doing something, even if it doesn't feel like it. Trust an old military man. I wouldn't delay you unnecessarily. You'll need your men excited when you leave, and that means a full belly and a good night's sleep."

Aaron sighed and nodded to his father.

Emmerich stood and faced the men in the room. "All right, crown prince, I'll make you a deal. We'll have a feast—not a proper banquet, just the food. We can even begin early and have your men in bed at a decent hour. Tomorrow, you can all leave before the sun rises to get our princess back. After you leave, Jerome and I will ready the army, so as soon as we get word you have succeeded at establishing peace with Betruger, we'll leave for Warren."

Emmerich glanced back at Aaron and winked at him. Aaron couldn't help but smile.

How do you step into all those roles so easily—father, Emmerich, warrior, King of Datten? I blink, and a completely different man stands before me.

"I accept your terms." Aaron choked on his words. "We'll uphold the long tradition of sending our men off to battle with a celebration."

"Excellent," Emmerich shouted. "Your men deserve to celebrate that they're the first cavalry to be led by the next King of Datten."

Aaron clutched his brother's sword and looked up at his father's council, all these men who had years of wisdom and who had watched him grow from a little boy following his brother to the man who stood before them. When he really looked at them, they were all smiling, even if they were trying to hide it.

You all believed in me, except for the Rassgats. I know my father thinks threatening to take away my crown gave me the push I needed to be Crown Prince of Datten. But it was all to be worthy of her.

Aaron bowed to the council, and they all nodded to him. Then he strode to his mother. Guinevere held her arms out and embraced Aaron.

"I'm so proud of you, my love."

Aaron leaned down, and she kissed his forehead like she'd done when he was small. Aaron, in turn, kissed her cheek and squeezed her trembling hand.

Emmerich looked at Aaron and smiled. The mask slipped for an instant again. "Good, tell your men the news. We'll prepare for the meal."

Aaron bowed one last time and turned to leave the room, not only with his brother's sword but also with his mother's love and his father's pride. Holding back the feelings that threatened to overwhelm him, Aaron headed out to update Michael and Cameron.

"A FEAST? Why can't we leave now? Every day we stay is a day longer she stays there," Michael groaned.

"This is royal politics. If you thought Warren was complicated, Datten is worse," Aaron said.

"I'll leave early and make sure the horses are ready to go before dawn tomorrow," Cameron said, wiping his dusty hands on his pants as the three of them stood outside the stables.

"I'm sure you can handle the Warren men, Michael, while I make sure the Datten men are all up and ready too," Aaron said, and Michael nodded. "Then I'm going for a run before this feast. I need to clear my head and figure out what our next steps are."

Aaron had fully intended to run off some of his nervous energy but found himself standing in front of the old burned-out stable where Daniel had lost his life. A light breeze blew through the overgrowth as he walked down the path Alex had cleared through the plants. He stopped at the same spot they had when he'd brought her here. The flowers around the field were so plentiful they filled the air with their scents as butterflies fluttered from one to the next. Despite all the fresh growth, the burned-out stable was bare. Every plant Alex had accidently sent back to seeds hadn't grown yet.

If I could do it again, I'd be brave and confess everything to her after she kissed me outside the Lion's Chest. I was so worried it was the ale that made her do it—but it gave her the courage to act first. If I'd have looked more carefully at her, I'd have seen her determination, her nervousness, her desire.

"I thought I'd find you out here."

Startled, Aaron turned to face his mother. She could move silently even in her enormous dresses, but today, she wore the simplest of gowns. It looked similar to the one favored by Alex.

"What are you thinking?" Guinevere asked.

"It's not important."

"If you're thinking about it, it's important to me. Tell me."

Aaron sighed and told his mother about all the things he regretted with Alex. She confessed that thanks to Lady Jessica, she was aware of most of them, but a few, including Alex's drunken Datten kiss, were a surprise.

"Aaron," Guinevere said, "do you really think so lowly of

yourself that you believe Alexandria would need to be drunk to want to kiss you?"

Aaron shook his head. "I didn't want to push her. She deserves so much more than I can give her, more than Datten will expect of her."

"Datten will expect of her what *you* tell them to expect. You want her to remain brave and fierce? Then demand they expect that." She placed her hand on his cheek, rubbing it with her thumb.

Aaron smiled at his mother; she looked at him with sadness.

Guinevere sighed, pulling her hand back. "I never wanted this for you, dear."

"Wanted what?"

"Being king. Daniel wanted to be king from the time he could talk. He was so much like your father, but you ..." She sighed. "You were always my sweet boy. From the time you followed Daniel around, we realized you were different. You were curious about things in a way your brother never was. When we would watch the knights, Daniel always grabbed a stick to imitate them while you were looking at the bugs or the sky, in your own little world."

Aaron couldn't help but chuckle as the butterflies flew behind his mother. "I know I'm different. I can't help being what I am."

"You were different, but then she came along. Aaron, something in you changed the day you met Alexandria. When we went to Warren for the introduction to the kingdom, every boy in all the noble families looked at the baby, nodded to Victoria and Edward as required, and took off to go play with their wooden swords. *Except you.* You stared at her. Victoria noticed it immediately. Any time you were around, Alexandria stopped crying. Once she could walk, she wouldn't leave your side, and as soon as she said your name, you were hers."

"I don't remember that."

"You weren't even five." Guinevere breathed deeply and took Aaron's hands. "I'm sorry."

"For what?"

"That I never told you."

"Told me what?"

"Victoria told me when Alexandria was born that the two of you would be the ones to finally unite Datten and Warren but that I had to let you two find your way to each other. That you'd both go through terrible heartbreak more than once but would always find your way back to each other somehow. I'm sorry I never told you. That either of you would have to be hurt once, let alone repeatedly, to be together was too much for me to believe."

"Always?"

"Pardon?"

"You said we would *always* find our way back."

"That's what Victoria said."

"Then I'll succeed. I'll get her back."

"Aaron, I think you're missing the point," Guinevere said, softly touching his arm.

Smiling at her, Aaron squeezed her hands. "No, I'm not. It doesn't matter how much pain or heartbreak we go through. It will strengthen us. We forge the strongest sword through the hottest fire and the repeated pounding of a hammer. Alex and I will be the blade that is born from this torture. And once I have her back, I'll make it my life's mission to keep her safe to the best of my abilities."

His mother's hand gently cupped his face, and he leaned down and kissed her cheek.

"I should change for the feast," he said. "May I escort you

back?"

Guinevere nodded, and they headed back to the castle together.

❦ ❦

DRESSED in his Datten knight attire, Aaron walked into the dining hall crownless. He waved at Michael and Cameron and was about to join them when Jerome grabbed his arm.

"Your Highness?" Jerome asked.

"It's Aaron, Jerome. When I'm leading my men, I'm Aaron, not the Prince of Datten, betrothed to the Princess of Warren, or their future king. If they entrust their lives to me, I'll eat, sleep, fight, and live as one of them. The privileges of my crown won't accompany us on this journey."

Jerome released him. "Then you'd best get back to your men."

Aaron bowed to his parents. Once they nodded back, he squeezed in between Michael and Megesti at the lower feast table and managed to snatch the last piece of bread before the servants switched the baskets.

Caleb and Cameron were across the table comparing stories about what trouble Aaron had gotten them into. Megesti won when he told about the time when Aaron was sixteen and they'd let the castle animals out. It had taken the knights a week to catch all the pigs. Aaron told them about how mad their fathers had been. Cameron made everyone laugh, telling about the first time Aaron fell off his horse when he jousted as a boy. Julius spit his ale out when Cameron explained how Aaron had bounced when he hit the hay. Aaron sat with his men, laughing, drinking, and feasting. When the roasted boar and deer came out, Aaron realized his parents had been planning this since they arrived.

His father had been right; the men deserved a boisterous feast before heading off to possibly face their deaths.

I should have realized it sooner. Lingering on my regrets won't help, but if teasing me makes them less nervous, especially with my inexperience ... then they can have at me. Aaron knew he had faults; the men must have realized too. If he couldn't hide them forever, why try? Once he was king, he'd need their support despite his faults.

While the feast went on longer than Aaron expected, he trusted his father. After the food was eaten and the stories shared, Aaron headed to bed. His and Daniel's rooms were in the middle and top floors of the west tower. He paused at the doorway of Daniel's untouched room and clutched his brother's sword. He needed to say goodbye to this space too. Like in Warren, their rooms were nearly identical. He went in and picked up his brother's copy of *The Iliad* from the bookshelf. As he leafed through it, an icy wind blew past him, chilling him to the core.

That's what Alex said it feels like when Daniel arrives.

"Daniel, if you're here, go back to Alex." He closed the book and looked around the ice-cold room. "Whatever happens, don't leave her. I have Michael and Cameron, but she's alone."

The chill left the room as suddenly as it arrived, and Aaron headed back into the stairwell and walked up the last of the stairs circling around the tower. He paused at the edge of his room; it suddenly felt so small.

This is my last night in this room. When I get Alex back, Mother will insist we use a royal suite if we visit. Wedding or not, I refuse to be separated from her again.

He returned his crown and sword to their spot on his side table, dropped his clothes before the wardrobe, and snatched a book off his shelf. On the way to his bed, he paused at his bear rug. "Wish me luck, Achilles."

Aaron tried to sleep, but he couldn't stop thinking about Alex. He hadn't expected those few nights with her to have changed him so much. Since they'd been separated, he'd woken up in the middle of every night searching for her.

I miss her smell, the strange little noises she makes while she sleeps, and the feeling of her curled up against me.

But tonight was different. It was worse.

Why can't I shake this feeling that something's wrong? That she's scared and being mistreated?

THE SKY WAS STILL DARK when Aaron and Michael arrived in the torchlit courtyard. The men were awake and loading their horses under Cameron's vigilant eyes. Aaron had made it clear to the men Cameron was responsible for overseeing the horses, so no one argued when Cameron adjusted their bags to ensure they weren't overburdened.

I'm glad I have you because I couldn't do this without you. Cameron, you can make sure our horses get us there, and Michael, without you, I couldn't be this calm. I understand why Alex made you her best friend. You have a calming influence on everyone around you.

"Are the horses safely loaded?" Aaron asked after Cameron returned.

"They are, but Caleb and Julius are arguing about who you made your second."

"It's Michael." Aaron slapped Michael on the back. "Having a Warren knight as my second will bring the men together. Plus, he's good for morale and knows Alex, so he'll be of help to predict what she gets up to. We'll also have Merlock, so if something goes wrong, he'll get the three of us out of there."

"What about the rest of the men?" Cameron asked.

Aaron glared at Cameron. "Merlock can only take a few people at once. I'm officially the future King of Datten— making my life priority. You and Michael matter to Mother and Edward as well as me, so he'll bring you too. But if I fail, everyone else will perish."

"That's a lot on your shoulders," Michael said.

Aaron scoffed. "I know. It always is. Still want to be king?" he asked Cameron.

"No. You were born for this, Aaron. No one can do this the way you can."

"Do what?"

"Lead."

"Think we have enough light yet to head out?" Michael asked. He pointed back to the castle. Merlock was heading for them.

"I think we do. Merlock, are we ready?" Aaron asked.

Merlock nodded, and Aaron moved toward the men before them.

"All right, everyone. We're ready to go, but before we do, I want to thank you for having faith in me and volunteering to go get Alexandria back. When this is over, I'll see to it you're all rewarded for your loyalty and bravery. Now mount up. We leave for the Ogre Mountains."

Aaron smiled at his men as they mounted their horses and got into formation. At Emmerich and Edward's insistence, they were all dressed in Datten crests as they were now the crown prince's cavalry.

Aaron called to his men as he mounted Thunder. Then, as one, the group headed toward the mountains with Aaron, Michael, and Cameron leading them. When he looked up, Aaron spotted Jerome and his parents watching him from the top of the keep. It was the same spot he'd watched his father leave from as a boy.

CHAPTER 9

ALEX

"Are you even paying attention?"

Alex's eyes snapped back to Moorloc. He was glaring at her.

Lygari sat at the table, mocking her failed attempts. He was wearing his ostentatious violet robes again. Alex worked exceptionally hard not to laugh at how ridiculous they looked on his gangly body. The robes were similar to Megesti's, but Megesti trained enough with Aaron that he had some muscle. Lygari was all skin and bones, so his robes hung off him.

"This is valerian, *not* angelica," Moorloc said, thrusting the jar back at her.

Lygari snorted at her, and Alex finally lost her temper. She threw the jar at his head. Moorloc caught it and gave her a warning look, making Lygari cackle louder.

"I won't warn you again, little titaness. You'll show me and Lygari the proper respect or there will be consequences. I've been trying to avoid using the harsher methods with you. One doesn't use force with a girl, but you're turning out to be even more stubborn than your mother and significantly more spirited than Lygari was in his youth."

Alex growled at Lygari, but Moorloc cleared his throat at her.

"Temper, temper, Harbinger. Better get the angelica leaves," Lygari said.

Alex squinted at him angrily, but she turned and trudged to the shelves. None of the plants had labels, and she was so exhausted it took a minute to remember. She returned with what she hoped was the correct plant and held the jar out to her uncle, turning away to hide the fear she knew would show on her face.

"Now that wasn't so hard, was it? Next, we need the gryphon feather and powdered snake skin."

Alex nodded and gathered the requested ingredients. Moorloc had her summon the water for the potion. She collected the exact amount for the pot they were using on her first try, and it thrilled her. Once the fire was going, Lygari left, leaving Alex and Moorloc to complete the potion.

"What's the potion for?" Alex asked. Moorloc had written the recipe on a slip of paper with no additional information on it.

"It's an old family recipe for helping with sleep issues. Victoria and I perfected it over the years. I've noticed you aren't eating, appear tired, and are lacking concentration in your studies. I thought it might help you," Moorloc said.

Alex gasped but hid her face as she stirred the pot. *I didn't think you'd notice—or care.* Swallowing hard, Alex asked a question she'd been dying to ask. "What was my mother like at my age?"

Moorloc smiled and let out a sharp laugh. "Your mother was a force to reckon with. When she got an idea in her head, there was no stopping her. She is the reason we left the Forbidden Lands."

"Really?" Alex asked, looking at Moorloc carefully. She remembered the story in her mother's journal but was curious to hear Moorloc's side of it.

"She pretended it was our idiot brother's idea, but I saw through her. Victoria forgot that while she could see through my deceptions, I could also see through hers. Merlock had a vision that scared him enough he wanted to leave, and she went along with him. What she didn't tell him was that she'd had that same vision for weeks before."

"Did she tell you about her visions?"

"When it benefited her. Your mother was quite the opportunist and would use whatever she could to get her way."

Alex stopped stirring. That her mother was anything other than wonderful had never occurred to her.

"Let me guess," Moorloc said. "No one has ever uttered a word against your mother?"

Alex looked back at him and shook her head as the potion bubbled. Moorloc stood, strolled over to her, and sniffed the pot. He motioned for her to do it.

Alex sniffed and pulled back. *It smells like lavender, but there's none in it.*

"Like potions, sorcerers are complicated. Titans are the most mysterious and complex beings in this world." Moorloc looked down at her. "To imply your mother was perfect would dishonor her memory. She wasn't wicked or unscrupulous, but she had faults, as everyone does. She had a temper, was stubborn—especially when you disagreed with her—and was exceptional at manipulating people to get what she wanted. I never figured out why she did it."

"Did what?"

"Picked your father. Of all the men in Torian, she picked

the Prince of Warren to be your father. She saw something in him I could never see."

The logs in the fireplace roared to life as Alex's temper sprang to life. "She loved my father."

"In time, she did, but when she took him to bed—and I promise you *she* took *him*—she was looking for something. And since you're standing before me as both the Heart and Crown Princess of Warren, whatever that was, he had it."

Moorloc waved his hand, calming the fire in the fireplace. In that instant, everything she'd known about her mother was tarnished. Alex couldn't believe that everything people had said about her mother being with so many men was true. The idea that she'd have pursued Edward for anything other than love was devastating.

"The potion can cool while you spar against Lygari. Tonight, you can take it to help you sleep. A good night's sleep will allow your healing powers to help you heal faster."

Alex spun to look at him, wide-eyed and trembling. "Do I have to? We both know I'm going to lose."

"Yes. You need to learn, and if you're unwilling to spar with your cousin, that leaves me. The choice is yours; however, I will point out that I am more likely to interfere on your behalf with Lygari than he would be if we sparred."

Spinning her bracelet, Alex ran her finger over the line marks. After a month with Moorloc, half the line marks were black—the Celtic leaf, Merlin's infinity symbol, the Cassandra sun, Poseidon's waves, and Salem's flames. If anyone had doubted the claim that she was the Heart, her range of powers proved them wrong, even if her ability to effectively wield them wasn't there.

Alex exhaled. Her hand rubbed the burn scar that remained on her shoulder despite hours of trying to heal it. "Can we get it over with?"

Moorloc nodded, and Alex followed him. Lygari was waiting in the courtyard. He'd changed out of his fancy robes and was back in his pants and a violet shirt. Alex sighed. She gripped her mother's necklace and begged for strength from whoever might listen as she took her place on the dirt patch across the courtyard from Lygari.

He crossed his arms and smirked. "Seeing as you still haven't got a grip on your powers, I'll let you go first again. I've defeated a dozen of the Betruger king's best men in one shot, so you're not really a challenge."

"Is it fair to consider beating mortals the same as a sorceress?" Alex asked. "I know the Betruger men are skilled warriors, but I don't think you're one to fight fair."

"Why on earth would I fight fair if I don't have to?"

Alex sighed. She closed her eyes, and the soft summer breeze tickled her skin and brought the scent of the sea. As a calm washed over her, she reached deep for her Celtic powers. When she opened her eyes, thick vines covered in thorns snaked their way into the air, weaving into each other until they formed a shield in front of her.

"That's not completely terrible," Lygari said. "But it'll burn."

Her shield was so thick she couldn't see, but she could hear the sound of Lygari slapping his palms together. The crackle of fire followed as his fireballs struck her vines. They burned immediately. Alex jumped back and brought a second layer of vines from the ground. These were thicker than the first and wove together more tightly. Then she kneeled and touched the ground, summoning water. As her Poseidon power flooded her, Alex touched the vines with her free hand, soaking them with water. When the first shield fell, the second one was ready to go—and stronger.

Lygari's laughter carried across the field. Alex slunk to the side of her shield and risked a peek. She watched as he created a fireball, stretched it out, and then hurled it. The entire shield shook as the fireball hit. Alex lost her footing and stumbled back. As she righted herself, the ground beneath her rumbled while Lygari's laughter grew louder.

Alex fell back onto the ground as the soaked vines burst into flames. She struggled to get more vines up. When she spared a glance, Lygari was sending more fireballs at her. Alex threw her arms around her head to shield herself. The surrounding air became colder than the forest camp in the winter, and an icy wind caressed her face. When she dropped her hands to look, ice entombed her.

Lygari's flames struck the ice, and water ran down the walls. Fear filled Alex as she desperately tried to refreeze the ice, but the fresh ice built up inside and closed in on her. As the ice turned orange from the flames fighting to get through, Alex pushed herself as far back as she could.

"Enough, Lygari," Moorloc shouted. Alex watched as the receding flames burned a hole through the ice. Lygari's smug face appeared, and the look of it was enough to make her sick.

"Like I said last time. Silly little mortal princess. That's all you'll ever be."

Rage erupted out of Alex, making the entire ice dome around her melt and soak her in seconds.

"At least I knew my mother!" Alex shouted at Lygari as she struggled to her feet on the slippery ground. Lygari whipped around and threw a fireball at Alex's face. But before it could reach her, Moorloc cracked between them, and the flames vanished in front of him.

"I said enough." Moorloc stepped toward Lygari. "Sparring is over. It's time for dinner, and I prefer to eat in peace." With a wave of his hand, Alex's clothes were instantly dry, and they all headed inside to dinner.

When they reached the hall, Moorloc went inside, but Lygari grabbed Alex's wrist, dragged her back around the corner, and shoved her into the deserted armory.

"Let me go," Alex ordered.

Lygari slammed the door behind them and stared at her. "You don't realize what's going on here, do you?"

"You mean other than you being a Graham?" Alex pushed him away.

"A what?"

"A weak, stupid male who thinks they can scare me."

"I'm not the one you need to worry about, *princess*." The words came out in a snarl. "I know you think I'm annoying and cruel and that my father is trying to help, but I promise you it couldn't be further from the truth."

Alex stared at her cousin. "Why would I believe you? You're a murderer who has repeatedly made my life difficult, if not outright horrible."

"That's true. But those are nothing compared to what my father is capable of. He tells you about your mother—but he is *selective* of what he tells you. He tells you what will get you on his side."

"That's a lie," Alex said, tears welling in her eyes. "He told me my mother was a whore who picked my father to breed with rather than out of love."

"I hate to tell you this, but what's said about your mother is true. Sorcerers are not as uptight about sex the way mortals are. So if your mother wanted lovers, she'd take them. Simple as that."

Her eyes widened, but Lygari kept talking.

"Humans live for fifty years. They get fifteen to twenty good active years to have children and never know when or if they'll have one. Sorcerers can have children from the age of eighteen until our death, and we can choose when we have them. We enjoy a much longer age of *exploration*. You need to realize that your mother was young for a sorceress when her family came here. Our amorous stage lasts until well into our seventies or eighties."

"Catch your tongue. I don't want to know this, least of all from you." Alex turned to leave, but Lygari blocked her path.

"Would you prefer to hear it from my father when you turn twenty and your hormones turn you into a lustful, crazed sorceress? Or would you rather have the time to prepare yourself? Because I can promise you my idiot cousin or uncle thought to warn your betrothed."

Alex froze. "What do you mean, 'warn' Aaron? I'm here until your father says otherwise. Why would they need to warn him of anything?"

"Unlike my father, who's locked himself away in this castle since he arrived in Torian, I've worked with Betruger. I understand what Datten is capable of and what a territorial Datten prince will do to get back something he thinks belongs to him."

"I don't belong to any man," Alex growled, setting the torches in the room blazing.

"Maybe, but that won't stop him from coming for you. Especially if you found your way into his bed before you left. That whole honor nonsense in Datten makes them stick to someone once they've ..." Lygari looked her up and down. "So did you help him? Or do you *know* he's going to be successful?"

Alex stared at Lygari, trying to absorb everything he'd told her.

"So no vision," he said. "If you didn't know he would come for you, why on earth would you have agreed to come here?"

"Do you really not understand the notion of love? That I would give my life to save Aaron's in a heartbeat?"

"Sorcerers aren't built that way. We can love, but we value our lives too much to give them up so freely for another."

"Then I pity you, Lygari."

"Why? Because I'm not willing to sacrifice myself for some mortal whelp?"

"No. Because you never had anything *worth* sacrificing yourself for."

"Both our mothers sacrificed themselves for us. What good did that do to anyone?" Lygari asked.

"What do you mean?" Alex asked, but before Lygari could answer, the door flew back and hit the wall, making her jump.

Kruft's second-in-command, Doyle, filled the doorway. His purple eyes fixed on Alex. His blond hair was tied behind his head, and his brown skin almost vanished in the dark doorway.

"Why are you hiding in here?" Doyle asked.

Alex swallowed and moved behind Lygari.

"Get out," Lygari said to Doyle.

"I'm following orders. Your father wanted to know where you vanished to. Should I tell him I caught you alone with her in the armory?"

"She's my cousin, you imbecile," Lygari said, snarling at the mountain of a man before him.

"Betrugers value family above all else."

"Then you should understand me having a word with my cousin. So get out before I set you on fire."

Doyle looked suspiciously at the pair of them until Lygari summoned a fireball to his hand. Seeing that, Doyle left, slamming the door behind him.

"Why tell me all this?" Alex asked.

"Because I believe you're going to have to kill my father to leave."

"I can't kill my family."

"Why not? I'd help you."

"Why would you offer to help kill your father?"

"Survival. My father believes he'll eventually break you and be able to control you, but I know better. When it comes down to you against him, you're going to win, and I need to make sure I'm on the right side of that fight."

"I won't give you an oath, Lygari—*any oath.*"

"I know. I'm trusting that mortal sense of honor you inherited from your father will keep me alive. Let's hope my faith isn't misplaced." Without another word, he opened the door and walked out.

Alex stood in disbelief, wondering if that conversation had really happened. *Could Lygari actually be on my side? Is he trying to get me to trust him so he can betray me? What if his actual plan is to kill me? I don't know what to think anymore. But ... maybe he'd help me get a letter to Aaron.*

Clinging desperately to that last shred of hope, Alex opened the door to find Kruft's two favorite guards, Tristan and Doyle, waiting for her.

CHAPTER 10
AARON

"Do you think we're pushing the horses too much?" Aaron asked Cameron on their third day of hiking up a challenging stretch of the mountainside. Michael had gone ahead to scout with Julius and Caleb, leaving Aaron and Cameron to bring up the rear.

"Not yet, but if we don't reach the peak today, they'll need a day off tomorrow. Father gave you the best horses we breed, but even they can't go forever."

"Another lost day," Aaron groaned.

The endless days were infuriating, but on top of that, there was nothing but rocks, dirt, and a few scattered trees on this stretch of mountain. Nothing to hide them if trouble came.

"Buck up," Cameron said. "You didn't think we were going to get her back in a month, did you?"

"No, but we should have made more progress."

"You *want* us to have made more progress, but we've moved exactly as far as I expected. It's like my father says. Things take as long as they take, and we can't force them even if we'd like to."

"You sound like your father."

"I'd rather sound like my father than yours."

Cameron laughed, and Aaron snorted, scratching his face. He still wasn't used to the beard that had sprouted since they'd set off on their journey.

Aaron heard horses trotting and looked up to see the scouts. "So what did you find?" he called to them.

"We're about an hour away from the top," Julius said, a big grin spreading across his face.

"Good. We'll stop here for a brief rest and some food and then carry on to the top and into the next valley," Aaron said. Julius rode ahead to tell the men.

They'd been riding for weeks, following the small valleys that broke up the expansive mountain range, and finally made it across the mountains. At first, the men grumbled about the rough terrain and joked about whether Aaron really knew where he was going. He'd allowed the gentle ribbing, knowing the men needed to focus on something while they adjusted to the mountain terrain. Soon, the joking vanished, and they followed him without question.

Reaching the massive peak, he realized they were almost at the end of the mountain range. Smaller mountains still stood between them and the Oreean Sea. Staring at the blue water, Aaron couldn't stop his mind wandering to Alex. He missed her so much he couldn't stop replaying the night of his birthday. They'd gone to the bowels of the castle to calm down after Lygari and the mercenaries attacked. They had talked about their parents and life. She'd let him hold her to keep warm. It was the first time he'd let himself see how she really looked at him.

Even after a battle, you followed me, trusted me. I miss you so much and hope you aren't being mistreated. If anyone hurts you, I swear on my crown I'll—

"What are you thinking about?" Michael asked. "You have your serious brooding face on."

"My what?"

"That's what Alex calls it when you're lost in thought like that."

"What else does Alex say about me?" Aaron asked.

"Oh no. I won't break the confidence of my princess."

Aaron turned to look at Michael, who wasn't smiling as much as usual. "Let me understand. You'll fight at my side, risk your life to convince the King of Betruger to come with us and attack the most powerful sorcerer in Torian, but you won't tell me what my betrothed says about me when I'm not around?"

"Correct."

Aaron laughed. "Why not?"

"I've been keeping Alex's secrets as long as I've known her. She's family, and I don't have much of that. She'll tell Jessica not to marry me if I upset her. Also, she sets things on fire when she's mad."

"Fair points," Aaron said.

A whistle came from the group.

Aaron pushed Thunder forward and trotted toward the men with Michael behind him. Heading into the valley, Aaron decided they'd travel parallel to the sea and search for the Betruger castle hidden in the mountain valley. The air smelled more fragrant as they moved away from the rocky terrain, and they saw crops and trees. This land was more fertile, and soon they found scattered bits of forest and bush to hide and hunt in.

They split the work evenly, and that included Aaron. He was grateful the men accompanied him, and he made sure to assign tasks according to each man's strengths and took the duties everyone hated. The men noticed both, and it quickly built strong morale.

We're all taking the same risks, so I'll treat everyone as equals, regardless of their station in the kingdoms. After years of hearing the knights complain about how they hated it when my father traveled with his army and left them to handle his and his council's share of the work besides their own, I'll do it better. I'll be fair and make sure I listen to their concerns.

So when the men talked about seeing people nearby, Aaron took it seriously.

Aaron declared that they would travel by night so they'd remain hidden as they foraged off the land, hunted for food, and slowly climbed their way across the remaining rocky landscape. He stressed to the men they were not to be seen.

On a sweltering predawn morning at the end of July, they reached the peak of another challenging mountain and finally found what they were searching for. Perched atop of the mountain over the next valley was Betruger Castle. Aaron let out a sigh of relief.

It was smaller than Datten's or Warren's castle but looked as if it were climbing up the mountain—they'd built the castle *into* the mountain. Daniel had told Aaron the Betruger people lived in caves high up on mountain ridges, but clearly he'd been wrong.

Before them stood an architectural wonder. Aaron marveled at the stone towers and spirals that rose higher into the air than any Aaron had ever seen before. Like the one in Datten, a massive wall stretched around and surrounded both the castle and the town, except Betruger Castle seemed to have an opening in the middle. Aaron realized they must have cut a path through the wall to allow the men to move unseen. *Their builders thought of everything.* In the predawn light, the castle was visible, but during the day, it would be camouflaged against the rocks of the mountain.

They had made it to Betruger Castle, and Aaron squinted to

see the town in the distance. The houses were built similar to those in Warren, featuring narrow roofs of alternating heights but close together. The army was too far away to tell if the houses were colored like Warren's or made of dirt and rocks. Aaron wondered if they'd been built together because of space or to foster community, as Warren had done.

The men dismounted in a small valley and tied their horses. Some men began foraging for food while others gathered water for the horses. They did their best to remain out of sight since hiding fifty horses was no easy feat.

Aaron, Michael, Cameron, and Merlock hiked up the peak to get a better look and come up with a plan. The men stayed quiet as Aaron studied the castle and wall. The sun was over the mountain, sending a bright light onto the castle before him.

"We found it, but now what?" Michael asked.

"Now I figure out how to see the king," Aaron said.

"You mean meet the king without being killed," Cameron added.

"Exactly." Aaron forced his voice to sound more confident than he felt.

"Your father would head up and *demand* to be seen," Merlock said.

"I don't think that's a good idea," Michael said. "Datten is known for being aggressive. Betruger could kill first. I'm supposed to keep him safe. I promised her."

Aaron looked him over. Michael's entire demeanor had changed; he was more serious and stood with a stiffness that made him resemble Stefan.

"I agree with Michael. We need the Warren approach," Aaron said. "I'll take a small group of volunteers. We'll arrive on foot and ask to see the king. Perhaps without an overt show of force, they'll allow us in."

"If they don't …?" Michael asked.

"We hope they let us leave to come back," Aaron said.

"What if they don't?" Cameron asked.

"If we don't return, take everyone home," Aaron said to him. "If we don't come back in ten days, you'll know we're dead."

"*Ferflucs*, Aaron!" Cameron said. "Even if I'm furious with you, my place is at your side. You haven't thought this through."

"Thinking it through is all I've done since we left Datten. This is the only way."

"You can't truly believe I'll agree to stay behind—that I'll sit here like a coward while you risk your life."

"It has to be you, Cameron. I brought you here for your expertise with horses, not to fight. If anything goes wrong, *you* need to return to Datten to tell my parents. They won't believe anyone else."

Cameron swallowed hard but nodded before pointing an accusing finger at Aaron. "You're not allowed to get yourself killed. I don't want to tell your mother she's burying another son."

"She won't get to bury him if we die here," Michael said.

Aaron and Cameron both turned to look at Michael. The somber look on his face as he stared at the castle was unnerving. Aaron realized he'd worried so much about the men, he'd neglected Michael. Alex expected him to take care of Michael, but he hadn't noticed how much worrying about Alex and Stefan was weighing him down.

When I have a few minutes, you and I are going to have a long talk, Michael. If we get Alex back and she comes home to a broken Michael, she'll never forgive me.

Aaron turned to head back down the valley to talk to a few more men.

"Aaron?"

Aaron caught Cameron's face in the morning sun. Under the beard and messy hair, he looked like the boy Aaron had grown up beside. He looked scared.

"Cameron?" he asked.

"We're good." Without another word, Cameron turned and continued toward the horses.

Aaron smiled as he watched his cousin leave. At least one thing was getting better.

"Wait!" Aaron shouted after him. "Did you say that because you think I'm going to die?"

Cameron didn't turn around but waved at Aaron as he disappeared down the hill.

"Michael, let's go," Aaron shouted up the hill.

Aaron, Michael, and Merlock headed over to the men Aaron hoped would join them. Julius, Caleb, and Henry agreed before Aaron could finish asking. It took less than an hour for them to prepare to head to the castle on foot. Aaron packed his satchel with the pearl nestled inside. When he looked at Michael's glum face, Aaron considered leaving him behind. *If things go wrong, I'd need Michael and Stefan to get Alex from Moorloc—and get her through my death.*

The castle looked increasingly intimidating. Aaron swallowed hard. The others had gone to refill their water skins, leaving him and Michael.

"You can stop staring at me," Michael snapped.

Aaron had never heard him use such a harsh tone. "There's no shame in staying behind. You could look after Cameron," Aaron said.

Michael dropped his arms to his side and glared at Aaron. "You think I'm a coward because I didn't grow up with knights? That I'm not willing to die for her?"

"I don't doubt your loyalty, Michael," Aaron said. He

moved closer to Michael and lowered his voice. "I'm thinking about what happens if we—if *I* fail and don't make it back. Who would save her ... take care of her?"

Michael swallowed and looked at Aaron. "Stefan would. He's spent most of her life protecting her. If you don't realize he's already made *several* plans with General Nial, then you don't know Stefan. Besides, I promised Alex."

"What?" Aaron looked at Michael as fear flooded him.

"After we came back from the castle. You were in Datten being stitched back together, and we sat at Stefan's side. She cried in my arms like she always has and made me swear to take care of you. That if anything ever happened to her, that I'd look after you, and, um ..."

"And *what?*"

"I told you in Warren. She made me promise if something happened to her, that I'd make you find someone else."

Aaron's heart stopped. "There is no one else, Michael."

"I know."

"Will she give up?" Aaron bit back a gasp as the words rattled out of him.

"We all have our breaking point. But as long as she stays angry or hopeful and not sad, she'll be strong. She just needs *one person* there to connect with. If she can find someone to give her a piece of what Stefan or you or I do—*just one*—she'll survive until we get there."

"If she can't?"

Michael looked away and exhaled. Aaron waited with bated breath for Michael to turn back. "Then we may get the princess back, but the Alex we knew will be gone. She said that after losing her mother, she couldn't handle another heartbreak. That it would destroy her."

Aaron breathed deeply and wiped the tears from his eyes. "Then move faster."

Michael and Aaron marched to gather the others. The sun was up, and they had to work hard to avoid being seen by the people who were out living their regular lives. It took longer than Aaron would have liked to sneak down and back up the single valley, but the forest area was smaller and thinner than the Dark Forest where he'd grown up. To ensure they weren't spotted, they continued to travel at night and into the early morning hours.

THEIR PATIENCE and careful movements paid off. In the early morning light, two days after leaving their group, they made it to the castle wall without being spotted. The morning air was cool and crisp, and the dew made their shoes and pants wet as they slunk through the thinning woods. The group of six men inspected the castle walls from the dense surrounding trees, looking for a way in, until they found the gate. The massive stone bricks were different from those used in Datten and Warren. They were the same shade of brown as the surrounding rocks, and despite the harsh climate and nearby sea, they didn't appear weathered. Instead, they were polished to an even smoother finish than decorative stones in Datten. Aaron admired the beauty of it from their vantage point inside the tree line.

Michael grabbed his arm. "Are you sure this is the best way, Aaron?"

"Best? I can't say. It's my only option. Alex told me to trust my instincts, and they're telling me to use the Warren way. We have to show trust and peace first. Besides, I brought a gift." Aaron held up his satchel and grinned.

Michael and Merlock flanked Aaron as he strode out of the

safety of the woods right up to the castle gates. The others remained close but a few steps behind.

"I'm Crown Prince Aaron of Datten. I'm here to seek an audience with the King of Betruger. I—"

A group of armed guards sprang from the wall and surrounded them. They appeared from the stone as if they were made of it. Aaron couldn't believe how well they'd been camouflaged. Each guard was fully clad in leather armor colored to match the surrounding rocks. Hoods, also colored to match the rocks, covered their hair and faces. As they removed their hoods, Aaron started. The stories in his family's library told of monsters, but these men looked like any of the knights in his father's armies with their varying shades of brown skin, black and brown hair, and normal knight build. The only things that differed were the eyes—all shades of purple—and the men were all taller, making Jerome look short by comparison.

Aaron glanced around at the wall behind them. He still couldn't see where the Betruger knights came from. He'd admired the stones for a long time in the trees and didn't notice that they hid their guards.

"Stand down," Michael ordered the Datten men.

Aaron held his hands up. "We're not here to fight. I wish to speak with your king. I have come to make peace and brought a truly special gift."

The oldest of the men snarled at Aaron as he scrutinized him. His skin was a dark brass, his black hair was speckled with gray, and he stood nearly seven feet tall, but it was his lilac eyes that made Aaron stare.

I've never seen purple eyes. Is it the altitude? Does everyone here have them?

Aaron remained composed, his face calm and stoic as the guard's stare intensified. One of the younger Betruger guards muttered something, and Aaron's palms sweat. The senior one replied in a language Aaron couldn't understand. The younger man looked at Aaron's crest and then punched Aaron in the face.

Michael leaped to his aid, but Aaron held his hands out and straightened himself while he wiped his bloody lip and nose with the back of his hand. The senior guard shouted at the others, and the younger guard was shouting at his companions. Aaron watched the senior man and noticed he had yellow stripes on his uniform's shoulder. *Do those depict your rank?*

As soon as the senior guard shouted, the younger guard stopped yelling, and two of the other guards took him away. Aaron wiped his face again and swallowed the blood in his mouth, not wanting to risk offending the senior guard by spitting it out. Aaron rolled his shoulders and stood tall, trying to show this wouldn't deter him.

"*Despite* what happened, I desperately need to see the king."

The guard shouted something in Betruger, and the gate opened. Aaron tried to peek inside, but another dozen guards stormed out and seized them. These men were better trained than the younger man, and before Aaron could order his men, two of the guards grabbed each of them and hauled everyone toward the gates. Aaron scanned the faces of his men, and while they weren't happy, they weren't panicking either.

That's good. Stay calm while I figure out what to do. Aaron held his hands in front of him when the one in charge moved toward him.

"I'll come freely. You don't need to drag me."

The guard nodded and pointed to the gates.

Readjusting his satchel to secure the pearl, Aaron straightened his back, fixed his tunic, and marched proudly through the gates before his men. Grumbles sounded behind him.

Aaron glanced back. His men had been released and were doing their best to emulate his calmness.

Once they arrived inside the wall, the gates slammed shut behind them. Sensing the agitation of his men, Aaron stood taller. Only Merlock seemed unaffected by their predicament. Aaron tried to look around, but it was impossible with so many guards in the cramped space. They were being corralled down a narrow pathway between two large brown stone walls.

I was right. There is a path here. That must be why we didn't see them moving.

The air quickly grew stale and hot as the guards pushed them along. Each man had two guards around him, and the stench of their sweat in the confined space was unbearable. By the time they stepped out, Aaron was sweating and gasping. As his men followed, they rushed to his side. Julius, Caleb, and Henry tried to flank Aaron, but he shook his head softly and put his hand on Henry's shoulder to drill home his order not to draw their swords.

"We're guests. Even if we're slightly being held hostage. No fighting," Aaron said, raising his brow to them.

Michael came up beside Aaron and chuckled.

"What?" Aaron asked.

"So many kinds of apples." Michael pointed at the large fruit trees that lined one side of the courtyard.

Aaron recognized the apples, pears, peaches, and nectarines but couldn't identify any of the others. Michael started laughing, looking at Aaron.

"Now what?" Aaron asked.

"Alex will hate the beard. She can't even eat peaches because they tickle her."

Aaron pushed Michael playfully. He rubbed his bearded chin as he looked around to survey the area. *Then she is definitely going to laugh at my beard when we get her.*

From the outside, the inner castle had looked small, but this space was amazing. The grass was as green as Alex's eyes. The trees were lush and bowing with fruit despite the rocky soil outside. Aaron noticed training equipment similar to what they had in Datten—wooden swords, dummies, and barrels of archery supplies. Surprisingly, the men wore leather armor, nothing metal—neither those sparring or training, nor the guards watching him and his men.

Aaron spotted a pair of older men working with a group of boys. They were working on footwork. Their speed and agility were amazing. Even the smallest boys moved around with finesse. Aaron's own men were nimble, but compared with the Betruger knights, they moved like drunkards. He watched until the senior guard stepped in front of him.

"Move back," the guard said and stared down at Aaron with a glare that would make Jerome nervous.

Aaron opened his mouth to speak but decided it would be prudent to obey. Moving back with his men, Aaron continued to take in their surroundings—towers, walls, weapons, anything they might have in common. But his eyes kept coming back to the boys. They reminded him of his own training with Jerome and Matthew.

"Why do you want to see our king?" the guard asked. He stood at ease, but Aaron knew he was ready to attack if necessary. His stance was identical to the one Jerome took when he was training new knights.

Aaron gave the guard his most charming prince's smile. "I need his help. I come with an offer of peace and a gift."

"You're of Datten." The guard pointed to Aaron's crest on his tunic and wrinkled his nose and lips in disgust. "Datten doesn't make peace. I should end you and be done with this."

As the guard moved his hand to his sword, Michael and Caleb reacted. But Aaron threw his arm out to stop his men.

Next, he undid his sword belt as the guard watched. As he held it out to the Betruger guard, Aaron's men gasped.

"What's your name, sir?" Aaron asked.

"Macht to you," the guard replied.

Aaron nodded as Macht took his sword. Aaron grunted to his friends and thrust his head at Macht. The Datten men removed their swords and handed them over to the Betruger men.

"As you can see, Sir Macht, we mean no harm. I meant what I said—we want peace. I've studied the Betruger kingdom. You won't hurt me because we're here on behalf of King Emmerich. Even if you doubt who I am, you won't risk killing me without your king's order. Betruger is as honorable as Datten."

Macht scoffed as he grasped Aaron's sword in his hand. "We have more honor than you. But here, you must first best our general to meet with our king."

Aaron looked up at Macht. "If I must fight the general to earn an audience with the king, I'll do it."

"Very well." Macht turned around and shouted in Betruger to the older men. One turned and headed off across the yard toward an elaborate stone doorway.

None of them knew what they were waiting for, but it was clear they were to stay put. The minutes spent waiting felt like an eternity until the older man returned with a younger man.

Aaron eyed the man carefully. *This is the general?* Younger than the guard before him by at least a decade, the general wore a simple green tunic, black pants, and boots and lacked the leather armor the guards wore. Wiping his hands on his pants, he strode in with a false confidence that Aaron recognized. He'd spent his life surrounded by men trying to prove their importance to other people either by clothing or mannerisms. The general's posture appeared forced. He was clearly new to his role and uncertain about what he would do about this situation.

"General, we caught these men trespassing," Macht said as the man arrived at his side.

"Regards, Macht." The general nodded at Macht and slapped him on the back before he stepped toward Aaron. While shorter than Macht, he still towered over Aaron. His skin was a cool bronze, and his black hair was short and curly. But it was the general's eyes that Aaron fixated on. Like Macht, the general's eyes were purple, though a darker violet shade. Aaron had never seen anything like them before.

"Who speaks for you?" the general demanded in a deep, commanding voice.

"I do." Aaron stood taller and stepped toward him. Macht grunted, and Aaron stilled.

The general glared at him, moving his eyes from Aaron's golden blond hair down to his royal crest and back up to his face. "You're from Datten."

"I am."

"We hate Datten. Your kingdom has done nothing but attack us for six hundred years." He turned to Macht. "End them."

"No." Aaron thrust his hands out, and both Macht and the general shifted their stance toward him. Feeling the sweat drip down his neck, Aaron exhaled slowly. "Please spare my men. They came at my command, followed my orders. They're innocent of this hatred you feel toward Datten."

"And you aren't? It takes a King of Datten to attack a kingdom. Knights merely obey," the general said with a sharp tone as Macht crossed his arms.

"Kings and princes can lead men."

"Aaron, this isn't going well," Michael murmured before the guard behind them struck him.

Aaron spun around and shoved the guard back. "Don't touch him." In response, the other guards drew their swords, but Aaron remained unmoving, staring down the three men to protect Michael.

"Macht!" the general snapped, and Macht shouted at the men in Betruger. They immediately backed down and stood at attention again. Aaron turned back to the general to find him observing Aaron with his head cocked to the side.

"Such loyalty to your men. But who are you to give commands?"

Aaron nodded to Merlock. The sorcerer snapped his fingers, and Aaron reached into his satchel. The Betruger men moved for their swords, but the general's hand shot up. Swallowing hard, Aaron pulled out his crown. He placed it on his head and stepped up to the general.

"I'm Prince Aaron Edward Johnathon Arthur, Crown Prince of Datten and, through betrothal, Prince of Warren. I have come to speak to your king and beg him to help bring my betrothed home and to end the centuries' old war between our people."

"Peace from Datten? Liar! Our king will never agree to see you. If you leave immediately, I'll spare your lives." The general turned around to leave.

"Please," Aaron called after him. "We share an enemy. Your kingdom's former adviser, a sorcerer named Lygari, killed your king."

The general stopped and turned back to Aaron. "How did you know?"

"I'm a crown prince who prefers to hide as a knight among my people. I have learned many things that way, including rumors of the betrayal and death of King Ehre. Twelve years ago, that same monster murdered my brother, and now, he and his father have taken my betrothed, the Crown Princess of

Warren, and are holding her captive. If we have any chance of bringing her home, we need to join forces with you. United, we can defeat them."

Macht looked at the general, and they both chuckled.

"The illustrious Prince Aaron of Datten. Your reputation precedes you. We had high hopes for when you became king. Yet here you are, inviting death by trespassing in my kingdom."

Aaron ran his hand through his hair and tried not to think about all the things his own father had said about his shortcomings as a leader.

The general continued. "You bring few men, fewer weapons, and no horses. You're clearly not here to attack— either that or you're very foolish."

"Many have called me foolish. I'm young and inexperienced but not foolish enough to arrive alone. The rest of my men are in the mountains. If I don't return in a week, they'll consider us lost and go home."

"Where your mother would mourn another son," the general said.

"Yes," Aaron replied.

"All right, Crown Prince Aaron," the general finally said. "To have an audience with our king, you must fight me. Win, and he'll speak to you, and you'll leave unharmed."

The general motioned to Macht, who grunted, and the guards held back the Datten men. Aaron handed Michael his satchel and stepped toward the general. The other guards quickly sent the boys off the field.

"If I lose?" Aaron asked.

"Then you'll be dead."

Aaron could sense Michael and Merlock's panic behind him. Slowly, the general circled him. Aaron stood tall, ensuring his crown remained straight on his head. The sun was high enough that the dew vanished, and sunlight warmed his face.

He thought of Alex and how her eyes sparkled in sunlight. It helped him withstand the scrutiny of the military man before him.

"All right," he said. "I accept your terms. Without the king's help, we're lost, and I'm willing to risk everything to get Alexandria back."

The general headed over to the young boys and older knights while Macht and the other Betrugers pressed the Datten men toward the wall. The young boys scattered but remained close enough to watch. When the general returned, he was wearing a gigantic sword on his hip and holding two shields—one circular and one oval. He held them up for Aaron to choose.

Aaron took the oval one, and Macht returned his sword.

"Aaron, don't do this," Caleb said. "Let one of us fight in your place."

"Who?" Aaron asked, handing Caleb his crown. "You and Julius are better with a bow. Merlock can't fight. Michael doesn't know the formal rules, and I always beat Henry."

"But, Aaron—"

"*Sir Reinhart*, I've heard your protests, but it's *my* choice."

Caleb nodded and fell silent. Aaron turned and adjusted his belt. The general was watching him. Swallowing the fear in his throat, Aaron moved toward the man. This close, Aaron could see his entire chest move with every breath.

"I'm ready," Aaron said.

The general motioned for Aaron to follow him to a large circle of dirt in the middle of the courtyard. The grass surrounding it was barely alive. Everyone in the yard stopped and watched them. Even the guards on the top of the wall had stopped their duties to watch their general fight with Aaron. There had to be at least a hundred of them. Aaron looked up at the general. He'd had his pride handed to him many times by Jerome and was prepared for it again.

I hope I do well enough to earn an audience with His Royal Highness.

"Have you had a sword match before?" the general asked as he moved to one side of the circle, ensuring they both had the sun on the side of their faces. The general was older, outweighed him, and had the height advantage.

Is this how Alex feels when she has to spar with Stefan, Jerome, or me?

"Of course. I've sparred with my father's general many times and had my share of fights in tournaments." Aaron took his place opposite the general and adjusted his shield.

"So why make war on the sorcerer? We heard you hate war."

"Who told you that?"

"I have my sources in both Datten and Warren. Now tell me your side."

Gripping Daniel's sword, Aaron took the proper stance before replying. "I lost my brother as a boy. I grew up seeing what that did to my parents and swore I'd never cause that pain and grief to another parent."

The general drew his sword and took a similar stance to Aaron. Immediately, Aaron noticed an odd red sheen to the general's blade as they began to slowly stalk each other around the circle.

"Yet you came here." The general moved slowly to Aaron's left.

"I had to."

"I've enjoyed this recent peace between our people."

Aaron smiled at him. "I have too. When your guards appeared out of the walls, I finally understood the legends of the Betruger knights disappearing into the land."

"It seems you are as well read as people say."

Aaron watched the general's calculated, slow moves. Speed would be Aaron's advantage in this fight. Darting toward him, Aaron slashed at the general. He moved his shield in time, and the hard blow made Aaron's arm shake as he leaped back from the massive Betruger sword that swept at him.

Aaron faked to the right and slashed at the general's left, but his opponent evaded Aaron's swing at the last second. When the general swung, his sword collided with Aaron's shield, sending it into Aaron's shoulder. Pain ripped through his arrow wounds despite Alex's work healing them. Fighting the pain, Aaron gripped the shield tighter. A few more sweeps, slashes, and stabs later, both men were starting to pant.

A cry from above distracted Aaron for the briefest second, and the general took full advantage. He raised his sword and slammed it into Aaron's shield. Aaron saw the blow at the last second and dropped his sword to hold the shield with both hands. A crack resounded through the courtyard as the shield split in two. The general and Aaron looked at each other, shocked for a second.

"Aaron—stand down," Michael shouted.

"No," Aaron said. He dropped half the shield and swung the remaining piece at the general.

CHAPTER II
ALEX

"Snooping again? I thought you learned your lesson last time," Tristan said. He wasn't as tall as Doyle, but he was extra mean to make up for it. His tan skin looked darker in the dim light and his black hair vanished, but his gray eyes had a cruelness behind them as they fixed on Alex.

"I wasn't snooping. Lygari dragged me in here. Doyle caught us," Alex said.

"I don't know what you're talking about." Doyle smirked.

Alex's temper roared to life, but she breathed deeply to calm it, knowing Moorloc would be furious if she set something on fire. "I wasn't snooping, and I did nothing wrong. Now *move*. I'm late for dinner."

"I say otherwise." Doyle grabbed for her arm, but Alex easily slipped away from him using Stefan's defensive moves. Annoyed, Doyle pushed her as Tristan stepped forward to block her. Anger turned to fury, releasing her fire powers. Above them, the ceiling burst into flames. Alex jumped back, moving close enough to Doyle that he slapped her behind. Alex spun around and shoved him—but, like with Stefan, their size difference meant nothing happened.

Doyle and Tristan both laughed at her obvious frustration. Alex turned and punched Tristan with an uppercut to the chin.

Tristan screamed, and Doyle tried to grab Alex from behind, but she elbowed him in the gut. He groaned and grabbed his stomach. Alex spun around and kneed Doyle in the groin, sending him to the ground. Tristan had recovered and seized her wrist, slamming it into the wall.

Alex threw her right hook. Footsteps sounded behind her, and Moorloc and Lygari rounded the corner in front of her as her fist connected with Tristan's face. Everyone heard the crunch when his nose broke and began to squirt blood.

Alex shook her hand, realizing she was rusty and hadn't positioned her thumb properly. *That punch would have gotten me a lecture from Michael.*

Strong arms gripped her waist and pulled her away from Tristan as he started swearing at her.

"Enough!" Moorloc shouted. "What happened here?"

"They harassed me again," Alex said, trying to squirm away from Kruft's vise grip on her middle.

"Nonsense," Kruft said over Alex. "I found her punching them when I came around the corner. I know my men. They're completely loyal to me, and they wouldn't have done anything to her."

"That's a lie," Alex screamed, trying to pry Kruft's hands off her. "*All* they've done since I arrived here is belittle and harass me. Moorloc, you've seen them do it."

"She's lying. We caught her in the armory snooping again. We said we'd report it to you, and she went crazy," Doyle said, glaring at her.

"Stupid witch even set the ceiling on fire," Tristan said, wiping his face.

Alex desperately turned to Lygari, but he turned his head before his father looked at him. Lygari shrugged at his father and smirked as he looked back at Alex.

"She has a history of snooping and a preference for violence," Lygari said.

"I tire of your insolence. I try to be kind and understanding, yet you persist in showing nothing but disrespect for my home and people."

"Kind and understanding?" Alex wanted to scream and set the entire hallway ceiling on fire. "It doesn't matter how kind you are. You manipulated me, and I don't *want to be here.* If you were kind or understanding, you'd let me out of the oath and have me come for training after having seen the value of what you can offer me."

Moorloc moved toward Alex and looked at her carefully. Kruft released her so suddenly that Alex stumbled when her feet hit the ground. Moorloc nodded, and Kruft struck her across the face. A metallic taste filled her mouth. Her eyes watered instantly, and a ringing filled her ears. The shock made her breath stop as she looked at her uncle.

"Sir Kruft, bring my niece to the tower."

"The tower?" Lygari asked.

"If she insists on claiming she's a prisoner, then we'll treat her accordingly. She'll remain there until breakfast the day after tomorrow. No food, no water, no comforts from her room. That should put her back in line. Lygari, fetch the Celtic books I assigned her and bring them to her new room. She obviously needs time with them to learn the peaceful aspect of that line."

"You can't do this," Alex cried, desperate to get away from them.

Doyle moved to grab her arm, and her defensive instincts kicked in again—but excruciating pain hit as her powers failed her. Alex looked down to see her bracelet had turned the same color as the red steel blades.

Temporarily losing her magic didn't impact Stefan's teachings. She punched and kicked Tristan and Doyle when they tried to contain her. Alex knew she'd done damage when more blood came.

"ENOUGH!" Moorloc roared. "I am out of patience. Kruft, deal with my niece as you see fit."

Kruft's monstrous smile sent a shiver down Alex's spine as he rushed her.

"You're as stuck-up and entitled as your mother was. You think you're better than us? We'll give you something to cry about."

He grabbed Alex's arm and twisted it as he dragged her the entire way to the tower. Alex cried in pain at how he held her. Each struggle against his grasp made him laugh and squeeze harder. Lygari had cracked away during the scuffle, and when he returned, he followed them with the books. Once they reached the tower, Lygari opened the door, and Kruft threw Alex onto the floor of the room. Alex slammed into the ground so hard it knocked the air out of her and cut open her chin. Kruft's horrible laughter echoed through the room as he headed toward the courtyard.

Lygari glanced back quickly and dropped the stack of books on the floor. "Happy reading, *princess*," he shouted before whispering, "I'm sorry."

He slammed the door hard enough that the tower shook. A click sounded. Alex ran to open the door, but it was locked. She realized she'd learned how to manage magical locks but not how to pick normal ones. Merlock and Megesti never expected Moorloc to use a key lock.

Alex sobbed and pressed her back into the door and sat

down. Her arm throbbed, and her stomach rumbled. She'd picked at breakfast and missed dinner completely.

It's going to be a long day.

Alex pressed her head to the door. All her hard work undone. They'd been working on Salem, Moorloc's dominant power, and she was improving. He'd trusted her and controlled all the near accidents she'd had. She'd been on her best behavior; she listened, learned, and, most importantly, obeyed without question. Moorloc was pleased with her progress, and she'd thrown it all away on those two idiots.

A small crack sounded. Alex looked up, and Aaron's cloak was on the floor in front of her.

Thank you, Lygari.

Alex grabbed the cloak. She hugged it to herself, pulled her knees to her chest, and cried until she was out of tears. Then she got up from the cold ground and looked at the small, dirty, broken bed. She grabbed a Celtic book and climbed the rickety stairs to the tower above the room. At the top, she leaned on the ledge and watched the sea. Moorloc had been right about the sea refilling her powers. Even looking at it helped energize her. Filling her lungs with the salty air, she climbed up on the ledge and reached up into the rafters. After a few tries, she found her journals and jumped down.

Alex opened a journal and began her daily letter to Aaron. She described the sparring match and her confusion about what Lygari had told her and Kruft. Tears hit the page as she wrote, *I miss you all so much. Thinking of you hurts, but I can't stop. I need to remember you to keep going.*

Alex looked at her arms. Bruises were already forming.

I wish I could send you a letter to ease your fears and my own. Maybe Lygari would help me.

"What will his next punishment be?" She shuddered. To

take her mind off it, she made a list in her mind of what Stefan and Aaron would do to Kruft for giving her those bruises.

Alex picked up a plant book. Even if she couldn't remember all of their names, plants were a power she excelled at. In the month she'd been there, she'd mostly separated her Celtic powers from her emotions and could control plant growth at will, even if the odd tree or plant got away from her.

Alex read until she couldn't keep her eyes open anymore. Then she moved to the small bed on the main floor and sent a wind to remove the musty smell. Lying in the bed, she fell asleep dreaming of Aaron's smile.

Moorloc was true to his word. Alex spent the next day alone and not a scrap of food or a drop of water was brought. She used her time to memorize every plant in the plant book she didn't know. Alex took her mother's ledger and practiced the plants by guessing what ailment her mother was treating based on the plants she'd used. A Rassgat had needed help with virility. The Lady Elizabeth Veremund needed help to conceive. The Datten king had gout. The Wafner general had muscle and joint pain. Her mother helped so many others with the garden on her roof.

Would a princess even be allowed to help heal people? Could I be like her one day?

Thinking of her mother made her think back to what Lygari and Moorloc had told her.

Was what everyone said about her true? Could sorceresses really be that different from mortal maidens?

With her head spinning, full of more questions than answers, Alex went to sleep early that night, hoping to sleep through her hunger pains.

She found herself on the beach by Moorloc's castle. Breathing the sea air, she listened to the waves lap at the sand. She'd had this dream often since she arrived. It never changed. She strode out into the water, stopping at waist height. Her magic drank in the sea's power as her fingers skimmed the top of the water.

The hair on the back of her neck stood up when he arrived, and Alex turned to look at the man on the beach. His hair was obsidian-black except for the streak of gold that ran through it starting above his left eye. The streak matched his golden eyes. He watched her with an intense stare that only Stefan could best. Alex knew he could see the real her, the parts of her she hid from the world and herself. Tall and handsome, he wore the ugliest robe Alex had ever seen in her life. When he tilted his head, the burnt orange collar would slip, exposing two small marks on his neck: an ax and a crescent moon.

Alex felt terrified and excited. Her heart pounded painfully in her chest, and her palms became clammy when his stare grew more focused. He held his hand out toward her, and it brought Alex toward him with a force she couldn't resist. She grasped his hand, and the cold seawater swallowed her.

Alex woke up gagging on seawater. She was soaked and freezing. Dreams had never been dangerous before. She stood and searched the wardrobe to find a single pair of old pants and a stained tunic. They were too big, but at least they were dry. She was too shaken to dry the bed. As soon as she finished changing, the door clicked, and Kruft opened it.

"Get up and get out here," he barked at her and walked away, leaving the door open.

Alex rushed out the door, hoping to avoid angering Moorloc further. The gulls were already active on the sea. Their cries carried all the way to the courtyard, and with the surrounding silence, she could hear them even here. The sun was barely up, and the morning dew sparkled like jewels in the grass as she cautiously scanned the yard. Moorloc and Lygari stood at the center. Moorloc appeared stoic, and though

Lygari's lips were pursed, his eyes were wide. Alex managed a few steps before Doyle and Tristan grabbed her.

"Let me go!" Alex demanded, but they held her arms firm and far enough away that she couldn't kick them. Digging their fingers in her arms, they dragged her out to the middle of the courtyard before Moorloc, Lygari, and Kruft.

Kruft's smirk spread across his face, and his eyes sparkled with delight. "I'm going to make an example out of you, little princess witch. I've seen royal entitlement my whole life, and I'll not tolerate it in my house."

"Entitlement? You *lied* about what your men did to me and had me locked in a tower for two days!"

"You broke a guard's wrist and another's nose," Kruft said.

Glancing at Doyle and Tristan, Alex noticed the bandage on Doyle's free hand, and Tristan's nose was slanted to the left. Rage seethed through her. Alex had to fight hard to keep her fire under control—if she didn't, it would get worse.

"I fought back because they won't leave me alone. Their injuries are their fault."

"If you get angry, I'll get to put you in your place," Lygari snarled.

Alex swallowed her rage and looked at the ground.

"After thinking it over all day and discussing the options with Kruft, we have decided on your punishment," Moorloc said.

"Locking her up without food or water wasn't the punishment?" Lygari asked.

"That was the punishment for snooping. The punishment for injuring the men was up to our head guard," Moorloc said.

A wicked grin spread across Kruft's face. "As punishment for your violent actions toward my men, you'll receive thirty lashes. Fifteen for each man you wounded," he said.

Alex's blood turned to ice as she shook her head in disbelief and stared at Moorloc. "That's barbaric," she said. Her voice wavered as her breath came out in sharp rasps.

"You need to learn your place here, little titaness." Moorloc spoke calmly, as if he were asking her to hand him a book.

"No," Alex begged, desperately trying to back away from everyone. "I'll behave—please!"

"It's too late for begging," Kruft sneered. "Kreiger, Adolf, hold her."

Two giant men Alex didn't recognize took her arms from Tristan and Doyle. They moved her to the free wall that led into the hall and pressed her against it. The stone was cold on Alex's face, and the jagged edges cut into her cheek and wrists as she struggled against their iron grips. When she struggled, they pressed her harder into the wall, so she stilled.

Alex could hear Kruft talking to his men. When he went silent, sweat dripped down Alex's face and back while her legs trembled. A hand gripped her shirt, and Alex bit down her scream. Kruft laughed as he pulled her shirt away from her back. It choked her for a second before it ripped. Chilly morning air hit her clammy skin, and Alex swallowed down the bile rising up her throat. He ran his rough and calloused hand leisurely down her bare back, ensuring her shirt didn't cover it. It made her stomach lurch as her flesh prickled from the crisp air.

Kruft pressed her shoulder blade against the rough rocks as he leaned toward her ear. His breath was hot against her skin and smelled of old ale. She desperately wanted to turn away from him, but they still pressed her into the stone.

"I could be persuaded to come up with an alternative punishment. One that wouldn't mark your beautiful flesh so permanently."

He grabbed her braid and, giving it a tug, moved it off her back. Alex jerked backward.

"Get your hands off me," she growled.

"Mouthy, like your mother. She thought she was too good for me, and all it got her was dead."

"Just get on with it, Kruft," Lygari snapped, and Kruft stepped away from her.

"No temper tantrums, little one. Take your punishment like a proper sorceress, or I'll have to resort to magical punishments, and I assure you those are much worse," Moorloc said.

Alex gulped and thought of Stefan's training in the woods, remembering the times he forced them to stand on tree stumps for hours or hold logs above their heads or run without knowing when they'd stop. It had hurt and burned, but he'd prepared her for this—for the time he wouldn't be there to protect her.

A crack filled the air before the first whip struck. Alex bit down hard but didn't make a sound. The pain was terrible, but not seeing it coming was infinitely worse. Alex knew she'd never forget the sound of that whip. She tried to focus on something else around her, but there was nothing except cold stone and the unseen whips behind her until an icy wind encircled her.

Daniel.

Cold surrounded her and numbed her back. Daniel was holding her, desperate to protect her from a pain he couldn't stop.

I'm not alone.

Using Daniel for strength, Alex closed her eyes and took her punishment.

134

AFTER IT WAS OVER, Moorloc cracked her back into her room. She'd been relieved of her studies for the rest of the day. She stared at her bed, trying to focus on anything but her back. She'd made her bed that morning. It wasn't perfect, but she was getting better at it. Food had been brought to her, but the pain was so unbearable she couldn't eat. After a few hours, Reinhilde appeared long enough to deliver new food and take away her untouched plate from before. Kruft accompanied her to ensure she didn't help Alex. The smug look on his face when he saw her broken hurt more than the scars. Through it all, the room remained ice-cold, no matter how much wood Reinhilde put on the fire. Daniel refused to leave her side. He sat with her and rubbed her back to numb it and dull the pain.

Alex's rage was so intense she couldn't function for the rest of the day. She spent it lying on her stomach to give the wounds time to heal. It took every bit of energy in her not to set the castle on fire.

Don't burn the place down. You'll burn too. Think of water. Think of Aaron.

She focused hard to dull the pain on her back and treated the wounds as best she could with the skills she'd learned as a healer growing up in the woods, but she couldn't reach the wounds, so her Cassandra powers were of no help.

Once night hit, Reinhilde slipped into the room with Lygari. Daniel watched them both with suspicion, but Alex didn't care. They brought a basin of clean water, some rags, and new books. Lygari warmed the water and kept watch as Reinhilde tended to her back. Alex could smell a combination of herbs in the water and tried to figure out what they'd used.

She lost consciousness more than once from the pain of Reinhilde cleaning her wounds, but she knew it would help stave off infection. Finished, Reinhilde caressed Alex's cheek and left the room with her supplies, leaving Alex alone with Lygari.

"Why?" Alex asked as Lygari placed her new books within reach on the bed.

"As bad as this is, sorcerer punishments are worse."

"Worse how?"

"You wouldn't want to know—trust me."

"Why help me?"

"Because of what you said the other day. There was *one* person who loved me ... who was kind to me. I can't bear to disappoint her."

"Your mother?"

"No. My mother died in childbirth. There were complications, and it was me or her. My father didn't even hesitate." Lygari moved to the door, and Alex had to twist to look at him.

She thought of Megesti and wondered how Merlock handled the loss of Megesti's mother and raising an infant alone. "Then who?" she asked.

"The only person to ever show me love and kindness was your mother." Lygari spoke so quietly Alex barely heard him. He turned and left without another word, closing the door behind him.

That night, Alex shivered in the cold air. She couldn't sleep on her back, nor could she tolerate her scratchy blanket over the still raw, bleeding flaps of skin that covered the whole of her back. She cried, thinking of her mother, of what Lygari said, of her father, and, most of all, Aaron. She longed to be in his arms. She could crack to him now that her skills had improved, but she'd never be able to save him or Stefan when Moorloc undid the healing. Trembling, she wished she'd wake up from this horrible nightmare to find Stefan teasing her about her stupid dresses or Michael ribbing her about how much Aaron made her blush.

As the night wore on, Alex whimpered and tears rolled down her face, soaking her pillow. "Mother, I can't do this anymore. I need help from someone who has my level of power. It's growing faster than I can control. What am I going to do? I don't know how to make Moorloc happy with my powers. Please don't let them break me."

CHAPTER 12
TITAN OF MYSTICS

espite the setting sun, the forest air was hot and muggy with a heavy, sweet smell of flower nectar. Flowers and leaves of every color filled the trees while butterflies fluttered around, attracted to the nectar feast. Gryphon took a deep breath and watched them flit and float past him. Summer in the Celtic forest was the most beautiful in all of Torian.

After what I went through to get Birch this book, she better be happy to see me. Last time, she berated me for not visiting her sooner. Not exactly the best way to get me to come back.

The sun was setting, so he quickened his pace to find what remained of the overgrown stone path. It didn't matter how many times he'd walked this exact trail; he never remembered where the path was. Knowing she'd be livid if he hurt any of her *babies*, he took extra care with his step, a courtesy few received. As darkness fell, he sent an orb of flames before him.

Another day of chaos and idiocy. I can't understand why anyone even listens to Garrick anymore. The older he gets, the angrier and more insane he becomes. If this happened to my grandfather, it doesn't bode well for me when it's my time to be Head.

A small red fox appeared on the path, and he stilled to let it pass him. Tired of waiting for it to move on, he gekkered back at the fox, and it bolted. He straightened his robe, shifted the massive book, and continued along the path. The wind picked up, sending his wild hair swaying across his forehead, and a small voice whispered, *"Help me."*

Gryphon froze. He scanned the surrounding woods, but with every heartbeat, the forest grew darker. "Is someone there?"

Silence—except for the buzzing of insects around him and an owl waking up. Sweat gathered on his forehead as he strained to hear. *I must be more tired than I realized.* Satisfied, he exhaled and took a step.

"Help me, please."

He spun back toward the path and sprinted until the cottage came into view. As soon as he passed the invisible protective barrier, a tremor rippled through him. Panting softly, his senses heightened, and he listened. The owls and bats had woken and were out hunting for their evening meals, but there were no voices. Unable to silence his loud breathing, he threw open the door of the cottage.

"I can't do this anymore."

"Birch? Birch, where are you?" He raced into the simple wooden cottage. A mug of hot green liquid was waiting for him on the small table between the door and kitchen. He lifted the beaten old mug, sniffed it, and groaned, turning his head.

"Drink it," Birch said from the couch in the sitting area. Several birds sat on the back of her chair, watching him.

Gryphon winced. "It smells like feet."

"Drink it anyway. They can't know you came here."

He sighed, drank the entire cup in two gulps, and then

shook his head. "It's not terrible. Did you add berries this time? It tasted sweeter."

"It's the nectar in the flowers this time of year. Did you find my father's journal?"

When he held up the book, a smile spread across her entire face, lighting her eyes. The green in them matched the moss growing on the walls of her cottage.

"Thank you, Sprout. I know it was risky." Birch's raven-black hair fell across the acorn-colored skin of her shoulders as she stood and took the book from him. "How was the titans' council?"

"Tedious as always. Every meeting gets longer because of how much my father likes to hear his own voice."

"You'd think after a century as Head, he'd be tired of it."

"Sadly not." Gryphon smiled at his aunt. "They still haven't found a Celtic powerful enough to remove you as titan."

Birch smirked. "He's trying, though, isn't he? I've been feeling a surge of power lately."

"He is, but I felt the surge too. So has Lynx."

"So everyone's felt them? Do they have any ideas?"

"My father thinks the Heart has come into their full powers. He remembers these sorts of ripples when his Heart came into his power, though those were nowhere near as strong."

"That seems unlikely, unless ..." Birch trailed off.

"Unless what?"

"Unless your Heart is a Merlin or Cassandra. Their line has been missing for almost a century." The unease in the room grew heavier.

"You know where they are, don't you?"

"Don't ask questions you don't want the answers to, Sprout."

"Fine. Lynx and Kharon send their regards. They miss having you at council since my parents banished you again."

"Of course they do. Celtics and Tiere have a close connection. Without me, Lynx has to talk to Ridge, and sorcerers in the Mire line are as exciting as the dirt they play with. Kharon and I went to school together, so clearly they'd miss me. Anything of note come up?"

"Ember and Phobos were too busy trying to win my father's approval to give a proper update on the Salem and Ares lines. Ridge, Pearl, and Penelope had little to add and looked bored."

"Mire and Poseidon are close with Celtics too. I'm surprised Ridge and Pearl didn't have more to say about a new Celtic titan."

"They mostly complained about all these power ripples we've been having. So what do you need help with?" he asked.

"What do you mean?"

"You called for help while I was outside. Said you couldn't do it anymore."

"No. I've been waiting for you. I didn't say anything."

"That's strange."

"Maybe you're getting your answer."

"I'm going outside to figure it out. Sorry I can't stay." He kissed her cheek and turned back to the door.

"Your Mystics powers can pick things up further away than anyone else."

"Better me than my father." Gryphon headed out the door into the pitch dark. Not bothering with a glowing light, he focused, opening his well, and releasing his Mystics powers. By the time he crossed the boundary, his entire body was glowing with a faint blue light.

He barely made it two steps when the voice returned. *"Please don't let them break me."*

Something inside him stirred, making his blue glow deepen.

"What the Ares? I don't recognize that voice."

As he looked down, his usually golden bronze hands glowed even brighter blue. It dawned on him. The Heart was calling for help.

CHAPTER 13
AARON

One strike, and the shield was ripped from Aaron's hands. Jumping back, he tripped over the other half and landed on the ground hard as the general stalked toward him. In seconds, the blade pressed against Aaron's left shoulder, piercing above where Alex's arrows had.

Panting, Aaron stared up at the general.

"Do you yield, Prince of Datten?" The red in the general's sword was more obvious so close up.

"I yield," Aaron said.

The general handed his sword to Macht and held his hand out to Aaron. Grasping it, Aaron allowed himself to be pulled up before he collected his own sword.

"You fought bravely and with better skill than I expected," Macht said.

"Believing there are better options than war doesn't mean I'm not trained to fight."

"How many armies have you led?" the general asked, looking back at the Datten men beside his own.

"They're my first. I feel I'm too young to lead an army, and my father believes I'm too old to learn—somewhere in the middle lies the truth. But I won't allow the brave men who followed me to lose their lives for my failing. If you require a sacrifice, then I'll forfeit my life."

"You'd end yourself for your men?" the general asked, twisting his head sharply at Aaron.

"Yes. They followed me out of honor and a desire to rescue the Crown Princess of Warren. So if you take my life, I beg you to still help them free her. She shouldn't suffer because I'm better on my horse than with a sword."

"Your offered sacrifice is enough, Your Highness. You have won your audience with our king," the general said.

Aaron bowed low. "Thank you, Your Royal Highness. I have many matters to discuss with you and have brought you a truly precious gift to start us on the correct footing."

The king paused. "You knew?"

"As you said yourself, I'm well-read. The General of Betruger is the king, even if he has a dozen sons. The king leads the army himself. I may not believe in war, but I've learned a great deal about the other kingdoms."

"Yet you fought me still," King Harold said, tilting his head to the side.

"I needed to prove myself worthy of an audience with Your Royal Highness."

"You may address me as King Harold."

"Then please address me as Prince Aaron. What of my men?"

Harold eyed the men with suspicion, especially Merlock, before pointing at Aaron. "I'll speak with you. *Alone.* Macht, take his men to our dungeons."

Aaron nodded to his men and headed for Michael and Caleb to collect his crown and satchel. Macht stopped him and took the bag. After he'd rifled through it, he returned it to

Aaron. The Datten men went away peacefully with the guards while Aaron followed the king through the courtyard and into the castle. Several guards flanked them as they walked until Harold waved them away.

As they strolled down the hallway, Aaron couldn't help but feel awe at the building they were in. The stones used to build the castle had been cut with a precision that he'd never seen in any of the other kingdoms. Harold allowed Aaron to walk a few steps ahead of him down the lengthy hallway. The stones on the floor were well worn, but those on the wall between the decorations sparkled as if they were gems. The walls were covered with paintings of stunningly beautiful women without a man in sight. Even the colors used were richer than any he'd seen in Datten.

"Are these your queens?"

"Yes." Harold stopped at one of the paintings and smiled. "We value our wives and mothers more than anything. We learned long ago that if you want a legacy, you treat your wife with utmost respect."

"I couldn't agree more," Aaron said, but Harold scoffed behind him.

"You come from Datten, where men *own* their wives like property. What do you know about valuing a woman?"

"My mother is from Warren, where women are encouraged to have opinions. I was raised differently," Aaron said. "Speaking of unusual, do all Betruger speak the common tongue as well as you? I didn't know Betruger were bilingual. There's nothing in our books about it."

Harold sighed. "That's one good thing to come from that horrible sorcerer. My father insisted he teach everyone your common southern tongue. My generation speaks it fluently, but our older men less so." Harold motioned toward a narrow hallway. "What else was wrong in your books?"

"Plenty," Aaron said. "My brother told me you lived in caves, and the books I read as a boy told of monsters who could rip a grown man in half with their bare hands."

Harold chuckled. "Ours told of ugly, short, stocky men whose skin was translucent and whose hair would blind you in the sun. They were also said to be violent and angry."

"That is a fairly accurate depiction of many former kings of Datten."

When Aaron arrived at the door, he opened it to reveal a library filled with floor-to-ceiling bookcases. Aaron smiled. *Alex would love this room—she'd probably insist we make our library match it.*

"I'm sorry for what my kingdom put you through."

Harold paused at the large table in the center of the room. "What do you mean?"

"I've read the kings' journals," Aaron said. "I know Datten attacked first, even if no king would ever admit it."

Harold took a seat at the table and motioned for Aaron to join him. Aaron sat to his right rather than across from him. Alex's words echoed in Aaron's mind: *The king had purple eyes.*

"That older man you brought—he isn't a knight." There was a suspicious tone in Harold's words.

"No. Merlock is my father's sorcerer."

Harold crossed his arms and looked at Aaron. Sighing loudly, Aaron explained how Merlock, Megesti, Victoria, and Alex fit in with Lygari and Moorloc and how they'd come to be in Datten and Warren.

Harold shook his head. "I have no faith in sorcerers. We learned that their kind cannot be trusted and that they'll turn on you when it suits them."

"Our truce can't begin with lies. I know Lygari made you doubt the sincerity of sorcerers, but I hope to dispel those beliefs."

"It isn't so simple. I have *many* doubts, and I knew what your man was the moment I saw him. I nearly put him in chains."

"I know it's hard for you to believe that a sorcerer could mean no harm, but our sorcerers are different." Aaron told the long story of the sorcerers, of family connections, powers, and failings, including Alex's accident that injured him. "Her guilt from hurting me and Stefan is how Moorloc managed to take her from us."

"She left willingly?"

"She sacrificed her freedom to save us, something I can't live with."

King Harold sighed. "Thank you for your honesty. I am aware of the princess's unusual powers *and* this incident at her mother's castle. I was testing your honesty ... and honor."

"Real peace can't begin with a lie. I'll give you complete honesty in anything you ask," Aaron said.

"How do I know you speak truthfully?"

"Because of the gift I brought you," Aaron said. He reached into his satchel and pulled out the velvet bag. Harold stared as Aaron slid it across the table to him.

Cautiously, Harold grabbed the bag and opened it. "What's this?"

"It's called the pearl, and it shows your memories. It came from the Forbidden Lands with the sorcerers and ended up in Warren with King Edward. He's giving it to you as a sign of appreciation for helping get his daughter back."

"How does it work?"

"You hold it and think of a memory. Then a fog appears, showing you that memory like a dream before you. It'll show you I speak the truth because it can't lie. It merely shows memories, including details you may have forgotten."

"You could be lying."

"Believe your own eyes then." Aaron held his hand out and waited for Harold to hand him the pearl. Aaron placed it in his free hand. "Watch and then try for yourself."

The fog spread around them, and Edward's table appeared. Aaron's conversation with Edward, Emmerich, and the generals detailing their plan of getting Alex back played out before them as ghostly apparitions in the fog. Harold snorted when Aaron snapped back at his father that he wasn't asking and would get Alex back, even if it meant going alone.

Next, the fog swirled around and replaced Edward's room with Alex's old bedroom.

"Aaron—" Alex whispered before Aaron was on her, holding her face in his hands.

"Alex?" Watching himself, Aaron could not believe the nervousness in his own voice.

"Stop being honorable and kiss me," Alex said, and Aaron grabbed her face and finally kissed her for the first time.

The pearl clinked as it hit the table in front of Aaron.

"I can show you Alex distracting me so I was knocked off my horse while jousting, or when she shot me with her bow the day we found her, or dozens of times where she was trying to show me she had feelings for me and I ... had no idea."

"Clearly she had feelings for you if she shot you."

"I don't understand," Aaron said.

"An old Betruger custom. Here, if a maiden shoots a man, she's claiming him as hers. If he agrees, he gives her a horse, and they marry."

Aaron stared at Harold, shocked. "Why would she shoot him?"

"It shows she is proficient enough with a bow to help provide for their family. It hasn't been used for some time."

Aaron held up the pearl to Harold. "Would you like to try?"

Harold reached out and took the pearl. "So I hold it, and it'll show my memories?"

"Yes. It can't lie or change them. We hoped you'd try it and confirm my sincerity."

Harold gripped the pearl tightly, and the fog spread around them again. Before them appeared a woman singing a beautiful song Aaron had never heard before. She had dark bronze skin with long, curly black hair and deep turquoise eyes. She smiled as she sang. A boy's voice joined hers to sing the same song.

Glancing at Harold, Aaron suspected he was looking at the last Betruger queen. The same curly black hair, only shorter, sat on Harold's head as tears filled his eyes. Aaron racked his brain to remember what happened to her.

"She ended twelve years ago. She became sick." Harold answered the question Aaron wouldn't ask. "It happened around when your brother ended. It's why my father never took advantage of Datten's sudden lack of interest in fighting."

"I'm sorry," Aaron said.

"My father wasn't a usual Betruger family man. He expected our mother to tend to us, so when she ended, he didn't know how to be a father," Harold said.

"Us?"

"My younger brother and I. He ended when we were boys. There was an accident." Harold said.

"I know that pain. I never realized Lygari was the culprit until recently. If I had spoken up sooner, perhaps your father would be alive," Aaron said.

"Even if you had, my father wouldn't have trusted his sources. He was heartless. Someone would have ended him eventually. I'm surprised it took that long." Harold went quiet for a moment. "What is it?" Harold asked, looking Aaron over.

"I don't know how to make you believe this, but I'm not my

father's son. When I rule, I intend to bring Datten into a new age like Warren. I don't intend to spend my entire reign at war —with you or anyone else."

"I understand. I am not who my father wanted me to be either. His rule was brutal and violent. Our people were willing to follow him, but he could never see past how things had been or let go of old hate."

"My father lost his desire for war when my brother died. I intend to do what I can to keep that peace," Aaron said. He sighed, imagining himself and Alex on his parents' thrones one day, bringing Datten into the modern age.

"What will happen if you change your mind when you take your throne?"

"I won't."

"How do I know you will honor your word?"

"All I can do is give you my word and hope you'll accept it. I don't have any honors yet to prove my worth as a prince, but I can tell you that the most important people in my life are my betrothed and my mother. Both women came from Warren and are not afraid to tell me when they aren't happy with me."

Harold narrowed his eyes as a sheepish grin spread across his face. "A Datten crown prince who obeys his mother and betrothed?"

Aaron smiled. "Yes. I've been told my whole life I'm too much like my mother. When you meet her, you'd assume Alex was the Datten heir."

"Oh?"

"She has a temper and doesn't like when people don't listen to her. But I suspect you two are going to get along fine," Aaron said.

"Putting your cart before your goat."

"She was right. You're my Edward," Aaron said, pointing at Harold.

"Your what?"

"Just something Alex told me that I'm only beginning to understand."

Harold leaned against the table and stared at Aaron. "You didn't travel all this way to compare childhoods. What exactly did you hope to achieve?"

Aaron explained how Moorloc had stolen the books that would have let Alex control her powers and then attacked. He also confessed how he'd declared war on Moorloc and intended to get the books back. Finally he explained how Alex had left and how badly he'd reacted at finding out.

Harold shifted his elbows onto the table and rested his chin on his hands. "You still want to marry her?"

"More than ever," Aaron said. "We have a connection I can't explain."

"What do you need from me? Men? Access to ships?"

"I need help to locate Moorloc and Lygari's castle. I hoped that you might have an idea where they are after Lygari lived here for so long."

"I believe so," Harold said. "Over the years, our ships have witnessed odd things happening on our northeast shores. Our men see a castle appear and vanish. I wouldn't hold much faith in drunken sailors' tales, but too many men have seen it for me to simply ignore."

"It's a start and more than I had before," Aaron said.

"Recently storms arrive in that area without warning."

"Storms? Alex has power over the weather."

Harold eyed Aaron carefully.

"So have you decided whether you'll work with me or if you'll kill us all?"

"I would never end you," Harold said.

"My father thought I was mad for coming here. He didn't believe that you could see past centuries of hate."

"I'm not my father, and you have something about you." Harold shifted and sat back in his chair. He watched Aaron long enough that he started to sweat. "I think we'll make a good pair. Prince Aaron, I'll grant you your truce. I accept Datten and Warren's terms for now. I'll work with you long enough to hunt down this deceptor Lygari—and help you free your beloved. Whether we maintain our truce afterward will be up to you and your men."

"But—"

"But?"

"You must have something to add," Aaron said. "I would."

"You're right. I have one condition," Harold said, standing up. "When we find this castle, *I* settle our score with Lygari."

"I'll do everything in my power to get you that."

"That's a Warren answer if I have ever heard one. You have spent much time with Edward."

Aaron stood, holding his hand out to Harold, and they shook.

"Now, straighten your crown, Prince Aaron. We'll retrieve your men from our dungeon. I'm still impressed you got so far without us knowing. I clearly need to brush up on Datten warfare."

"You'll want to study Warren warfare." Aaron followed Harold down the narrow hall and explained how they traveled at night to avoid being seen and then sent a small party once near the castle.

Sir Macht was waiting for them in the larger hall. Harold spoke quickly in Betruger. Macht nodded to the king but glared at Aaron.

"I don't think Sir Macht likes me." Aaron smiled at the guard, who scoffed back.

"Macht suspects everyone. Any requests for our feast?

Datten is landlocked; do you even eat fish? What about mountain goats?"

Aaron laughed. *That's what you're worried about? Feeding me?*

Harold looked at him. "Isn't it proper royal protocol to ask your guest about their food tastes?"

"You're worrying about my food preferences, but my men are in your dungeon. Will you release them so I can send for the rest?"

Harold's eyes went wide for a moment. He jerked his head toward Macht and nodded. Immediately, the guard headed down the hall.

"How many did you bring? We'll want rooms prepared for everyone."

"We're fifty, including those here," Aaron replied.

"We can room fifty easily," Harold said as he stopped a young servant who was going past. He spoke quickly in Betruger, and the servant stared wide-eyed at Aaron before hurrying off.

"I understand if it isn't possible, but could I have a tour?" Aaron asked. "I find the differences in our castles fascinating." Aaron looked up at the ceiling and realized theirs were taller than Datten's and arched at the top.

Harold crossed his arms and gave Aaron a crooked half smile as he looked him up and down. "I think a small tour would be possible."

They continued to discuss customs as Harold explained how the queens' portraits ran along the west side of the castle because the queen's suite was on that side. Aaron learned the kings' portraits were on the east side with the king's suite. Just then, a rush of footsteps sounded behind them. Macht came around the corner with Aaron's men. They were still missing their swords but otherwise looked perfectly fine.

"Are you all right?" Aaron asked them.

"We are, Your Royal Highnesses." Michael bowed to Harold and then to Aaron while the others stayed back.

Almost right, Michael. The bowing was great, but I'm just Highness, though Alex would've been impressed.

"What do you need us to do?" Julius asked.

Aaron turned to Harold.

"We're having rooms made up for all of you," said the king. "Tonight, you'll enjoy a feast and dine as our guests. Sir Macht will accompany you to retrieve your companions."

"Michael and Caleb, would you take Merlock and Sir Macht to bring back our men? King Harold and I still have much to discuss."

"Of course, Your Highness." Merlock nodded to both royals. "Your Royal Highness." He followed Sir Macht to fetch their men, Michael and Caleb hurrying behind him. A minute later, the servant was back, and Harold instructed him to take Julius and Henry to their room.

Harold took Aaron on a tour of the castle, showing him their orchard, training grounds, stables, and shipping yard. It fascinated Aaron to see the size of their horses. He couldn't wait to tell Cameron about them, and Harold agreed to let Cameron see the stables as well. So much of the kingdom of Betruger was the same as Datten and Warren.

Did my ancestors purposely lie about Betruger, or were they too ignorant to know better?

After the tour, Harold left Aaron in his room to freshen up.

Aaron dressed in the finest shirt he brought, and while it was appropriate, it didn't feel proper for the occasion. He was surprised by how similar his room was to Warren and Datten guest suites. There was a large four-poster bed, a wardrobe, and a table where his satchel, sword, and crown rested. Aaron's room was on the outside of the castle and had a balcony with a view of the sea. Aaron reached into his shirt and gripped Alex's ring. He crossed the room, opened the balcony doors, and stepped to the stone railing.

The gulls flying overhead cawed as the waves crashed on the beach, sending the salty air into his nose. It made him think of Alex and their time spent at the pier visiting the little bookstore. He smiled, thinking of how she'd bite her lower lip if she read a very interesting part of a book. Part of him hoped she was watching the same sea as he was right now.

Of course she isn't. That's absurd. She's probably locked in a tower or library. The sea makes her happy, so I doubt Moorloc would let her anywhere near it.

Aaron returned inside but left the doors open to fill the room with the fresh sea air.

A knock on the door revealed Michael and Cameron.

"Merlock and some Betruger men took the others down to the feast, so we came to get you," Michael said.

He was wearing the cleanest Datten tunic he had. Cameron was, too, though he'd packed a proper shirt despite the trip being across the mountains.

"You packed your formal Datten tunic?" Aaron teased.

"Obviously you didn't." Cameron pulled off his formal shirt and offered it to Aaron. "You know, your room is twice as big as everyone else's, and we're sharing."

Aaron smiled slyly, taking off his tunic and tossing it to Cameron before putting on the formal one. "I'm the Crown Prince of Datten. I suspect Harold is trying to be a gracious host. If we establish peace, it'll end six hundred years of war."

Cameron wandered onto the balcony while still adjusting Aaron's simpler shirt. Aaron began fastening his sword to his hip when Cameron looked back. "Leave the sword."

"Why?" Aaron asked.

Michael slapped his bare hip. "Every knight we've seen was swordless. I don't think they carry them inside the castle."

"It would make sense," Cameron said. "They're so far away from the other kingdoms it isn't as though an army could sneak up on them."

Aaron put his sword down, grabbed his crown, and placed it on his head. "After dinner, we're meeting with King Harold and Sir Macht to go over the plan."

"You want us with you?" Michael asked.

"Of course."

"Then we'll be at your side," Michael said, standing taller.

"You're in a better mood," Aaron said, watching Michael join Cameron on the balcony.

Michael exhaled. "Something about this place reminds me of Alex. I can feel her presence here. Maybe it's all the flowers ... or the sea. It smells like her, and that feels like a sign."

Cameron sighed and crossed his arms. "Michael's right. I feel it too. She's with us here. If they agree to help, I think we'll get her back."

"But no pressure, right?" Aaron asked his friends.

"Oh no, there's lots of pressure," Michael said. "I want my best friend back, and you're the one who can convince King Harold to work with your father."

"I want her back as badly as you do, Michael," Aaron said.

Cameron playfully pushed Aaron. "We don't want to be late for dinner. That would make a terrible impression. So lead the way, Your Highness."

CHAPTER 14
AARON

Aaron shoved Michael and Cameron when they bowed to him. The three of them wandered along the large arched hallway toward the stairs. The stones absorbed the sound of their footsteps as they headed down the stairs from the third floor to the first floor, where guards were heading to the main hall.

How can a hall feel so familiar and foreign at the same time?

Like the dining halls of Datten and Warren, four tables were laid out. Here, though, the king had several head tables on either side of him, a symbol of his importance. Macht sat at the closest table with a few other men beside him. Aaron's men were scattered at different tables. He'd expected to have them all in one place, but they sat in pairs between the Betruger men, laughing and enjoying themselves.

The decor had none of the usual paintings of royalty, but bloody battles were vividly depicted around them. In one painting, several Betruger knights were slaying a massive roaring green dragon while it devoured a fallen warrior. Another showed the aftermath of a battle against an ancient

Datten army. Betruger was the clear winner in a field of bloody Datten corpses. Aaron looked at his crest and rubbed his tunic as he looked over at the head table. The painting behind the young king depicted a copper-skinned black-haired woman holding up a bloody severed head. Aaron elbowed Cameron and pointed to the bloodiest one. In it, a pack of wild boars impaled a pair of men who were tied together in front of a stand of cheering people.

"It's a wonder they can eat anything in here looking at these," Michael said, gulping so hard Aaron heard.

"They're probably used to it," Cameron said.

Harold waved them over to the front of the room. The table to his left was empty except for Merlock.

"It looks as if we'll be dining with the king," Aaron said.

The three of them made their way up the aisle and took their seats at Harold's left. Aaron took the seat closest to the king. *If we were visiting Warren, this would be my father's seat.*

"I hope you enjoy our food. You never gave me answers about what you liked," Harold said. With a clap of his hands, servants swarmed the room, carrying in a wild boar on a spit, an entire mountain goat on a massive platter, countless baskets of every bread imaginable, and trays upon trays of carrots, beets, turnips, and parsnips.

Aaron's mouth watered at the smell. After weeks of living off what they could catch, looking at the feast made him realize he was starving.

"Everything smells amazing," he said as a massive mug of ale slammed the table in front of him. "Boar is one of my favorites."

Harold summoned the servants holding the boar, and they gave Aaron a huge helping and then continued serving the other Datten men. Picking up his ale, Aaron looked around the room, watching his men interact with the

Betruger men. Everywhere he looked, he saw excited, friendly chatter, exactly what he'd see at any meal back home.

"Sorry about the decor," Harold said, taking a sip of ale.

"The colors are ... vibrant," Michael said.

Harold chuckled as Aaron elbowed Michael.

"We use this hall for court proceedings as well as meals. These paintings have been up for centuries. When I became king, I decided to leave them up to remind us where we came from and to ensure we don't fall back to old ways."

"All kingdoms have a darker past than we'd care to acknowledge," Cameron said.

"Some more recent than others." Aaron took a sip of his ale and thought of Arthur's brutality toward his people and family.

"It's ridiculous. Centuries of war over slights that no one remembers anymore," Harold said.

Aaron nodded and held his ale out to Harold. They bumped mugs and toasted, and the room erupted in cheers.

The chatter throughout dinner was exciting. The Datten men were clearly thrilled to be clean again, have a hot meal in their bellies, and looking forward to a proper bed tonight. They celebrated finding Betruger and giving Aaron the chance to create peace.

"After dinner, we'll go to my library and work through your plans," Harold said. "Bruno—I mean Macht—has some suggestions, and once we've agreed, we'll be closer to an official peace."

Aaron nodded. He kept a slight smile as he ate to hide how much everything was weighing on him, but the looks Michael and Cameron gave him throughout dinner made it obvious he wasn't succeeding. Any peace would be temporary unless he found a way to capture and hand over Lygari.

Keeping the sorcerer alive was never part of the plan, but for Alex, I'll do whatever it takes.

Harold finished eating first and excused himself with Merlock. He had specific things he wanted to know about sorcerers, and Merlock had volunteered to answer all his questions. Before leaving, Harold insisted everyone continue feasting and enjoying themselves.

Lost in thought, Aaron finished his food and got up. When he did, Cameron and Michael jumped to their feet. He hadn't even noticed they were waiting for him. One of Macht's men escorted them down the hallway to the library for the meeting.

"Did you update your father?" Cameron asked.

"Merlock delivered a letter to Datten before dinner. Once he's finished talking to Harold, he'll return for my father's reply."

"That's good news," Michael said.

Aaron shrugged. "I got us this far, but we'll need some more experienced men to help come up with a plan if we want to get Lygari alive."

"I think we should let the men rest up while we try to figure out how to find Moorloc's castle," Cameron said. "Did the king have any suggestions?"

"He has a suspected area, so that will get us closer."

They reached the library, and the guard knocked on the door and opened it for them. Macht stood guard on the inside of the door. He nodded to them and pointed to the far side of the room where Harold and Merlock were sitting at a table looking over a book. They were so deep in conversation they hadn't noticed the Datten men. Aaron looked around the room again, which featured floor-to-ceiling books and the table in the middle. There were ancient weapons and statues on display Aaron had missed the first time.

"Maybe instead of trying to charge the castle, we can get Moorloc and Lygari to come out to us," Michael said.

"That would be safer for Alex," Aaron said. "We even have the perfect bait."

"What is it?" Cameron asked.

Aaron sighed. "Me."

At this, Merlock finally came toward them. "I can't let you be bait, Your Highness," he said.

"Why would he want you anyway?" Harold asked.

"I'm unfinished business. They blame my father for Victoria's death." Aaron explained everything they'd learned at the tournament.

"Ending you punishes your princess," Harold said.

"That doesn't matter. My brother will suspect Alex would be easier to control if Aaron were dead," Merlock said.

"Could Alex have made demands, such as no harm coming to you or Stefan?" Michael asked.

"I suspect so," Merlock said. "She's clever enough to make it part of the deal. It explains why they haven't attacked us or sent anyone else after Aaron."

"Then we have one advantage—a grim one." Aaron turned to Harold. "If we fail, I need you to hurt me, Your Royal Highness—*severely* hurt me to break her oath and set her free."

"Aaron, your father would not approve of this," Merlock said.

"I don't care. I'm going to free Alex in any way necessary." Aaron looked to Harold. *Please agree with me.*

Harold grimaced and leaned back in his chair. "I agree, but only as an ultimate resort. For now, let's try to come up with a less violent plan. We have chains made of red steel. If we get close to the sorcerers, we can trap them."

"You have red steel?" Merlock asked. His eyes widened, and he moved away from the king.

"What's red steel?" Cameron asked.

"It came from the Forbidden Lands. I don't know how it's made, but it's said to prevent a sorcerer from using their magic," Harold said.

"That's possible?" Michael asked.

"According to legend, it's toxic to sorcerers," Harold said.

Everyone turned toward Merlock.

"It is. They make red steel from ore that was soaked in dragon blood. A nick will weaken us. A severe cut will lead to death. A long and excruciating one." Merlock winced.

Harold explained, "My father doubted Lygari's loyalty and managed to get some before he was ended. We turned it into shackles but never got to use them."

Merlock stood quietly for a long time before he addressed the king. "Do you know where my brother's castle is?"

"We don't know the exact location, but we have an idea. Bruno, our map."

Sir Macht took a giant sheet of paper from the bookshelf and unrolled it on the table for them. Harold pointed at a location and explained everything he'd told Aaron earlier.

Aaron looked at Merlock, his breath held as he waited for confirmation. He felt as if his limbs had all turned to water and become useless.

"Water and weather powers are some of the safest powers for a young sorceress to learn," Merlock said. "I expected my brother to start with her water and plant powers."

Moving his finger a bit to the south of the inlet, Merlock tapped the map. "And this is the area where I suspected my brother was hiding."

"We've been there, Your Highness," Macht said to Aaron. "There's nothing."

Aaron exhaled and turned to Harold. The king crossed his arms and tilted his head, focusing on the map.

"I'd prefer you call me Aaron. If you're going to come with us—fight alongside us—you call me Aaron."

A smile spread across Harold's face. "You're a peculiar prince."

"Sorry, Your Royal Highness," Cameron said. "He's always been like this."

"Good—because I like you, *Aaron*. You speak honestly, even if you know it isn't what I want to hear."

"Alex says he's honorable to a fault," Michael said, and Aaron scoffed.

"I agree to drop our titles *if* you call me Harold. But I have one last request. If we're going to take this journey together, I would like a meeting with your Kings of Warren and Datten."

"I can retrieve them," Merlock said.

"Are you comfortable with that, Harold?" Aaron asked.

"Yes. He has answered many of my questions about magic," Harold said. With a nod from Aaron, Merlock vanished with a loud crack.

Michael looked at the empty chair, Cameron, and the royalty in front of them. "Would you like us to go?"

Aaron paused before answering. "You both should be part of this meeting, but we need to check on the men. You and Cameron can go. Make sure they're behaving themselves." His friends nodded and followed Macht out, leaving Aaron and Harold alone. Aaron gazed at the map, tapping his fingers on the table.

"Nervous about facing your father?"

"A little," Aaron said, scratching at his beard. "My father has his own way of doing things, and we rarely see eye to eye. But Edward wasn't doing so well when we left Warren. I'm worried."

A crack came from the large hall, followed by an eruption of cheers. "That will be my father and godfather and probably their generals," Aaron said, getting up. "I hope that your invitation extended to their guards as well."

"I expect kings to travel with guards. Sit beside me, Aaron. My men will bring your kings to us. Let's show these old kings what this generation of Torian royalty is capable of."

Aaron straightened his crown and sat with Harold on a large bench until Macht escorted the kings and Randal, Jerome, and Stefan into the library. Rising for the senior royals, Aaron and Harold glanced at each other for a moment before Aaron made the introductions.

Once everyone was introduced, Cameron and Michael returned, and the meeting got underway. Aaron couldn't help but notice his father's satisfied smile and boisterous demeanor. Edward, on the other hand, slumped beside Emmerich, putting up no fight against any of Emmerich's wild suggestions. His eyes had lost all of their vitality, and Randal had to keep bringing his attention back to the conversation.

Harold smiled kindly. "I'm deeply sorry your daughter was taken, Edward. I want this peace, and if helping get Alexandria back provides peace, we're at your disposal. Our motto is 'legacy never dies,' and that comes from how much we value our wives *and* children. My knights honor their oaths to me and their wives equally. It's their wives who provide our warriors with their legacies."

Emmerich tapped his fingers on the table impatiently. "Yes, yes, we all know a soldier needs food, wine, and a good *legacy* to come home to. What do you propose for the matter at hand?"

Aaron and Harold explained their plan, showing the various meeting spots on the map, including the final valley near Moorloc's location. They intended to swap knights— lending a few Betruger men to Datten and Warren's armies to better prepare them. Cameron agreed to return to Warren to help with the horses, and Stefan volunteered to replace Cameron in Aaron's cavalry.

Harold scrutinized Stefan before turning to Aaron. "He's her other one, isn't he? Who she hurt?"

"I am," Stefan said. "Does that matter?"

"Yes," Harold said, placing his hands on the table. "Your insistence on helping to save her after what happened speaks volumes not only of your character, but that of all Datten's men."

Aaron noticed Jerome straighten at Harold's compliment of Stefan.

"I've spent half my life keeping Alex away from danger. That I failed to keep her safe from *this* has been eating me since I woke up. I have to make it right," Stefan said.

"So," Aaron said, "Datten will deal with Kruft, and Betruger will deal with Lygari. Merlock and Megesti will be our messengers to ensure all of us arrive at the same valley."

"Agreed," Emmerich said, sitting back satisfied.

"How will we see the castle?" Macht asked from the side. "Our ships can see it, but to this day, no one has ever seen it on land."

"My son can," Emmerich said.

Aaron held his scarred palm up to Harold and Macht. "Before she left, Alex gave me her blood. It should let me see the castle. It won't help to get our army inside, but it'll tell us if we're in the right place." Aaron stood. "I think we're all set to start preparations."

"Tomorrow we'll go to war—*together*," Harold said.

Edward and Emmerich stood and shook hands with Harold and Macht. Looking at the kings, Aaron's stomach dropped, and his heart stopped. His father was giving him a look he'd rarely seen before—smiling at him with pride.

CHAPTER 15

ALEX

The pain was so excruciating that Alex couldn't keep anything down. When the first lash had struck her, she'd bit the inside of her cheek so badly that drinking water was painful too. As her energy drained away, her nightmares worsened—memories of the whipping and her mother's murder. That strange man on the beach. Every dream ended with her drowning in the sea until a flash of orange light woke her up.

Whenever Reinhilde brought food and drink, Kruft stood behind her, watching. Finally on the third day she arrived alone. Reinhilde tried everything to get Alex to eat, but after a few bites of bread, Alex retched. The next day, her cheek had healed enough that she gave in and drank some tea and eventually broth. It took six days lying in bed without moving for her back to heal enough that she could move without ripping open the wounds or sobbing. Even so, she stayed in bed.

What is the point? I'm not ready to practice spells or face the guards who laughed when I was punished.

The next time Reinhilde visited, Alex noticed her hands

were dirtier than usual. "What have you been doing?" Alex asked as Reinhilde handed her a tray of bread, cheese, and a peach. Alex took the bread and pushed the tray back to Reinhilde.

"Someone had to take care of that large garden and orchard you grew in the woods." Reinhilde winked at Alex as she picked up the peach and ate it.

"You found it?"

"I did. Thank you. The others are excited to have something different to eat. We don't want you to get into any trouble, but we do appreciate your choice of plants."

Alex smiled weakly. "I was ordered to work on my Celtic powers. Moorloc never told me what I had to grow. Do you have any requests?"

"More tomato plants."

"I'll take care of it the next time I'm out there."

Reinhilde grabbed Alex's plate and held it out, wiggling it. Alex sighed and took the cheese piece off the plate.

"I don't like peaches. The fuzz itches."

"They're my favorite." Reinhilde smiled and placed the peach pit on the tray.

The next day, Moorloc assigned her readings from the Celtic and Hades lines, and she forced herself out of her room. During the day, Alex stayed in the library, and while everyone else was at dinner, she retreated to her room. She managed a few hours of sleep at night. If she didn't wake from nightmares, she'd wake from the pain.

Once Alex could move without crying, Moorloc again let her have free rein of the unlocked parts of the castle and surrounding grounds. Still, Alex was hesitant to leave the safety of her library. After a few more days, she remembered what Aaron had told her in the Warren throne room.

I can't hide forever. Every walk around the castle will not result in a severe beating.

She forced herself to walk the main floor. Alex spun her bracelet and admired the engravings of Celtic, Cassandra, Poseidon, Salem, and Merlin that had tarnished with age. The ones of Hades, Ares, Mystics, Mire, and Tiere still had their golden hue. She spent a day walking through every room on the main floor, though she avoided Moorloc's bedroom and the kitchen.

The next evening, she'd planned to go to the basement, but after spotting Kruft heading down the stairs, she turned around and ended up on the second floor. It was a maze of hallways that broke down into smaller hallways, all of which led to the guardrooms. The stones on the second floor were not as worn, but they were dirty, and there were no flames to light the halls, only a few scattered torches.

"Figures Moorloc would only care about what he sees," Alex said. She'd realized a few mornings before that she hadn't spoken to anyone outside of brief chats with Reinhilde in a week. When Reinhilde came, Alex would ask her questions about Warren when her mother was alive, trying to piece together anything that would explain why her grandfather had killed her mother. But she never stayed long.

"So I talk to myself. *Since nobody else will.*" Her voice echoed in the dim hallway.

Her fingertips grazed the wall. The stones were crumbling and weak—more like a dungeon than a castle. Alex scrunched her nose. Up here, it stank as if an army had marched through. Without the ceiling flames, the scattered torches barely lit the way from one hall to the next. Alex walked slowly, listening for the whispers of her family's books, but there was nothing.

It was getting late, so Alex made her way down the stairs to the main floor. The fire overhead crackled as she walked down the hallway to her room. Lost in thought, she didn't notice Daniel's icy warning until it was too late, and a sweaty hand pressed over her mouth.

"Hello, witch."

Kruft's voice sent a wave of terror and revulsion through her, but Stefan's training kicked in. She bit down hard on his calloused finger with all her might. When he yanked his hand away, she screamed. He released her, but before she could run, he slammed her into the cold stone wall. Her scars ripped open, sending burning pain down her back. He wrapped his hands around her neck and choked her. Alex scratched and clawed at his face, desperate to make him release her neck, but even as blood ran down his face, he squeezed tighter. She saw Daniel watching helplessly as her vision went dark.

"What the Merlin is going on out here?"

At the sound of Lygari's voice, Kruft loosened his grip enough to let Alex gasp for air. She coughed from the force of her ragged breaths.

"Nothing," Kruft said, a menacing smirk spreading across his lips.

Lygari scanned her and returned his glare to Kruft. "My father made it perfectly clear you were to keep all your filthy parts to yourself. Release her—NOW!"

"Why do you care?"

Lygari didn't break eye contact with Kruft as he tilted his head to the side with a pop. "Because if you break her, I'll get blamed, and I'm sure as Hades not sticking my neck out for you, especially after you disturbed my sleep."

When Kruft didn't remove his hand from Alex's neck, Lygari's eyes widened, and he flicked his wrist. A fireball appeared, hovering over his palm. "I'm not in the mood for your *ferflucsing* stupidity."

Kruft stared at Lygari, nostrils flaring, but then he removed his hand from Alex's throat and stepped back.

"Leave," Lygari said. Kruft cursed under his breath as he left. Lygari closed his hand, extinguishing the flames.

Alex was hyperventilating now that her lungs could take their fill. She fought to calm herself.

"Be more careful because my father won't keep him in line —and Kruft won't stop coming for you."

"What did I do?"

"Nothing. His vendetta is against your mother. Clearly your resemblance has struck a nerve."

"What did she do to him?"

"Turned him down. Boorish Datten men need nothing more than a woman refusing them to go ballistic. Remember that. I can't always be around to save you."

Alex swallowed and nodded to Lygari. When they reached her bedroom door, Alex turned back to her cousin; he was still watching but not looking at her. Daniel arrived beside her. The ghost looked at her. His chin quivered, and he vanished.

You didn't fail me, Daniel. I wasn't paying attention.

Looking back, she saw Lygari had left, so Alex stepped into her room, closed the door, and sank down on her knees.

Alex massaged the painful bruises already forming on her neck. She tried to bury her fear and rage deep inside, but her hands burned, and tiny sparks jumped between her fingers. She slammed her hands onto the cold stone and drew water from it to extinguish her fingers, causing a hissing sound.

As she watched the water work, Alex wondered if she'd ever learn to manage her powers and be able to leave. *Or did I curse myself to remain here until I lose control and kill everyone?* Exhaustion and pain flooded her, and she dragged herself to the bed. Alex sighed as she ran her fingers across Aaron's shirt and pulled her own shirt off. The amount of blood on it confirmed that her back had ripped back open again. Getting dressed would make it worse, so she gingerly lay on her bed and fell into a restless sleep.

⁂

She woke at dawn and headed to the library. Moorloc had left a stack of books for her, and she'd finished the last of them when there was a loud thump. Alex looked up to see Lygari dropping another pile of books on the table in front of her.

"What are these?" She picked one up and looked up at Lygari hesitantly. "You've only been giving me books about the powers of lines I don't have. These are books on powers that I already have."

"These are the titan books. A titan wrote each one. My father's version of an apology. He shouldn't have let Kruft go that far and suggests you start with the Salem, Celtic, or Poseidon ones."

"Is he going to start instructing me or just more books?"

"He won't be teaching you for a while. Your juvenile behavior and lack of control is not something he's willing to contend with. After your powers have settled and you've learned what he wants you to know, he'll try again. For now, he's approved you to leave the grounds unsupervised to practice on your own. He hopes this will encourage you to test your limits, especially since he knows how much you like the woods and sea. But tomorrow you'll be expected to complete your required reading."

"When will the bracelet come off?" Alex asked, glancing around the room to make sure the doors were all closed.

"Not for years, most likely. He doesn't trust you not to run to the Datten idiot." Lygari pulled an Ares and Hades book from her pile of discarded books and walked to the door.

"Lygari ... will he ever let me see my father again?"

"Your father?"

"I miss him. I barely had any time with him when I got home."

"He blames Edward as much as Emmerich for your mother's death. You're lucky he hasn't killed your father already."

Alex gasped as she thought of losing her father too. The idea of never getting to see him, never saying goodbye, made her heart hurt.

Sensing her pain, Lygari said, "I'm sorry. I know you didn't get to say goodbye to either of them. It seems our line is destined to be abandoned by our parents. You and I must forge our own path."

Alex sniffled back tears as Lygari left the room and slammed the door behind him. He did it any time he left, and while it bothered her, she understood they had to keep up appearances despite the fact that she was starting to trust him.

She couldn't be in the library anymore, so she picked a few books from the pile and brought them to her room. She plopped on her bed and flipped through them. Not a single mention of the Cassandra line. Moorloc was staying true to his word about not letting her learn to heal.

She balanced a Celtic book in one hand and a Poseidon book in the other.

"If I practice Celtic powers, I could grow those tomato plants. But Poseidon would cool the burning in my back."

She tucked the Poseidon book under her arm and headed to the beach.

The gulls were exceptionally active as she methodically walked down the overgrown trail to the water. She moved as gracefully as possible to not aggravate her back but kept an eye out for Kruft. She'd been allowed to visit the sea under Lygari's supervision for the past week to wash out her wounds. She'd done enough damage to Doyle that the other men kept their distance to avoid risking an altercation with her. Alex knew she'd made Doyle and Tristan bleed for their crimes enough to buy her a temporary reprieve from the others' cruelty, while Kruft seemed determined to make her pay for her actions.

She took a deep breath and let the salty sea air fill her lungs. The gulls sang their songs overhead as Alex removed her shoes and rolled up her pants before she walked cautiously into the water. As the cool water hit her knees, Alex closed her eyes. She pictured Edward's face and then Aaron's. Edward smiled at her while Aaron's mischievous grin filled his face—the one he got when he shared a secret with her. She could hear Edith's giggles, Jessica's sighs, Michael's laugh, and Stefan's groan. Tears streamed down her face, dropping into the sea.

Suddenly, a hot tingling erupted throughout her body, sending every hair on her arms and neck straight up. For once, the chaotic magic wasn't coming from inside her. Alex's eyes snapped open. The beach had gone silent. There were no sounds of waves, gulls, or anything until an eerily familiar voice brought her back to reality.

"How can you stand being out that far in the water? Don't you get cold? Ares, I hate the feeling of being wet."

Alex whipped around. A man was standing on the beach's waterline. His hair was as black as obsidian except for a gold streak that ran from above his left eye through his hair. It suited his golden bronze skin perfectly, making him devastatingly handsome. He looked Aaron or Michael's age, and even from the water, she noticed his gold eyes.

Like Lygari and Moorloc.

Alex froze and stared at him wide-eyed. *You're the sorcerer from my dream.*

She could feel the power radiating from him. It beat like a

drum in her ears, calling to her, and it made tingles spread through her body. When she looked at him, it both terrified and excited her.

Alex sensed he wasn't as young as he looked. He gave off an air of authority like Lygari, but he dressed in a burnt orange robe that was oversized and ostentatious like Moorloc's.

That's a truly ugly robe.

The man cocked his head. "It isn't nice to make fun of someone's clothes," he said. He snapped his fingers, and his robe was replaced with an outfit similar to hers, though her tunic was gold and his was a rich blue.

"Do you prefer me like this, princess?" He smirked at her.

Alex straightened her back and raised her chin. "My name is Alexandria. But how do you know I'm a princess?"

"I know practically everything about you, *Alexandria,* daughter of Victoria, this generation's true daughter of Cassandra, and the last of your line."

Alex's hands trembled, but she moved closer as she always had in her dream. A branch snapped, and the sorcerer's head spun toward the castle. For a moment, Alex spotted his sorcerer line marks on his neck: an ax and a cloudy crescent moon.

When she looked up at the beach, her stomach dropped. It was Kruft. Her hand shot to her bruised neck. She swallowed hard and trembled as she backed further into the water, soaked up to her waist. Her heartbeat was like a thunderstorm in her ears.

Kruft smirked at her until he noticed the sorcerer on the beach watching him. "Who in the Forbidden Lands are you? No one goes near the witch. You aren't new, so leave before I make you regret the day they ripped you from your mother's cunt."

"No," the sorcerer said. He calmly crossed his arms and turned to face Kruft.

"Boy, if you think you're getting into her pants, you're in the wrong place," Kruft continued. "She broke the nose of the last man who touched her, but I messed her up real good after that."

The sorcerer looked at Alex. "Is that true?"

She didn't reply, so he softened his voice and spoke again. "Alexandria, I can't help you if you don't talk to me. I need to know if he hurt you."

Alex swallowed hard. She should fear this sorcerer, but after what happened with Kruft, she'd take her chances with the stranger. *At least if he kills me, he might make it quick.*

"Help her? Who in the Forbidden Lands do you think—"

The sorcerer held his hand up to Kruft without taking his eyes off Alex. Kruft froze in place. The sorcerer stood there, waiting for her answer, but she was too scared to reply or even breathe. She couldn't take her eyes off Kruft. It looked as if he'd been petrified. As if he sensed her struggle, the sorcerer cracked—soundlessly—to Kruft. He circled him twice and then placed his palm on Kruft's forehead. Turning back to Alex, the sorcerer grinned and winked. His eyes flashed the same bright blue as his tunic, and Kruft's face tensed for a moment before the sorcerer stepped back.

"Well, Sir Rassgat," said the sorcerer, "you're going to leave here and forget ever having seen me. You'll go straight to the kitchen, find the hottest boiling pot, and stick those hands into it until someone pulls them out." The sorcerer didn't glance away from Kruft for even a second. His manner was full of confidence and unbridled power. "And if you ever put a hand on Alexandria again, it'll be your face in that pot."

Kruft nodded and then turned around and marched away from the beach as if nothing happened.

Alex's entire chest moved with each raspy breath, but she managed to shift her feet into the Wafner stance. When the sorcerer finally turned back to her, she used her power to throw a massive wave of water on him. She tried to run, but she was out too deep.

In a blink, he was standing before her in the water with his hands out in front of him. "Alexandria, it's all right. I won't hurt you."

"Why would I believe you?" Alex shouted. Her voice faltered with panic. "I watched you order Kruft to stick his hand in boiling water, and he obeyed!"

"If I wanted to hurt you, I would have. How do you have pity for him? He's a brute who whipped you so badly you're bleeding through your shirt. Who—" His voice softened. "Who tried to choke you. I made sure he'll never touch you again."

Alex looked down at the blood on her shoulder. "How did you ...? Who are you? What do you want?" Tears streamed down her face as he moved closer to her. Common sense screamed at her to run, but her magic was telling her to stay.

"I want to help you. Let me show you." He held his hand out to her.

"How do I know you won't make me do things?"

"Because it works on weak-minded mortals—and you, princess, are *neither* of those things."

He moved closer, exactly as in her dream. She'd always woken up before she could take his hand. The tingles of raw power that came from him grew even stronger, and he smelled of burning wood. Despite her fears, Alex couldn't resist the draw. She bit the inside of her cheek and took his hand. The instant she did, he closed the distance between them and slid his hand along her temple.

The vision came, but she was looking through someone else's eyes, like when she'd used the pearl to show her memories.

Around them was a beautiful forest with leaves and flowers of every color. She couldn't stop herself glancing around. Then she heard her own voice crying out, just as she had after the whipping.

Alex ripped away from him. "I don't want to hear myself begging for help."

"I'm sorry I didn't come the first time I heard you. I didn't realize what I was hearing," he said. "If I had, I could have spared you."

"You're a Mystics sorcerer?"

"I am. Ares too. That's the one most people see first, and the reason for the orange robe you find so ugly." He pulled down his collar and turned his head to the side, letting Alex get a better look at his line marks.

"Are all of you this powerful?" Alex asked.

"No. We—as in you and I—are exceptional, princess," he said, smiling smugly.

"How many heard my call?" Alex nervously played with her necklace.

"You mean your desperate cry for help? Only me. That's for the best since there isn't anyone who's as qualified to help you as I am."

"How do you know so much about me?"

"Daughters of Cassandra are easy to identify."

Alex groaned. "What's your—"

"Gryphon." He bowed, grabbed Alex's hand, and kissed it the way her previous suitors had. She scowled at him, pulling her hand back.

"None of that, *Gryphon*. I'm betrothed to the Crown Prince of Datten, and my future father-in-law has quite the temper."

"Betrothed? That means ... How old are you?"

Alex scrunched her nose. "Nineteen. Why?"

"No, I mean your actual age, not how old you look."

"Nineteen," Alex repeated, frowning. "You look twenty-five. How old are you really?"

Gryphon's face went pale. "Sixty-four. How are you *this* powerful at nineteen?"

Alex moved out of the water toward the beach. Before she even lifted a hand, Gryphon waved his hand, and warm air surrounded them for an instant. Her skin tingled and she smelled like a campfire, but she was completely dry.

"How did you—"

"My father also gifted me with Salem. Like you, I have more than two lines. But you didn't answer my question. How are you so powerful?"

Alex sighed and explained how her powers came in.

"That explains the begging for help. Moorloc is the most useless titan I've ever read about. Well, I'm happy to train you. We'll go to the cottage and—" Gryphon grabbed her arm, but Alex ripped it away.

"I can't. I gave him my oath."

Gryphon frowned. "Why would you do that?" He crossed his arms and stared at her, waiting for a reply.

"I *had* to," Alex snapped. She explained how much damage her temper had done to her friends and her failure to heal them.

"That explains why your back is bleeding."

"How do you—"

"The brute's mind. Not a delightful place to be. Lots of hatred and violence in that one."

A shiver ran through her. *Violence.*

"You flinch every time you move. You must be in excruciating pain."

Alex looked down and realized she was playing with her hands. Stefan's reminder not to show weakness sounded in her mind. She exhaled and then snapped her head up and stared at him.

"I could cauterize the wound," he said. "It'll hurt, but it would stay shut."

Alex stared at him. "You can do that?"

"Yes. I would seal the wounds over permanently, and I'll even bring you an ointment for the pain. My aunt is the Titan of Celtics. She'll make you one."

"I thought sorcerers rarely had more than one child."

Gryphon laughed. "Says the daughter of a thirdborn child with twin uncles. Twins are even rarer than multiple children in our world—many magical rules are tied to twins. My aunt was adopted. Her parents died in an accident, so my hexa and hexen took her in."

"Huh?"

"My parents' parents."

"That's really sad."

"It's better to have no parents than terrible parents," Gryphon said.

Alex thought of Michael. "I disagree. Everyone deserves to know where they came from."

"Cauterizing or not?"

Normally, Alex was suspicious of new people—a consequence of hiding from her grandfather for the last twelve years of her life. *But there's something about you. I can't understand, but my gut says to trust you—and my magic seems to be drawn to you in a way I've never known before.*

"Yes, cauterize it. Please."

"I should warn you—it's going to hurt. Turn around." Gryphon uncrossed his arms and stretched them out, cracking his fingers.

Alex turned her back to him and crossed her arms. Gryphon gently pulled her bloodstained shirt up, and she gasped as the cool breeze hit her back. A moment later, he tapped her shoulder and she took the hem of her shirt from him, leaving his hands free to work. Warm fingertips skimmed her shoulder blades before they gently touched the skin around her wounds. They grew warmer and warmer until they became like hot coals searing her flesh. Gryphon was right. It was agonizing but nowhere as harrowing as the whipping that made the marks.

Alex closed her eyes to visualize Stefan and Michael and all the tricks they'd taught her over the years to withstand pain and remain brave through anything. As Gryphon's fingers moved across her back, tracing each mark, a faint sizzle confirmed each sealed wound. Alex stilled her breathing, but it didn't help. The cracks of the whip echoed through her mind like it did in her dreams. She kept her composure and didn't utter a sound while her tears fell. After what felt like an eternity, Gryphon pulled her shirt from her fingers, and it fell back into place.

"I'm finished. It looks hideous, but it won't bleed again."

"Thank you." Alex wiped away her tears before she turned around. "Why are you here?"

"I told you. I came to answer your cry for help." The impish smile that spread across his face made Alex's throat go dry.

"Can you help me learn to control my powers?" Alex asked.

"Yes, but only if you let me. Our level of magic requires special training. You need to be taught control before attempting the complex magic each line possesses."

"What happens if I don't?"

"Bad things."

"Such as?" Alex needed to know what she'd face.

Gryphon groaned. "Untrained sorcerers of our magnitude wreak havoc on the world around them. If you lost control of your weather, you could send a tornado through your kingdom. Fire could burn down a castle. Earthquakes, sunken ships, floods, dead crops—"

"Enough," Alex said, biting her lower lip. The fear of decimating Warren with her powers was too real to her.

"I'll help you in other ways. I'm sure they've starved you of civilized conversation as well as food," Gryphon said. He cocked his head to the side, and Alex tugged on her tunic, conscious of how weak she'd become after a week of not eating.

"Conversation?" Alex realized that this was one of the longest conversations she'd had since she arrived at the castle. But the look he was giving her made her cheeks flush. She recognized it from the suitors in Warren.

There is no reason for you to look at me like that. You just met me. "Somehow, I don't believe *conversation* is what you were implying."

Gryphon grinned. "Can you fault me for trying? You're rather lovely, and I'm attracted to power. An Ares's only weakness."

Alex rolled her eyes. "What do *you* get out of teaching me?"

"You mean besides conversations with you? Why, the warm fuzzies for helping a fellow sorcerer, of course."

She stared at him coldly.

"You're exceedingly guarded, princess. If you want me to help you—really help you—you're going to have to let me in."

"I let people in. I'm picky about *who* I let in, and it takes longer than a few minutes for me to trust anyone." Alex crossed her arms. *And you appear about as trustworthy as a fox in the henhouse.*

"While that is fair in normal circumstances, you and I are not normal. You *asked* for my help. For me to give it, you're going to have to trust me. To do that, you have to let me in.

Otherwise, there's no point in me trying to help you," Gryphon said.

"Why?"

"While I don't have premonition powers, I know you're going to be extraordinarily important to not only our world but, one day, to me."

CHAPTER 16
ALEX

"What does that mean?" Alex asked. Stefan's voice told her to move away from him, but she stepped toward him instead. *Magic, behave.*

"Your importance to our world is a long story, and I don't think you want to spend all our time today learning about that when I could help you learn to wield your power better. History and legends can wait."

I feel you have something up your sleeve, but you're right. Help first. Suspicions later.

"Where do we begin?"

Gryphon stood in front of her. She only came up to his chest, forcing her to look up to watch his face. He smiled at her, and her stomach flipped.

"Stand like you normally would if you were going to do a spell. A big one that requires focus."

Alex stepped back a few paces to give herself room and moved into her usual fighting stance, her legs spaced for balance and her elbows bent. Gryphon crossed his arms and cocked his head to examine her. She was sweating from the intensity of his stare. He kneeled at her side and frowned at her hips and arms.

She let out a loud sigh and turned to glare at him. "What are you doing? You're supposed to be helping me."

Gryphon smirked. "I was looking at your arms." Heat rushed to Alex's cheeks as he looked up at her. "You're dropping your elbows."

"What? They taught me to stand like this."

"Well, it's wrong." Gryphon stood up.

She growled in annoyance. "Are you going to help me and show me or just stare?" she snapped. *Who does he think he is with that cocky smirk? He probably doesn't even know what he's doing.*

A grin spread across Gryphon's face as he stepped forward, examining her.

Can you hear everything I think?

Gryphon winked and held his hands out to her. "May I?"

Alex swallowed and then nodded. "It went faster if I let Michael and Stefan fix my position. So ... do that."

Gryphon moved behind her, and Alex flinched. The closer he got, the more magic pulsed through every cell in her body. The moment his hands touched her, the magical pulsing stopped, and a calm swept through her. Softly, he pushed her feet into a wider stance and gently twisted her right foot forward. Alex relaxed until he slid his hands down to her hips. It startled her enough that she straightened her back and hiccupped.

"Much better. Stay straight." Gryphon gripped her more firmly, twisting her hips forward. Finally, he slid his hands down her arms and pushed her elbows up. "Don't drop your elbows. This isn't a fight. Magic moves through you. You need to lock your core, then *raise* your elbows. That will give you more force to send it out."

Alex looked back at Gryphon and blushed. She was concentrating so much on committing to memory how he'd positioned her that she hadn't been aware of how close he was. Instinctively, she turned, but he gripped her waist and twisted her hips back into place.

"In the Forbidden Lands, our power comes from the magic in the land. In the mortal world, it comes from the elements around you and your natural stores. Your power starts in your core. Here." He squeezed her middle, tickling her. "Think of it as coming from your belly button. When you use it, you force it up through your chest and out through one or both of your arms. If you hold your arms straight, it flows faster and, therefore, more powerfully."

Alex's mouth dropped open. "No one has ever explained it like that to me. It finally makes sense."

"Try it. Whatever spell you want to do." He stepped away and examined her stance. The heat burning through her evaporated the instant his hands left.

"It's a new one," Alex said, feeling self-conscious. "I've never tried it before."

"That's fine. Try anyway." Gryphon smiled encouragingly at her. "I won't laugh."

Alex swallowed and turned back to the sea. She closed her eyes, and when she opened them, her power shifted. As the power flooded her, it became impossible to focus on the spell since her magic kept pulling her toward the sorcerer standing behind her.

Stop pulling me to him. I don't know what you think is going to happen if we go to him. She scolded her magic as if it were a living thing and would listen.

Alex thrust her hands straight out with her palms touching. Gryphon's breath hit the back of her neck as he came behind her again.

"Steady," he whispered.

Her magic swelled inside of her as she released a store of it she didn't know existed. Gently, his hands ran down her arms and pushed her elbows straight to lock them. As she dragged her palms apart, the water in the sea moved. She held her breath but didn't stop. Soon, a path out into the sea emerged. She lowered her hands and looked at Gryphon.

"Impressive." He smiled as his eyes fixed on hers. "And I mean impressive for a sorcerer, not for a nineteen-year-old. Controlling the entire sea is an advanced spell for the Poseidon line."

"Does that mean other sorcerers could feel it?" Panic rushed through Alex, making her feel seasick.

"No. Despite the impressiveness of this spell, you'd need to perform a spell reserved for titans to draw their attention. It signals competition for their position as titan, and my father doesn't react unless something is annoying his titans. So you're safe."

Gryphon's smile calmed her fears.

"I can't believe I did that," Alex said. She stepped awkwardly toward the water, unsure what would happen to the sea.

"Let's go see it."

"Is it *safe*?"

"Are you planning to put it back while we're out there?"

"*I* have to put it back?" Alex asked, her eyes widening with shock.

"Yes. But don't worry. I'll help you."

Together, they walked out into the sea. Even looking right at it, Alex couldn't fathom what she was seeing. The water stayed in place on either side of them, and the seabed was bone-dry. Alex watched the fish and creatures swimming around on both sides in what looked like a solid wall of water.

She reached out and her hand pierced the surface, but the water around her hand stayed in place.

"You'll *really* teach me?" she asked.

"Yes," he said. A wicked smile spread across his face.

"When? How?" Alex realized she should hide her excitement, but that was impossible for her. *Control!*

"When can you get away? Since you can't come with me, I'll come here."

"We could meet here every morning before sunup. We'll go as long as possible before I'm summoned for my lessons after breakfast." They headed back to the beach. Alex couldn't help running her fingers along the wall of water as they walked.

"I'll be here then. Every day before sunup."

"What if we're caught?" Alex asked, tugging on her shirt hem again.

"We won't be."

"But I'm watched." Alex held up her wrist with the bracelet on it, and Gryphon burst out laughing.

"That? We use that on children who develop their powers before they're of age or those whose powers are undetermined. As for being watched, I can take care of that while we train."

Alex looked out to the sea and back to him. "If you're sure."

"What other powers have you found so far? So I can come prepared tomorrow."

He held his hand out to Alex, and she gave him her wrist. He closed his hot hands around hers and cracked them onto the beach. Standing in the sand, he pulled her hand close to his face and examined the bracelet. "What else can you do?" he asked.

"I have premonition dreams, I can see the dead, and I can grow plants and control the weather and sea. I've healed people accidentally, cracked accidentally, and I can work with fire. Though I have trouble controlling fire, thanks to my temper."

"The fact you have any real fire powers reflects how truly powerful you are. Few sorcerers can manage opposite elements."

"What will we do next?" Alex asked. She tried not to sound too eager, but with his help, she'd managed a spell she thought was impossible.

"Salem is one of my mastered lines, so how about we play with fire?"

"Aren't you worried I'll hurt you?" Alex asked.

Gryphon laughed even harder. This time he had to rest his hands on his knees to catch his breath. Alex took a step back as her cheeks flushed. Gryphon noticed and stood, straightening his tunic smugly. "I'm not worried you'll hurt me. Unlike Moorloc, I'm an expert in fire to the point I can take fire from anywhere. I'm also several decades older and more powerful than you, so you can't hurt me."

"Your arrogance is as attractive as your orange robe," Alex said.

"It isn't *arrogance* if it's true."

Alex crossed her arms.

"I'm sorry. I said I wouldn't laugh. I only meant it's common for Salem sorcerers to have control issues. It's a hard power to master."

Alex looked away. "I lose control when I'm angry."

"Are all your powers tied to emotions?" There was a curiosity in his voice Alex hadn't expected.

She nodded. "They started out that way. Moorloc believes I'm the Heart."

"He's right."

"How do you—"

"My father is the current Head. Logical. Powerful. Like me.

I'm the next Head—your Head. Now put the sea back and then light me a fire."

Alex jumped away from him. "You're the Head?"

"Future Head."

"But *if* you're the Head and I'm the Heart, why didn't you kill me?"

"As I said earlier, you're going to be important to our world."

"What does that mean?"

"We've only ever had one other Heart who was a sorceress, and you would be the first Heart to have ten lines too. There has never been a Head or Heart with Merlin until you. So you're *unique*—and I have an inclination to protect extraordinary things, princess."

"Don't call me that," Alex snapped.

"You're a princess," Gryphon said. "I thought that was how mortals addressed someone of your station."

"It is, but it's the tone you use when you say it. You say it the same way Moorloc addresses me. It's condescending, and it isn't my name." *I'm sick of people calling me whatever name or word they think fits.*

Gryphon stepped toward her. "What does he call you? It clearly upsets you."

Alex sighed. "I'm named after my grandmothers, like all mortal princesses are, and I go by Alexandria, or Alex to my friends. Moorloc calls me titaness or Harbinger, and Lygari calls me princess. If you call me princess, I'm calling you Sunset after that ugly robe."

"What would you like me to call you? I'd be honored to be allowed to call you Alex, but I understand if you would prefer I not."

Alex's stomach flipped. Her powers were still trying to pull her to him. *Stop it.* She scolded them again. *I need a friend here.* "Alex is fine."

Instantly, the impish smile was back. "Enough stalling. Fix the sea and show me your firepower. Don't hold back. I can take whatever you have to throw at me, *Alex.*"

Alex turned back to the sea and adjusted her stance. She glanced at Gryphon, and he scrunched his face at her. Alex groaned. "Help."

Gryphon pulled her shoulders back and gently patted her thigh, making her shift her right leg inward. "Better."

Alex closed her eyes and searched for the hidden power she'd tapped into earlier. She struggled to find it. Hot breath hit the back of her neck, sending a shiver down her back.

Gryphon whispered, "You're trying too hard. Let go of your need for control. You can't force your magic to bend to your will any more than you can make your eyes not green. It's a part of you."

Alex thought of Michael and the calm he'd brought out in her whenever she was losing control of her powers. When she opened her eyes, her magic shifted within her. Thrusting her arms straight out before her, she slammed her palms together, and the sea collapsed into itself. It threw off a gust of wind that knocked her off-balance. Before she hit the ground, she gasped as heat surged through her. Gryphon's arms gripped her tightly. Surprised, she broke away from him.

Gryphon shrugged. "Sorry. Instinct. If you prefer, I'll let you fall next time."

Alex exhaled. "No. I'm not used to help from the living."

After successfully putting the sea back, she spent the rest of the day working with Gryphon on her Salem fire powers, and true to his word, no one came looking for her. At the end of the day, she'd learned more from him than Merlock and Moorloc had ever taught her. Just him standing beside her and fixing her stance repeatedly made a difference in her control. Every time she tried using her magic, a calm came over her body. By the time the sun went down, Alex's powers were drained, and her energy was vanishing.

"I think we overdid it today. Let me help with the weakness." Gryphon held his hands out to Alex, and she slid hers into them, causing a warmth to spread through her body. For a moment, her skin glowed faintly orange before dissipating.

"What did you do?" Alex asked.

"I shared my power with you."

"Sorcerers can share their power?" Alex asked.

"No. We're special. It's a Head and Heart thing."

Alex rolled her eyes.

Gryphon smiled at her. "You should go before Moorloc comes looking for you," he said. "I can hide you from mortals, but he might see through my spell, and he won't appreciate you working with me," he said.

"Why not?"

"Because of who I am. He's not a fan of my father."

"How could he even tell who your father is?"

Gryphon chuckled and pointed to the blond streak running through his black hair. "This runs in the men of one family, though my father's hair has turned gray."

"Moorloc knew your father?"

"My father is why your family fled. The twins didn't like him around your mother, and when she rejected him, it got … dangerous. They wouldn't have had a chance against my father or his friends. Moorloc *maybe* could have stood up to a few of my father's friends—he is a titan, after all. But Merlock is a secondborn son and doesn't have many powers. Even in your generation, Lygari's nothing special, and Megesti … well, he's lucky to have the powers of his mother's line, and you—"

Alex's head whipped around. "Wait—what? Megesti's mother was mortal."

Gryphon laughed. "No. It's why I know as much about your family. I know his mother. Megesti is a full sorcerer, Lygari is half, and you ..." Gryphon cocked his head to the side as he stared at Alex. "You I can't figure out. You should be half human, yet you're more powerful, and I don't know why."

"How can you tell I'm more powerful than half?"

"I'm an Ares. We're the most powerful of the ten lines, and we can sense the power in others. It's helpful in finding their weaknesses. When someone powerful is around, my magic lets me know."

Alex was about to tell him that her own magic hummed in his presence, but she stopped herself. "What does that feel like?" she asked.

"A pleasant tingle." He winked at Alex, but she crossed her arms and scowled.

Gryphon's forehead wrinkled as he stared back at her. "When a powerful sorcerer is near, I get a sensation similar to the tingles you get on your skin when you come inside a hot room after being outside in the blistering cold."

"That I can understand." Alex uncrossed her arms, relaxing.

Gryphon looked across the sea for a moment before he turned back to Alex. "And being around you feels as if I walked into the fire itself."

Alex gulped as Gryphon leaned down toward her. "Until tomorrow, princess. Get some rest." He cracked away.

"Until tomorrow," Alex whispered as she headed back to the castle.

The moment Alex arrived inside, Reinhilde dragged her to Kruft's bedroom. It was complete chaos. Kruft sat with his hands laid out on a table. They were so blistered that his skin was peeling off. His face was pale as he looked up at Alex. Her breath hitched when she thought he'd out her, but he snarled at her and went back to looking at his deformed hands. Alex wasn't sure if he'd ever recover.

Good. Alex thought of every slap, manhandling, and attempt to choke the life out of her those hands had committed.

"Nice of you to show up," Lygari snapped as he came back into the room with an armful of plants. "I've been dealing with this all day. How about you get to work, *Cassandra*?"

"What should I do?"

Lygari shoved the list of plants at her, and Alex needed three trips up and down the tower stairs to collect them all. Moorloc barked orders at her to work harder. She spent the entire night working with Moorloc to heal Kruft's hand. After all the potions and ointments were complete, Moorloc left, and when he returned, he was carrying an ancient spell book. Alex realized quickly it was from the line of Cassandra. *The books are safe, and I can get them back.*

Moorloc placed the book on the table and stood behind her. Repeatedly she spread the ointments and uttered the incantations, but it made little difference. It took Alex countless tries until it worked, and she healed his burns. It was sunrise when she looked up at her uncle, hoping for praise or approval.

"I relieve you from your morning studies to rest. I'll expect you in the lab this afternoon." He dismissed her with a wave of his hand.

Swallowing her disappointment, Alex crept into the hallway. As soon as she was away from prying eyes, she ran down the stairwell and out to the beach. Gryphon awaited her, a tin of ointment in his hand.

He looked more handsome than the day before. He was

dressed in the same clothes as her, but today, he sported a royal blue tunic with his black pants.

As much as I hate blue, that color suits him much better than the orange did.

When he turned his gaze to her, Alex couldn't stop her heart pounding. It had been months since anyone looked at her with genuine excitement to see her, though she could have done without the pity on his face when he looked at the bruises Kruft had left on her.

"What happened to *you*?" he asked.

Alex looked down and realized she hadn't changed. She had sand, herbs, and potion all over her.

I must look dreadful after not sleeping or even bothering to run a brush through my hair.

Trying to hide her embarrassment, she turned away and undid her braid in an attempt to tame all the loose strands the gentle sea breeze kept blowing in her face.

"You don't have to feel embarrassed in front of me," Gryphon said. "I think you're beautiful no matter what you wear."

Why do I even care so much? This is Jessica's doing. Alex gripped her braid and whipped her head to face him, scowling.

"Don't blame me. I've had a thing for sorceresses with brown hair and green eyes. Not to mention we revere Cassandras in the Forbidden Lands—especially the titans—and I'm attracted to power. You, princess, check all the boxes."

His arrogance sent a heat through Alex that she was too familiar with—rage.

"Calm down. I'm teasing you." Gryphon moved in front of her. "You look like you could use someone to play with."

Alex stilled. Had Michael or Stefan said that to her, she'd have shoved him into the water, but she was so tired and didn't know if she had it in her to play with someone like that.

Instead, she looked down at the sand and sighed. Something hit her leg. Alex startled. Gryphon was kicking sand at her.

"You're incredibly annoying," she said. *But you're also right. I need someone to play with. I miss them, and this place is breaking me.*

"You'll learn to love it." Gryphon smiled down at her, making Alex roll her eyes.

"Today we'll start with history since you seem tired. What do you know of the Forbidden Lands?"

Alex told him the little she'd learned. Gryphon then explained about the seventeen generations of sorcerers who'd lived, including all the Heads and Hearts. To date, Alex was only the second sorceress Heart.

"That makes you extraordinary, and it means your well runs deep."

"My well?" Alex asked.

"Did your uncles never explain your powers to you?" Gryphon's eyes grew wide as his lip curled into a scowl. "Did they do anything with you other than beat you and make you feel ashamed when your clothes are dirty from being up all night making potions?"

Alex wrinkled her nose at him and growled. "Yes, but they constantly contradict each other. It's hard to know who's right."

Gryphon nodded and crossed his arms. "Tell me what they taught you, and I'll tell you who's right."

"Merlock told me my powers come from within me; Moorloc said they come from the elements. Because I'm so strong in Celtic and Poseidon, the woods and sea strengthen me."

"Both are right but also completely wrong."

"And yet you ask why I'm confused," Alex said, throwing her arms in the air with a huff.

Gryphon laughed and grabbed her hands, locking eyes with her. The intensity of his eyes made her unable to look away.

"Your powers are a well with a lid. Around the well are buckets with various amounts of water in them. When you do easy magic, you use a bucket, and when you need more, you have to push the lid off the well. That's when you feel that rush and your eyes change."

"Do all of our eyes—"

Gryphon put his finger against her nose. "Let me finish, and I promise I'll answer anything you ask."

Alex knocked his hand away.

"The rush tells you when you're accessing the well. When you perform a large spell, like parting the sea yesterday, you draw from the well. As the Heart, your well is exceptionally deep, but you need to be careful. Young sorcerers usually can't control how much they draw from their well. Sometimes you'll draw far too much when a small bucket would have sufficed. *That's* when things go wrong. Has anything happened like that?"

Alex dropped her shoulders and nodded, looking at the ground. "I set my father on fire and made a tornado explode."

"That's drawing from the well when a bucket would do. There is another risk. The well replenishes itself, but only as long as you leave enough in it. Take too much, and it'll take longer to fill back up, leaving you vulnerable and unable to pull from it if you need to."

Alex's head snapped back up. "What happens if I drain the well?"

"You die."

Alex's eyes grew large, and she gulped.

"Which is why teaching you control will be our second

lesson. Your first was posture. You're slouching, by the way. Sorcerers stand up straight."

Alex groaned but straightened her back, earning a smile and a nod from Gryphon.

"Now, you were asking about our eyes."

Gryphon explained that since titans were the living embodiment of their lines, their eyes flashed their line color whenever they drew from the well. Those born to become titans could do it. He explained the line colors: Hades had gray, Salem red, Celtic and Tiere green, Mire brown, Mystics and Poseidon blue, and Ares orange. Alex asked about black eyes, but Gryphon laughed and assured her no one had black eyes.

Gryphon held his hands out. "Take my hands. I want you to feel when your eyes switch. I'll let my powers pull yours."

Alex squeezed Gryphon's hands and closed her eyes. She pictured the sea beside them and willed it to become smooth as glass. When the familiar rush of power tore through her, Gryphon's hands squeezed hers tightly. Opening her eyes, Gryphon was watching her, and the sea behind him was as smooth as a blade.

"You felt the pull, didn't you?" he asked.

"I did."

"Then let's work on drawing enough power to accomplish what it is you want to do. And your form is important. The harder it is for the magic to come out of you, the more magic you'll use for the same spell."

"Really?"

Gryphon nodded. "Fire, please."

Alex bit her lower lip but did as she was told. Her actions were slow and calculated as she copied what she'd seen Lygari do so many times in their sparring. Facing the sea, she pressed her palms together and rubbed them until they became hot. Gryphon stood beside her as she pulled her palms apart, creating a small ball of fire. Alex considered asking him to move away, but at that moment, he stuck his face next to her fire. Alex screamed and slammed her palms together.

"Why did you stop? Your fireball was adorable," Gryphon said, winking at her.

"Do you have a death wish?"

"No. I'm not frightened of you or your powers. I know that's hard for you to realize, seeing as everyone else around you is."

Alex scowled and was about to snap back when she pictured her friends' faces. Every single one of them had looked at her with fear at least once, and that was before her full powers came in.

"I'm sorry." Gryphon put his hand on her shoulder and rubbed it softly. "I know what it feels like to have everyone afraid of you for something you never asked for. If it helps you concentrate, I can stand behind you, but you need to understand that your fire can't hurt me." He opened his palm, and fire erupted in it. The flames raced up his arm, around his torso, and down his other arm. They danced across his skin, his clothes, and his hair, but nothing burned. Alex watched in awe as Gryphon merely closed his fingers into fists, killing the fire.

"If the Head and Heart pattern holds true for us, you'll be strong in everything I'm weak at and weak at everything I'm strong at. My father is a Salem sorcerer, so your Salem will never be an issue for me to handle."

"Really?" Alex asked.

"Really."

Alex exhaled and let her shoulders drop in relief.

"But if you need me behind you to perform the spell, then I'll stand behind you. I can't see your fireball as well, but I do enjoy the view."

Alex shoved Gryphon as her power flowed through her. "Pig."

"And you're in the well. You're welcome." Gryphon stepped behind Alex. His fingers brushed her hip but stopped.

"Just correct my form," Alex grumbled.

Immediately Gryphon pressed his thumbs into her lower back, forcing her to stand up straight, and he twisted her hip forward again.

Alex took a deep breath and started a new fireball.

"Don't bend your elbows, *princess*," Gryphon whispered in her ear. The heat of his breath on her neck made her stomach lurch.

"Catch your tongue, *Sunset*," Alex said back, growing her fireball before releasing it into the sea.

"Well done." Gryphon crossed his arms and looked out at the sea. "Can you make it bigger?"

ALEX AND GRYPHON continued to meet in secret in the early mornings over the next weeks and months. They were never caught or disturbed, and while Alex wasn't sure how Gryphon managed it, she didn't worry enough to ask. She let him help and teach her. She often showed up with bruises, and whenever Gryphon tried to discuss them with her or comment about how much her appearance changed, she'd leave. Eventually he stopped mentioning it.

Under Gryphon's tutelage, Alex learned to handle her Poseidon and Celtic powers, and she could soon manage her Salem fire with ease. When she cracked, it was controlled and silent, unlike the way the rest of her family did it. Gryphon had explained that weak or improperly trained sorcerers made the sound. Alex loved working with plants so much that, little by little, the area around the castle became lush and green despite being in the desert mountain range, and the garden she'd made in the woods grew large enough to feed all the servants.

One morning after two months of training, Gryphon arrived with a serious look on his face. He handed Alex a slip of parchment.

"This is the spell that will put an end to all this." He pointed at the bruise on Alex's arm, and she moved her hand to hide it.

"It'll break your uncle's control over this place ... and over you."

Alex's eyes grew wide. "You mean I could leave? But Aaron—"

"Should be fine. The protection spell is extremely complex, and I suspect it was cast by your mother and uncle. So removing it would require at least two, which is what your uncle was banking on to keep you here even as your powers grew. I figured while we're at it, we might as well break your oath too."

"We?"

"Yes, we. A non-blood oath can be broken if three titans cast a counter spell. I'm the Titan of Mystics, and you're the Titan of Cassandra, even if you're still in your sorcerer awakening."

"What's a 'sorcerer awakening'?"

"Your uncles didn't tell you that either? It's when you turn nineteen and your powers come in."

"Moorloc called it 'sorcerer puberty,' and Merlock said it was 'coming into my powers.'"

"They didn't use the proper term for anything."

"Moorloc still refuses to use my name. He calls me little titaness."

"Considering you're the Heart, that's incredibly degrading."

"I assume it's because it's painful to use his mother's name."

"*No*," Gryphon said. "Sorcerers like Moorloc have a reason for everything they do."

Alex went silent, thinking about everything Gryphon had said. "You said we need three titans."

"I'll get the third."

"Is it safe?"

"Honestly … the spell is risky. Three titans might use enough magic to attract attention from my father, and if done incorrectly, it can hurt the sorcerers."

"Why does everyone tell me to stay away from the Forbidden Lands? You've been helpful."

Gryphon's eyes widened. "Sorcerers like my father only want power, and you, princess, are the most powerful sorceress I've ever met. They would take everything and everyone you love and destroy them to get your power on their side. Don't let them anywhere near you or those you love."

"Okay." Alex swallowed, folded up the spell, and slipped it into her pocket. "Then we should wait for them to come for me to perform the spell. That would be safest."

"Them?" Gryphon asked.

"Datten and Warren. Megesti told me before that Aaron will come for me."

"And if he isn't coming?"

"They are. I know they are." An icy chill ran down her spine as Daniel appeared behind Gryphon.

"So that blond ghost who follows you around told you?"

"You can see Daniel?"

"Daniel?"

"*Prince* Daniel. Aaron's brother."

Gryphon turned and looked at Daniel. Both looked each other up and down, scowling.

"You're the one who died to keep her safe?"

Daniel nodded, crossing his arms.

"Thank you," Gryphon said.

Alex stood, shocked, as Gryphon turned back to her.

"Try the spell."

CHAPTER 17
AARON

Aaron woke up before sunrise on the cold, hard ground with his journal stuck to his face. Michael was snoring louder than usual on the other side of the tent. In the dim morning light, Aaron dropped his journal on the blankets and dragged himself out of bed. He rubbed his arms as he walked out. Laughter and the scent of pork wafted toward him. The men were busy preparing breakfast. Aaron began running through the morning routine in his head but struggled to remember who was assigned which duties.

Is it my turn for breakfast duty? Not my favorite, but I refuse to be like my father and let my men do everything. They entrusted me with their lives, so the least I can do is scrub a few pots. When he reached the edge of the camp, he surveyed the valley they would travel through today. He could see the other side not far off, but it was deceptive. Moving fifty men was slow, but moving over a thousand took forever, even with the Betruger knights' expertise in moving across the rocky terrain.

They'd been traveling for weeks but everything in the mountains looked identical, and Aaron felt as if they were going in circles. But last night they'd received word from Randal and Jerome that the Warren and Datten armies had passed Verlassen Castle and would be at the meeting point in a few weeks. Harold told Aaron they were a week from it. The fall mountain air sent a chill through Aaron, and he pulled his cloak tighter. He watched the sky lighten as the sun crept over the next hill. Footsteps crunched behind him.

"It's colder on the mountains than valleys," Harold said.

Betruger uniforms were the same shade of brown as the surrounding earth. Aaron laughed the first time he'd seen them. But that leather explained why his ancestors could never defeat Betruger. Leather colored to match the rocks allowed the entire army to vanish. Harold's traveling clothes were lined with fur inside and out, even his boots, though Aaron suspected those were for show more than practicality or warmth.

"You allowed your men to accept our gifts of warm traveling clothes, but you yourself wouldn't take them. Why?" Harold asked.

"I'm more alert when I'm cold," Aaron said.

"At least wear this then. You stick out." Harold handed him a brown fur-lined cloak. "When we arrive at their castle, we want our numbers hidden."

"When we arrive, I *want* them to notice me. I intend to be front and center. Have you decided how you plan to handle Lygari?"

Harold's posture tensed, and he clenched his hands into fists. "I have some ideas but haven't decided yet. You?"

"Kruft will pay for betraying my father, Datten, and Alex. I can't stop thinking about how horrible he could make things for her. I intend to handle him personally."

"She changed you this much? Everything we heard of you was about how kind you were."

"I'm still kind, but I have the notorious Datten temper, and only a few things trigger it."

"Such as Alexandria?"

Aaron nodded. "I watched Lygari kill my brother. I need him to suffer."

Harold sighed. His eyes went dark, and his lips twisted into a scowl. "I intend to use our chains on him and burn him alive. He made my father suffer a slow and painful death. I'll return that favor and send him to wherever sorcerers go in agony."

"I approve of your plan," Aaron said. "It settles me to know that if we can't free Alex, I have someone capable of following through with our backup plan."

"I'd prefer not to kill you."

"You agreed to the plan. If anything goes wrong, you break her oath."

"Love makes fools of all of us." Harold shook his head. "But it won't come to that. Her uncle would have to be mad not to surrender when our three armies arrive at his door."

"I've seen Moorloc once," Aaron said. "I wouldn't classify him as sane."

A strange voice came from behind them. "Of course not. He's unhinged."

Harold and Aaron turned around to see a man in a hideous orange robe.

The man continued to speak to them brazenly. "Lygari—well, he's a monster for his prior actions, but he might have some redemption in him. At least that's what she seems to believe, and I'm not about to argue with her, even if she's adorable when she's angry." He looked around. "Where are the others? There's supposed to be ..." He waved his hand dismissively at them. "*More* of you."

"Where did *you* come from?" Harold asked, moving his hand to his sword.

"My mother. And you?"

"Who are you? And how do you know Moorloc and Lygari?" Aaron asked.

"It's my job to know about *all* sorcerers—and that includes the supposedly dead Merlin and Cassandra lines." He strode up to them and shoved his way between the royals to look down into the valley.

"Do you know him?" Harold muttered.

Aaron shook his head as the stranger turned back to them.

The man yawned lazily and stretched his arms in the air. When he finished, he cocked his head at Aaron, scrutinizing him. His eyes locked on the Datten crest. Neither Aaron nor Harold was wearing their crowns, but this man kept looking at the top of their heads. Finally, he crossed his arms and scowled.

"So you're Aaron, the illustrious Crown Prince of Datten? I expected *so* much more. I'm waiting for you? Princeling, I'm disappointed. Any man in Torian, and *you're* the one she pines for? I mean, look at the handsome mass of muscle beside you. She should've at least picked one who can protect her, and rumor has it Betruger men know how to take very good"—he glanced down Harold's fur-lined body—"care of their wives."

Aaron opened his mouth, but the man shoved his way between Harold and Aaron again. He held his hands up and wiggled his fingers while moving his hands in small circles in the air. Frustrated, he scoffed and slammed his hands on his thighs.

"Where is Merlock? I can't even sense him, and I need to talk to him *now*. I'm in a hurry and refuse to make her wait because of you."

"I'm not calling anyone until—"

"Fine. I'll do it." His eyes flashed blue for a second, and the crescent moon tattoo on his neck glowed. "Merlock! I don't have all day. Get over here."

A crack sounded as Merlock appeared beside them, looking annoyed.

"Aaron, I was in the middle of—" When he saw the stranger, he gasped and stumbled back. "Gryphon! What are you doing here?"

Gryphon sneered and stepped toward Merlock. "I came to speak with you."

"How did you find us?" Merlock asked.

Aaron watched his trembling friend. *I've never seen you this scared in my life, and you're afraid of this cocky idiot?*

Gryphon glanced at Aaron and snarled before turning back to Merlock. "She summoned me."

"She can't summon anyone," Merlock argued back.

Aaron's head whipped around to Harold. *She? Alex!*

Gryphon laughed. "You'd be in awe of what she's capable of. I suppose she *called* for help rather than *summoned,* but either way, it did the job."

Merlock crossed his arms. "She called you? She doesn't have Mystics powers."

"She shouldn't, but here I am. She's unbelievable, Merlock. Beautiful, smart—powerful. Oh, *so* much power. Being near her makes my magic pulse with excitement." Gryphon smirked at Aaron before he turned back to Merlock. "But, as you'd expect, Moorloc hasn't taught her anything."

"You're helping Alex? You've seen her?" Aaron asked.

The sorcerers ignored him. "You weren't even alive when we left," Merlock said to Gryphon. "How in Hades would you know what Moorloc is like?"

"Birch told me. She says hi, by the way. You remember her, don't you? The sorceress who decided helping her sister raise me was more important than you and your son?"

Aaron watched Merlock's face turn red as he clenched his jaw harder.

This woman meant something to you—who is she? And who is this ferflucsing arrogant ass?

Merlock's words came out in a growl. "Do *not* speak of her like that."

"I only ever speak the truth, Merlock, and can't help it if women prefer me over the lesser men in their lives. I'm sure it'll happen again soon enough, but we have matters to discuss." Gryphon whipped his head at Aaron and winked. "And I don't want to keep Alex waiting."

Aaron moved toward him, but Harold grabbed his arm. "No. I've dealt with cocky sorcerers—do not provoke him," Harold said in a low voice.

Merlock's skin went pale, and his eyes bulged as he moved toward Gryphon. Aaron's own heart raced, and his breath quickened. He'd never seen Merlock this out of control.

"Do your parents know where you are?" Merlock asked.

"I'm reckless, not stupid. Can you imagine what my father would do if he found out I was helping train the Heart instead of killing her? Or that she's the daughter of his one true love? We both know how he feels about Edward after that tantrum he threw when Victoria wouldn't come back with him after she'd conceived their little Heart."

"Gryphon, enough!"

"Now, my mother and grandmother ... Well, you know them, so I won't go there."

Merlock sighed and rubbed his face with his hands. "So Victoria was right? She is the Heart?"

"Of course she is. She has powers from six lines. Not to mention the tingles that being around her sends through me. It feels like when your powers first come in. Like another awakening but deeper," Gryphon said.

Aaron's eyes flashed. "You'd better explain what that means."

"I have powers in nine lines, but I'm decades older, and I've trained my entire life. She's Merlin. She can have *ten* lines, but your narcissistic brother is making a mess of her," Gryphon snapped at Merlock. "We have to get her out, and if you want her trained properly, she has to come with me."

"You're not taking her anywhere!" Aaron shouted at Gryphon, pulling away from Harold. *I'm done being ignored and listening to you talk about Alex like you know anything about her.*

"Quiet, princeling. The grown-ups are speaking," Gryphon said.

"I will not." Aaron lunged and shoved Gryphon. "You're not planning anything with my wife! Do you hear me?"

"She's not your wife yet, *boy*." Gryphon regained his balance and spun around to face Aaron. His eyes flashed blue as he stalked toward Aaron like a wolf toward its prey. "Even after you marry her, it means nothing. They're only words. Sorcerers bond themselves for life. A bond we feel every moment of every day. Mortal wedding vows won't keep me from her."

Gryphon stared Aaron down, but the prince's temper had awakened. "You've known Alex for a month, and suddenly you're an expert on what she needs?"

Aaron heard footsteps behind Gryphon and spotted Michael coming over from their tent. *Good. The* actual *Alex expert is here.*

Merlock grabbed Gryphon by the shoulders. "Behave yourself. The entire point of Birch going back to help raise you was so you wouldn't continue the cycle of unmitigated rage that runs through your line. Do *not* let her sacrifice be in vain."

Michael stopped at the edge of the group with crossed arms and spoke up. "Also, if you hurt Aaron, you might break the oath, but Alex will never forgive you—not after what she sacrificed to protect him. I don't know who you are, but if you actually want to help her, you should be quiet and listen to us."

Gryphon turned. "Michael. You're as recognizable from her description as the princeling is."

"Stop calling me princeling!" Aaron clenched his jaw to stop himself from attacking Gryphon again.

"So why are you here?" Harold asked. Aaron was in awe of his composure. "I doubt you came to upset Prince Aaron. From what Merlock said, you've risked yourself in coming here."

"I risk myself every day I go to help her. My parents would feed me to their dog if they discovered I was in the human lands. There is an old score to settle between our families."

"Old score?" Aaron asked.

Gryphon turned to Merlock. "Your brother is useless, and his methods are barbaric. You wouldn't believe what he allows to take place under his roof. Everything she learned has come from *me*. I'll continue to help her afterward, but you need to get her out."

"He's keeping the Cassandra books from her, isn't he?" Merlock asked.

Gryphon nodded.

"Is he even bothering to train her?"

"No."

"If he can go see her, why can't you?" Aaron asked, frowning at Merlock.

"Because they're twins."

"My brother would sense me the instant I arrived there and, knowing him, would use it as an excuse to say Alex broke her side of the oath and kill you and Stefan," Merlock said, sighing.

"Her powers are astounding, but she can't heal, and she won't use them for self-defense. She's worried any indiscretion might make Moorloc end the oath and cause the princeling's death."

"How bad is it?" Aaron asked, terrified of the answer.

"I would have taken her away from there the first day I found her if I could have."

"Why?" Aaron asked.

For the first time since appearing, Gryphon's smugness vanished. He hung his head and shook it softly before darting his gaze between them. "What she's suffering isn't mine to share. But I figured out who hurt her, and he paid ... dearly."

"What did you do?" Harold asked, putting a hand on Aaron's shoulder.

"The details aren't important. I gave him the idea that he should cleanse the hands he hurt her with. And if he does it again ..." His feral smirk returned. "It'll be his face."

Cleanse?

Michael looked at Aaron with wide, terror-filled eyes as Gryphon's satisfied smirk grew larger.

"The most powerful Mystics possess mind control powers," Merlock explained. "Did it work?"

"Somewhat. She arrives at our lessons with bruises and is becoming weaker and more withdrawn, but nothing like that first day. She keeps coming back—there's a strength there—but you're taking too long. It's been months. I worry she's losing hope. We all have our breaking point. I don't want to know what happens when she hits hers."

"How close is she?" Aaron asked. His voice trembled.

"We aren't there yet," Gryphon said, his mocking demeanor shattered. "But I worry if she breaks, we won't get her back. I won't let it get so bad she'd hurt herself. I'd burn the *ferflucsing* place down before it came to that."

"Gryphon!" Merlock said.

"Don't patronize me, old man. I'm not some petulant child.

You know what I'm capable of." His head whipped back toward Aaron and Harold. "Now get off your insignificant mortal *asses* and get there. I can help her break the oath, but you need to get there after she's mastered the spell."

Aaron barely understood what was being said. All he could do was think of Alex in pain and hoped they'd get there fast enough.

"You'd better not put Birch in danger," Merlock shouted.

"Of course not! I'd never risk her," Gryphon said. His eyes flashed blue as he clenched his fists.

Are his hands glowing?

Merlock sighed. "You're using Kharon, aren't you?"

"Of course. No one ever cares what the Hades line gets up to. For Ares's sake, any of us can talk to the dead if we do a summoning spell, and we don't have to walk around looking like we're mad, talking to ourselves all the time. Oddly, Alex can see them too. The first princeling follows her around, scowling at me whenever I touch her."

"Why not be useful?" Aaron snapped. "If you're so powerful, crack us there."

"I'm more than capable, but I won't."

"Not so talented, are you?" Aaron asked. He puffed up his chest and moved into Gryphon's space, staring at him.

"Cracking your army would use too much magic. It would draw attention here. Sorcerers would investigate, and Alex isn't strong enough to face all the titans, even with my help."

Aaron swallowed as the memory of Daniel's death at Lygari's hand came back.

"I'd never risk her," Gryphon continued. "We treasure Cassandras in our world, and she's our last. The best thing I can do is keep her hidden from our kind for as long as possible and train her myself until she's strong enough that they aren't a threat to her anymore. This army isn't all you have, is it? I've seen Moorloc's men. He has a lot of them, and they're larger and better trained than you, princeling."

"Of course not," Aaron said. "We're meeting the armies of Datten and Warren."

"Together, we'll move to his castle," Harold said.

Gryphon sighed in relief but then looked at Michael. "What does she like to eat?"

"Eat?" Michael asked.

"She's grown weaker since I met her, which means she's not concentrating as much as she could be. I want to bring her something in the morning for training."

"Apples and bread. She'll never turn either down," Michael said.

"Really, it's that simple?" Gryphon asked.

Michael smiled and shrugged. "For a princess and a sorceress, she's always had simple tastes."

Gryphon raised his eyebrows, glanced at Aaron, and snorted.

"Is there anything we can do to help? Perhaps if her friends wrote to her?" Harold asked.

"No," Merlock said. "It's too risky. Gryphon's powers allow him to hide from my brother and keep Alex's memories of him locked away. But Moorloc would discover *any* contact from us, and it's too risky."

"So what can we do? There has to be something," Michael said.

"You can let me try to beat the princeling to break the oath."

Aaron looked at Gryphon. "I'll try anything so long as it doesn't put Alex at risk."

"He's not fighting you, Aaron," Merlock said.

"There is another option," Michael said.

"Is he awake?" Harold asked as Gryphon frowned.

Aaron turned to Merlock. "I need Stefan." Merlock nodded and vanished with a crack.

"Her guard? The one she calls her brother?" Gryphon asked.

A crack echoed again, making Gryphon groan and stretch his arms as Merlock reappeared. Stefan was in his sleeping clothes, looking annoyed and half asleep. He immediately fixed his eyes on Gryphon.

"Who are you?" he demanded.

CHAPTER 18
ALEX

"Leave him alone, Daniel. He's trying to help," Alex said and took another bite. "It's a big deal that Moorloc lets me train alone in the mountains. It gives me the chance to try more challenging things away from prying eyes."

"You shouldn't talk with your mouth full, even to ghosts," Gryphon shouted from across the rocky field. "Now hurry and finish that apple. We have work to do."

Alex took another bite of her gigantic green apple. It was tarter than she usually liked, but the extra juice made up for it. She wiped her chin with her sleeve and watched Gryphon set up targets from her seat on the rocks. He'd been bringing her bread and apples every day for the last few weeks. Apples from the Forbidden Lands were so huge it took Alex two hands to hold them and three days before she figured out how to eat them efficiently. The bread made her suspicious.

How did he know those are the foods I can't turn down? I know I look rough, but I didn't think anyone realized—or cared. Her bracelet, once snug, spun freely on her wrist, so it wasn't just her pants that were looser.

Daniel's icy breeze circled her. He came to her when she trained with Gryphon. Despite his continued silence, his opinion of Gryphon was adamantly clear from his scowls, glares, and gnashed teeth. Lately, Daniel even stood between them. But knowing Gryphon could see Daniel gave Alex a feeling of peace regarding her ability to see the dead. Her tutor found Daniel's protectiveness hilarious. He walked through Daniel at every opportunity and purposely lingered when he touched Alex just to rile him.

While it annoyed her that Gryphon messed with Daniel, she enjoyed the sorcerer's friendship and his touch. Outside of Reinhilde, the rest of her contact was abuse, so she allowed him to touch her the same way she would Stefan or Michael.

"I'm glad we're in the mountains," she said. "It's better than being stuck in that castle all day with the mercenaries." An icy gust touched her forehead. "And I'm thankful to have you back, Daniel. I feel safer with you looking out for me."

Gryphon watched her with that look of pity she hated.

"I think we're ready to try the other side of Salem," he said.

Finishing her apple, Alex headed toward Gryphon, moving cautiously across the jagged rocks. Fall was in full swing, and the mornings were chilly. Alex avoided thinking about what winter in the mountains would be like, especially considering how cold her room was already. She didn't know if she'd get warmer clothes—Moorloc hadn't provided any new ones since she arrived. She remembered the cold winters in the camp at the base of the mountains, the forest trees sheltering them from the worst of the storms.

I expect it'll be so much worse up here. Maybe he's hoping I'll freeze to death. Alex tossed the apple core as far as she could.

"If you like apples so much, why don't you grow fruit trees?" he asked.

Alex smiled. "I did, but I leave the fruit for the servants. Moorloc doesn't treat them as well as he does me."

Gryphon's eyes flashed blue—a sign Alex learned meant he was angry but not with her. Since they'd started training, he'd never once been angry at her, but every time she arrived with a new bruise, he would become angry with an outright feral intensity.

Are you angry about what's happening to me, or that you're powerless to do anything to stop it? What's going on in that head of yours?

"He treats them worse than you? How is that possible?" His eyes moved to her forearm. There was a massive bruise where Lygari had grabbed her violently two days ago. He'd done it to get her away from the men who were harassing her. By dragging her away and screaming at her, he'd protected Alex from their violence. She didn't know how to explain the strange kinship that had formed between them. While she didn't fully trust Lygari and probably never would, he'd proved himself to be on her side.

"I have an actual bed," she said, "and while I don't like the food, I'm offered two meals a day every day. I don't eat it because it's gross." Alex looked away from Gryphon. It was the first time she'd acknowledged her visible weight loss.

Gryphon grabbed her hand. "I'm sorry. Not only for what you're enduring but also for what you're being forced to witness. I wish I could do more."

Alex looked down for a moment as he ran his thumb over the back of her hand. His touch no longer had the same effect on her as it had originally. As her skills grew more powerful, the pull from her magic to Gryphon's had intensified, and the heat and awkward feelings from his touch had abated. They'd settled into the mutual affection she shared with Michael and

Stefan—except for the times she'd catch Gryphon looking at her the way Aaron did.

You're looking at me like that again. Stop it. Alex pulled her hand back and adjusted her shirt hem.

"You are helping," she said. "Most days, you're my only conversation. Do keep bringing me your giant apples. I'd much rather eat them than violet fish."

"He feeds you Eitur fish?"

"You actually know what that is?"

"It's a delicacy in the Forbidden Lands. I'm impressed he's able to get it every day."

"Well, *I'm* not," Alex moaned. "Now, what am I working on today?"

"Explosions." The impish grin that spread across Gryphon's face made Alex think of Michael when they were about to get into real mischief. "I know you didn't feel safe doing them by the castle, but here, we're far enough that you should be willing to at least attempt them."

"And this will tell Moorloc if I succeed?" Alex asked, shaking her bracelet.

"Yes. I set up different targets, and I want you to destroy them."

"Is it terrible that I think that might be fun?"

Gryphon stepped up to Alex and looked down at her. His gold eyes sparkled in the morning sunlight as he moved her braid from her shoulder. "No, because it *is* fun. I would be more concerned if you weren't excited."

An icy wind went down her back, and she gasped. "Daniel, if you're going to behave like that, you can go. That last thing I need is you scaring me so I explode myself."

"I don't think your ghostly guard likes me, princess."

"Well, Sunset, if you told me about where you got that

black eye, he'd warm up to you." Daniel glared at Gryphon, making Alex laugh. "Why *do* you have a black eye?"

It's been a week since you gave me that spell, and a day later, you arrived with that shiner. I wish you'd trust me enough to tell me.

Gryphon moved right up to her face, and her stomach twisted. "I didn't tell you last week, so what makes you think I'm going to tell you now?" he asked.

"I keep asking nicely?" Alex bit her lip to stop the laugh from escaping.

"My black eye is not important."

"I think it is. I care when my friends get hurt."

Gryphon crooked his head as he looked at her. "You think I'm your friend?" *Just wait. I'll be so much more.*

"Of course you are. You fixed my back, you play with me, help me with my powers, and feed me. You make me feel safer here, and you're doing it despite our family history. So tell me."

Gryphon's face turned red, and he lit and extinguished fire in his palms. "I tried to break your oath, but it didn't work."

Alex waited for him to explain, but he didn't. She thought about it, and her eyes widened when she realized what he was saying. "You went to see Aaron? Is he okay? Wait, you *fought* him? What were you thinking? Did you hurt him?"

"No." Gryphon brushed dust off his tunic. *I stole his journal.*

"What journal?" Alex asked, but Daniel's scowl distracted Gryphon.

"Of course, I didn't fight the princeling. The funny one made it clear it would put me in your shit books."

"So what *did* you do?"

"High Hades. I fought the red-headed one, what's his name—"

"Stefan," Alex replied.

"Fine. I fought Stefan and lost. Apparently, decades of

magical power don't mean you're a natural physical fighter." *Even if you're fighting a brainless oaf.*

Alex laughed. "Everyone knows better than to fight Stefan."

"Merlock and I both believed that if harm came to Stefan or Aaron, it would break your oath. Everyone—including Stefan —refused to let His Highness be the test, so they chose Stefan instead. But you're still tied to this place with the same magical pull and force you were before."

"Thank you for trying, and I'm sorry about your eye. But Stefan isn't an oaf, so if you fought him, you're lucky that's all you ended up with."

Gryphon shrugged. "I never called him an oaf."

"Yes, you did. I heard you. And you mentioned a journal. Why would you steal Aaron's journal? Is there something in it you don't want me to know?"

"I never said those things." Gryphon's eyes went large as he cocked his head to the side. "I thought them."

"*Thought* them?" Alex looked at Gryphon and then nervously glanced at her bracelet before pulling her sleeve down to cover it. "Maybe explosions are a bad idea today."

"You don't have to worry about my eye. I have explosive powers, so this bruise is nothing. You'll find that out soon enough."

Aaron. You saw Aaron. She moved toward Gryphon and ran her hand down his arm. "How are they? I miss them."

Gryphon smiled kindly and held his hands out to Alex. "Let's test your Mystics powers." Alex gave him her hands, and Gryphon placed one on his cheek and the other on his temple. "I'm going to open up the memory of seeing your princeling and his friends."

"Princeling? He hated that, didn't he?"

Gryphon said, "Promise not to be angry about anything I said."

Alex pursed her lips. "I promise." She closed her eyes and focused. Looking through Gryphon's mind was like seeing a vision in her dreams. Snippets of memories spun around her.

"Focus on the one you want," Gryphon said, caressing her arms.

Alex thought of Aaron. A rush of wind hit her, and then she was looking at Aaron through Gryphon's eyes as their entire encounter played out before her. She struggled to catch everything, distracted by seeing Aaron before her. She cried out as it ended suddenly and threw her from Gryphon's memories. She wobbled dizzily and released Gryphon's face.

He moved with animalistic speed, pulling her against him to steady her. "Sorry. I should have warned you about how draining it is to leave someone's mind."

Alex glared at Gryphon as she pinched him. "You were mean."

He crossed his arms as he leaned down. "That's because I'm *not nice,* princess. I'm known as deceptive, egotistical, and boorish. It's expected because of who my father is. The men in my family are Heads, and kindness is not something we're allowed."

Alex swallowed. "But you're kind to me."

"You're different."

"You were cruel to Aaron but especially to Merlock. Why?"

"Our family history. And he's fun to rile up. Given the chance, I'd do worse to Moorloc, but the power needed would attract too much attention. As for the princeling ..." Gryphon exhaled and looked her over slowly. "He irks me."

"There's something you aren't telling me," Alex said, crossing her arms and staring Gryphon down.

"You and I are special. There is a legend in our world that

the next sorceress Heart would bring about a new golden age of sorcerers. You mean something to our world. But you'll mean even more to me."

"So I'll do that?"

"You're the first Merlin descendant to be a Heart. Merlin was exceptionally powerful. For once, I think the Head and Heart will be a much closer match, so we'll work together to create a better world for our kind."

Alex's power tingled at the idea. Looking at him, something deep inside her rumbled out to the surface. *No. No. No. You aren't attracted to him. It's the magic, the loneliness. He's a friend. Only a friend!*

"So you ask why you're different?" he continued. "It's because you and I end up changing our world. I know this princeling of yours is temporary." Gryphon took her hands in his. "And once he's gone, you'll be my queen."

"I'm marrying Aaron. He won't be temporary." Alex's voice came out as barely a whisper.

"Go ahead. Mortals live decades. We get centuries. I'll rule alone until you're ready." Gryphon leaned down to her face. "For you, I'll wait."

Alex stared at him, and her cheeks flushed despite herself. "You have some imagination if you think I'm going to believe that."

"You're a premonition sorceress, so you'll see it eventually. That tingle you feel in your powers when I get close? It's unique to me. It's my powers calling yours. No other sorcerer will have this effect on you."

"What tingle?" Alex lied. She raised her finger and poked Gryphon in the chest, pushing him back. "The only man who makes me feel anything is Aaron. You're my friend, nothing more."

Gryphon smirked. "We'll see."

"You won't see anything." Alex scowled.

Gryphon smiled at her. "I've been around a lot of sorceresses. I get the same tingle but only around you."

She backed away, trembling as she clutched the necklace around her throat. *This conversation is getting dangerous, and yet* ... "What happens after we break the spell?"

"You ride off into the sunset with your love. Get married. Have some blond babies."

"I mean with us. Will I ever see you again?"

"Aww, getting attached?"

Alex looked away, avoiding Gryphon's face. "I mean, are you going to keep helping me?"

Gryphon's hand went to her chin, gently turned her face to meet his, and closed the space between them. "Do you want me to stay?"

Alex looked up at him and saw his bravado vanish. In its place was something she couldn't read. She sensed hope in him, and it made her blush. "I enjoy having someone around who understands what it's like to hold this much power inside," she whispered.

"I'll have to stay away for a while to keep you safe and make sure the rest of our kind don't find you. But you'll see me again, and I'll be able to hear you, so if you run into trouble, you can call for help and I'll come." Gryphon ran his thumb across her cheek. "I'll always come when you need me."

Alex tried to stop it, but a heat spread through her. It was the kind she hadn't felt in a long time. She needed him, but there was an implication behind his words. She knew she wasn't supposed to like it, but a small part of her did. *You're betrothed—ignore this smooth-talking, charismatic sorcerer. He's exactly the man Stefan warned you about. It's okay to enjoy the attention because you're lonely here, but—*Ice hit her back suddenly, and she stepped away from Gryphon. "Daniel! Stop it."

Gryphon laughed. "Ready to break some big rocks?"

Alex gulped and nodded. She looked at the field, but he grabbed her wrist. They looked down at her bracelet, and the crescent moon of the Mystics line was dark too. Alex sighed and pulled her hand back. *I keep getting more of these, but I'm never learning the one I need.*

"What?" Gryphon asked.

"Nothing. Is it the usual stance?"

Gryphon moved behind her as she positioned herself. Alex closed her eyes and thought of the rocks Gryphon had stacked for her. But the memory of Gryphon arguing with Aaron kept creeping into her mind. She couldn't unsee Aaron's pained face at the idea of her starving and alone. *And where did that hideous beard come from?*

She felt so stupid for never having thought of what could happen after she was widowed. *I assumed the Head would kill me after Aaron died or I'd end up alone. But what if Gryphon's right? What if I end up with a sorcerer afterward? I can't imagine loving anyone the way I love Aaron.*

A wave of power engulfed her as heat burned down her arms. Rage and flames exploded out of her with a force she'd never experienced since the day she burned down the mill in Kirsh, the day her Salem powers came in. The rock she was aiming for exploded as if something inside were trying to break out. Gryphon cheered, but the heat grew stronger, and another rock exploded. This rock was closer and not set up for her. Several small pieces of rocks hit her, and her hands trembled.

Seconds later, her hands seared themselves as multiple explosions erupted out of her at once. A force slammed into Alex as she screamed in pain and was knocked to the ground so hard the air left her lungs. A rock slammed close to her, dirt pelting her cheeks.

Hands flipped her onto her stomach as a mass landed on top of her. The burn was still raging through her as a faint orange glow reflected off the surrounding ground. Finally, the heat drained from her back. Turning her head, she saw that Gryphon's eyes were blue, but he wasn't looking at her. Alex's eyes followed his, and she realized all the rocks she'd exploded were hanging in midair. As the heat left her, Alex grew weaker while the pain in her hands intensified.

Once all the heat vanished, Gryphon's arm looped under Alex's waist, pulling her against him.

"I need you to trust me," Gryphon said without taking his eyes off the rocks.

"I do."

"Good."

Gryphon squeezed her harder and released the rocks. Before they hit the ground, Gryphon cracked himself and Alex to the beach at Moorloc's castle.

Several rocks came with them and struck Gryphon as he protected Alex from her projectiles. One hit her cheek hard enough to draw blood. She knew it would need stitches, but she was too worried about Gryphon to care about her face. Alex clambered out from under him, and he collapsed onto the ground, groaning. Alex kneeled beside him to check. One rock had struck his shoulder, cutting deep into his flesh.

"Your hands," Gryphon said.

Alex looked down and realized her hands were glowing gold. Gently, she put them on Gryphon's shoulder. The light left her hands and flowed into him. It vanished into his body before it reappeared in the wound. Alex watched in awe as his injuries stitched themselves together before her eyes until it was completely healed. When the light faded away, Gryphon pushed himself up and stood before Alex.

"I'm so sorry," Alex said. Tears poured from her eyes. Gentle hands cupped her face to make her look up.

"For what? The rock or the explosion? Because both are nothing new to me."

Alex's lip quivered at the idea of what almost happened.

"None of that." Gryphon gently ran his thumb over her cheek. "I'm fine. So are you. Explosions are hard to master, so that's going to happen a lot."

"No." Alex shook her head as tears flowed down her cheeks. She couldn't stop picturing Aaron and Stefan's injuries from Verlassen Castle. Her mind twisted them with Gryphon's near miss, making her shake uncontrollably. "I'm not doing that again ... you can't make me."

"You have to *because* you don't want to. Explosive powers are dangerous if you can't control them. They get sorcerers killed."

Alex started crying so hard her chest was heaving.

"Then take them. I don't want them—any of them. I want to go home, see my father, marry Aaron, and have a normal life!"

Gryphon pulled Alex to him. She wrapped her arms around him, letting the warmth of his arms and chest engulf her. The smell of burning wood filled her, and she cried until she'd released all the fear, guilt, and pain. He stayed silent and comforted her.

"Did you get it all out?" he asked softly when she'd stopped crying. Alex nodded.

"I can't take your powers, Alex, but I can help you learn to wield them. I know it's scary, and I mean that. The same intense powers rush through my blood every second of the day. It's overwhelming—sometimes terrifying. But if you let the powers rule *you*, we all lose, and I don't think you want that for your friends, your father, or yourself."

Alex pulled away and looked up at Gryphon. "You forget Aaron."

Gryphon smirked. "He underwhelmed me, so I left him off that list."

Alex scoffed and shoved Gryphon. He let himself fall dramatically to the ground, feigning injury—the future Head of sorcerers pretending to be wounded and twitching on the beach before her.

"Tomorrow, we'll try again. And the day after, and the day after that. It's onerous, but if you don't want to accidentally explode things, you need to learn control."

Alex wiped her tears away. "I should head back for dinner."

Gryphon looked up from the sand and nodded.

Alex exhaled as Gryphon cracked away, and then she cracked herself into her bedroom to change before dinner. Reinhilde was waiting for her as usual. The moment she spied Alex, she was on her feet.

"What have you done to yourself?" she scolded, grabbing Alex's chin to examine her cheek. "This one will scar."

"Good. Maybe everyone will stop telling me how much I resemble my mother."

The old woman sighed angrily, and Alex regretted her behavior. Gryphon and Reinhilde were the two people who were truly kind to her, expecting nothing in return.

"I'm sorry," Alex said. "Explosive magic is harder to control than I expected."

"Sit. I'll be right back," Reinhilde said as she left the room.

Alex touched her face, and her fingers came back with blood. She stripped off her dirty, sweaty training clothes and put on clean ones from her wardrobe. Then the door opened, and Reinhilde returned.

"I said sit."

Alex immediately obeyed.

The old woman grunted, putting down the basin of water, and picked up Alex's dirty clothes, tossing them by the door. She dipped the rag into the basin and washed Alex's cut. Alex bit the inside of her other cheek to avoid flinching in pain. Once her cheek was clean, a needle and thread appeared from Reinhilde's apron. She handed Alex the needle while she fussed with the thread. Alex closed her eyes and sent fire to her hand and then water, cleaning the needle. Opening her palm, it glistened like new. With lightning speed, Reinhilde took the needle and threaded it before turning to Alex.

"How am I ever going to repay you?" Alex asked.

"I told you, I'm honored to help, Your Highness."

Alex held still as best she could as the needle pierced her flesh. It took a minute for the gash to be stitched, but tears streamed down her cheeks.

"Where did you learn medicine?" Alex asked, trying not to touch her stitches as she wiped her tears away.

"When I was in Warren, I worked at the castle." Reinhilde turned her attention back to the basin. She picked it up and headed toward the door.

"Wait." Alex stood and gently grabbed Reinhilde's arm. "If you worked in the castle, how did you end up here? Surely you could have received help from my father."

"I was sent away when your father was an infant. I lost the favor of the king, and his wrath was swift and harsh. Even being a noble wasn't enough to spare me. He cast me out. I found work, had a family. I was happy."

"What did you do?"

"I found a healer and was trained to work under them."

"So that's when you learned medicine." Alex smiled.

"Yes. I enjoyed helping people. But then my employer died,

and soon after, my son became deathly ill, and no one would help me because they feared your grandfather so much. Out of desperation, I summoned Moorloc. He gave me a choice: my son's life for mine. It wasn't a hard decision. I gave up my freedom so my son would live."

"Do you ever regret the choice?"

"Never. My son was married with children of his own, and I was a widow. They needed him more than they needed me. Once you become a mother, you'll understand the depths we'd go to in order to save our children."

Alex had no words as she watched Reinhilde give her a half smile and head to the door.

"Did you ever meet my mother?"

Reinhilde stopped and turned around, closing the door behind her.

"I did. She was exceptionally kind and wanted to help anyone who needed it. Many of the noble families wouldn't be what they are today without her help."

"What do you mean?"

"Your mother had a way with healing potions. She could help with everything from infections to wounds to the inability to conceive. And she would only accept what someone could afford, so she helped everyone regardless of their station in life."

"You seem to know a lot about my mother." Alex squinted at Reinhilde, but the woman smiled back.

"As I said, I trained with a gifted healer. If you'll excuse me, I have some time before the next chores, and I'd like to visit the garden."

Alex watched her leave and thought about everything she'd learned. When she visited the Strobel estate, she'd learned from Cameron's parents about her mother giving them a potion for infertility. Without Victoria, Cameron would never have been born—but Alex hadn't considered how many others her mother might have helped.

Lost in thought, Alex didn't notice the room grow colder until goosebumps erupted down her arms and back. She glanced at the fireplace and saw it burning brightly. The fear that swallowed her told her the cold wasn't Daniel. She slowly looked behind her to find her grandfather's horrible face staring back at her.

CHAPTER 19
ALEX

She had no appetite after seeing her grandfather. She'd run from the room and nearly knocked over Lygari trying to get into the hall for dinner. It was the same pungent violet Eitur fish and bland root vegetables. Alex poked at the fish and managed a few bites, but she mostly ate her potatoes and took extra portions of bread. No one asked about the cut on her face. No one cared. Looking around, Alex realized Moorloc's face was paler than normal, and the men seemed especially lively at dinner.

"Is something going on?" Alex asked.

"New slaves arrived today," Moorloc said. The calmness in his voice made Alex's skin crawl. The idea of owning *people*, as if they were nothing more than possessions, made her feel ill. Alex pushed her barely touched plate away and brought her legs up to her chin.

"What are they going to do?"

"Work," Moorloc said, picking up his goblet to sip his wine.

"For how long?"

"For however long I say. They need to work off their debts. I told you before. Magic is expensive."

Alex slid her feet back onto the floor. "I want you to let them go."

Moorloc's head snapped toward her as he slammed his goblet down. "What did you say?"

"Release them. Whoever you had here before today, let them go. I'll take their debt."

"You have nothing to offer," Moorloc said and turned back to his wine.

I must have something, but what do you want? She considered for a minute when it hit her. "I'll spar with Lygari. If I lose, I'll give you a blood oath. I'll never leave."

Ice flooded her veins, and her magic trembled.

Lygari and Moorloc stilled as they turned toward her.

"But if I win or you interfere in any way, you'll set the people free."

Moorloc narrowed his eyes. He reached for her wrist, but she pulled back and jumped to her feet, putting her throne between them. Moorloc rose to his feet, and everyone turned to look at them.

"Do you accept my terms?" Alex asked. Her heart was pounding in her ears louder than Flash's hooves when he cantered. This would be her chance to help the slaves and make a difference.

"Alexandria," Reinhilde came up behind Alex. "Your parents wouldn't want you to do this."

"Silence, old woman," Lygari snapped.

Moorloc approached Alex, carefully scrutinizing her. "I agree. If you win or I *interfere,* I'll let the old servants go." He extended his hand out to her.

Alex nodded and moved to take it, but he snatched her

wrist and twisted it around to see her bracelet. His eyes widened at the black crescent moon. The only marks still gold were Tiere, Mire, and Ares.

"You'll spar," Moorloc said, releasing her.

"But it's getting dark," Lygari protested.

"Scared of the dark, cousin?" Alex asked. The image of Gryphon holding up her uncontrolled rocks filled her mind, giving her more arrogance than she'd ever have dared to show before.

"I'm not scared of anything, least of all a sad little mortal princess. I'm worried you wouldn't be able to see me coming."

"I'll be fine."

"Excellent. Then let's go before the sun sets." Moorloc moved from his throne. Alex followed close behind, with Lygari trailing her. Before they even hit the hallway, the sound of benches scraping overtook all other sounds.

I may have done something reckless. I'm sorry, Gryphon. I hope I'm as good as you think I am.

When they arrived in the courtyard, Alex took her place on the side closest to the central tower. She shook out her arms and legs to release the tension and positioned herself in the stance Gryphon had taught her, shifting so her legs were wider than her hips and holding her elbows up. Around the grounds, mercenaries and servants looked on.

"Elbows up," Alex muttered to herself. She struggled to see Lygari's expression in the setting sun. Moorloc clapped and summoned floating spheres of fire to light the yard.

"Witches first," Lygari said, smirking.

Alex closed her eyes and dug her heels deep into the dirt, just how Stefan had taught her when she needed to hold her ground. When her eyes opened, the rush of power hit her as she pushed the lid off her well. Vines ripped through the ground into the air, grabbing Lygari's arms and legs and slamming him into the dirt.

Lygari shouted curses as he struggled to free himself from the ever-growing vines, but Alex grew them thicker and squeezed tighter. When Lygari finally freed a hand, he grabbed the vines, and they burst into flames. Kneeling to catch his breath, he placed both hands on the ground, and the grass before him erupted in flames. Before Alex could react, the fire rushed and encircled her, springing up into the sky. Lygari brushed himself off and laughed.

Alex thrust her arms straight out, palms together, then drew them apart, twirling her hands in a circular motion. An icy gust of wind rushed toward the fire. She replaced the wind with water, dousing the flames. When she thrust her hands forward again, the flood of water hit the ground and surged for Lygari, drenching him and extinguishing everything it touched.

Alex had no time to consider her next move. The ground around her trembled and rose up; she lost her footing and fell hard on her hip. As she cried out in pain, the ground quickly encased her in a tomb of dirt and stone. Fear slammed into her as the earth closed in.

She pressed her hands against the wall of stone. Gryphon's lessons echoed in her mind, sending tingles down her spine.

Don't be afraid of your gifts. Reach deep, embrace them, and, most importantly, do not let them control you.

Adrenaline and heat rushed from her core, through her chest, and into her arms. As pain engulfed her, she clenched her teeth and pounded her throbbing hands into the stone.

The tomb exploded in a shower of burning rocks. Lygari and Moorloc dodged them, but Alex didn't even notice when they hit her. Pain shot through her shoulder as blood ran down her arm, but she fixed her eyes on Lygari. Flames danced across her hands and joined into a fireball. Little sparks of lightning shot from the ball as she stepped toward Lygari with narrowed eyes. She slowly raised her hands above her head, sending more lightning from the fireball. Finally, she threw her arms forward, but an icy blackness hit her. The same chest-crushing pain from when she fell through the ice as a child filled her, and she dropped to her knees.

"Enough!" Moorloc shouted, stepping between Alex and Lygari. "You win. I'll release the mortals."

Alex panted and felt the extra power drain from her, leaving her weak. She dropped her hands to her knees as a burning pain spread across her wrist. Alex looked down. Her bracelet had turned red and tightened so much that blisters were forming on her skin. Alex ignored it and faced her uncle.

"You'll let them go?"

"Yes. I keep my word, little titaness. Something you'd do well to remember." Moorloc's warning tone made Alex gulp. He turned toward Lygari with a scowl on his face. Before Lygari could speak, Moorloc struck him across the face, splitting his lip open and sending blood running down his chin. Moorloc stalked back to Alex, grabbed her chin, and pulled her face to his. Alex could smell the fish on his breath and gagged.

"Curious. I've never seen a sorcerer's eyes turn black. It happened during the vortex at your mother's castle too."

Shoving her face away, Moorloc looked her over but then turned and headed into the castle, muttering to himself. Alex stumbled over to check on Lygari. He wiped his bloody lip with the back of his hand and shoved her as he rushed back to the castle. Shakily, Alex dragged herself to her room.

She was trembling all over but couldn't tell if it was from adrenaline or exhaustion. The bracelet pulsed red, and Alex's magic completely abandoned her.

When she got there, she leaned against the closed door. "I did it!"

"What you did was nearly get yourself trapped here," Gryphon scolded. He sat on Alex's bed, reading the book she'd left there last night.

"How did you get in here?"

"Any sorcerers can enter. A basic spell, but it would serve the purpose here."

Suddenly the room started spinning, and she leaned her head back on the door. Gryphon dropped the book and rushed to her side. Finally, she looked at her shoulder, and her sleeve was soaked with blood down to her wrist. Gryphon kneeled in front of her, lifted her hand, and spoke in a strange incantation. Alex's bracelet popped open and fell onto the floor.

"Brace yourself," Gryphon said.

The smell of burning flesh hit her nose seconds before the pain. Gryphon squeezed her hand, and she clenched her jaw, trying to keep from screaming. Whimpers escaped her as she stared into his eyes to distract herself.

Please, seal it so I can heal it in my sleep. Ferflucs, that hurts!

"I've got you. Let's get you cleaned up. You'll be okay." Gryphon's voice was soft and reassuring as he helped her sit on the bed. He picked up her wash basin and summoned water to it before sticking a burning hand into the water.

"Aren't you worried about Moorloc sensing you?"

"No. I can hide from him. It's *you* I can't hide from." Gryphon opened her wardrobe, and Alex pointed to her old, looser training shirts and the box of rags. He carried them over and knelt in front of her.

"When I was fighting, I felt a surge of strength. Was that you?" Alex struggled to pull her tunic off, so he helped, leaving her in a blood-soaked undershirt.

"Perhaps. I did nothing, but my presence influences your powers."

Alex sighed and slipped her arm from her shirt. "If you're going to scold me, let's get it over with."

Gryphon wrung out the rag and began to wash Alex's shoulder. "No scolding, just a reminder. You aren't here to free people who willingly made a deal with your uncle. You're here to learn and go home."

"I know, but—" Alex spotted something, and a hotness surged within her. "Did you read my journal?" She reached for it, feeling her Salem powers trying to rise, but she struggled to catch her breath.

Gryphon finished washing her and sat the basin down. He held her shirt over her head the same way Aaron would and closed his eyes. Alex clenched her teeth and pulled off the bloodied shirt before letting the new shirt cover her.

"You used far too much magic," Gryphon said. "I'm surprised you're still functioning."

Seeing spots again, Alex groaned and rested her forehead on his shoulder as he sat down beside her. Gryphon ran his hand along her cheek, and an orange light swept through her, filling her with a gentle, comforting warmth.

"Better?" Gryphon whispered, and Alex opened her eyes to see the journal in front of her. "Open it, princess."

Alex took it from his hand and flipped to a random page. Her breath hitched as she recognized Aaron's handwriting.

"I stole it from his tent when I visited him. Your funny friend snores worse than Cerberus. It took me a week to enchant it, so hide it well and stop being reckless. Remember what you have to lose." Gryphon rubbed Alex's back and stood up.

Alex hugged Aaron's journal to her chest. "Gryphon ..." *I don't even know what to say.*

241

"Yes?"

"Thank you."

Gryphon bent over and picked up her bracelet and whispered to open it. He smiled and handed it to her. "Put it on your wrist in the morning. It'll lock back up." Then he cracked away.

CHAPTER 20
AARON

"You're barely more than a boy! What do you know about planning battles? And besides—"

"I respectfully disagree," Harold said, interrupting Emmerich again.

Aaron tried to hide his delight as Emmerich's eye twitched, a clear sign he was ready to snap. Every time Harold interrupted him, the Datten king's face would get redder. Aaron usually struggled to hide his frustrations from his father, but this was worse. Emmerich was intent on arguing with Harold about every detail of their plan. Harold took it all in stride.

I can't believe how well you're handling this. Listening to my father prattle on is one of the most tortuous things I've had to endure.

Jerome shifted his stance—*again*. He was struggling to keep his king in line. Edward hadn't spoken, leaving Warren's opinion to Randal. Stefan and Michael sat silently beside Macht. In Alex's absence, Aaron had insisted that her opinion be represented at the table. His father had demanded Aaron pick one person to represent her, so he'd assigned the role to

Stefan and put Michael in place as his general. Stefan had broken his usual stoic composure long enough to laugh at Michael being a general of anything. But it achieved the intended goal: both of them being part of the planning.

They were in discussion for hours. Aaron listened to everyone's opinions, but he couldn't take the squabbling anymore. *Time to let out my Datten side.*

Aaron slammed his fists on the wooden table, toppling goblets that spilled their contents onto the floor. Everyone went silent and stared at him with wide eyes.

"We're *done* discussing this. You assigned me the job of getting back my betrothed. I've made Michael my general, placed Stefan on this counsel to speak for Alexandria, *and* made peace with King Harold. I respect the rest of your opinions, but it's the four of us, along with General Macht, who have decided what plan we follow."

Harold sat back and smirked at Emmerich. Emmerich opened his mouth but closed it without saying a word when Aaron glared at him.

"So what is the plan, Your Highnesses?" Randal asked, breaking the tension.

"We will go to the castle in three days," Harold said.

"Why three days?" Jerome asked.

Aaron smiled. "The last group of Datten and Warren men just arrived. They need rest before the final journey and battle. So while we wait for them to recover, I have something planned, since I remember things about the men I serve with."

"What are you talking about?" Emmerich started, but someone cleared his throat at the tent door. Everyone turned to see Julius smirking, but before he could say anything, Edith burst through the entrance, practically knocking the knight over. She was dressed in her sparring clothes, and her raven-black hair flew behind her as she whipped her head until she found her father. When she did, a smile broke out across her tawny face and her brown eyes twinkled like her father's.

"Happy birthday, Daddy," she said.

A moment later, Jessica entered the tent. Her red hair was twisted upon her head, and she curtsied in her simple red Datten gown before speaking. "Forgive the interruption, Your Highnesses. Happy birthday, General Nial, and happy early birthday, Father."

"Edith!" Randal stood and opened his arms. Edith ran and embraced him with such enthusiasm he'd have fallen if Macht hadn't steadied the pair.

Jerome watched Randal and Edith, horrified, while Jessica stepped gracefully to her father. Jessica stood on her toes and kissed her father's cheek. The Wafners were opposites of the Nials with their pale skin and cool greetings.

"King Harold and General Macht, may I introduce Lady Jessica Wafner, daughter of General Wafner, and younger sister of Sir Stefan. Lady Edith Nial is the youngest daughter of General Nial. These are Alex's best friends," Aaron said.

"We also serve as her lady's maids," Jessica said as she curtsied.

Still busy with her father, Edith waved her hand. "It's a pleasure. Daddy, I brought presents, come see," she said, pulling him toward the door.

"Edith, sweetheart, we're in a meeting," Randal said.

Edith's head jerked, and her eyes fixed on Aaron's face.

"You can go, Randal. I'm afraid to find out what Edith would do if I try to say no."

Edith giggled and pulled her father out of the tent.

"Is she always like this?" Macht asked.

"Yes," Jessica answered. "Edith is one of the kindest ladies I have ever known, but her endless exuberance is exhausting."

Edward stood up, brushing himself off. "It's because

Randal raised her like a boy. If you'll excuse me, I'm going to go for a stroll. I think the fresh air will do me some good."

"I'll join you," Emmerich said. "Jerome, you're free to spend time with Jessica." He turned to Harold and Aaron. "We'll finish our planning later."

"If by 'finish' you mean go over *our* plan, then, yes, we will," Harold said, grinning mischievously at Emmerich.

The tent emptied, leaving Aaron alone with Harold, Michael, and Macht.

"So, King Harold, what did you think of the ladies?" Aaron asked.

"Lady Jessica seems like a proper lady."

"She is," Michael said suspiciously.

Aaron grinned at Michael. "Are you going to ask for her hand?"

"I am. I have permission from Jerome."

"Took you long enough." Aaron laughed.

"Should we talk about how long it took you and Alex to admit your feelings?"

"I'd rather not."

"What of Lady Edith?" Harold asked suddenly. "Is she ... spoken for?"

"No," Michael said.

"Edith is a challenge, as Jessica would say," Aaron said. "Randal encouraged her to learn skills normally reserved for sons. In Datten, she's considered too wild for nobility. In Warren, no man will court her because of who her father is."

"They won't court her because her father is their general?" Macht asked. His lip curled in disgust.

"Not exactly. Everyone knows Edith is Randal's favorite. Her sisters, Abigail and Diana, are both happily married, but to marry Edith, you not only need Edith's approval, but you need the general's as well, and he's known to dislike the idea of Edith marrying and leaving home."

Outside, a loud commotion erupted. Aaron and Michael looked at each other and laughed.

"What?" Harold asked.

"It'll be Edith. She's not even here half an hour and she's into something," Aaron said. "Let's go see what it is because I can guarantee you if Edith's involved, it'll be fun."

Exiting the tent, they followed the shouting through the clusters of tents and found Edith with Caleb in an open field. Julius was at her side with a quiver of arrows, and Lucas was helping Caleb with his. Randal waved them over to him. "Someone said she got lucky at the tournament, so Julius pushed them and started a whole thing. So they're going to have a shoot-out," he explained. "If she'd been born a boy, she'd be the next General of Warren."

"I think Alex likes her just the way she is. She might not be a general, but she'll be on Alex's council," Michael said.

"I think you're right, Michael," Randal said, smiling.

Aaron noticed Harold was watching Edith intently.

"Are you all right, Harold?" he asked.

Flustered, Harold turned his attention back to Aaron. "Of course. She reminds me of someone."

"That painting in your throne room. The one behind you of the dark-haired girl," Aaron said.

"The one holding the severed head," Michael added, shuddering.

"Yes—Odette. She was our first Queen of Betruger and fought alongside her king to establish our home. She bore him seven children and ruled at his side for decades. She is what all our queens strive to be. Edith resembles her."

Aaron grinned at Michael as they watched Harold stare at Edith in awe. Aaron had seen that look on Michael's face when he looked at Jessica. Standing with Randal, they watched a pair of knights run down the field to set up a target. It was so far away, Aaron wondered if it was part of their contest.

Edith kissed her father's cheek for luck. Caleb bowed, allowing her the first shot.

"Is she good?" Harold asked.

"She's the lady from the tournament we told you about," Aaron said.

"The one who came second?" Macht asked.

"Yes, out of all the archers in Torian," Randal said. "Though she got an earful from her mother after we got home."

"Oh?" Michael asked.

"Judith worries Edith will never find a husband if she carries on like this. But any man who tries to change my little girl isn't worthy of her," Randal said.

A hush fell over the crowd as Edith positioned herself. Meticulously, she nocked her silver arrow, pulled back, and lined it up with the target. When she released the string, the arrow shot straight for the target and struck with a loud thunk that made everyone from Warren cheer. Aaron couldn't help but cheer alongside the men.

Edith stepped aside, letting Caleb stand where she had. He smirked at her as she held the bow out to him. Snatching it from her, he stood and nocked his golden arrow. Again, the group fell silent as he drew back the bowstring and released. The arrow whistled as it sped and struck beside Edith's. Caleb handed the bow back to Edith.

People in the crowd were squinting, trying to see which arrow was closer to the center when another arrow sped by. Lucas spun around, and everyone turned to Edith. She nocked another arrow.

"Are you mad? What are you—"

Caleb never got the rest of his sentence out before Edith

released the third arrow. She glared at Caleb, tossed Hunter the bow, and then took Julius's arm and sashayed back to her father.

"Oh my kings! Caleb!" Lucas shouted.

Edith released Julius and smiled broadly at the men before her.

"Edith, what did you do?" Randal asked.

"I split our arrows," Edith said. "Walk me to your birthday lunch? I hear a certain crown prince made sure we had enough swordfish for everyone."

"Of course." Randal and Edith left as a group of men crowded around the target, still shouting about Edith's arrows.

"I knew she was good, but I didn't realize she was that good," Michael said.

"We all have our secrets, Sir Michael," Harold said. "Now let's go before we're late for lunch."

The lunch bell rang through the camp as Aaron and Harold headed toward the food. Having Edith and Jessica around helped the men's morale. Edith encouraged them to shout "huzzah" whenever her father took a drink. They ended up getting so rowdy that Randal stopped drinking. Michael excused himself early, leaving Aaron to finish eating with Harold. When Edith hurried over to them, both men were quickly on their feet.

"Aaron, we have to go," Edith said. "Now."

"Why?" he asked as Edith grabbed his arm and pulled him from the table. Harold followed them, motioning for Macht to stay behind.

"Hurry," she said. "Michael is going to propose to Jessica, and if you don't move, we're going to miss it." Edith dragged Aaron out of the tent.

"We're going to go spy on Sir Michael asking Lady Jessica for her hand?" Harold asked.

Edith stopped and spun around to face him. Her eyes gleamed. "Yes. How else are we going to tell Alex what happened? Keep up or stay here."

Aaron snickered while Harold followed silently. Edith led them away from the camp across a rocky field toward a small wooded area. They slowed at the edge and crept behind a gigantic pile of rocks. As Edith leaned on a rock to get a better look, she lost her footing. Harold caught her and beamed. For the first time, Aaron witnessed Edith blush.

"Go on, or you'll miss it," Harold said, releasing Edith.

Edith leaned on the rocks next to Aaron, and together they peeked over the top of the rocks. They were too far away to hear what Michael was saying, but it was clear he was nervous by how much he was fidgeting. Harold knocked a rock loose, making Jessica and Michael turn toward them. Aaron and Edith ducked behind the rocks and sat unmoving.

"Do you think it's safe to look?" Edith asked.

"I'll peek," Harold said. He stuck his head up and waved his hand to signal it was clear.

Edith gasped and covered her mouth as Michael took Jessica's hand, kissed it, and got down on one knee. Jessica's mouth dropped open, but she nodded vigorously and then held her left hand out to Michael. He took it, and the others couldn't quite make it out, but it was obvious he was putting a ring on her finger. Then he stood, and Jessica wrapped her arms around Michael's neck, kissing him.

Edith's squeal was so loud Aaron suspected it would take a few days for his hearing to come back in that ear. Jessica and Michael both spun around as Edith sprinted toward them.

"Your princess has some delightful friends," Harold said as they stood and followed Edith toward the happy couple. "Congratulations, Sir Michael," he said once they got closer.

"Thank you, Your Royal Highness."

"Royal Highness? When did Aaron get a royal before his name?" Edith asked, examining Jessica's ring. Aaron winked at Michael. Tradition in Warren and Datten stipulated if a royal guard took a bride, the royal closest to that guard gifted the ring. In Alex's absence, Aaron let Michael choose Jessica's ring from the Datten collection. Michael had selected one with a large sapphire with two silver pearls on either side in the middle of a gold band.

About as Warren as you can get.

"I didn't," Aaron said. "Congratulations to both of you. My parents and Edward will cover the cost of your wedding. Considering you've both sacrificed so much to ensure that Alex stayed safe, they wanted it to be a proper celebration."

"Thank you, Aaron," Jessica said, hugging him. Despite her tears, she couldn't stop smiling.

"Michael called you 'Royal Highness,'" Edith said.

"No, I called King Harold 'Royal Highness,'" Michael said, gesturing to him.

Edith's face went ashen before her cheeks turned bright red. "I'm so sorry, Your Royal Highness. I didn't realize who you were. If my inappropriate behavior made you uncomfortable or embarrassed you, I'm terribly sorry."

Harold smiled at Edith. "No, Lady Edith—I enjoyed having someone other than Macht and Aaron be their true self around me. I hope you'll continue to be yourself around me. I especially enjoyed when you beat Sir Reinhart at archery and didn't even stay to listen to what he had to say. He needed to be knocked down."

Edith's smile filled her face. "It's my father's birthday. I didn't want to sacrifice my time with him for a boy who thinks he's Torian's greatest archer. He's good. I'm better. Now, we have an engagement to announce."

Jessica and Edith led the way back to the camp, giggling

about the ring and wedding dates and which kingdom's style of wedding dress Jessica should wear.

Everyone was thrilled by the engagement announcement, and all three kings agreed to tap the barrels of extra good ale in celebration. Michael and Jessica left to talk specifics with Jerome and Edward. Aaron asked Edith to give him a few pointers with a bow, so Harold joined them on the rocky field.

When they arrived at the target, Harold looked at her inquisitively. "Why didn't you go with Lady Jessica? I thought you were pleased about this development."

"I'm thrilled," Edith said, "but when we get back, the wedding is all we're going to talk about. There has been a lot of wedding talk at court since Aaron proposed to Alex. Uniting Datten and Warren through marriage is history. I'm tired of weddings. Please don't tell Jessica. I don't want to take from her excitement. It's just that my two sisters got married in three years."

Aaron laughed. "I can't even imagine *one*—and with Jessica's, you'll be in wedding number four."

"So where's this new sorcerer?" Edith asked. "Michael keeps writing about the vain and annoying sorcerer with a loud mouth and magnificent hair."

"Come on, he didn't write 'magnificent hair,'" Aaron said.

"He did." Edith grinned. She picked up the bow and showed Aaron how to grip it properly before nocking the arrow.

"Was someone asking for me?" Rocks crunched as Gryphon appeared. He stopped short and winked at Edith. "Hello, Edith."

Aaron and Harold both stepped in front of Edith. "What do you want, Gryphon?" Aaron asked.

"My ears were ringing, so I assumed you missed me, but I can see you have company. Should I tell the princess you're spending your days carrying on with her lady's maid rather than trying to save her?"

"You wouldn't," Harold said.

"I certainly would." His gaze shifted toward Aaron. "It would break her heart to know you're gallivanting with another woman while she's desperately trying to free herself and reading your journal every night."

"That's where my journal went."

"I thought it would help her, but I wonder if I shouldn't have left it. I mean, if you're writing about other women, it'll do more harm than—" An arrow struck the ground in front of Gryphon. He yelped, and the three of them looked up at Edith. She narrowed her eyes and scowled at Gryphon.

"*Never* speak ill of my princess or her betrothed. Next time, I won't miss."

"Where's the red-haired one? She's supposed to be civilized," Gryphon snapped back.

"Lady Jessica is occupied, having gotten engaged today, so you're stuck with me." Edith nocked another arrow.

Gryphon sighed. "Pity. No matter, if I tell Alex about this, she won't feel so bad about me getting her on her back yesterday."

Another arrow flew between Aaron and Harold, hitting Gryphon in the upper thigh. He screamed out in pain as Edith looked on.

"Peddle your lies somewhere else. No one here believes a word of them," she said.

"Merlock," Aaron called, and a crack echoed through the field.

"*Merlock*," Gryphon said, smirking.

"Merlock, take Edith to Randal. We'll be there in a minute," Aaron said.

Merlock held his hand out to Edith. When she accepted it, they both vanished.

Gryphon's nostrils flared. "Alex is getting reckless," he said.

"Clearly, if she let you put so much as a hand on her," Harold said.

Gryphon ripped the arrow out. Blood ran down his leg as he fixed his eyes on Aaron's face. His hand lit up bright orange like metal pulled from the fire at the blacksmith. Without looking away, he placed his burning hand over the wound. Aaron grimaced as Gryphon's skin sizzled where he touched his skin and sealed the wound.

Gryphon sneered. "I was going to ask for your help on how to minimize Alex's dangerous behavior, considering she offered her uncle a blood oath, but if you're too busy, then by all means, continue your archery lesson."

Gryphon's head snapped to the side suddenly. When he looked back, his eyes flashed blue, and he cracked away, leaving Harold and Aaron alone in the field.

"I'm sorry. I shouldn't have upset him," Harold said.

"That departure was about more than the arrow or you," Aaron sighed, running his hand through his hair. "We should head back to camp. If he wants our help, he'll be back."

CHAPTER 21

ALEX

lex woke up feeling hopeful for the first time in ages. Moorloc had kept his word. All the slaves who had been at the castle when Alex arrived could leave if they wished. However, Alex's joy was soon squashed when half of them refused to leave. A few had come from so far away that they didn't want to go while others didn't have anyone left to go back home to. Alex begged them to go and make new lives; she even offered to crack them home, but many were so afraid Moorloc would take back the healing he'd performed on their loved ones they wouldn't risk it. Even Reinhilde wouldn't leave. When Alex asked why, she explained that she'd said her goodbyes already and her family didn't need her, but Alex did.

"You cannot stay here out of loyalty to me. My grandfather threw you out. You owe Warren nothing," Alex pleaded with her.

Reinhilde crossed her arms. "I don't need you to tell me who I owe what to, young lady. I'm more than capable of making decisions on what is best for me."

"Then why won't you leave?"

"I made a promise to a dear friend, and I haven't finished it yet, so until I do, I'll stay here."

"What kind of friend would want you to stay here? They couldn't possibly know what they were asking you to do." Alex slammed her pillow down on her bed and looked back at Reinhilde, the only friend she'd made in this horrible place. She was bossy but had Alex's best interests at heart. Alex decided that Reinhilde was like the grandmother she never had.

"Don't you have spells to work on?" Reinhilde waved her hands at Alex, dismissing her.

Frustrated at her failure to change so many of the slaves' circumstances and her inability to get through to Reinhilde, Alex cracked herself onto the rocky field where she'd trained the day before. It was unrecognizable. What had been a flat rocky place was a crater-filled mess. Alex sighed and gingerly moved around the jagged rocks to look inside the first hole. It was so deep she could disappear inside of it. Looking around, Alex counted another nine such holes. When Gryphon had cracked them away, he'd saved her from being crushed by the debris that littered the surrounding ground.

Alex's breath hitched as she thought of what would have happened if she'd been training alone. Fear crept up her spine, and she looked behind to find Lygari watching her. He strolled up beside her and looked into the crater.

"Did you do this?"

"Yes."

"When?"

"Yesterday."

"So *that's* why you stood up to my father." Lygari paused a long while before nodding to her. "You got lucky. It won't happen again."

Alex swallowed hard and brought her hand up to grip her necklace. She looked at Lygari's swollen lip and wondered how much he'd endured over these years. Behind him, Gryphon silently appeared for their lesson. When he noticed Lygari, Gryphon stalled, and his hands became glowing orange fists.

Please behave, Gryphon. I'll explain later. His hands stopped glowing, and he vanished.

Lygari turned to look behind him. "What are you looking at?"

"Daniel. Aaron's brother follows me around. Seeing him is my Hades power your father was so uninterested in," Alex said, waving the bracelet at him, but Lygari slapped her hand away. Alex stepped away from him and the crater.

Gryphon's voice sounded in Alex's head. *If he lays another finger on you, he won't make it back to the castle.*

"Why are you following me?" Alex asked.

"I wanted to see where you were going every morning when you don't come to breakfast. You've gotten better so quickly, I wondered if you were getting help. Salem isn't a simple power to manage, especially not for a little mortal half sorceress *girl* like you."

"Why do you insist on calling me 'mortal' and 'half sorcer-ess' when you're exactly like I am?"

"I am nothing like you!" Lygari screamed in her face. "When you aggravate him, he takes it out on me. What keeps you safe from my father's wrath is the fact that you look like your mother. Victoria was the only thing he has ever loved in this world, and he intends to use you to get revenge on everyone he blames for her being gone."

"I would never hurt Datten or Warren. He can't possibly think I would do any—"

"Are you that naive? He doesn't need you to hurt them. *He*

can hurt them or make me do it. What he needs you for is to hurt the sorcerer who started this."

"Who?" Alex asked.

"Garrick. Only the new Heart or Head can defeat the old one."

"But he must be two hundred. I won't stand a chance."

"Which is why you aren't going anywhere until you're ready. It'll take decades, so if you were smart, you'd tell your bed warmer to go home and not waste his life coming for you because *if* you're lucky, you'll be allowed to attend his funeral."

"No!" Alex shouted at Lygari and pushed him as hard as she could.

He stumbled for a moment but caught himself. His face twisted into a snarl, and he grabbed her wrist and threw her to the ground at the crater's edge.

"You're never leaving, and the sooner you understand that, the better. Stop playing games with my father because you'll lose, and I promise that you'll live to regret it."

"I'm never going to give up, never going to stop fighting to get back to Aaron, my father—all of them."

"The reason I've been nice to you is because I thought you'd take the focus off me, but your rebellious streak has made him worse than ever."

"So you came here to yell at *me* ... because *he's* a monster?"

"Before you, I could at least control him to a point. But your powers keep growing and, with them, his plans for you."

"I'm sorry," Alex said, cowering. "I didn't know."

Lygari groaned and held his hand out to Alex. She accepted it, and he pulled her up. "If you have any hope of ever seeing your loved ones again, you need to get stronger."

"Why? He won't let me go."

Lygari smirked. "So you can kill him. That's how you get free."

"You want me to *kill* your father?"

"How else will I become titan? You can have Cassandra. I want Merlin."

Alex swallowed and backed away from Lygari. "I'm not capable of that."

"You're a sorceress. It's only a matter of time before you realize what you're capable of. Try not to get yourself killed," Lygari said as he cracked away.

"Can I kill him yet?" Gryphon asked, coming up behind Alex.

She looked down and went silent. *He's the least of my problems here.* Gryphon's warm hands squeezed her shoulders while Alex sniffled back tears.

"Are you okay?" Gryphon asked.

Alex shook her head and faced him. "Is what he said about the Head true? Is killing my uncle the way to get out of the oath? Can your spell even work?"

Am I capable of murder? Would that make me worse than him?

"You're asking and thinking too many questions at once for me to keep up. Ask what it is you really want to know ... *princess.*" Gryphon rubbed her arms. Every touch from him sent her magic racing, making her body feel as if she'd explode like the rock piles around her.

"Is your father the reason my mother left her home?"

"Yes."

"How did he make them leave?"

"My father was infatuated with your mother. When she rejected him, it got messy, and so the remaining lines of Merlin and Cassandra vanished. Many thought my father had them killed, but I knew they fled."

"Why?"

"Birch told me. She was friends with your mother and Merlock."

"You know Birch?"

"I do, but we don't have time to get into her right now. We have to figure out how to handle Moorloc."

"But—"

"Another day, Alex."

"Fine. Will your spell work?"

"If you master it, and I can get another titan to help."

"If we can't?"

"Then you have Lygari's idea."

Alex pulled away from Gryphon. "I don't know if I can kill Moorloc." Bile crept up her throat, threatening to bring up what little food was in her. It was too much. She couldn't do everything fast enough. The servants wouldn't leave, she'd failed at her explosions, and Lygari's cruel words kept repeating in her mind.

Could I really kill my own blood? Am I as much of a monster as he is?

"You're not a monster. You're a princess, a sorceress, a titan, and my Heart. You'll do what needs to be done."

"What if I fail?"

"You won't."

"I wish it was that easy for me to believe you." Alex sighed and looked down. *How much more blood do I need on my hands?*

Gryphon sauntered over and held his hands out to her. "You need cheering up. Your magic won't cooperate if you're in a mood. We need to loosen you up. Dance with me."

"No."

"Why not?"

"I don't dance." *With anyone but Aaron.*

"Why don't you dance?"

"Because I'm terrible at it."

"So—you don't do things you're bad at even if they're fun?"

"I prefer not to embarrass myself publicly."

Gryphon chuckled. "You do an awful lot of magic that you're pretty terrible at."

Alex's mouth dropped open. "Catch your tongue!" She shoved Gryphon as hard as she could, trying to push him into the pit she made, but it didn't stop his laughter. *Michael would have said that. You're not allowed to act like Michael.*

Gryphon flung his fingers out, and the surrounding earth was flat again. Looking at her with a small smile, he handed her a giant apple. Alex didn't want to know where he'd hidden it. Despite everything she was feeling, she smiled back. Gryphon put his hand on her cheek and turned her face to the side.

"Whoever stitched your cheek did an outstanding job. You might not have a scar."

"Reinhilde. She's the other person who's kind to me. Moorloc assigned her to be a sort of lady's maid to me. Really, she's the first servant I met, and my charms can't manipulate her."

Gryphon winked. "You won her over, didn't you?"

"I didn't have to. She knew both my mother and grandmother."

"So either Moorloc is as foolish as I believe, or he's got something planned."

"I don't think it's either. I think he is so indifferent about his servants—or *slaves,* as he calls them—it never occurred to him to check which kingdom she came from."

"I need you in a happier mood for our lessons ... The funny one proposed to the red-haired one."

Alex's head snapped to Gryphon. "Michael did *what?*"

"I went to the camp yesterday. Apparently it was a birthday, and your princeling arranged to have your ladies visit. The funny one took advantage of the situation."

Alex couldn't breathe. She was so excited. "Michael proposed to Jessica. How are they? Is everyone okay?"

"The army has grown significantly, and your friends all seem to be doing well. I don't like Edith. She's feistier than you are."

"What did you do?"

"Me? I did nothing, and she shot me. So I don't like her."

"Edith shot you? Where? Let me see."

Gryphon grinned and pointed to his upper thigh. Alex groaned.

"Still want me to show you?"

Alex straightened herself. "I'm a healing sorceress. It's my duty to help. You're fortunate Edith has such exceptional aim or things could be much worse."

"You're right. A little to the side and she'd have hit something precious to me."

Alex rolled her eyes as Gryphon untied his pants to show Alex the injury. Once the wound was on display, she squatted down. She couldn't help glancing to the side and snickering.

"You were being rather generous to yourself," she said.

Gryphon leaned down to her and whispered, "If getting shot is what it takes to get you into my pants, it was worth it."

Alex pinched his thigh. "Magician."

"Owww," Gryphon shouted and gave her a dirty look.

"The burn is healing incredibly well, and there's no infection. You may put your pants back on." She looked sideways again and smiled. "You look cold."

"For that, we're doing explosions again today."

Alex gulped as she stood and brushed the dirt off her hands. "Fine."

"Now get ready."

Alex sighed and took the proper stance.

The day flew by. After dinner, Alex took a quick nap and

then waited for everyone to go to sleep. She braided her hair and wore her dirtiest tunic. It was a dark shade of gray.

Thank you for being so worried about me, Gryphon, but I'm going to find our books. My mother left them for me, and I'm getting them back. Alex left her room and crept along the deserted halls.

She padded down the long hallway to get to the southwest tower stairwell. The east tower was closer, but the armory was rarely unguarded, and the kitchen was deserted at night. When she reached the stairs, Alex grabbed a torch off the wall and stepped softly on the stairs. She glared at the torch as she held the end, and a flame erupted exactly where she wanted it.

There was no fire-lit ceiling in the bowels of the castle. The air was heavy with moisture from the rain-soaked dirt floor, and everything stank of decay and mold. A cavernous hall stood before her, built with the same decrepit stones that made up the rest of the castle. The arch in the doorway swallowed much of her torchlight. Dirt and rocks crunched beneath her feet as Alex sped up to get away from the stairs. The dark halls seemed to go on forever. Beneath the castle was a maze of halls and passages leading into one another with doors virtually everywhere. Alex had expected a mess of things to investigate down here, but this was overwhelming.

She moved down the halls, opening every unlocked door she found and looking for anything that might hide books. She remembered the bookcase doors and kept her eyes open for anything that seemed out of place as she inspected the rooms. Many were empty or had nothing but a few beds in them. Alex was beginning to feel frustrated when she noticed a door down a narrow hallway. Letting the torch light her way, she tiptoed until she found herself at a door off another main hallway. The old, rusted handle made a small click as she pulled it open and snuck inside.

This room was larger than the others, but the air smelled stale. It seemed to be filled with items that were discarded from various parts of the castle. Alex placed her torch in the holder on the wall beside the door, managing to light the space with a faint glow. There was a large, solid wooden table, and in the corner was a heap of broken chairs. Whoever left them couldn't even be bothered to stack them. On the other side was a pile of rusted armor that had clearly been thrown in the corner. Beside the armor were several chests with flat lids. Moving toward them, Alex counted eight before the bookcases on the back wall caught her attention. Immediately she rushed to them, but there were no whispers. Frustrated, Alex grabbed a book, and the door behind her slammed shut.

Alex nearly jumped out of her skin as she turned around.

"Well, Tristan, what do we have here?"

Alex's blood ran cold as she saw Kruft's men. Doyle and Tristan stared at her, blocking the only door to the room. Their size prevented most of the torchlight from reaching her.

"It looks as though we caught our guest snooping again, Doyle."

"I suppose the little witch needs a lesson in manners."

Alex grabbed for her magic, but her terror and rage were so bad they interfered with her powers. After the Verlassen Castle incident, she was too scared of hurting herself to unleash her powers, something she now regretted not telling Gryphon. She clenched the book to hide her trembling hands.

The men came toward her. She looked around but there was nothing, so she threw the book she was holding at Doyle and grabbed another. Doyle dodged, but the second book hit Tristan as he lunged for Alex. Still, he managed to grab her arm. Alex struggled against him as Doyle came up before them. He grabbed Alex's neck and jerked her head to face him as Tristan locked his hands on her arms and held her in place.

Squeezing her neck, he brought his face close enough to hers that she could smell the ale on him from dinner.

"Fighting us won't help you, but it'll make this more fun for us. You didn't think you could embarrass us in front of our men and get away unscathed, did you?"

Alex spat in his face, and he released her and stepped back in disgust. She knew that no matter what she did, they were going to hurt her. They wanted revenge ever since she beat them in the hallway.

"Gryphon!" Alex screamed, causing Doyle to slap her across the face with his open palm. Alex winced and tasted blood.

"Go ahead and scream. No one can hear you, and your annoying cousin won't save you this time," Doyle said as he yanked on Alex's braid, making her wince.

"I'm not afraid of you." *They know I'm lying.*

Doyle slapped her again but cursed when Alex whipped her head back and spit blood at him. "It's pathetic that you need Tristan to hold me down to hit me," she snarled. "Second-in-command can't handle a little princess."

"I don't need anyone's help to handle you," Doyle said.

"You aren't surprising us this time, so try to give us a challenge," Tristan said, squeezing her arms hard enough to make her hiss.

"What should we do first?" Tristan asked. "Break her arm? Knock some teeth out?"

"We could strangle her. Fast and easy," Doyle said, sneering.

Gryphon, where are you? HELP!

"No opinion?" Tristan asked, twisting her arm behind her.

"Now she catches her tongue." Doyle grabbed her chin and tilted her head back and forth. Alex could smell the ale and body odor from both of them and tried not to be sick.

"We could give her a scar to match the one her guard gave Kruft. Do you think he'd like that, *princess?*" Tristan asked as he pulled her back and shifted his grip on her.

Gryphon! Please! How do I summon my powers when they won't come?

She reached into her well and came up empty. She closed her eyes and exhaled. *My magic has become a crutch. I need to focus, to remember Stefan's training.* Adrenaline washed through her as her forgotten training bubbled up from the depths of her mind.

Doyle tried to pull her forward by her tunic, but it was so worn it ripped, exposing her stomach up to the bottom of her breasts.

"Any old scars we can reopen?" Doyle laughed but then turned his attention on a scar on Alex's side from when she fell out of a tree.

Alex knew that was her chance. She stomped on Tristan's foot, making him release her and step back, giving her space. Immediately, she threw an uppercut at Doyle, striking the bottom of his chin. The blow was audible to the three of them as a rage and strength Alex didn't know she had flooded her veins. Time slowed down, and she focused on getting revenge for everything any man had ever done to her. They'd bear the punishment for her grandfather, Kruft, Wesley, inappropriate suitors, and Graham—everyone who ever hurt her.

Alex threw her left hook at Doyle. Her wrist exploded in pain as he stumbled backward. He slipped on the books she'd thrown that were scattered on the ground. Tristan grabbed Alex and slammed her into the wall between the bookcases so hard her head bounced. Spots flooded her vision, but she refocused and brought her knee up exactly how Michael had taught her to, and Tristan dropped like a stone.

Doyle recovered and rushed toward Alex from across the

room, and something inside her woke up. Her adrenaline spiked, releasing a new power and rage. They swirled together into a violence Alex never thought she was capable of. Cracking herself behind him, she threw her leg up and kicked Doyle so hard he landed on top of Tristan. Her hands were glowing orange. She saw the stack of chairs and grabbed one. She smashed it into the wall, leaving the thick, carved wooden leg in her hand. She held the end with both hands and stalked toward the men still struggling to stand.

She struck Doyle in the neck as hard as she could. She heard his bones crunch as she turned to Tristan and struck him in the face. His nose exploded, and blood splattered her skin as she kept beating him with the chair leg. The more she attacked, the darker orange her hands glowed and the angrier she became. When Tristan stopped moving, Alex returned to check on Doyle.

Wind hit her, and Gryphon appeared in front of her. Panic-stricken, he sniffed the air. "*Blood.*" He frantically scanned the room. "Alex, are you all right?"

The instant his eyes locked onto hers, he erupted in an orange glow. Alex looked down and saw that her entire body glowed orange like his. Gryphon stepped toward her, and his eyes switched from gold to blue. Power crackled off him, sending a monsoon of emotions through her while stirring the rage more. Alex couldn't focus or think. She wanted to hit Gryphon, too, but when he stalked toward her, the power in her intensified and replaced her rage with a desperate longing.

"Gryphon?"

Looking him over, a painful desire and arousal overcame Alex. Without thinking, she dropped her weapon and leaped into his arms, locking her arms around his neck. He caught her easily and wrapped his arms around her waist.

She stared at him for a moment before she kissed him. He

stumbled and then reciprocated her kiss with gusto. As his tongue slipped into her mouth, a fire lit inside Alex that she'd never known before. Her powers all awoke at once, as if Gryphon had summoned them to the surface.

His hands gripped her against him as Alex shifted her legs and locked them around his waist to deepen their kiss. When her backside hit the table, Gryphon ripped what remained of her shirt off. In response, she reached into his collar and pulled, listening to each stitch of the fabric stretch and tear in her bare hands. His entire torso was glowing a dark orange. Alex ran her hand across his perfectly muscled chest, and her powers screamed at her to take him, to claim him as hers.

Gryphon gripped her face with his hands and kissed her again. She gripped his hips to pull him against her and moaned softly as Gryphon alternated between nipping and kissing her neck. He pressed her against the table with his weight, and Alex's mind emptied, and her body took over. Her hands wound their way into Gryphon's hair as she pressed against him. He switched to biting her neck.

Alex moaned as she struggled to get closer to him, to feel more of him. Losing all sense, Alex panted his name. "Gryphon."

Gryphon's eyes snapped from blue to gold, and he pulled Alex's wrist, pulling her away from him. "No," he said firmly.

Alex growled, desperately trying to press herself against him. The need and desire were excruciating. "Please," she said, trying to take control of the situation. "I need you."

Gryphon shook his head and backed away. "You think you do, but it's your magic. Your Ares powers are calling mine. Ares sorcerers are like opposite sides of a magnet in that they are uncontrollably attracted to each other. And there is no pair more powerful than us. But this isn't *you*."

Alex slipped from the table and stalked toward Gryphon.

Before he could stop her, she grabbed his face and kissed him again, but this time, she became tired and weakened. When she blinked her eyes open, Gryphon was staring down at her. He opened his mouth, but Alex didn't hear what he said as everything went black.

CHAPTER 22

GRYPHON

Gryphon sighed and surveyed the damage. "You left a disgusting mess, and you're drained of power again. We're going to have to talk about this tomorrow—assuming you have the courage to look at me. First, I need to get you cleaned up and into bed. Tomorrow will be horrible for you when you remember tonight." He slid his arm under Alex's legs and scooped her up.

He cracked her back to her room and laid her on the impeccably made bed. He found her basin of water and grabbed a rag from the wardrobe. After heating it, he washed the blood from Alex's body. He paused for a moment, examining her necklace before dressing her in the oversized Datten shirt he found under her pillow.

Your bed warmer's shirt, judging by the lingering stench.

Tucking Alex into bed, Gryphon leaned down and kissed her forehead.

"You're incredible. Sorcerers don't settle down until they're a hundred years old, but at nineteen, you forged your own path and committed yourself to him, even if it's only for a few decades. But he—no, *they*—failed to protect you. If any experienced sorcerers showed up, they'd all be dead, and you'd be taken before my parents. I promise I'll do everything in my power to never let that happen."

Gryphon's skin prickled. He looked up to see Alex's annoying ghostly guard staring at him.

"Go play with a hellhound."

Daniel crossed his arms and sneered.

"Sorry, dead princeling. You may not like that I saw her naked, but I wasn't going to put her to bed all bloody. That would have made tomorrow worse."

Daniel didn't stop sneering.

"Where exactly were *you*?" Gryphon growled. "I thought you were protecting her. Shouldn't you have warned her before those two morons found her? I'm fairly confident your brother wants you guarding her, not checking up on him playing commander."

Daniel looked down and dropped his shoulders.

That's what I thought.

Gryphon picked up her bloody clothes and threw them into the fireplace. He summoned fire, and in moments they were reduced to ash. He turned back to Daniel.

"Don't leave her. I'll be back when I'm done dealing with them."

He cracked back into the storage room. The two brutes lay on the floor, unmoving amid the other broken castle waste. He crossed his arms and kicked one with his foot.

"You're lucky she killed you. I'd have made you suffer until you begged for death. No one hurts my Heart and lives. Tonight, I'll visit Kharon and make sure the Titan of Hades sends you exactly where you deserve. I hope you like dogs because the hellhounds are going to enjoy ripping you apart."

Gryphon cracked their bodies deep into the mountains and

then used his powers to scrub the blood from the stone floor until all that remained were dust and rat droppings.

She has Ares powers. But not small, weak ones. How are her powers so strong even compared to mine? Ares ... her bracelet.

Returning to Alex's room, Gryphon took Alex's hand and whispered an incantation to turn the Ares mark gold again.

Better they don't know yet what you're capable of.

Alex's hand turned and gripped his. She was sound asleep, but when he tried to pull his hand away, she whimpered. Gryphon looked up at Daniel. The ghost rolled his eyes and vanished. Gryphon sighed and slid onto the bed beside her. Holding her hand, he brushed the hair off her face and watched her sleep.

"All I want to do is take you away from this horrible place, but I can't because it would hurt that boy you love. You are such a rare thing, and my family would slaughter everyone here to get you. I'll do everything in my power to keep you safe and hidden as long as possible. We have a destiny to fulfill, and it won't happen if our families—yours or mine—interfere."

Alex sighed and squeezed his hand before she nuzzled his shoulder.

Staying with you right now is a terrible idea. I'm already dangerously attached to you.

Ares sorcerers were extremely territorial, especially when guarding a claimed sorceress.

But I can't claim you. Not the way my line claims their bonded partners. Every sorceress in the Forbidden Lands would consider it a high honor, but you were raised by mortals. You'd resent me for taking you from the princeling.

For now, you want him, but one day, you'll be the mother of the greatest sorcerer to ever walk Torian. Our son will be a Head like we'll never see again. I need to convince you to come back with me and not waste the next few decades with that princeling.

CHAPTER 23
ALEX

lex jerked awake in her bed, gasping and soaked to the bone. Adrenaline roared through her, and her body ached as if she'd been in a fight. She was in Aaron's nightshirt and cleaner than she had been in days, though she had no memory of washing. She trembled as she stood and found hand-shaped bruises all over her arms as the night before came flooding back to her.

She covered her mouth and crumbled to the ground. She could still feel a trickle of rage coursing through her blood and the immense power that came when she glowed orange. Alex spun her bracelet on her wrist to the Ares ax. It was still gold, not black.

I don't understand. How is that possible?

Gryphon's face flashed in her mind before the crunch of the chair leg contacting Doyle's neck and Tristan's face. She grabbed her basin from her bedside table and threw up.

"Did I kill them?" Alex shoved the basin under her bed and pressed back against it, shaking at the idea of having committed murder. It had been self-defense, but then the memory of Gryphon's lips on hers hit her.

I kissed him, touched him. I would have—How am I going to explain that to Aaron? He's never going to forgive me.

Stifling a scream, Alex pressed her forehead against her knees, trying to force her body to breathe as her vision tunneled into blackness. She'd just gotten her breathing under control when the door flew open and Lygari appeared.

"What are you doing? We're supposed to be sparring. Your bet with my father didn't exempt you from our monthly test of your powers."

"I can't," Alex said, keeping her face pressed to her knees.

Lygari stormed into the room, grabbed a shirt and pants from Alex's wardrobe, and threw them at her. "Unless you want to see what my father is like when furious, get up and do what you're told."

Alex glanced at the clothes before looking up at Lygari. "*Please.*"

"I'm not sticking my neck out for you. Kruft's on a warpath because he can't find Doyle. I'll not be adding my father's anger to that shit pot. So get your *ferflucsing* rear up and get dressed or else I'll drag you out of here in your nightshirt. And if you think the men are horrible now, I can promise they'll be so much worse if they see you practically naked."

Lygari slammed the door as he left. Alex's legs trembled as she stood and dropped Aaron's shirt on her bed. His smell had all but vanished from it, but she missed him so much she couldn't stop wearing it. Alex took a few deep breaths to settle herself and dressed. She braided her hair as she hurried to the courtyard to find Kruft arguing with Moorloc.

"He wouldn't leave. Doyle was loyal," Kruft growled.

"Do mercenaries understand loyalty?" Moorloc asked. "If you can't find your second, that isn't my problem."

"Have you tried asking Tristan?" Lygari asked, rolling his eyes.

"He's gone too."

"Again, not my problem," Moorloc said before turning to Alex. "Look who finally graced us with her presence. I don't care that you aren't a fan of sparring matches. I expect you to be punctual. Get to your place so we can see how your powers are progressing."

Moorloc pointed to her spot, but Alex looked at it. "Please, I can't," she whispered, looking at Moorloc and begging him with her eyes to not make her.

"Get to your spot or I'll have Kruft drag you there," Moorloc barked at her.

Alex whimpered as she shuffled to it. Lygari fixed his hair and shouted at the servants as he made his way to his place. Alex lifted her head and looked over at the group of men and women who worked in the kitchen.

"Move faster, you useless mortals. I want everything in the kitchen before we're done sparring or I'll set your rooms on fire," Lygari shouted at them.

Alex glanced at them. These were the people whose freedom she'd risked her life to win, but they'd remained. Alex had asked Reinhilde about why they'd stayed, and while Alex understood their fear, she was frustrated that they were still being mistreated by Lygari and the men despite her deal with Moorloc. Alex's breath sped up as she watched the women hauling bags of root vegetables while the mercenaries sat on their butts waiting for the sparring match. Rage seized her, and a quiver rushed through her chest as she stared at Lygari.

"You could give up, princess. I killed your bed warmer's brother and the Betruger king, so what chance does a nobody like you have?"

His cockiness made her sick. Lygari rolled up his sleeves

and slammed his palms together, and when he pulled them apart, a swirling sphere of fire hovered between them. The fire grew to the size of his head. Lygari smirked before he hurled the fire directly at Alex.

The same feelings of the previous night threatened to overtake Alex, and her inner well erupted with power. On instinct, she sent a burst of water from her hands, stopping his fire before it made it halfway to her.

Raising an eyebrow, Lygari cocked his head to the side. Moorloc and Kruft stopped bickering and focused on them. Alex watched Lygari produce a half dozen fist-sized fireballs. He flung them all at once and then snickered and crossed his arms. Time slowed down for Alex as the fireballs flew toward her. She summoned her water and weather, making snowballs, and sent them after Lygari's flames.

Alex raised her chin at him, and Lygari stopped laughing. He glanced toward his father. Moorloc gave him a nod, and her cousin closed his eyes. A heaviness came over the courtyard. Closing her own eyes, Alex let the rage that she was holding in flood her body. A rumble left her, and when she opened her eyes, Lygari's face went pale. The surrounding grass was dead, and dark black clouds filled the sky above them. Thunder rumbled across the yard, and lightning struck outside the castle. Alex thought of Daniel, of the Betruger king, and all she'd endured at Lygari's and Moorloc's hands.

Revenge.

What happened the previous night was eating her alive, threatening to take her. She could end this—permanently. But Alex refused to surrender to the darkness burning her soul. She pushed through and held her hands out, palms up, to change the game they were playing.

A crackling sound erupted across the field. Lygari's arms

trembled as he formed a fireball larger than ever before and hurled it at her. Alex threw her hands out, and when the fire reached her, she caught it.

Fire can't hurt Salem. That's what Gryphon said, and I'm stronger than Lygari.

Before anyone could react, she threw the fire back at Lygari along with a bolt of lightning from her hands. Lygari reacted a second too late, and the fire singed him before he cracked away. But the fire and lightning continued through the empty space and struck a servant in the back, sending them flying to the ground.

At that moment, time caught up for Alex. She cracked across the field to where the servant had been hit and collapsed on the ground. Dreading what she'd see, she turned the woman over. The other servants had gathered around and looked on in horror.

"No, no, no, no. *Moorloc!*" Alex screamed, cradling the lifeless body of Reinhilde. The heat from where the bolt had struck her was so hot, Alex's hands blistered, but still she held her. The smell of singed flesh hung in the air and filled Alex's nostrils. Her hands glowed gold as she poured out her healing powers with such force that she almost drained her well and felt weak. The woman gasped once more, a long, horrifying rattling breath, but there was no light left in her eyes.

"It's too late," Moorloc said behind her. "The magic of Cassandra can only fix so much."

Tears streamed out of Alex as she clung to Reinhilde. *Three! I murdered three.* An animalistic howl burst from Alex's lungs. The guilt, her rage, her pain, and her grief all at once was too much. Inside her, something shattered, and Alex made a choice. It gutted her. *There is no controlling my powers, no coming back from this. I'm unforgivable. This will end here.*

"Put her down. We'll dispose of the body," Moorloc ordered.

"No."

"Alexandria." The tone was a warning, but Alex didn't care.

"No! I will bury her. Properly. I don't trust you to not leave her body for the wolves." Alex whipped her head to look at Moorloc, and his eyes widened, his face ashen. Alex saw fear in his eyes. Whatever broke in her showed on her face because he stepped back.

"Kruft, get her a shovel."

ALEX CRACKED Reinhilde and herself to the edge of the surrounding woods she'd grown. None of the other servants had dared come with her after seeing the terror on Moorloc's face. But Alex was determined to memorialize this spot so they could come visit Reinhilde if they wanted to. It took her the rest of the day to dig a plot. She refused to use her magic, and at the end, her clothes were caked in mud, her nails were broken, and everything hurt. As gently as she could manage alone, she lay the old woman in the pit and filled it in. Despite the time of year, she grew flowers around the entire area before she collapsed beside the grave, weeping.

"I'm so sorry," she repeated.

An icy chill brushed over her as the ghost of Reinhilde appeared beside her.

"Please forgive me," Alex begged as she looked up at the ghost. Reinhilde bent over and kissed the top of Alex's head before she disappeared, but the tears wouldn't stop. Alex sobbed at the grave until there was nothing left in her.

Then she walked back to the castle and her room. Still covered in mud, she collapsed into her bed and didn't move.

Whatever had scared Moorloc and Lygari was enough that they didn't bother her. Alex stayed in her room with her thoughts and guilt.

I'm a monster.

Everyone who loves me ends up hurt or dead.

Reinhilde. My mother. Daniel. The Wafner family. Cameron. Stefan and Aaron. If I marry him, I'll end up hurting him ... or worse.

When she closed her eyes, all she saw was their bodies: her mother, Reinhilde, Tristan, and Doyle. The consequences of her sorcerer blood and rage. Whenever Alex managed to fall asleep, violent nightmares plagued her, leaving her more tired than when she fell asleep.

I'm a horrible, violent monster.

Completely unworthy of love.

Aaron could marry someone worthy. Stefan could stay in Datten with his family. Michael would go with him and prove himself worthy of Jessica. My father wouldn't have to try to make a half sorceress fit into his perfect kingdom.

If I was gone, the kingdoms would be safe. Who knows what sort of uncontrolled, violent magical mishaps would befall my people if I came home?

They'd be better off ... if I disappeared.

Finally, after four days, Alex got up in the middle of the night. It was silent in the castle. She picked up her journal and, still in her muddy clothes, climbed the stairs to the center tower. Sitting on the cold stone floor, she ripped pages from her journal and wrote a stack of letters: one each to Aaron, her father, Michael, Stefan, Jessica, Edith, Gryphon, Randal, and the Datten royals. After finishing, she ripped the list of spells out of her first journal, crumpled them in her hands, and turned them into ash.

"Disgusting, violent monster," she whispered as she held

her hand open and watched the ashes vanish into the surrounding blackness. She closed her eyes and whispered, "The beast must be contained, or she'll meet her end."

⋙⋙⋙ ⋘⋘⋘

SHE WOKE up on the cold stones of her tower. She hadn't brought a blanket or cloak with her, and the damp air chilled her to the bone. The sun was rising, and the trees she'd grown over the last few months were becoming barren in the late fall chill. Her guilt still gnawed away at her. She'd known guilt and sorrow before but nothing like this. Inside, she felt dead. She picked up the letters she'd written and went back down the stairs to her room.

Daniel appeared, shaking his head and begging her to stop. "I'm sorry. Don't follow me." Alex grabbed Aaron's cloak and cracked onto the beach.

She stood in silence and watched the sea, letting her lungs fill with salty air. After some time, she folded Aaron's cloak and placed it on the beach. She put all of the letters she'd written on it and set a rock on top. Finally, she placed her shoes and her mother's necklace beside the cloak. Then she left them there, walking slowly down the beach to the waterline, watching the sunrise.

What will happen to the line of Cassandra after I'm gone? Will it pass to Megesti or Lygari's daughter? What if he doesn't have a daughter? It doesn't matter. The sorcerers will sort that out.

Her feet hit the icy seawater, and she shivered. Soon, her shins were soaked, and the cold had spread up her legs, freezing her entire body, but she was so numb it barely registered. When the water hit her waist, a tremor rushed through her powers.

"This feels familiar," Gryphon said, chuckling.

Alex stopped moving and turned back to face him.

"What's this?" Gryphon was holding her letters in his hand.

"Nothing," Alex lied and took another step backward in the icy water.

"This one has my name on it." He waved it and grimaced. "We have to talk about the other night. I've come every morning since, but ... you scared me."

"I know," Alex said, taking another step. The water was up to her chest, and she was so cold she couldn't stop her teeth from chattering.

"Ares's powers are challenging when they come in, but I'll help you. We'll get through this, I promise."

She didn't react.

He held the letter in front of him. "Dear Gryphon," he read in a high-pitched tone, imitating her, and smiled before looking back down.

Alex knew what he was reading and acted quickly. She closed her eyes and cracked herself far away from him, right into the Oreean Sea. Under the water, it was dark and silent. The freezing ice cold crushed Alex's chest like the river had done when she fell in as a child. She opened her mouth, expelling the last breath of air from her lungs, and let herself sink into the murky darkness.

A blinding orange light surrounded her.

Air barely filled her lungs when Alex cracked herself away again, but this time, the light came faster. A hand grabbed Alex's as she tried one last time. This time, when she hit the water, it was warm. Gryphon's hands locked onto hers. He shook his head at her as his orange light encompassed them.

Back on the beach, Alex's lungs ignored her demands and

sucked in deep breaths. She was lying on the cold sand looking up at the sky when Gryphon's face appeared above hers. Drenched to the bone, he was furious, but when his eyes landed on hers, his face softened. Alex sat up and pulled her legs to her chin.

"Talk to me, Alexandria. Whatever this is, whatever broke you, let me help. Let me in."

"You can't," Alex said, fighting back tears. "You can't fix it. No one can, and I can't live with it."

Gryphon kneeled beside her. "Is it what happened in the basement?"

Alex nodded but then shook her head. "I beat Lygari sparring and … and …" She couldn't get the words out. She took his hand and placed it on her face as the images burning into her mind flashed by.

Gryphon's eyes widened, and he swallowed hard.

"There was an accident. You hurt someone."

Alex nodded and sobbed.

Gryphon didn't say a word. He put his hand on her leg and sat with her. The harder she cried, the worse she felt. Having him near her made the betrayal too real. Knowing how she'd acted, how much she'd *wanted* it, she didn't know how Aaron could look at her again. Finally, she couldn't take feeling alone anymore. Gryphon held her as she cried and what happened with Reinhilde spilled out of her.

"I'm sorry, Alex, but you can't drown yourself over this. We each have a purpose in our lives, and you haven't completed yours. Think of what losing you would do to your father and that princeling who's fighting so hard to get here. Putting them through that is selfish."

Alex pulled away from Gryphon. She didn't want to hear from him how important she was to Aaron—not after what they did in the castle basement. Gryphon stood and offered his hand, but Alex pushed it aside and stood up.

I ruined everything with Aaron. For what? This dark-haired sorcerer in the hideous robe? I'm an idiot and deserve everything that's ever happened to me.

"You don't deserve what's happened to you." Gryphon stepped up to her, sliding his hand over her cheek. Alex looked down and pulled away.

"You don't know everything I've done." She turned to gather her things, but Gryphon drew her back.

"I know you deeper than you realize. Haven't you had a premonition for what comes after ... Aaron?"

"No," Alex said sharply. He looked at her, and Alex's heart pounded painfully in her chest. *Aaron. I love Aaron. Whatever this draw is to Gryphon, it's a lie or a spell.*

"I'm sorry, princess. It's not a lie or a spell."

"Get out of my head."

"*I'm* the after," Gryphon said. "Sorcerers live centuries. Don't you want to be happy again ... after Aaron?"

"I don't believe you."

"Then I'll show you."

Alex froze and looked at him. "You can't. You're not a Cassandra."

Moving closer to her, Gryphon slipped his hands around hers. "When I was young, I snuck into my father's library. He forbade me from going in there, so I did it often. One day, I found his secret magical artifacts area left open. So I took the black pearl and demanded it show me my future partner, my equal."

"Gryphon—" Alex didn't know if she could handle this.

"It showed me you, Alex. You on the beach, exactly how we met—and our family."

Alex looked away. The early morning sun glistened across the ocean waves. Then she looked him in the eye. "Show me."

Gryphon moved Alex's hand to his temple. "Brace yourself."

Alex nodded, and Gryphon placed her other hand on his temple, and they closed their eyes. The feeling of entering Gryphon's mind felt like falling. When she oriented herself, Alex was on the beach when they met, watching herself through his eyes. She saw herself rolling her eyes at him, and he playfully grabbed her waist, and she kissed him.

She was in a bedroom, looking down at herself. She heard herself moan, calling Gryphon's name.

Now, she held a baby girl with brown hair and emerald eyes as a young man with black hair with a brown streak through it looked over the chair to see the baby.

Then they were in the middle of a hall Alex had never seen. Gryphon wore a crown and a royal blue robe, Warren's color. Alex was in gold, also wearing a crown, and they stood in front of a group of sorcerers, one for each of the ten colors of the lines. The children from before had grown and were wearing blue and gold robes. Megesti was also there. He was smiling at her in his violet titan robe.

Alex pushed Gryphon away and stumbled backward. Gryphon grabbed her and pulled her against him.

"I can't know this!" Alex said. "How am I supposed to live with that after what I did? Aaron's never going to forgive me."

"He forgave you for kissing his cousin—how can you doubt his love for you so much that you think he'd let me come between you?"

Alex pushed him away. "I don't care, Gryphon. Go."

"No. I don't trust you alone right now. I'm not letting you destroy yourself over some stupid kiss that—"

"It isn't that. It's everything that's happened here. All the things I've done." Alex trembled as Reinhilde's face flashed into her mind.

Gryphon squeezed her shoulders and breathed deeply. "What if we took them away?"

"Took what away?" Alex turned to look at the sea.

"Your memories." He gently rubbed her arms, and a warmth spread over her, drying her clothes and hair as the sun cleared the horizon.

"Can you really take away my memories?" she asked.

"I can try."

"Can you take the whipping?"

Gryphon nodded.

"And last night?"

"You'll never remember what happened with those men or me."

"And this morning. I don't want to remember anything from here or the sparring accident."

Gryphon sighed. "Yes, but nothing more. That's all I can do. Are you absolutely sure about this?"

"I'm sure. Take them," Alex said, her lip quivering.

"It's an incredibly complex spell, and how well it works depends on many things, but there are risks. I could take the wrong memories or hurt you, but the biggest risk comes if you get the memories back, and that happens more frequently than I'd like."

"Then we make sure I don't get them back. What about my journal? And if others ask about today?"

"I'll remove the pages from your journal and change your memory that your maid left when you freed everyone."

"I'd notice missing pages."

"Then I'll take the journal. Alex, I need you to understand. If the memories return, whatever you are feeling will be much, much worse. This won't fix things. Trying to run away from your problems has a way of catching up with you."

Alex looked up into his eyes as he gripped her arms. "I don't care. If I keep them, even if I go home, part of me will always be trapped here. There's no one here who cares. No one to help me. If the memories come back, at least I'll be with people who love me—people who will help me get through it."

Gryphon took her hands and squeezed them. "All right." He moved himself directly in front of her.

"How do you do it?"

"The easiest way is ... if I kiss you."

"What?" Alex scrunched her nose at him.

"I'm not trying anything. A kiss creates the strongest connection because we drop our guards. I can use that to get in your head."

"Okay. Do it before I change my mind."

"Alex, if you have any doubts about this—"

She grabbed his tunic and kissed him. He leaned into the kiss, pulling her close to him. A heat erupted through her body, running up from where his hands held her, tingling through her until it reached her head. Her head throbbed, and everything went black.

Alex blinked. She was looking up at Gryphon from the sand.

"What happened?"

He squatted beside her. "You pushed too hard training after you won your first sparring match with Lygari. We've talked about limits, and you didn't listen. How do you feel?"

"My head is pounding, and I can't even remember beating him."

Gryphon held her hands and pulled her up with him. "You need rest," he said. "You probably hit your head when you blacked out. We'll skip the rest for today, but I do have a surprise for you." Gryphon grabbed her hand and cracked them away.

Alex looked around. She was standing on an unfamiliar mountain ridge looking into a massive valley. Turning around, she saw more mountains, and the other way showed the sea. Alex held her hands out and summoned a breeze from the sea. It brought the sounds of the waves and the smell of the salty air. She noticed her magic tingling as Gryphon appeared beside her.

"Where'd you go?" she asked.

"I left your bracelet in the field near the castle. We'll get it on the way back."

Alex shoved Gryphon. "How dare you risk the man I love for training? If Moorloc found it there, he'd consider my oath broken." An overwhelming sense of rage filled her, but Gryphon grabbed her hand and pulled her reluctantly to the edge.

"Look."

Alex huffed as she looked into the valley. The earth was the same shade of brown as the rocks of the mountains here, but far below, she could see linen tents and small dots moving around them. Larger ovals of dark colors congregated near the edge, a few sparkling in the sunlight. Her eyes darted from one place to another and another until they met Gryphon's. "There must be thousands of people down there. Where are we?"

"That is your salvation, princess. Warren, Datten, and Betruger. All coming to retrieve you."

Alex's eyes grew larger. "They're all down there? Aaron? Stefan and Michael?"

"Your father and godfather too. Hopefully that nasty maid left," Gryphon said. His hand slid along her shoulder, and he held her snug against him. Where his hand touched her, a pleasant heat warmed her cold skin and then moved deep inside her. She rested her head on his shoulder.

"No matter how hopeless or dark your thoughts, remember this: they love you, and they are coming for you. We will all fight for you."

"Can I at least tell them something, anything?"

"No. That is too risky with your oath. But you can give them something."

"What?"

Gryphon smiled impishly. "You can't touch them, but your magic can. Those horses look hungry and thirsty. Some fresh grass and an abundance of water might be a pleasant change."

Alex smiled and breathed deeply. Gryphon removed his hand, and she shifted her stance. "But I thought I used too much power this morning," she said.

"That's why I gave you some."

"The heat?"

Gryphon nodded, and Alex couldn't help blushing. She wouldn't admit it, but Gryphon made her feel safe the same way Aaron did when she doubted herself. She turned back to the camp, took a deep breath, and pushed the well lid off. Immediately, her body filled with so much magic her skin glowed. Scared, she turned to Gryphon, but he nodded to her, and a moment later, he was glowing orange beside her.

"Why are you glowing?" she said.

"Reach deep into that well, princess," Gryphon said, smirking at her.

"Know-it-all Sunset," Alex said and stuck her tongue out at him. She thrust out her hands, locked her elbows tightly, and pictured green rolling fields. Her arms glowed darker, and then green appeared at the edge of the camp. A second later, a wave of green washed over the earth, turning all the brown dirt vibrant green. Once that was finished, she imagined the river along the camp in the Dark Forest, and fresh water erupted from the ground in the valley below them. Blinking, Alex watched the little dots scatter around all over, but her eyes landed on a small cluster at the edge of the grass.

"We have to go. We've been spotted," Alex said.

"You go to our training grounds, and I'll be right there. I need to have a few words with that princeling first."

"Behave yourself, Sunset," Alex said and cracked away.

CHAPTER 24
AARON

"Merlock!" Aaron shouted the moment the grass appeared at their feet. "Merlock, she's here!"

Harold, Michael, and Stefan came running from their tents.

"What are you shouting—" Stefan began but stopped as the grass appeared before him.

"What is that?" Harold asked.

"Look up." Michael pointed to the top of the mountain before them.

Aaron looked. On top of the rocks were two glowing shapes. One glowed orange and sent a surge of annoyance through him, but the figure next to it shone with a golden light. Aaron swallowed hard as the ground shook and a massive river of fresh water appeared before them.

"Merlock!" Aaron shouted again, and a loud crack sounded as both Merlock and Megesti appeared.

"What?" Megesti asked.

"Take me there!" Aaron pointed to the rocky cliff face and grabbed Megesti's arm.

Without a word, Merlock cracked them to the cliff edge, but it was deserted. Aaron spun around, looking for the gold light he'd seen when Gryphon appeared.

"Are you really that stupid?" the sorcerer asked.

"For wanting to see the love of my life after being away from her for months?" Aaron shoved Gryphon.

"No, you foolish mortal. For risking everything when you're so close to having it back!" He shoved Aaron. "Useless humans and your inability to see the bigger picture. Didn't you think for a moment that if she'd seen you, her oath would have been broken? And then you would have died right where you stand. *In front of her.* Are you trying to destroy her? Because—trust me—that place is doing enough of that!"

"What do you mean?" Merlock asked.

"I mean they broke her." Gryphon said, glaring at Aaron. "And I had to fix her."

"Fix her how?" Megesti asked.

"By taking away what broke her."

"Gryphon, what did you do?" Merlock demanded.

Rage burst through Aaron as he looked at the fear on Merlock's face.

"I did what I had to," Gryphon said, turning to face Merlock.

"What did you do to her?" Aaron lunged at Gryphon. He caught him off guard, and his right hook collided with Gryphon's face, sending him to the ground. "If you did anything to her, I swear I'll make sure you pay with your life."

"Ares, you're a real pain in my ass." Gryphon staggered to his feet as Aaron shifted into his fighting stance. "If I fight you, it'll upset Alex, and I'm not about to risk my future with her for your stupidity."

"You don't *have* a future with her," Aaron shouted. His rage made him begin to see spots.

"Of course I do." Gryphon moved to Aaron and clenched his orange fists. "She *needs* me. I'm the only one who can train her. I'll stay, help her, and wait for you to die. Humans live to fifty, and you're already twenty-two. Not to mention you're a tad rash. In another decade or two, you'll be dead, and when you're cold in the ground, I'll be the one warming Alex's bed. The one who makes her scream at night. I'll have her longer than you were even alive!"

The little restraint Aaron had left on his Datten temper snapped, and he attacked Gryphon. He got a jab and an uppercut in before Gryphon struck him back with a left hook. Pain exploded in his nose, and Gryphon hit him again before Merlock and Megesti pulled them apart.

"I'm going to make sure you never get near her again," Aaron shouted. "If you touch her, I'll hunt you down."

"What if *she* touched me?" Gryphon wiped the blood off his lip and stared down at Aaron. "Remember, she went after you. What makes you so sure I'm pursuing her? She's been alone in that castle for months. Women have needs the same as men, *bed warmer.*"

"Catch your tongue, Gryphon," Megesti said.

Aaron struggled to get away from Megesti, but his grip held tight. Gryphon jerked free of Merlock, and a journal dropped to the ground. His eyes burned with rage at Aaron.

"You're an idiot, and she deserves so much more than you'll be able to give her."

"Do you think she's ready?" Merlock asked as Megesti finally released Aaron with a stern look.

"Her powers are coming along beautifully. But don't ask her to explode anything yet. Her aim is terrible." Gryphon's gaze went to Aaron. "Or maybe ask."

Aaron picked up the journal and flipped through it. "This is Alex's. Why are there pages missing?"

"Because things happened to her that aren't your concern."

"If it pertains to Alex, it is."

"Not these. If she wants you to know, she can tell you. But I sure as Hades won't."

"Why should I trust you?"

Gryphon looked at Merlock and Megesti and sighed. "Because if I hadn't been there, you wouldn't have a princess to rescue anymore."

"What does that mean?" Megesti asked.

Gryphon shook his head, and Merlock pursed his lips.

"How long do you need?" Gryphon asked Merlock.

"We'll go to the kings at once. We're a day away—two at most."

"We'll be ready," Gryphon said, and then he faced Aaron. "Never question me about what I'd do for Alexandria again. She's your princess, but she's *my* Heart—even if you have hers."

Before Aaron could reply, Gryphon vanished.

"You don't have to antagonize him like that," Merlock said as he cracked them back to the camp.

"You're blaming me?"

"I'm not blaming anyone. You don't know the depth of a sorcerer's bond. It ties our magic to another in a way mortals could never understand. You love Alexandria so much that you would die for her. No one denies that. But understand this: Gryphon is the next Head, and she is the Heart. There has only ever been one Head and Heart pair that didn't kill each other. I have no idea how deep of a connection those two share now that they've found each other."

"No," Aaron said. "I'm the one she's going to marry."

Megesti sighed. "Aaron, you're mortal. You won't live as long as we do. She can marry you and have an entire life with you—children, ruling together, really live. But when you die of old age, she'll look exactly as she does today. And Gryphon—he'll be there, waiting, and they'd still have centuries together," Megesti said.

Aaron stared at Merlock. *Him? No. She can have another love after me but not him.* "No. I don't want him anywhere near her!"

"At that point, Aaron, it won't be your decision anymore," Megesti said.

AARON LOOKED through the tent doorway at the Betruger, Datten, and Warren armies. All these men had come together to help him get Alex back. He knew they would succeed, but part of him still worried. In his entire life, nothing had ever meant as much to him as Alex did. Not his brother, not his mother, not even his crown. Nothing compared to the love he had for her.

I miss her so much. The way her hair falls in her face. The way she wants to race when we ride. How perfectly she fits in my arms. That she still blushes when she catches me staring at her.

Harold stomped on his foot. Aaron turned back to the group around the table and realized his father had been talking.

"Sorry, I missed the last part," Aaron said to the surrounding kings.

"Harold has offered to go to the front lines with you," said Emmerich. "The two of you, along with Michael, Macht, Stefan, Megesti, and Merlock, will lead the armies to the castle. The generals, Edward, and I will follow behind. If you need us, we'll be right there, but she's your princess, and this is your battle, son."

"Thank you, Father. I'm ready, and we'll get her back."

Aaron turned to Harold. "How long will it take to get there from here?"

"With packing up camp? A day," Harold said. "What happens if we get there and can't see anything?"

"Then we hope that idiot sorcerer is good for something," Aaron said.

"What idiot sorcerer?" Edward asked.

"The cocky sorcerer with skunk hair who talks to Merlock as if he knows everything about their family. He's obviously powerful and claims he's been teaching Alex. Hopefully he's been helping her and hasn't been torturing me for fun," Aaron said.

"Two hair colors? Black and gold? How old?" Edward's eyes widened.

"Looks my age," Aaron replied.

Edward had tears forming in his eyes as he turned his back to Aaron and Emmerich. "We have to get her. Rally the men."

Harold shrugged at Aaron. "I'll get the men ready."

"Thank you." Aaron stopped beside his father. "Do you know what's going on with Edward?"

"No," Emmerich said.

Aaron moved toward Edward and gently put his hand on his godfather's shoulder. Edward spun to face him. "The sorcerer was young, right? You're sure?"

"Yes."

"So he can't be Garrick," Edward said. Aaron realized Edward was talking to himself.

"Garrick?" Emmerich asked. "The sorcerer Victoria was—?"

"Yes, him." Edward scowled. He was pale and sweating the same way Alex did when she was nervous or scared.

"I don't understand," Aaron said.

"He's a monster. He would have rather killed her than let

her be happy with me. But Victoria cursed him and sent him away. He's why she put the protection spells on the castles. What if he helped my father?"

"He had two-colored hair?" Aaron asked.

Edward nodded and tapped his hand on the table.

"Likely, we have the son," Emmerich said to Aaron.

"If his father tried to kill Victoria, can we trust him?" Aaron asked.

"Yes, we trust Gryphon," Merlock said from the open tent doorway. "There is a sorcerer legend that one day there would be another male and female Head and Heart. For the entire time we've existed in this world, only once has a sorceress been a Heart. All the rest were sorcerers. Alex is the sorceress we've waited a millennium for."

"What does that have to do with trusting Gryphon?" Emmerich asked.

Merlock sighed. "Gryphon is Garrick's son and the next Head. If the legend is to be believed, he needs her more than anyone. They will bring the golden age of magic to the sorcerers ... but *only* if they do it together."

"So he won't hurt her?" Edward asked.

"No. He has too much to lose."

"We've got to get my daughter back," Edward said, looking up at Aaron and Emmerich.

"We will," Aaron said, and Emmerich patted his shoulder.

Edward stared at Aaron. His eyes were wild. "The day we get her back, you're marrying her. We'll have the kingdom weddings later, but I need to know that no matter what happens, she'll be protected."

"Edward, I'd never let anything happen to my goddaughter," Emmerich said.

"It's not enough," Edward said, slamming his fist on the table. "I know firsthand how a king can turn on his own. I need you married, so no matter what happens to me, Datten will always be there for her, and for the rest of your life, that sorcerer has no claim to her." He didn't wait for Aaron to respond. He stood and stormed away from them.

"I'm worried about him," Aaron said to his father.

"You and me both." Emmerich patted Aaron's shoulder. "Let's go get your princess back."

CHAPTER 25

ALEX

Gryphon made it back to her shortly but refused to tell her what he'd said to Aaron or why his lip was bleeding. After working on her explosive powers, Alex was drained and begged to go back. Gryphon relented. He replaced the bracelet on her wrist and vanished without another word.

What did I do? Alex cracked back to her room to change. She worked in the library and ended up falling asleep on the table while she read the spell books.

The table shook beneath her. Alex woke up and jerked back in her seat so hard she almost knocked it over. Lygari was leaning on a Hades book and didn't bother to wait for her to greet him.

"My father wants to see you. Now."

Alex hurried after him to the door that connected the lab and library. Lygari opened it and, once Alex walked through, slammed it shut. Moorloc stood at the table grinding some herbs. The air was heavy, and the room smelled of mint and sage.

Moorloc looked up from his work. "It would seem your whelp isn't giving up as sensibly as we'd hoped. Kruft's scouts have seen the armies on their way. They're close. Apparently Betruger has joined them."

"Betruger?" Alex asked. "They've been fighting against Datten for centuries."

"Indeed. But it seems your charming prince brought them to heel. Their new king is not happy with my son," Moorloc said, glaring at Lygari.

Alex rolled her eyes and looked at her cousin.

Lygari smirked at Alex. "I dealt with a problem as I saw fit. You're lucky my father is so hell-bent on protecting you. Otherwise, you'd be dead."

Alex scoffed. "I'm not scared of you."

"Truly?" Lygari stepped right up to Alex, but she stared him down. She could see the crater-filled field and hear Gryphon's words. *You're the Heart ... You have the power of seven lines ... Lygari is half sorcerer, and you should be, but somehow, you're more, and I don't know why.*

"Care to take this outside, cousin?" Alex asked.

Lygari gulped before he scowled again.

"You two can spar again tomorrow," said Moorloc. "Right now, my little Harbinger, I need you to go tell your betrothed it's over and you're done with him."

"No."

The air was sucked from the room as Moorloc set down his tools. "What did you say?" His nostrils flared, and the vein in his neck throbbed.

"I said no. If he's coming for me, let him. I hope he burns this castle to the ground." Alex braced herself.

"You remember our deal, Alexandria. You took an oath to stay here and train until I decide you are—"

"I am ready!" Alex snapped. "You're in denial, and you can't keep me here forever."

Moorloc slammed his fist on the table and lunged at her. He grabbed her face and forced her to look at him. "Do not interrupt me! You're a child and will do as you are told! *I am* the titan of this line—your line. Your mother is dead, and that makes you my charge. You'll tell the Crown Prince of Datten to go home, or you'll regret it."

Stomach churning, Alex thought she might throw up, and it took everything in her to keep herself from trembling as Moorloc squeezed harder.

"No. He's coming, and I intend to leave with him."

"Your oath will keep you here," Moorloc replied with a cocky attitude.

"Not if you're dead."

The color drained from Lygari's face, and Moorloc struck her. It knocked her head back, and a metallic taste trickled into her mouth. He struck her a second time, sending her to the floor and making the room spin. The rage that erupted inside Alex ignited her Salem powers, and the fire roared to life. As she staggered to her feet, a feeling of vengeance coated her insides like sticky blood.

She held out her arm, and the green and gold staff flew from the wall into her hand. Time slowed for her, making the sorcerers move at a snail's pace. With incredible speed, she cracked Moorloc in his ribs with the staff.

Her eyes burned as power and rage coursed through her and swirled together into a violence Alex never suspected she was capable of. Lygari ran at her, and Alex used the staff to sweep his legs out from under him. He landed on his back with a loud grunt. Moorloc stood, holding his ribs as Alex snarled at him like a feral animal. She could feel the new power singing in her blood. It was calling out to another, and she knew exactly who was going to answer her call as she gave herself to the rage.

"How are her eyes black?" Lygari coughed, and he got up, moving away from Alex. She stepped back toward him as the staff she held glowed dark orange.

"Ares! You have Ares?" Moorloc's eyes went wide, and he gasped for breath. "Calm down, Alexandria. We can't bring them here, not with what you are. You think you're ready for me, but you're not ready for them. If you use too much Ares, you'll attract the Titan of Ares. Their power calls to others. It draws them to their own kind."

"Yes, it does." Gryphon's voice cackled behind her. "What exactly have we here?"

CHAPTER 26
ALEX

Moorloc and Lygari leaped toward the wall, leaving Alex in the middle of the room. Gryphon circled her like a wolf circling prey. He'd always looked at her with kindness. But the look on his face as he took in her cousin and uncle was cold and malicious. Turning his gaze on her, he looked Alex up and down slowly, lingering on certain feminine features. His carnal gaze made the tingle and rage in her blood flourish and sent heat through her. Swallowing the lump in her throat, she trembled as she stepped back. Alex held the staff out to distance them, but Gryphon moved on her with lightning speed. He grabbed the staff and threw it aside, closing their distance in a blink. His eyes bore into hers, and Alex's breath quickened. The calling coming from her powers intensified with each breath.

"Well, well, well, Moorloc. Perhaps you aren't as useless as my parents claim." He leaned toward Alex and sniffed her.

Alex looked down, too afraid to meet his eyes. The playful Gryphon who'd helped her control her powers for the last few months was gone. In front of her stood the terrifying sorcerer everyone else knew: the Titan of Ares. Something told her not to fight him in front of Moorloc, that any attempt at dominance would get her into trouble. And yet, the power emanating from him was intoxicating and made her dizzy.

How is it that our powers are calling to each other? That doesn't happen during training. Is it because I found my Ares powers? It made her painfully aroused and nauseated. Alex wasn't sure if it was him standing up to Moorloc or her use of his power that changed him. Looking at him, Alex couldn't help but feel frightened of Gryphon.

"I take it you're Garrick and Imelda's son," Moorloc said.

Gryphon snarled at them. "Correct. Gryphon, the next Head, and you, Moorloc, son of Hermes, have found my missing Heart. We were wondering if there wasn't one. But lo and behold, she was hiding in the mortal lands, and most peculiar ... my Heart is a lovely sorcer*ess*. Perhaps the legends of another Tabitha and Grindal are true."

"I've been training her for *you*," Moorloc muttered to him.

Gryphon circled Alex again, grabbing the wrist with her bracelet. He spun it, glancing at the line marks. "I can see that. The power coming off her is truly impressive, and it doesn't hurt that she's exceptionally pleasant to look at either. Though, what is she wearing?" Gryphon snapped his fingers, and Alex found herself in a beautiful gold sorcerer's robe. "Much better."

"I'm surprised she hasn't growled at you yet. She's nineteen, but she's as bullheaded as her mother. I've never seen her this quiet," Lygari said.

Alex sneered at Lygari, and he lunged at her. Gryphon snapped his fingers, and in a blink, Lygari was lying on the ground.

Gryphon stood above Lygari and looked down at him.

"That, *boy*, is because you don't know how to handle a powerful sorceress."

Gryphon slipped his hand around Alex's waist, and his voice came clear as a bell in her head. *I'm sorry about this. Please forgive me.* A second later, his lips found hers, and all the rage and violence drained from her. Alex's heart pounded as Gryphon held her tightly to him. His lips were soft, but Aaron's face flashed in her mind, so she shoved him away and slapped him.

Gryphon looked at Moorloc and smirked. "I've never had one say no. This will be fun. Leave us."

Moorloc said, "Sir, I don't mean to be rude, but—"

"Get out!" This time it was an order.

Her neck burned, and she noticed Gryphon's neck was glowing. Moorloc bowed, and Lygari followed him out of the lab without another word. As soon as they left, Gryphon turned back to Alex, and she slapped him again, harder this time.

"Owwww! I deserved that, but let me explain." Gryphon grabbed her wrist and pulled her against him before she could slap him again.

"Let—me—speak."

"No," Alex snapped.

"Alexandria, you were spiraling. It's normal for young Ares sorcerers when their powers erupt as powerfully as yours do. But it draws attention. Ares sorcerers sense when another of our line is using too much power. We're attracted to chaos, and if you'd have kept going, you'd have attracted other Ares from the Forbidden Lands. I had to stop you, so I took your power away, and the easiest way was to kiss you. We have a connection as Head and Heart. You can deny it all you want, but I won't ignore fate."

Alex shoved Gryphon away and rubbed her neck. "How did you know?"

"I felt your power erupt. After months working with you, I can sense when your power shifts, and as the most powerful Ares sorcerer, I can take someone's Ares powers from them."

Alex's rage left her. "This changes things. You being here, I mean. What do we do?"

"I'm going to convince your uncle I'm here to kill your betrothed in order to get you for myself. If princeling were out of the way, you'd be mine."

"I don't belong to any man—mortal or sorcerer."

Gryphon rolled his eyes. "Oh, *I'm* well aware of that. But Moorloc isn't. Go to your room. I'll come as soon as I can."

"Gryphon." Alex grabbed his hand. "What's this?" She touched her neck.

"Our mark. We've found each other, so the Head and Heart marks have appeared. The crown is the Head, and the Heart is obvious. They are combined because we're both alive. As you grow older, yours will darken and mine will fade."

"You won't hurt Aaron, will you?"

"No. I promise I won't hurt your precious princeling."

She stood on her toes and kissed his cheek. "Thank you, and I forgive you for kissing me."

He winked at her as she left the lab.

Alex took the long way around the castle. Her adrenaline was pumping from the fight in the lab, and she needed to calm down. As she got close to Moorloc's room, she heard familiar whispers. *The books!* She froze and stopped breathing to listen carefully. She quickly checked behind her and then hurried to Moorloc's door. He'd locked it, but her unlocking spell took care of it.

The room was empty but reeked of Moorloc—musty books and strange herbs. Alex scanned the wardrobe, a gigantic bed with violet bedding, a table with chairs, and a bookcase. She rushed to the bookcase, and the whispers grew louder, though they were muffled.

He could come in at any moment.

Alex went to the right side and started frantically grabbing books and tilting them until a click sounded and the wall moved. Alex's hand went to her mouth to silence the gasp that escaped her. The entire alcove was bookshelves stacked with the books her mother had hidden. Alex jumped when the door behind her slammed shut.

"You're not supposed to be in here, nosy little witch." Kruft locked the door behind him.

Alex reached inside but found herself empty. Gryphon taking her Ares powers had drained her. Fear enveloped her as Kruft sauntered across the room.

"Did your magical temper tantrum leave you too weak to fight back?"

Alex backed away from Kruft and bumped into the corner. She'd have to fight him without magic. She silently cursed Stefan and Jerome for not forcing her to practice dealing with being cornered more when she was with them. The sound of her blood pumping silenced the books' whispers. She balled her hands into trembling fists and moved them up into position.

Kruft lunged for her. Alex punched him and tried to rush past, but he grabbed her robe and yanked her back.

Gryphon, why did you put me in this ferflucsing robe?

Kruft slammed her so hard into the bookcase she screamed in pain as her wrist snapped in her bracelet.

Kruft struck her. "Catch your tongue. I'm finally going to get revenge for what your mother did to me." He ignored her whimpers and ripped her robe, exposing the simple shirt beneath it. He groped her breast and pressed himself against her. Alex closed her eyes, trying to crack, when he unexpectedly let go.

Alex slumped against the shelf and opened her eyes to see Gryphon standing behind Kruft. His face was feral—his brows furrowed, his lips scowling. His eyes glowed blue, and they were fixed on Kruft. Neither said a word, but Kruft turned around and left the room.

When the door shut, Alex crumpled to the ground. Gryphon rushed to her side and looked her over, pausing at her wrist. Alex tasted blood in her mouth as her face stung. Kruft had struck her exactly where Moorloc had earlier. She cradled her broken wrist and looked up at Gryphon with tears welling in her eyes.

"How did you know?"

"I heard you. Since the first day I came here, I've heard nearly everything inside your mind. I'm still trying to figure out how to keep your thoughts out. So when you cursed me for the robe and Jerome for corners, I put it together."

Gryphon stood and selected a golden book from the shelf and then closed the hidden alcove.

Alex tried to get up, but the terror had left her with nothing. She fell back down. Gryphon bent and scooped her up in his arms. He cracked them back into her bedroom and gently put Alex down on the bed.

"Do I want to know what you made him do?" Alex asked.

"No."

"Gryphon—" Alex said, but the fire still burning in his eyes stopped her.

"No," he growled, trembling. "I read minds. I know exactly what he planned to do to you. No man will ever touch you without your permission and go unpunished. The fact he's alive is a testament to my mercy."

Alex swallowed hard and looked down.

"I'm sorry," Gryphon whispered and sat on the edge of her bed. "I didn't mean to scare you. Let me see your wrist."

The rage on his face had vanished, so she slowly gave him her wrist.

Whispering the incantation, he took the bracelet off and threw it across the room. After examining her wrist, he handed her the gold book and walked to her wardrobe. He returned with wrappings and her sleeping clothes. He set the clothes down and wrapped her wrist tightly. "When you wake up refreshed, you can heal it," he said.

Alex narrowed her eyes at him before she examined her wrist. *Not perfect, but it'll work.*

"Sorry. I'm a destroyer, not a healer." He took her wrist again and began tightening some of the wrappings.

"Stay out of my head," Alex said, trying to play with him.

"I already admitted that I can't, even if I wanted to."

"I'll work on thinking quieter ... Gryphon?"

He looked up from finishing with her wrist. "Yes?"

Alex's lip trembled as she whispered, "Thank you."

He squeezed her hand softly. "I meant it. *No one* will hurt you and walk away as long as I'm alive."

"Please don't go. I don't want to be alone. I'm scared."

Gryphon raised his brow at her and sighed. "I'll stay. I've seen the bruises, but things changed today, and I won't risk your safety. Get some sleep. You'll need your strength tomorrow."

Alex stood and looked Gryphon over for a long time. "I trust you. Would you turn around, please? I'd like to change."

Gryphon spun on his heels and faced the door, letting Alex change in privacy.

"Finished," she said. When he turned around, she handed him the gold clothes, which he made vanish.

Alex rubbed her sore wrist. Gryphon was pacing around

the room. "Do you think the army will be here tomorrow?" she asked him.

"If not tomorrow, then the next day."

"What are we going to do tomorrow? I mean, how am I supposed to act?"

He paused and looked at her. "Probably like you want me dead. As far as your uncle knows, I have forced my way into your bed tonight and intend to kill your betrothed tomorrow, all so I can whisk you away from here."

"Wouldn't you take me, though?"

Gryphon raised an eyebrow at her.

"If you wanted him dead, wouldn't it make sense to take me? Me leaving breaks the oath and results in Aaron's death."

"No. You need to see him die. Otherwise, you'd hold out hope."

"That's dark," Alex said, trying to adjust the bed.

"I told you before, I'm a monster." Gryphon reached over her, untucked the blankets and moved the pillows into Alex's favorite position.

"How did you know—?"

Gryphon tapped his temple.

"You're not a monster. No matter what others think." Alex climbed into bed and adjusted her blanket with her good hand. She watched Gryphon's face as he glared at the door. Something was off, but she couldn't put her finger on it. Stefan and Michael had watched over her countless times, but there was still a feral rage emanating from Gryphon.

"You need to rest too." Alex patted the spot beside her in bed.

Gryphon's eyes widened. He slipped beside her but lay on top of the blankets.

"Goodnight, princess."

"Goodnight, Sunset."

CHAPTER 27
AARON

The men rode late into the night before making camp. A rested army would fight more fiercely. Riddled with anxiety, Aaron didn't expect to sleep, but he was out as soon as his head hit the pillow. It was still dark and cold when he was awakened.

"Sorry, Aaron," Stefan said. "We're ready for you."

Aaron scrambled out of his makeshift bed on the ground and hurried into his clothes. He'd been wearing the same ones for weeks, but this morning the gold lions on his shirt, which embodied his Datten title and lineage, seemed to weigh a ton. Stefan led the way while some knights took down his tent. They walked up the hill to Harold.

"We let you sleep as much as possible," Harold said. "Our scouts have returned. We're an hour away from the valley, so if we want to surprise them, we must hurry. The kings will bring up our rear, and since we're leading, we must go. Michael and Macht are preparing our horses. If everything goes according to plan, we'll have your princess back before nightfall."

Aaron rubbed the back of his neck and stifled a yawn. "Lead the way, Your Royal Highness."

Harold smiled at him, and they headed off to collect their armor.

❧❧❧ ❧❧❧

AN HOUR LATER, the sky was lightening. Aaron, Harold, Michael, Stefan, Macht, Merlock, and Megesti were riding through the middle of a valley when Aaron shouted to stop. The morning was frigid, and there was a strange mist swirling around the immense field. Aaron gazed up at the massive stone fortress that stood before them. *Reminds me of Datten. Not for living in but for guarding.*

The castle stones appeared to have been cut from the rocks of the surrounding mountain. Like Betruger Castle, it was smaller and built close enough to the surrounding mountains to allow it to vanish if seen from the sea. Aaron peered upward and noted a few men on guard at the top of the walls. Once the men spotted them, they ran inside.

"There's nothing here," Stefan said.

"You don't see anything?" Aaron asked.

"No. Do you?" Harold asked.

"Yes. The castle is right there." Aaron pointed.

Stefan squinted. "Strange. It looks like a field with lots of plants. What now?"

"We wait for Gryphon and Alexandria to do their part," Merlock replied.

CHAPTER 28
ALEX

Alex woke up soaking wet and gasping for breath from a nightmare she couldn't remember. Her back felt as if someone had slammed her into something solid. Fear and revulsion at the previous day's events flooded her, and she began to shake so violently Gryphon groaned. He was asleep on top of her blanket, having found another to cover himself. He was snoring softly again, and Alex didn't want to wake him. Rather than starting the fire, she whispered, and small flaming orbs appeared in the air, dimly lighting up the room.

She realized her bandaged wrist was on his leg and yanked it away, and pain shot up her arm. Wincing, she reached across the bed to grab the gold book. She traced the sun mark on the front and flipped through it until she found a drawing of a broken wrist. Gently, she rubbed her wrist in a counterclockwise direction. A gold light left her fingers and moved into her wrist. It tingled, and when Alex removed the bandage, her wrist glowed from the inside.

Gryphon moaned and rolled over to look at her. "The glow is where it's healing."

"It's strange that you know more about my powers than I do."

"As the future Head of our world, I was taught the same as a titan for every line except Merlin because your family stole the books." Gryphon rolled his neck and stretched his arms above his head.

Alex looked toward the virtually nonexistent window. She could still see the last few morning stars. "How will we know when they're here?" she asked.

"They're already here."

"How do you know—?"

"Mystics powers." Gryphon smirked. "I can hear Merlock and Megesti."

"What's going to happen? What will we do?" Alex asked. She stood and paced the length of the room.

Gryphon lazily watched her from the bed. "They plan to make themselves known soon, but we have to let them come to us or it'll raise suspicion. If I leave without you, Moorloc will know something is wrong. My hexa is starting to ask questions, so I can't summon anyone here, meaning our plan with three titans is out. I can't help you anymore with the spell to show the castle either, but you're strong enough to handle it. Honestly, I was going to be there for emotional support."

Alex's heart pounded as panic set in. "How am I supposed to do this alone?"

Gryphon leaped from the bed and grabbed her hands. "You're more than powerful enough to perform the spell to show the castle. You need a second sorcerer to balance it. I'll go out front with Kruft and Moorloc to assess the danger. Take what you need from Lygari. You're blood relatives, so say the spell and grab him. If you touch him, your blood connection will do the rest."

Gryphon released Alex and snapped his fingers. Her training clothes appeared on her, but the tunic had been replaced with one that bore her crests; the left half was Datten's crest and the right Warren's. Gryphon winked at her and placed Aaron's cloak around her. He snapped again, and this time he freshened himself up and was back in his burnt orange robe. Alex looked at him and snickered.

"I'll be easier for you to spot, princess."

"It's still ugly, Sunset."

"After you release the castle, the armies will begin fighting the mercenaries. But we still have to break the oath before you can leave."

"How are we going to get me out of here?"

"They'll demand Moorloc release you. If he doesn't, they'll fight him for you."

"Fighting him and the mercenaries won't free me."

"The battle won't, but we will. It's you, me, Merlock, and Megesti against Moorloc and Lygari. Moorloc thinks I'm on his side, putting the odds in his favor. He'll attack them, thinking he can win. He's wrong."

"How much power can you use without risking something bad happening?"

"Given the chance, I'd send an explosion at your uncle and all the mercenaries, but I can't risk drawing attention from my parents. I should be able to handle your uncle one-on-one if needed. It's surprising he's so cocky, considering he isn't even powerful." Gryphon paused. "There is one thing you should know."

"What's that?" Alex asked, pausing at the door.

"If something happens to one or both of your uncles, their powers may transfer to you."

Alex stared at him in confusion.

"It's rare, but with only you left for Cassandra and your cousins for Merlin, it could happen. Losing a line would be catastrophic for the sorcerer world, so when a line is at risk of dying out, its members concentrate their powers in the youngest of that line."

"Not today," Alex said.

"We're about to walk into a battle. Anything is possible. You're going to see things today you could never imagine. I might explode." Gryphon reached for the door handle.

"Ares can actually explode?" Alex whispered as she hurried after him.

"Yes." Gryphon grabbed her forearm, making her wince in pain. "Sorry. You need to be furious with me. Remember what they think happened last night and what they believe I'm going to do. Think of the Titan of Ares who showed up in the lab yesterday and look at me like that again."

Alex nodded and tried, but she couldn't muster any hatred for Gryphon.

"That's pathetic," Gryphon said. "You have to *hate* me. He thinks I claimed you last night—sexually."

Alex rolled her eyes at him. "I understand."

"Then look at me with *that* hatred."

Alex sighed and grabbed his hand. "I can't. All you've done is help and protect me. I don't hate you, and I can't fake hatred."

Gryphon stepped right up to Alex and stared down at her. "I've erased your memory—made you forget so much of your time here. You don't know what I erased or why."

"What?" Alex's eyes widened at Gryphon. Her temper roared to life in her, sending a tremor through her powers and bringing a scowl to her face.

Gryphon leaned down, making her step back until she hit the wall. "Did you know you're adorable when you're angry?"

Alex shoved him away and snarled.

"Closer, but not quite." Gryphon grabbed her arms and pressed her back against the wall. With lightning speed, he cupped her face and gave her a wide open-mouthed kiss. Alex froze for a moment before a sense of déjà vu hit her. She kissed him back for a moment before her rage returned and shifted to fury. Alex kneed him in the groin and shoved him off. When he smirked at her while adjusting his stance, she slapped him across the face with her hand, feeling as if it were on fire.

"Perfect." Gryphon grabbed her arm and pulled her through the castle into the lab. Moorloc jumped as the door slammed behind them.

You did all that to make me mad? But you sounded sincere.

"They're here," Gryphon sung.

"How do you know?" Lygari asked.

"Really, boy? You want to ask again?" Gryphon asked. He released Alex's arm and stalked toward Lygari.

Lygari went ashen and gulped, moving back against the wall.

"Gryphon, *enough,*" Moorloc said.

Alex could see Moorloc trembling too. Both were trying to hide it, but it was clear Gryphon terrified them.

Good. Serves you right.

Gryphon's voice echoed in her head. *Enough of that, princess. Remember, you need to be terrified of me too. Think of your princeling.*

Gryphon glared at Lygari. "Idiot. I can hear your uncle and cousin. Let's get out and deal with that worthless prince who thinks he has a claim on *my* sorceress. When I make an example out of him, the rest will fall into line."

"No," Alex said. She forced her voice to tremble as she

spoke. All the sorcerers in the room turned to her. "If you leave him alone, I'll go with you. Please don't hurt him."

"You'd give up your freedom to save his life?" Gryphon asked.

"Yes. Please don't hurt him. I love him."

Gryphon cocked his head at her. Even though she knew he was on her side, his intense stare made her breath speed up.

"Sorry, princess, but I won't risk it. You're mine, but as long as he's alive, you'll also be his." He turned back to Moorloc and Lygari. "We kill him."

"No!" Alex screamed and lunged at Gryphon, but he pushed her back.

"Useless one, stay and watch her. The grown-ups have work to do. Where's that head guard of yours? I want a shield. This is my favorite robe, and I'd hate for it to get bloody."

Gryphon and Moorloc cracked away, leaving Alex alone with Lygari.

"I'm sorry." Lygari was gasping, trying to calm himself.

"What?"

"I know my father isn't easy, but he's nothing compared to that one or his family and their fixation on Cassandras. This way."

Alex rushed after Lygari across the hall to the front tower. In no time, they ran up to the top floor and looked out. Gryphon stood out front with Kruft and Moorloc. On either side of them was the entire mercenary army. This time, they dressed the men in armor, but the sight on the field before them made Alex gasp.

"There are thousands!" Lygari said.

Knights in red, silver, and brown filled the field. The rising sun sparkled against the armies, forcing Alex to squint. In front of the soldiers was a row of men on horses. Two rode at the front—one wore brown, and the other man was dressed in gold on a black horse.

"They're in the proper position. How the Hades do they know where we are?" asked Lygari.

"Because I gave Aaron my blood before I left."

"You did what?"

Alex smirked at him. "He can see your castle, and in a minute, they all will." Alex whispered the incantation and grabbed Lygari's arm. Her well exploded, flooding her with power, and the sound of glass shattering tore through the castle.

CHAPTER 29
AARON

Even across the massive field, the sound of breaking glass was so loud it scared the horses. Aaron barely got Thunder under control as the other horses around him stomped and whinnied.

Aaron watched the mercenary army march out of the castle gates and split into two groups, leaving a large space between them. Even at this distance, he recognized the blond hair of the mercenary general. Watching Kruft march out toward the men made his blood boil.

"Whatever you're thinking, stop," Harold said.

Aaron realized all the surrounding horses growing more uneasy.

"I take it that's your cousin?" asked Harold.

"It is."

"Save it for afterward," Harold said.

A crack sounded as two men appeared beside Kruft. Aaron failed to hold back his snort as Gryphon's preposterous orange robe practically glowed even from across the field. Aaron glanced back at their armies. They outnumbered the mercenaries twelve to one, but Kruft's men were larger than any of the Datten and Warren men. Aaron looked at Harold. *How are you so relaxed when we're standing at the front of a battlefield?*

Harold looked at Aaron and smiled, answering the unasked question. "My father brought me along to battles, even when I was a child. I've been around more violence and bloodshed than I hope you see in your lifetime. Let's see if we can get him to surrender."

Aaron dismounted Thunder, handed Michael the reins, and marched toward the castle with Harold and Merlock on either side. They crossed the field, meeting Moorloc, Kruft, and Gryphon in the middle. Moorloc stood cold and stoic, wearing the same violet robe he'd worn when he arrived at the tournament to take Alex, but seeing him next to Gryphon, Aaron realized their robes were the same style, though with different colors and a different glowing image emblazoned on them.

Are all the titan uniforms this ugly?

Gryphon narrowed his eyes at Aaron before turning to Merlock.

"How quaint. A half-rate magician and the king of dirt, standing beside the princeling who believes my Heart belongs to him," Gryphon said. His eyes flashed blue, and his face was feral.

"You should leave before we're forced to hurt you," Moorloc said. A smirk spread across Gryphon's face, and Aaron needed every ounce of restraint to not run him through.

"Funny, I was about to offer to let you live if you broke the oath and gave us back Alexandria. You're clearly outnumbered," Aaron said.

Kruft opened his mouth to speak, but Gryphon's head snapped toward him, and Kruft's lips slammed shut without a sound. "Outnumbered not outmatched," Gryphon replied.

"You will not be taking her from us today," Moorloc said.

"Unless you foolishly believe you can defeat the greatest sorcerers in your world with brute strength alone?"

Aaron grit his teeth. "That's the plan." Merlock gripped his shoulder, ready to take them in a moment if needed.

"You'd risk the lives of all your men for one girl?" Gryphon asked. He held out his palm idly, lighting and extinguishing flames with a flick of his wrist while watching Aaron with a bored expression.

"I'd risk the world for that *woman*," Aaron said.

Moorloc opened his mouth to reply when a loud explosion rumbled behind them. They all spun to face the castle. Another explosion sounded, and the mercenary men broke formation, rushing away from the castle walls. Merlock cracked Aaron and Harold back to their armies as a monstrous cloud of dust billowed out, swallowing the mercenary army.

Safely back with their group, the men stood waiting for the dust to settle. When it did, a giant hole appeared in the castle's wall. A figure was struggling to get up from the ground. Someone had clearly thrown whoever it was through the wall. Aaron went to rush toward it when a hand grabbed Aaron's arm, holding him back.

"If it's Alex, then you can't go to her until we break the oath," Megesti said.

Everyone watched in silence as the figure staggered around. It moved slowly over the rubble, clearly in pain, but then Aaron spotted the golden glow emanating from a second figure stepping through the hole in the castle wall.

CHAPTER 30
ALEX

The field stank of piss, sweat, and fear. Despite the early morning, the sunlight reflecting off the men's armor lit the entire field in a burning fire. Alex maneuvered around the scattered rubble and scanned the field before her for her friends.

Gryphon's voice laughed in her head. *You have horrible aim, but at least you got the lid off your well.*

"Catch your tongue. I'm still furious with you," Alex shouted as she climbed up the last piece of wall and jumped down onto the battlefield.

Lygari staggered toward her. "You little witch!" he shouted.

"Sticks and stones, dear cousin. Your names don't hurt me," Alex said and sent a wind to break Lygari's concentration.

Lygari locked his eyes onto Alex and growled. He pulled his palms apart to create a massive fireball and sent it flying toward Alex's head. She quickly flicked her fingers, and water flew into the air as if she'd thrown a bucket. She couldn't help but smile at her control as the fireball vanished into a puff of steam.

Alex braced herself for another attack from Lygari, and the ground beneath her trembled. She jerked her head to the side, but the shaking wasn't from magic. Kruft and Moorloc had given the order to attack. The mercenaries were charging toward the Datten and Warren armies.

Aaron! Alex looked around, frantically trying to find her friends. They'd been at the front of the chaos, and now—

Gryphon cracked to Alex's side, placing himself between her and Lygari.

"Can you go to them?" she pleaded. "I don't want anyone getting hurt."

"I'm confident the men you want me to protect would prefer I stay here to protect you."

"She did this," Lygari screamed. "She found the spell that showed them the castle." Fire shot from his hands.

Kruft stopped shouting orders at his men and turned to face them. Unlike the mercenaries, who wore mixed pieces of armor, he was wearing the fancy armor of Warren. Seeing the scratched-out Warren crest enraged Alex.

"Figures the whore would cause all this," Kruft shouted.

Alex snarled at him, but Gryphon held her back.

Don't waste your powers on him.

"I'm not scared of you, witch," said Lygari. He clenched his fists, making fire grow on his hands.

"But you're terrified of *me*," Gryphon said, smiling menacingly.

Lygari's fire fizzled out. "Take her and go," he said.

"Seems he isn't smart either," Gryphon said to Alex.

Lygari went pale. "You were in on it?"

"Of course. Who do you think trained her? If I'd left it up to you two idiots, she wouldn't have learned anything. I found her months ago. You should have known better. You can't hide a Heart from the Head."

"Stop playing with my cousin," Alex screamed over the battle. The mercenaries had moved away from the castle and were fighting with Aaron's army in the middle of the field. She dropped to the ground, placed both her glowing hands on the earth, and summoned her Celtic powers to the surface. Her golden glow turned green as it entered the ground. Vines erupted from the rocky soil on the field before her and grabbed the mercenaries, pulling them off their feet and slamming them into the hard rock.

Gryphon's eyes flashed blue as he gazed at the battle. Orange light flowed from him into the ground and wound like snakes toward the fighting men. It bypassed the mercenaries, and headed straight toward the Datten, Warren and Betruger soldiers. The men it hit started to glow faintly.

"What did you do?" Alex asked.

"Gave them extra bloodlust."

A moment later, the fighting intensity increased so much Alex lost her focus on the vines, and the mercenaries ripped free. The ground beside Alex's hand exploded, sending rocks raining down on them. She shrieked and turned to see Moorloc's eyes glowing violet as he moved to attack them again. Gryphon yanked Alex to her feet as Lygari sent an inferno of flame where her head had been.

Gryphon growled at Moorloc. "I'm going to enjoy killing you." *Can you handle Kruft and Lygari?*

Alex nodded.

"Stay away from your friends until I handle Moorloc. Your oath is still unbroken."

"I'm aware."

Gryphon cracked in front of Moorloc only to have him crack away. Gryphon chuckled, turned blue, and cracked after him.

Alex looked around, making sure she didn't lose track of

Kruft as Lygari sent another fireball after her. Lygari cracked behind Kruft, deciding to use him as a shield while fighting Alex. She couldn't help but laugh at how ridiculous he looked cowering behind Kruft. Summoning her powers over the weather, Alex sent a gale force wind to force them apart.

Lygari tried to summon flames, but Alex's winds were too strong for them to spark. Kruft fought his way across the area to her. Alex dropped the wind in time to dive and grab a dropped sword off the ground. She threw it back up to block Kruft's swing at her head.

"Gryphon. I changed my mind. I need help!" she shouted.

Kruft pushed her back by shoving his blade into hers. Alex threw her wind at him, sending him back enough to scramble to her feet. Behind her, she heard Lygari crack away. Alex focused on the vines, and they wrapped around Kruft.

I need them to hold him until help arrives.

He cursed her as he hacked at the vines, but Alex kept growing them—with extra thorns—barely keeping up with him.

She scanned the field for her friends again but couldn't find them in the melee of clashing soldiers and mercenaries. She could feel her power draining out of her with the effort of keeping the vines growing. Suddenly, the ground beneath her feet trembled, and she looked down. In that second, Kruft freed himself and attacked her. Alex tried to avoid the blow but was too slow. Cold steel ripped into her forearm and sliced it open. Spinning to shield herself, she slammed into Lygari.

A burning pain ripped down her arm as he snapped the training bracelet on her wrist. It was glowing red, and her powers abandoned her. Kruft sneered and barreled toward her, but Lygari snarled at him, and he backed off.

"Now we end this the proper way." Lygari held Alex's

bleeding arm over the ground and whispered a spell. As her blood dripped down, the earth between the castle and the fighting split open, and out of the earth came pouring something that sent icy terror right through to her soul.

CHAPTER 31
AARON

Aaron saw the vines erupt from the ground and reach for the mercenaries charging toward the Datten, Warren, and Betruger armies. They slowed and entangled the men, but then the orange light surged through the ground and hit each of their men. He froze and waited to see what would happen. Within seconds, their armies shouted louder and charged for the mercenaries. Aaron glanced at Harold, who was equally confused.

"Gryphon is an Ares sorcerer. They inspire violence in others," Merlock explained. "You enjoy mocking his orange robes, but to sorcerers, orange is the most feared of all the line colors."

The mercenaries were getting closer to them, and the sounds of the battle were vibrating through Aaron. His men's armor reflected the morning sunlight and blinded him enough that he lost track of Alex. She'd stopped glowing, and the flashes of fire erupting over the men had ceased. Aaron was itching to get into the battle. He would fight his way to Alex with his bare hands if he needed to. Staying still and doing nothing was maddening.

"Aaron, you can't go rushing to her until we break the oath," Megesti said, ever perceptive. "If you get to her, you'll end up dead, and this will have been for nothing."

"Same goes for you, Stefan," Michael said.

"We can move closer, so long as Aaron and Stefan don't go near her," Merlock said.

As they fought and weaved their horses toward the castle, the ground shook beneath them. Michael lost control of his horse, and it bit Stefan's, setting off a chain reaction that ended with Michael being thrown. The group halted to make sure he didn't get trampled by the surrounding fighting. Stefan cursed Michael's horse as Aaron leaped from Thunder, rushing to get Michael back to his feet; Michael was embarrassed but uninjured. Once he was back on his horse, Aaron leaped back on Thunder. But they froze when Gryphon appeared in front of them.

"What are you doing here?" Aaron scolded. "You're supposed to be protecting her!"

"Trying to break the oath," Gryphon growled. "I'm trying to find Moorloc, but the coward keeps hiding."

"We can deal with him later. Right now, you need to protect Alexandria," Merlock said.

"That isn't what she wants, and she hit me once today. I'm not upsetting her again," Gryphon said.

The ground shook beneath them again, turning their attention toward the castle. The battle raged on between them, but those fighting closest to the castle had abandoned their skirmishes and fled deeper into the battlefield. Then the earth before the castle seemed to rip open, and a dark cloud poured from the earth. Merlock and Gryphon looked on, mouths agape —just the same as the mortals.

"What in the Forbidden Lands is that?" Aaron asked.

"Is it steam or dirt?" Harold asked.

The cloud continued to burst from the earth and went high into the sky. It spread out into a circle at the front of the castle and continued to expand.

"No, no, no, no!" Gryphon said.

"What is that?" Aaron asked.

"That ... is the mortal underworld. Someone with Hades powers has opened a portal. Who would they bring back?" Gryphon said.

Stefan and Aaron gasped at the same time.

CHAPTER 32
ALEX

The fog swirled faster and faster until it grew dense and surrounded them. It blotted out everything around it, and Alex couldn't even hear the sounds of the fighting behind them. It sent waves of uneasiness through her.

"What is it?" Alex asked.

"Unfinished business," Lygari said.

Another rumble shook the ground as the crack opened further. Alex backed up until she hit the edge of the fog. Her hand slipped inside the darkness—it was freezing and chilled her to the bone. Alex yanked her hand out and thought back to her lessons on the lines. Only one made sense.

Hades has control over the underworld, and Daniel is ice-cold. Could this be the underworld? We don't have Hades powers, unless my seeing the dead is a skill from Hades and not from being a Returned One.

"*You* have Hades powers?" Alex asked Lygari. He merely smirked at her. "You knew Daniel was following me, guarding me, and you said nothing?"

"Why would I help you with anything? Good luck, princess. Even as a Returned One, you're going to need it."

She watched in horror as the ground rose up and cracked open, revealing a dark tunnel. As Alex looked into it, a bright light flashed, and Lygari and Kruft vanished, leaving Alex alone with the door into darkness.

She scanned the circle and spotted a mercenary's sword stuck under some rocks. Her wrist burned as the bracelet Lygari had put back on her glowed red, stealing her powers from her. She could hear footsteps. Alex grit her teeth against the pain and wrenched the sword from the rocks. She turned and waited, keeping the blade aimed at the tunnel.

The silhouette of a man appeared inside the tunnel. Slowly, it came closer to the opening. Sweat ran down Alex's back as her breaths became ragged gasps. Nothing could calm her as the shadow stepped out of the tunnel opening.

Alex's heart jumped into her throat as the face of her nightmares stared back at her. He had the same black hair and rich brown skin as her father, but there was no love in his eyes.

You have my father's smile. Why did he have to get your smile?

Somehow, he was young and fit, and his brown eyes burned with pure hatred. Dressed in her family's crest, he stepped out from the tunnel and strutted into the circle without taking his gaze off her. A sword hung at his hip.

"Hello, little witch."

"Grandfather."

Alex tried to calm her pounding heart as Arthur unsheathed his sword and moved toward her. Alex screamed and brought her blade up to stop his attack. He leaped back, and she barely got the sword back up before he came at her again. He was in his youthful body, strong and trained to fight for hours, while Alex hadn't trained for months and was a shell of herself.

Gryphon! Please do something. I won't last long here!

CHAPTER 33
GRYPHON

Gryphon peered into the thick fog, but it was impenetrable.

"Who's Arthur?" he asked.

"The grandfather who murdered her mother," Michael said. "You don't mean—"

Gryphon cracked to the outskirts of the castle. The fog was as thick on that side, but he was shocked to find Kruft, Lygari, and Moorloc all outside of the fog.

"What have you done, you fool? You're ruining everything," Moorloc shouted at Lygari.

"She was never going to help you," Lygari said. "She was working with Gryphon this whole time. At least this way, her power stays with us." He smirked. "Or rather, with me."

"What did you do?" Gryphon asked, reaching to touch the fog.

"I opened the underworld and pitted Returned One against Returned One. Even you can't save her in there. Arthur's going to finish what he failed to do twelve years ago," Lygari said.

Terror ripped through Gryphon as he realized the magnitude of what Lygari was saying. He whipped his head toward the sorcerer. "After I get her out of there, and I will, I'll take my time destroying you." Gryphon cracked back to the mortals. They were gathered around the massive fog, trying to get into it.

"You can't enter it," Gryphon said. "Lygari made it so only Returned Ones can stay inside."

"What do we do?" Michael asked, his voice pitching higher.

"Hope her magic is strong enough to defeat Arthur," Merlock said.

"Something is wrong. I can't hear her thoughts. She should be screaming at me."

"You can hear her thoughts?" Harold asked.

"There must be something we can do," Merlock said, ignoring Harold.

"No, but there's something I can do," Gryphon said, turning to Harold and Macht. "Keep everyone away. No one touches us. Aaron, Megesti, come with me."

In their fear for Alex, the group had forgotten the fighting happening around them. Harold, Macht, Stefan, and Michael moved toward the battle that fortunately had migrated away from the eerie fog. The four took their fighting stances to keep anyone back.

"Give me your dagger," Gryphon said. "And for her sake, no stupid questions."

Aaron handed his dagger over, and Gryphon grabbed Megesti's hand. He sliced open Megesti's palm, then did the same to Aaron, and then both of his own palms. He clasped their hands in his, faced the fog, and burst into a blinding orange light.

"Blood of the oath taker," he intoned. "Blood of the oath maker. Bring forth the guardian and make him corporal."

A flash of lightning burst up from the center of the fog.

"What did you do?" Merlock asked.

Gryphon turned to Merlock with a smirk on his face. "I evened the odds."

CHAPTER 34
ALEX

Arthur struck Alex's blade so hard the blow reverberated down her arm, and she cried out in pain. The blood from where Kruft had sliced her had run down her arm, soaking her sleeve and causing her fingers to lose their grip on the sword. Pure terror and adrenaline were all that kept Alex moving as she and Arthur circled one another, playing a twisted game of cat and mouse.

"It's disturbing how much you look like your mother," he said. "Not a speck of my son. I'm still not convinced you're even his."

"It's a trait of our line," Alex said, hoping to stall him.

"I know. All the Cassandras are alike. Are you a whore like she was too?"

"Considering how much time you spent stalking me in my father's castle, you know I'm not."

"Not yet. How quickly will you abandon your Datten husband?"

"Why is everyone obsessed with my mother's sex life? Is there something wrong with a woman allowing herself plea-

345

sure? And my mother wasn't like that after she met my father. She *loved* him."

"Are you so sure? My research led me to believe sorcerers can't love. It isn't in their nature."

"What research? I read your journals."

"You read the ones I left for your father. I'm not foolish enough to leave my work out in the open."

Arthur lunged at Alex, but she expected it. She jumped clear of his attack and spun to face him. "If sorcerers don't care for others, why did my mother work so hard to heal people and help them?"

"Your mother took lives with her *healing,* as you call it. Spells went wrong. Things were allowed to happen that never should have been. And if your mother had cared about you, she'd have left the day she conceived you and never married your father. But she wanted the comfortable life. She ensnared my son, and since you all look alike, there would be no way to confirm paternity."

Rage engulfed Alex, and she lunged for Arthur. He dodged her attack and sliced her shoulder open. Then he kicked her in the hip, slamming Alex into the ground. He stood over her and smirked as he crashed his boot onto her shoulder, pinning her down.

"Clearly you're not a Warren. Otherwise you'd have been able to defend yourself."

Alex tried to wiggle out from under his boot but couldn't. As he raised his sword to strike, Alex closed her eyes and braced herself. A bright light flashed through the darkness of her closed eyes. The sound of sword on sword screamed above her.

Opening her eyes, a man with golden blond hair in a red tunic was beating back Arthur.

"Aaron?" Alex struggled to her feet as the man struck

Arthur's shoulder. But his face wasn't Aaron's; it had more Emmerich than Guinevere.

Daniel?

The Prince of Datten was in a man's body and attacked the King of Warren with the rage and demand for vengeance Alex carried in her own heart. She watched them fight, unable to move.

"Alex, run!" Daniel shouted. He struck Arthur's arm, sending him backward. "Go into the fog and don't look back or stop for anything. Run until you come out the other side. If you're still inside when it's pulled back into the underworld, you'll be trapped."

"What if I fall?"

"Don't. There are things much worse than your grandfather in that fog."

Alex ripped the bottom of her shirt and wrapped it around her arm. A few steps away, Arthur swiped and missed Daniel. He snarled.

Alex turned to look at the dark, icy fog before her.

"Go *now*!" Daniel shouted as he dove for Arthur. Alex took a deep breath and leaped into the blackness.

CHAPTER 35
AARON

"What do you mean you gave her *Daniel?*" Aaron asked.

"Lygari has strong Hades powers, but mine are better—and my teacher was too. I gave her Daniel in his adult body, not as an apparition," Gryphon said.

"Kharon would be impressed," Merlock said.

Gryphon smirked. "Now we need to get her out of there. If Daniel and Arthur finish one another before she's out, she'll get trapped in the underworld when the fog returns."

"How do we get her out?" Harold asked.

Michael ran toward the fog and tried to push his hand inside, but it was solid as a wall.

Gryphon groaned. "You aren't a Returned One. Only those who have died before can get inside."

"Then how do we help? Scream bloody murder so she hears us over the fighting and comes out?" Michael asked.

Gryphon's eyes widened. "Yes. But we have to be loud enough to drown out what's inside there with her too."

Aaron glanced at Stefan. He swallowed hard, and they each

took a spot along the fog and started screaming for Alex. Michael and Harold joined them while Macht continued to guard them.

"Alex! We're here!"

"This way, Alex!"

"What about the oath?" Megesti asked. "If she gets out and sees them, they'll be killed."

"Aaron and Stefan, stand on the furthest edges," Gryphon said. "Merlock, Megesti, and I will take the middle. She'll come to us."

"How do you know—?" Michael started to ask.

Gryphon took Megesti's and Merlock's hands, and the three of them lit up in violet and orange. Gryphon grunted as his eyes flashed blue, and the sorcerers started glowing brighter. Aaron had to shield his eyes.

"Alex!" Michael was shouting again.

"Alex, we're here!"

Swords clanged together behind them. Aaron turned to see Macht fighting back some mercenaries who'd left the battle and come after them. Stefan abandoned his screaming to help Macht keep them back.

"Why isn't it working? Where is she?" Aaron asked.

"Inside, the fog is significantly larger than it appears out here," Gryphon shouted over the battle behind them. "And she probably is hearing all manner of pretenders in there, calling to her. Even of us."

"How do we convince her we're the real ones?" Michael asked.

Gryphon raised his brows at him.

CHAPTER 36

ALEX

Inside the fog was the worst stench Alex ever smelled: a combination of rotting meat, stale blood, and human waste. She made it three steps before retching. The fog was as thick inside as it had been outside, and she couldn't even see her feet, let alone anything in front of her.

Don't fall. Please don't fall. I don't want to die in this cesspit. Holding her hands out for protection, she made her way toward what she hoped was the edge of the circle.

After a few steps, the voices started.

"Alex."

"Alex, help me!"

"Alex, I'm here. I've come for you!"

They were the voices of her loved ones: Aaron, her mother, Stefan, Michael, Gryphon, and her father. Each tried to get her to go a different direction, telling her they were real and wanted to help her—save her.

No, you're not real. Stop it!

Alex clamped her hands over her ears, desperate to drown out the terrible voices. Branches, thorns, and rocks appeared out of the fog. They grabbed and scratched any exposed skin. As warm blood ran down her cheek, a branch snapped behind her, and Alex lowered her hands.

The snarl that followed sent her heart into a canter as sweat glued her shirt to her back. Alex glanced back to see a pair of red eyes glowing as low, guttural growls came from either side of her.

Run!

Steadying her breathing, Alex faced ahead and ran as hard as she could. She tripped on a root, and more branches ripped her flesh as she slammed into the ground. She could feel a hot, putrid breath on her back. Something powerful and large was trying to rip through the bramble to get at her. She scrambled to her feet and kept running.

Gryphon, where are you? Help me, please!

Tears ran cold down her cheeks as she ran. The voices returned, but now they screamed her name. Their cries echoed in her ears.

You're all lies. You have to be lies. I don't know what to do! Then she heard the name no one knew.

"Alex! It's Sunset. This way!"

Alex turned and almost twisted her ankle but caught herself at the last second. A faint orange light flickered in the direction of that voice, and Alex broke into a run.

A hot wind blew against her back as a flash of light lit up the fog for an instant. Alex memorized as much of the path before her as she could, but the beasts that had been chasing her lit up too. Giant dogs ... but *not* dogs. They had matted or missing fur and red eyes with jaws and teeth the size of a bear's with spiked horns down their backs and a pair on their heads. One leaped at her. Alex dodged it, but the second one caught her back with its claws. Pain lanced through her, and she screamed, sending her body into a harder adrenaline-fueled run.

Ahead of her, the orange light grew brighter. Another voice rang in the darkness.

"Alex, run faster. It's finished."

Daniel!

The tree ahead of her was uprooted from the ground and flew past her, sucked back into the center of the fog. If she didn't get out now, she never would. Alex pushed herself so hard she tasted blood with each breath. Rocks and trees flew past. Alex struggled to dodge them as she forced one foot in front of the other.

"It's Sunset. Alex, please!"

Gryphon.

Their voices became clearer: Aaron, Gryphon, Michael, and Megesti.

The fog thinned, and the lights grew brighter. Tears flew from Alex's cheeks as she pushed herself into the sunlight.

Alex couldn't have stopped herself for anything in the world. When she flew through the fog, she slammed into the bright light at a full run, taking them all to the ground. Adrenaline pumping through her, the groans beneath her silenced as she closed her eyes, forcing her lungs to stop racing and slow her breath.

"If you wanted me on my back, princess, there are easier ways to go about it."

Alex opened her eyes to see Gryphon smirking up at her.

"Idiot," she snarled and punched him in the shoulder.

"Ow. Is that any way to thank someone for saving your life?"

"If you hadn't left her, she wouldn't have needed saving," Aaron snapped.

Aaron!

"No. I can't see you. The oath!" Alex covered her eyes as a pair of arms pulled her off Gryphon, helping her to her feet.

"I'm not Aaron, princess."

Alex opened her eyes to find a man larger than Stefan looking down at her. His clothes matched the earth coating her clothing, but his violet eyes were kind.

"Can you stand?"

Her heart finally slowed enough that she could breathe. She looked at the crest on his armor and nodded. "Thank you, Sir or King …"

"Harold. My pleasure, princess."

"Alex is right. Merlock, you need to get Aaron and Stefan away from her until we can find and deal with Moorloc," Gryphon said.

Another tremor shook the ground, forcing them all to fight for their balance. Alex looked up and watched all of the black fog disappear back into the crack in the earth. Another tremor, and the hill and the crack vanished.

Alex took a few steps toward where the fog had been when Daniel appeared in front of her. He was back to the young boy version of himself.

"Thank you," Alex whispered.

Daniel smiled at her.

"Could you always make yourself older?"

He looked toward his brother, and Alex watched the smirk spread across his face. Alex was about to tease him when he leaped forward and pointed behind her, his face twisting into a silent scream of terror. Before she could turn to look, a burning sensation erupted in her gut. A thick, hot liquid ran down her belly, soaking her tunic.

She looked down to see a blade sticking out of her.

"Oath broken. Goodbye, little titaness," Moorloc whispered

into her ear. He wrenched the blade from her and threw it in the dirt. The world felt distant and cold as he cracked away.

She touched her stomach, and her hands came back red. Faces and voices surrounded her, but they were muffled and distorted.

I'm cold. Why am I cold?

"Alex, look at me. Look at me!"

Aaron?

Something solid hit her back and legs and when she opened her eyes again, she was on the ground looking up at him.

"Stay with me, please." Aaron's hand cupped her face.

Fear. He's scared.

Pressure on her stomach stole her breath. People were talking, but she couldn't tell who.

"It hurts," Alex whispered.

"I know. Stay with us."

"We're going to fix you. You have to hold on," Michael begged.

"I'm cold."

"Don't you die on us." Stefan's voice sounded far, far away.

Alex moved her hand to Aaron's cheek and stroked it with her thumb, leaving a streak of red. "I love you. I'm sorry."

"No apologies. You're going to be fine," Aaron said, his voice breaking.

Daniel and Victoria's faces appeared above them.

"It's okay, Alexandria, we—" Merlock's voice vanished as Alex gasped for breath that wouldn't come, and their faces faded into blackness.

CHAPTER 37
AARON

Alex's hand slipped from his face.

No, no, no, no. You can't die. You can't leave me. Not you too. I love you. I have to fix this. I can't lose you.

Aaron cupped her face and kissed her.

Nothing.

No kiss back. No reaction. No breath. She was gone.

"*No!*" Aaron grabbed Alex's body and pressed her to him. Everyone around them vanished, and all he could see was her. He tucked her hair behind her ear and kissed her. Sobs erupted from him, his cry louder than he would have thought humanly possible. He cradled her and begged everyone to bring her back to him.

Afraid to look into her eyes, Aaron did anyway, and as Alex had described with her mother, her eyes had lost their sparkle. *Lost their life—lost her life.*

Time had no meaning anymore. It could have been seconds or days. Aaron held her and whimpered.

"She's here," Gryphon said, and Aaron snapped up, looking around, but he saw nothing.

"We have to move fast. We've waited too long already. Any longer and the transference may fail. Get him off her. Now!" Merlock's voice broke Aaron from his grief as Harold, Stefan and Michael ripped him off Alex.

"No." Aaron tore free from them and dove for her again.

"Gryphon!"

Gryphon threw his hands up, and the same invisible hands from the tournament gripped Aaron and slammed his knees to the earth. He couldn't move, couldn't get to her.

"Keep him there," Gryphon said. Harold and Stefan held Aaron down as the invisible hands released him.

"Let me go. Get off me, you boars!" Aaron fought as if his life depended on it, but their grips remained tight.

"Gryphon, keep everyone away from us—especially Lygari and my brother. Megesti, I need your help. You know what to do. We get one chance at this."

Unable to move, Aaron watched as Merlock and Megesti gently laid Alex on the ground. They placed her hands on top of the wound that had taken her from them. Merlock kneeled down at her head and laid his hands on her shoulders. Gryphon looked around and set his hands on fire. Flicking his wrist, he sent a circle of fire around them and then raised his arms, causing the fire to grow taller than even Betruger men. Moving into a fighting stance, Gryphon braced himself and nodded to Merlock.

You can't even take a proper fighting stance. No wonder you failed to protect her.

"All right. Megesti, stay back. Under no circumstances are you to touch us," Merlock said.

Megesti obeyed his father. He moved to Aaron and put his hand on his shoulder. Aaron looked up at him; the sorcerer's face seemed to say everything would be okay.

It can't be okay. She's dead. Nothing ever will be okay again.

Merlock kissed Alex's forehead and whispered. He whispered over and over a series of strange words Aaron couldn't understand or even try to repeat. A faint violet glow slowly appeared around him. Once it was bright enough, it left him and moved into Alex's body, which glowed too.

Aaron looked up to see Alex's ghost standing between Gryphon and Merlock, looking down at herself. A shadow appeared beside her and took her hand. As soon as she squeezed it back, the shadow became clear—*Daniel*. Aaron's brother nodded to him, and Gryphon shifted from his stance and took apparition Alex's free hand. He squeezed it, taking Alex's attention off herself for a moment. Aaron shuddered as she and Gryphon stared at each other in silence for what felt like an eternity. When her eyes shifted, they found Aaron's; their emerald color sparkled again as she mouthed, "I love you."

Aaron sobbed again. The hands on him loosened as they spotted the ghosts. Their gasps made Aaron's heart hurt, knowing he wasn't imagining it.

She's dead.

Whatever Merlock is doing won't change that.

I failed you. I'm so sorry.

Daniel shook his head back and forth at Aaron.

The light coming off Alex's body grew stronger and brighter while Merlock's dimmed. Gryphon released Alex's hand and moved toward Megesti, placing his hand on Megesti's shoulder as Merlock continued to whisper strange words. Megesti cried softly and pulled away from Alex and Gryphon.

Megesti heaved a ragged breath before moving his hands above Alex's body and whispering the same words as his father. The light spread all over Alex and into Merlock. Aaron wasn't sure what was happening ... and then more apparitions appeared.

Victoria appeared first. She took Alex's hand—the one Gryphon had released.

Merlock's voice boomed over the fire and chaos of the battle raging behind them. "I call on Cassandra and Hades, the first of their lines. Mother of my line, bring back to us your daughter Alexandria."

A rumble shook the ground as two cloaked figures appeared behind Merlock. The light they gave off was blinding, and Aaron had to look away. From the ground, he could see one glowed gray and the other gold. Together, they walked around Alex and kneeled to touch her and then Merlock before vanishing as quickly as they'd appeared.

"Alexandria, daughter of Victoria, I go into the dark, endless night in your stead. You must return. Fulfill your purpose."

When Merlock uttered the last word, a long, heavy silence stretched before them. Then, in a heartbeat, Alex's ghost vanished, and Merlock collapsed, no longer glowing. Megesti dropped to his father's side in tears. Merlock's ghost appeared beside Victoria where Alex's ghost had been. Victoria placed her ghostly hand on her brother's face and whispered to him. Aaron watched as more sorcerers he recognized from the Verlassen Castle hall paintings appeared behind Merlock and Victoria. They were whispering, but he couldn't understand them.

Gryphon raised his arms and lowered the flame wall around them. Moving slowly, he went to Megesti and put his hand on his shoulder. A crack sounded as Moorloc appeared beside them. He lunged at his siblings, but Gryphon thrust his hand in the air. A blue light surrounded Moorloc, and he vanished. Harold, Stefan, and Michael released Aaron and tentatively stepped toward the sorcerers.

After staggering to his feet, Aaron was frozen in place. He watched Victoria bend down and kiss Alex on her head. She held out her hand, and a tiny yellow orb appeared. Like a firefly on a summer night, the gold orb floated from Victoria, landed on Alex's chest, and disappeared into her. Next, Merlock did the same with a violet orb. They watched in awe as every apparition around her released a small orb that dropped into Alex. They were all different colors—violet, gold, navy blue, gray, and green. When they'd all dropped their orbs, Alex was glowing with a swirling combination of gold and violet with a few splashes of other colors.

Except for Victoria and Merlock, all the ghosts vanished.

Victoria looked at Megesti. She bent down and kissed the top of his head. "She'll be back soon. You won't have to be alone."

Merlock nodded to Megesti. "I know you'll make me proud."

Merlock kissed Victoria's hand. "Thank you," Victoria said.

She turned back to Alex and smiled. "It's time, sweetheart. They've suffered enough."

A bright light exploded out of Alex, forcing everyone to shield their eyes. It even stopped the battle raging on behind them for a moment. Aaron blinked at the ground until he could see again. When he looked up, Alex had vanished.

CHAPTER 38
ALEX

Time slowed as a bright light erupted from her. She searched her stomach for the wound, but through the rip in her shirt, she could tell there wasn't one. Her arm and shoulder had healed too. She touched it and turned around. Merlock and her mother stood behind her.

Victoria kissed Alex's forehead and vanished with Merlock.

The icy cold left her forehead when her mother disappeared. Power drummed through her veins like she'd never experienced before.

Twice. Twice returned. Does that change things too? She saw the pain in Aaron's eyes and swallowed hard. Time caught up with her.

Aaron, I'm yours, and you're mine. Nothing is coming between us again.

"Alex ... you're all right?"

She nodded at Aaron, and he rushed for her. Sobs erupted from him as he slipped his hands around her waist and pulled her close. Alex grabbed his face, and her lips found his. The cold inside her vanished as he brought warmth back into her entire body. Everything around them vanished in that instant —their friends, the battle, her fears. All that was left was him.

Desperate to hold on to him, Alex kissed him harder, feeling his love fill every dark, scarred hole Moorloc, Kruft, and Lygari had beaten into her. Finally pulling away from him, she opened her eyes slowly and looked into his perfect blue eyes.

"You came for me."

"I would go to hell and back for you," Aaron said, pressing his forehead to hers.

"I missed you."

"I missed you too."

"Aaron?"

"Yes."

"You smell terrible."

She could feel the laughter in his chest as he squeezed her tighter and kissed her again.

"Not all of us had endless access to water like you did."

"Stop hogging her," Michael demanded.

Alex laughed as Aaron struggled to let her go, and Michael hugged her so hard he almost knocked her over.

Stefan didn't even wait for him to let her go and hugged the two of them together. "If you ever pull a stunt like this again, I'm going to lock you in your room," he said, crushing them tighter.

"That won't work anymore. She's mastered cracking," Gryphon said.

Megesti ran his hands over his father's eyes to close them. He whimpered and accepted the hand Gryphon offered. On his feet, Megesti walked to Alex and looked her up and down.

"You're all right?"

"I am."

Michael and Stefan released her, and she threw her arms around Megesti's neck. "Thank you." She whispered so softly only he could hear her, and he wrapped his arms around her, hugging back.

"I hate to break things up, but our battle isn't over yet," Harold said.

Alex took Aaron's hand and squeezed it. Her chest surged with every deep, ragged breath she took. She spun around to take in the world around her: Megesti staring at Merlock, her friends in silent shock gawking at her, and Gryphon. Harold had joined another Betruger man, and they were struggling to keep the mercenaries at bay.

Are you ready for this, princess?

Ready for what, Gryphon?

Things are going to get messy and dark before they get better.

Alex nodded to Gryphon, and he held his hand out to her. She placed her hand into his, and he whispered an incantation. Her bracelet opened and dropped to the ground. He picked it up and carefully snapped it shut before offering it to her, but she shook her head. He slipped it into his pocket.

Alex scanned the field again, this time looking for Kruft and the sorcerers. "Where are they?" she asked.

"Hiding. Like the wretched cowards they are," Gryphon replied.

"Can you find them?" Alex asked. A feral smirk spread across Gryphon's face as his eyes flashed and the rest of him glowed blue. Chuckling, he cracked away.

"I thought he glowed orange," Michael said.

"Gryphon is the titan of two lines—Ares and Mystics," Alex said. "His Mystics powers will allow him to track them and bring them back."

Alex kissed Aaron's cheek and dropped his hand. She turned to the clashing armies and dropped to her knees. Aaron went to help her, but when she placed her hands on the ground, he stood and watched. Alex opened her well, and a pale golden light left her and rushed along the ground. The light went into the Datten and Warren armies, releasing them from the bloodlust Gryphon had summoned into them. Then the vines returned. They burst from the ground, twisted themselves around the mercenaries' ankles and wrists, and then retreated into the earth, binding the men to the ground.

"No more bloodshed. Not for me," Alex whispered.

The armies stopped and gawked at the mercenaries struggling on the ground. Alex accepted Aaron's help and stood slowly. She was drained. She started toward her friends when a crack erupted between them.

Lygari and Kruft appeared, and they were ready for a fight. Kruft dove at Alex with his sword. Exhausted, Alex could barely move, let alone react to defend herself, but Harold reacted with lightning speed. He leaped between them and struck Kruft's blade with such force Kruft dropped it. Then Macht and Stefan tackled him before he could try to attack again.

Gryphon cracked back with Moorloc as Lygari drew his fire and went after Aaron. Alex snapped. She screamed and thrust her hands out, sending wind and gold orbs out of her hands. They slammed into Lygari. He vanished with an explosive crack.

"What did you do?" Moorloc asked, but Gryphon shoved him to the ground. Alex noticed her gold bracelet was fastened to Moorloc's wrist.

"I don't know what I did. I hit him with a light. But I don't know what the light does." She swallowed and looked at Gryphon, hoping he'd know what she did. But the scent of pine overpowered her senses as Aaron came behind her and slid his arm across her shoulders, pulling her close.

Gryphon closed his eyes, and they all went still for a moment. "You banished him. He isn't anywhere I can see."

"How?" Harold asked.

"Regardless of what anyone else believes, she is extraordinarily powerful," Gryphon said.

Kruft grunted, trying to free himself, and Macht slammed his knee into his back, pressing his face into the dirt. As she looked at Kruft and Moorloc on the ground, rage bubbled up inside of her. Pain spread through her at a rate she couldn't stop. Alex stepped away from Aaron and held her hand out to Michael. He paused but then drew his sword.

"Alex—are you sure?" Aaron stepped between them, forcing her to face him before she could take the blade. His eyes locked onto hers, and she had to look away. She could see the vein in his neck throbbing, telling her his heart pounded as hard as her own.

"You're better than this." Aaron's words hit her like her own magical wind. "I know you, and you won't be able to live with yourself tomorrow."

She struggled to hold back her tears. "You don't know me anymore. You don't know what happened to me here, what they did to me ... what I've become."

"But I do. Better than you do," Gryphon said. *Remember, princess, I took your memories of the worst things you experienced here because you didn't want to lose yourself. I didn't want to let that hatred consume you.* "Killing your own is a serious crime for sorcerers."

"I don't care." Alex shook her head.

"Then get your revenge," Gryphon said, stepping toward her. "Prove you're the Heart and that you belong with me in the Forbidden Lands."

"What?" Alex snapped at Gryphon. Aaron and the others moved back as an orange light appeared on Alex's hands and moved up her arms.

"We're vicious," Gryphon said, stepping right up to her. Orange light swirled around him as he stared down at her.

"Prove yourself to be the monster everyone says we are. Kill them. Then you can join me in the Forbidden Lands, and we can rain hellfire on the world. Or stay here with your prince and show them Warren mercy. There is no middle path."

Her rage grew as the orange glow continued to spread across her. *I won't change my mind, but take this rage away before it gets too much. I need to make the choice as myself.* Alex looked at Gryphon, and he held his hands out to her. When Alex placed hers into his, the orange trickled away and, with it, the rage she felt.

"There is a middle path. I'll show the men mercy. They followed orders. But Moorloc and Kruft will pay. This is a Datten battlefield, and the final judgment is up to me."

Harold nodded to Alex. "Betruger has this too."

Alex spotted something over his shoulder. Bringing her hand to her mouth, she sprinted from their group. With the mercenaries contained, the kings and generals had made their way up the field to them. Her legs held out until she reached her father. Alex threw her arms around him and burst into tears. Edward lifted her in the air, squeezing her so tightly she couldn't breathe, but she didn't care. When he finally set her down, a firm hand squeezed her shoulder, and she smiled at Emmerich.

"I'm all right. I'm coming home," she said when Edward released her from his hug. He cupped her face and kissed her forehead as tears streamed down his face.

"I like your tunic," Emmerich said, grinning at her.

Alex laughed when she looked down and remembered Gryphon's combination of Datten and Warren's crests. He'd placed the Datten motto underneath and Warren's on top.

"I didn't want to pick," she said.

"And you'll never have to. What have you decided for your captives?" Emmerich asked as Harold and Aaron joined them.

"Datten and Betruger justice," Aaron replied, and Harold nodded.

"You don't have to finish this yourself, Alexandria," Emmerich said. "The generals will handle it for you. It's their duty."

"No. If I pass the judgment, I bear the burden of that punishment." Alex held her hand out to Aaron, and he placed the grip of his brother's sword in her hand. She seized it, let out a ragged breath, and moved toward her uncle.

"Moorloc, son of Hermes, son of Merlin. You told me before. You're the Head of this line, so the guilt for the crimes of the line lies with you. Your son has vanished, and the rest of your family sees you for what you are—*a traitor*. The punishment for treachery against our own and treason against Datten, Warren, and Betruger ... is death."

Alex glanced back at her friends. *Will you ever look at me the same after this?* Michael and her father were horrified, but the rest nodded with a quiet understanding that the guilty must be punished.

Moorloc stood and looked down at her. "You'll never come back from this, Harbinger. If you kill me, you'll make yourself a monster—make yourself the beast you strove to protect your loved ones—"

Alex drove Daniel's blade into his gut, twisted it, and ripped it out again. Moorloc dropped to his knees, gasping and struggling for breath as blood poured from the giant hole Alex had left in him. Alex suddenly screamed in pain, dropped the sword, and fell to her knees.

Gryphon rushed to Alex's side and pulled up her sleeve while turning her arm over. Three stacked x's appeared on her forearm as if burned there. "The mark of a betrayer," he said. "Given to any sorcerer who violently harms their own."

"He deserved it," Alex spat.

"I know," Gryphon said.

Another scream erupted from the group. Alex pulled away from Gryphon and rushed to her feet. Megesti was doubled over on his knees, clutching his stomach. He'd erupted in a violet glow, and his eyes flashed violet. Alex ran to him. Aaron was trying to hold him up as best he could.

"He's fine," Gryphon said. "Meet the new Titan of Merlin. The power rush is excruciating, as you know, princess."

"Does that mean Lygari is dead?" Megesti asked. His breaths were quick and ragged.

"Not at all. You were always the next titan. Why would the power go to a half sorcerer when a full one is available?"

"You're a manipulative, egotistical Ares. Why would I believe a word you say, especially about my parentage?" Megesti snapped.

"The truth will come out eventually, Megesti. It always does," Gryphon said.

Releasing Megesti, Alex turned toward Kruft. Macht and Stefan were still holding him.

Aaron grabbed her waist to stop her. "Kruft's mine."

CHAPTER 39
AARON

E mmerich said, "Aaron, you don't have to—"
Aaron looked at his father. "He's a traitor *and* our blood. He's mine to handle."

"Aaron—" Alex began.

"No." Aaron pressed his forehead to hers and ran his hands along Alex's arms. One was wet and sticky with blood. Aaron turned it toward him, afraid of what he would find. But there was no wound to explain the blood.

"When you said yes to marrying me," he continued, "you became Princess of Datten. And like it or not, it's my duty to defend you."

She gently squeezed his arm. "You don't have to prove your worth to me."

"I know. But to them, I do." Aaron nodded his head to the army.

Alex's eyes grew wide as she scanned the field of Datten soldiers watching them. The gold color faded from her eyes. They returned to emerald, and when she stared up at him, he saw fear in them.

"I don't want this to change you," she whispered.

Aaron kissed her forehead and pulled her to him. He could feel her trembling in his arms.

"It won't. Just like your new powers won't change who you are inside."

"All right," Alex said, releasing Aaron. "You handle Kruft. He betrayed Datten, dishonored your family, and assaulted your princess. You choose the punishment."

Emmerich nodded to his general, and Jerome strode to Aaron, taking his position behind him.

Alex was facing the kings, so Aaron couldn't read her. *What exactly did you mean by "assaulted"? What did he do to you? What happened here?*

Edward came forward and held his hand out to her. She looked back at Aaron, biting her lower lip. Aaron pushed her gently toward her father. Edward took her hand and brought her to where Emmerich, Harold, and Michael were standing.

Aaron picked up his brother's sword from where Alex had discarded it, wiped Moorloc's blood from its blade, and sheathed it at his side. Macht and Stefan removed Kruft's armor before finally releasing him. Aaron grit his teeth to contain his temper and turned to face his father's cousin.

"Kruft, as Crown Prince of Datten, I sentence you to death. I'll hold you accountable for the actions against your people and your king."

Aaron removed his sword belt and handed it to Jerome as Harold helped him out of his armor.

Kruft started laughing. "Punish me for what? Putting my hands on that little witch? And it's your problem because your fathers are friends? How sad for you, defending the daughter of a whore. How do you know she's a princess? For all you know, she's the bastard of whoever her mother bedded before bedding Edward."

"Aaron, don't listen to him," Alex pleaded.

"Don't worry." Aaron smiled at her. "I've seen too many of your father's mannerisms in you to ever doubt your parentage." He turned back to Jerome. The general held Daniel's sword out to him, but Aaron shook his head.

"Thank you, but I'll handle this the traditional Datten way —with my hands." He scowled as he turned to Kruft. "Punishing you, cousin, is my duty because you dared to disrespect my betrothed and the future Queen of Datten."

Kruft shook his head at Aaron as he cracked his neck and knuckles. "Considering you're already known as the lesser prince, I thought you would have been smart enough to find yourself a proper maiden. I suspect if you knew half of what went on in this castle, you wouldn't want to marry the little witch. It's like everyone says—she's exactly like her mother in all ways."

"Victoria was more honorable than you," Edward snapped.

"What my betrothed's mother did before she married Edward is her business," Aaron said.

"Fine, but what about this witch's behavior? If you don't believe me, ask the sorcerer who spent last night in her bedroom."

Bile rose in his stomach as Aaron looked pointedly at Gryphon. *I warned you before. If you put your hands on her, I don't care how long it takes. I'll kill you.*

"Should we talk about what caused those scars on your hands and other parts, Kruft?" Gryphon said. His hands glowed orange, and his face shifted to a sneer.

"Kruft's mine, Gryphon. But I'll deal with you later," Aaron barked before turning to look at Alex. Edward held her, and she gripped his arm. She was pale and clearly terrified for him.

Gryphon snapped his fingers, and Aaron looked down to see his crested shirt matched Alex's with the combined Datten and Warren crests. *Bribery won't save you from my temper if you so much as touched Alex.*

Turning his attention back to Kruft, a calm overcame Aaron. The sun was high in the sky, magnifying the stench of the battle that had been waged around them. Aaron ran his hand along the back of his neck and turned to look at his father and the army of Datten. All his men watched him in stoic silence. If he was soft, it would set a precedent for the rest of his life with Alex.

I won't let a single man think I can't protect her now that I have her back or that I'll tolerate anyone touching her.

Since the first attack on Warren, something inside him had shifted. Before she was even his to protect, Aaron knew he would kill anyone who dared harm her.

I couldn't protect you here, but I can avenge what happened to you. Aaron put up his fists and moved toward the man who betrayed his father and Datten. Jerome followed a few steps behind him.

The battleground was pitted and slick with spilled blood. Aaron tried not to think of how much blood was Alex's. Jerome moved to the side but stood ready to act if Aaron were in any danger. Aaron and Kruft circled one another slowly with their fists up. Aaron had watched Kruft spar enough growing up to know the man never made the first move. It didn't matter how long a fight went, he would never attack first. Aaron braced himself, knowing Kruft would probably land the first strike, and lunged at the man. Kruft was fast on his feet and dodged, striking Aaron's face with his right hook.

Alex's cry carried into the field, but Aaron didn't let it distract him. He shook off the pain, and when Kruft dove for him, Aaron spun away at the last moment, thanking himself for working so hard to teach Alex dancing. When Kruft turned, Aaron punched him in the nose and followed with an uppercut to the chin. Kruft stumbled forward, landing on his knees. Aaron wasted no time and slammed his elbow into Kruft's shoulder, sending him onto all fours. The men watching all cheered. Aaron glanced at Alex. Her face was ashen as she held onto her father with Stefan at her side as usual.

Kruft took advantage of Aaron's distraction and punched him in the stomach, right where his scar was. Aaron cried out and lurched away. Both men moved away long enough to catch their breath. Warm, sticky wetness spread down the side of Aaron's shirt. His wound was bleeding again. He struggled to straighten his stance and waited for Kruft to move. When the man came for him, Aaron slugged him with a right hook. Kruft grabbed his nose and roared, leaning back.

Again, the men cheered as Aaron moved toward Kruft.

Alex screamed, "Aaron, no!"

But he realized too late it was a trick, and Kruft headbutted him. Unimaginable pain exploded in his nose. As blood poured down Aaron's face, Kruft's fist contacted his chin, knocking Aaron to the ground. Kruft slammed his boot into Aaron's chest, causing him to struggle to breathe. Jerome hurried toward them to intervene.

No. I have to do this myself. Aaron held his hand toward the general, and he stopped but remained ready to pounce.

Emmerich and Harold both held onto Alex, who was struggling to break free.

"Don't worry, little whore," Kruft said. His voice sounded far away. "With a figure like yours, you won't have any issues finding someone else to fuck you when he's gone."

Alex's eyes flashed gold, but Kruft's insult snapped the remaining control Aaron had over the violent Datten temper he'd inherited from his father. Embracing his rage, Aaron punched the side of Kruft's knee, sending him to the ground. Both men rushed to get up, but Aaron was faster. He grabbed

Kruft's hair, kneed him in the face, and threw him on his back. His upper lip and eyes twitched from the force of his scowl, and Harold grabbed Daniel's sword from Jerome and tossed it to Aaron.

Slamming his boot into Kruft's collarbone, Aaron ground in his heel.

"No one insults my betrothed's honor and lives." Aaron raised his brother's sword over his head, and Alex screamed.

Aaron looked at her pale face. Her eyes were wide, and she was shaking her head at Aaron.

Why is she acting this way?

"Look away," Aaron said. Alex buried her face in her father's chest. Edward wrapped his arms around her as Emmerich, Jerome, and Harold all nodded at Aaron.

Sighing, Aaron raised his sword and plunged it into Kruft's neck, sending blood flying all over him. Kruft gurgled and choked for a moment before he stilled. Aaron ripped his sword from Kruft's neck and stormed toward the men roaring like a wild animal. The men erupted in cheers as he waved his bloody sword.

"Let it be known from this day on, if you dishonor anyone from Datten—especially your future queen—you'll not deal with the king. You'll deal with me. For Datten. For honor!"

The men repeated it back.

Aaron rejoined the group. Edward looked Aaron up and down slowly, refusing to make eye contact. His face was a compilation of horror and shock, and he kept his tight grip on Alex as if shielding her from Aaron.

You wanted to know I'd protect her.

Emmerich stood tall and had never looked prouder. Stefan, Macht, Harold, and even Gryphon looked at him with understanding while Michael hunched over and retched in the grass.

CHAPTER 40
GRYPHON

The cheers of the Datten army were deafening as Gryphon surveyed the carnage around them.

Is this how humans deal with this sort of mayhem? Interesting. Though I have to agree with the princeling. The brute deserved to die, and had it been up to me, it would have been slower and much more violent.

Gryphon looked for Alex and found her face hidden in her father's shirt. *How strange you had no problem dispensing justice against your uncle, but watching the princeling punish someone who hurt you was too much. You must really worry this will break him.*

"What about his mercenaries?" Macht asked, bringing Gryphon's attention back to the mortals before him. Most of them had stopped struggling against the vines and lay there waiting for their fate.

"Most of them appear to be Betruger," Stefan said.

Alex finally pulled herself away from her father and joined Aaron and Harold. She cringed at Aaron's blood-soaked shirt but accepted his hand when he held it out to her.

"What do you want us to do with them? I could *make* them behave, but you don't strike me as that sort of king," Gryphon said.

Harold sighed. "You're right. I'm not my father's son. He'd have slaughtered them. But I won't use sorcery to force them."

"They're your people, so the choice is yours," Aaron said. "Bring them home or leave them here. Our peace will last regardless of what you decide."

Emmerich and Edward nodded their agreement.

"Should I untangle them?" Alex asked.

Harold nodded.

Gryphon could hear how tired she was in her ragged breaths. *You're exhausted. Be extra careful with your powers.*

Alex stepped away from the men. She took a deep breath, closed her eyes, and raised her arms over her head. As she lowered her arms, her eyes flew open, and the vines shrank back into the ground.

Harold moved and stood beside her. "Betruger mercenaries! Hear your king. My ways are not my father's. I have spared you. We will move forward and bring any of you who wish to return back to your homes. If you remain here, you can take your chances with the knights of Datten and Warren."

With a wave of her hand, Alex released the remaining vines, and the mercenaries rose to their feet. Most of them dropped their weapons and came forward. A few ran off into the mountains. Gryphon rushed to Alex, sensing her powers were more spent than she realized. He caught her as she stumbled. He helped her to her feet, and she smiled weakly at him.

Thank you, Sunset.

Before he could reply, Aaron pushed him aside, taking over holding Alex.

Real mature, princeling.

Aaron wrapped his arms around her waist. She leaned on

Aaron, resting her head on his chest and nestling under his chin. Gryphon could feel his Ares powers rushing to the surface. As if to spite him, Aaron pulled Alex tighter to him and gently kissed the top of her head. Gryphon slammed the lid on his powers and clenched his fists. He turned toward the other mortals to calm himself.

Michael and Stefan were ashen and looked as though they might be sick. Neither could take their eyes off Alex. Michael covered his mouth with his hand as he looked on, teary-eyed. Stefan's eyes were wide as he scanned every part of her, assessing each bruise and scar.

Gryphon rolled his eyes. *I warned you.*

"Now what?" Aaron asked his father.

"Decisions will have to be made," Emmerich said.

"What decisions exactly?" Alex asked, finally releasing Aaron.

"What to do with Merlock and Moorloc's bodies. Not to mention the castle and everything inside of it. And there is the matter of that large hole in it."

A tremor ripped through Gryphon's powers. He looked up, and Alex was staring at him with intent on her face.

She asked, "Is the wall repairable?"

"Yes. It's simple to do. Would you like me to show you how, princess?" Gryphon asked, holding his hand out to Alex. She nodded and took his hand, letting him pull her away from Aaron.

Satisfaction rippled through Gryphon's magic when Alex squeezed his hand, and Aaron flinched. Alex pursed her lips and raised her brow at Gryphon in a clear warning to behave.

They walked until they were facing the hole in the castle wall. Pieces of debris were strewn around them. Gryphon released Alex and raised his hands, and the earth beneath them rumbled. Slowly, the rocks rose from the ground. Some were beyond repair, and these he replaced by summoning mountain bedrock from deep within the ground. He turned to Alex.

A little water, please.

Alex nodded and conjured water to rain down onto the dirt. Gryphon used it to press the muddy stones back into the wall. After that was done, he thrust his hands straight out and sent flames against the wall to heat the stones in place. In a matter of moments, the entire wall was back together.

Gryphon smirked at the others, and when he turned back to her, Alex was still watching him intently.

"Thank you," she said.

"Anything you need, princess," Gryphon said, grinning at her before he bowed.

CHAPTER 41
ΛLEX

"How am I going to send them all home?" Alex asked as she glanced at the massive group of men before her.

"You're not," Gryphon said. "*We* are."

"Aren't you worried your parents will notice?"

"Lygari opened the underworld, Megesti became Titan of Merlin, and the entire line of Cassandra transferred to you. Cracking an army won't be noticed."

Alex sighed at Gryphon. *Why do you look at me like that?*

Because you're exceptional, princess.

Aaron's hand slid into Alex's and brought her attention to him. Behind him, the kings stood waiting for Alex to speak.

"Your Royal Highnesses, what would you like us to do with your men?" Gryphon asked.

"Send Datten's and Warren's armies home," Emmerich said. "We will welcome each with a feast and victory celebration."

Gryphon turned to Harold. "And your men, Your Royal Highness?"

"Send everyone except Macht and myself back to our kingdom. I trust my men to make our wayward brothers feel welcome but also to keep an eye on them."

"Okay," Alex said quietly. "Gather whoever you want to remain. Then Gryphon and I will send the rest home."

Michael looked over the field. "What about the dead?" he asked.

"They go home too. Their loved ones deserve to bury them," Edward replied.

"How many dead are there?" Alex asked. She scanned the battle scene behind them, noting every silver and red tunic on the ground.

"We'll worry about that tomorrow," Aaron said.

"Princess," Gryphon said.

"Sunset."

Aaron snorted, and Gryphon scowled at him.

"How do we crack so many at once?" Alex asked.

"Take my hand, and I'll help you send them back. I need to see where we send them to, and I haven't been to any of your kingdoms."

"I haven't seen them all," Alex said.

Harold looked at Alex and held his hand out to her. Alex nodded to him and then took his hand and Gryphon's. Closing her eyes, she saw a beautiful castle on the sea. It smelled of flowers, and the sea filled her lungs with fresh air, helping her forget the stench of death around her. Gryphon squeezed her hand, and a moment later, something pulled on her magic as if he was summoning it. When she opened her eyes, the entire Betruger army had vanished.

Another pull on her magic sent most of the Datten army home and then the Warren one.

"That was amazing," Harold said.

Alex looked at the castle and sighed. She didn't want to go

back in there, but things needed to be done. She found Megesti standing over Merlock's body and went up to him and stroked his back without saying a word.

Jerome and Sir Reinhart were coming with a few men to retrieve Merlock's body, but Alex motioned for them to stop. She grabbed Megesti's hand, willing him to look at her. She gazed down at Merlock and her chin quivered.

Thank you for sacrificing yourself for me. I'm sorry I never got to truly know you.

"Where should we take him?" she asked Megesti.

"Datten. It was his home, and he's with your mother now," he said.

"Datten it will be," said Emmerich. "I promise he'll be given a place of honor. We'll bury him in the royal crypt. He will spend eternity with the Kings of Datten."

Aaron placed his hand on Megesti's shoulder. "He served four different Kings of Datten. He belongs with them."

"Five," Alex corrected. "You weren't king with him, but his influence on you will live on when you rule."

The knights began to delicately move Merlock into a cart to transport him home.

"What about Moorloc and Kruft?" Gryphon asked. Everyone turned to look at him.

Alex had been avoiding it, but she forced herself to look at where Moorloc lay in the mud. His skin was graying, and the wound had soaked his neck and chest in blood. Alex closed her eyes, and when she opened them, his ghost was standing over his body, staring at her with such hate-filled eyes she stumbled backward.

"I don't care. Just get rid of them," she said.

"We could bury him in the wooded area," Macht said.

"No!" Alex shouted. The idea of it brought bile to her throat and horrified her. "Not there." She was shaking uncontrollably as she looked at Gryphon.

"What if we threw them into the sea?" Gryphon asked.

"Yes." Alex nodded as Aaron rubbed her shoulders. Gryphon snapped his fingers, and both Moorloc and Kruft vanished.

"They can't hurt you again," Aaron said.

Alex pulled away and moved toward the entrance gate to the castle.

"What happens to it now?" Megesti asked Alex as they stopped outside the door.

"We need to decide what to do with the castle," Alex said. Everyone seemed to stay away from them, giving them space. She wished they wouldn't.

"What do you need from inside besides your line books?" Gryphon asked. "They're all together, so grabbing them should be quick."

"How do you know where the books are?" Aaron asked, eyeing Gryphon with suspicion.

"I don't answer to you, princeling," Gryphon said without taking his eyes off Alex. "Moorloc expected to win. He wouldn't have moved them."

Her heart beat harder in her chest. "I can't go back in there to get our books. Not after—" Alex gasped as Aaron's hands gripped her waist.

"I'll get the books. No one is going to make you go anywhere you don't want to," Gryphon said.

"I'd like to collect my things from my room. I can't go in there alone," Alex said. She wiped the tears from her eyes.

"You don't have to," Aaron said.

"I'll help," Megesti said.

"We all will," Michael said, and Stefan nodded.

"Tell us what you need, Princess Alexandria," Harold said.

Gryphon, help, please.

Gryphon nodded. "Take your princeling and clean out your room. I'll show Megesti and your guards where to find your family's books. After that, the Betruger men and I can handle the lab."

"What about the slaves?" Alex asked.

"Slaves?" Edward asked.

"Moorloc tricked and coerced many people into servitude." Alex glanced from Stefan to Aaron. "If you wanted his help to save a loved one, you ended up trapped here as a slave."

"That's horrible," Michael said.

"It is," Alex said. "I want to help those who remain. Some I managed to free a while ago, and they have already gone."

"After you won a very dangerous game," Gryphon said, crossing his arms. Alex turned to her father.

Emmerich and Edward shared a look. "Whoever they are, we will ensure they're compensated for their time here and ensure they can go home," Emmerich said.

Alex let go of Aaron and threw her arms around Emmerich. "Thank you."

Wrapping his giant arms around her, he squeezed her with the same gentle firmness Aaron would. "Anything for our princess."

"After we gather up what you need, then what?" Stefan asked.

"I'm not sure," Alex replied. "Torian law says the castle belongs to Megesti and me."

"I think we should burn it to the ground," Megesti said bitterly.

"No. Then he wins." Alex went silent and gazed at the tall walls for a long moment. "It would be a good outpost or training school for Warren, Datten, and Betruger. We could all station men here to bring our armies together more formally."

"That is an exceptional idea," Edward said. He placed his hand on her shoulder. "Now you're thinking like the Princess of Warren."

Megesti nodded to Alex, and she turned around to face Emmerich and General Wafner.

"You have a mind for strategy, Alexandria." Emmerich smiled.

Alex flushed and smiled weakly. "I had outstanding teachers," she said, looking at Stefan and Aaron.

"What do you think, Harold? Would you allow your men to train with ours?" Aaron asked.

"I'd be honored," Harold said.

"That settles it. You need to pick a knight to run your outpost, princess," Jerome said.

Alex looked at Emmerich and her father. "I think I'll ask my godfather to pick the first one. Datten is known for their guards and knights, after all. Perhaps Datten could spare one or two exceptional ones to help run the new training outpost."

"I volunteer to remain and man the castle." General Matthew Bishop nodded.

Emmerich said, "I can certainly suggest a few to join Matthew. We'll have a discussion after we get all the castle things settled in Warren."

Alex nodded to thank Emmerich and held her hand out to Aaron. He took it and kissed it lovingly. Smiling, she led Aaron and the others into the castle to explain what her ideas were and how it would need to be set up.

ALEX AND AARON managed to clean out her room. It would have gone faster had she not broken down in tears in a mixture of relief and exhaustion. Aaron made her laugh by complimenting how well she made her bed. Then they made their way up to the top of the central tower to collect Alex's hidden journals. When they finished their work, she tried to go help with the lab, but Aaron held her tight, refusing to let her go to any place that might upset her again. Megesti took charge of Michael and Stefan, making sure all the books in Moorloc's room were carefully sealed up for the trip back to their labs.

Alex sat in the courtyard and watched them carry crate after crate of books out of the castle. She sighed, knowing Megesti, Michael, and Stefan knew how to take care of something as precious as those family books. Aaron eventually relented and allowed her to help them pack up the library.

Crates full of supplies were carted out of the lab by what felt like half the Datten army. Alex watched them make trip after trip to pile everything in the courtyard beside the books. Alex watched until she couldn't stand anymore.

"I think we're ready to go home," Aaron said. "We can send more people back tomorrow to deal with settling everyone in. Matthew can put the Datten and Betruger men we're leaving to good use until then."

Alex turned to Gryphon. *Will I see you again?*

I promise you will, but I have to go home to keep you hidden from the rest of our kind. We used a lot of power today, but I plan to spin it to sound as if your uncles killed each other. Use the books and learn all you can. You're strong, but you're not ready to face them yet.

Please hurry back.

I thought you'd be sick of me, princess.

Don't make this awkward, Sunset. You're my friend and a brilliant teacher.

They looked at each other for a long time without speaking. Finally, Gryphon held his hand out to Alex. Alex noticed Aaron tense when she took it.

"You can do this, and if you need me, you know how to call me for help," Gryphon said.

"Are you coming with us?" Aaron asked, sliding his arm around Alex.

Gryphon shook his head. Alex nodded to him and released his hand. She closed her eyes and thought of home. She felt around for Aaron's hand and linked their fingers. Light flashed, and a gust of wind hit them.

CHAPTER 42
ALEX

lex's strength wavered as soon as they arrived in the throne room filled with portraits of her ancestors. Everything that happened in the last day suddenly felt like one of her nightmares, but Aaron was beside her. He held her hand and followed her as she took her first steps back in Warren.

Home. I'm actually home.

Silence filled the room, so Alex's footsteps echoed through the hall until Edward couldn't contain himself anymore and rushed to her. Alex let her father hold her. Twelve years and then another six months was enough forced separation for a lifetime. After he finally let her go, he cupped her face and kissed her forehead.

"Your ladies will be waiting. I suspect they're as eager to see you as you are them."

Alex smiled at her father. "Maybe Edith. I suspect Jessica is more excited to see Michael."

"How do you know about that?" Stefan asked.

"Gryphon told me."

"What else did Gryphon tell you?" Aaron asked, holding his arm out to her.

"You don't like being called princeling, and Stefan beat the snot out of him in a fistfight."

"I did too," Aaron said.

Alex stepped back from Aaron. "When did you fight him?"

"After you visited the cliff by the camp." Aaron held her face with his hand. "To say it disappointed me to have missed seeing you there would be a massive understatement."

Alex's hand moved onto Aaron's. "It would have broken the oath. I'd have lost you," she whispered.

"Why didn't Aaron and I get hurt when you saw us?" Stefan asked, moving toward her away from the kings.

"Because my death broke the oath."

The room fell silent and heavy. Alex tried not to think about the time she spent out of her body or the pain on Aaron's face when it had happened. It was a pain she knew would grace her own face one day when she'd have to say goodbye to him. *But not today. Right now, we're here and together.* Slipping her arm back into Aaron's, she whispered softly, "I'd like to see Jessica and Edith."

Aaron and Alex walked slowly to Alex's suite. When the door opened, Jessica stopped her pacing, and Edith stood slowly from the couch. As soon as she saw her ladies, Alex's hands went to her mouth, and she broke down into tears. The ladies rushed to embrace her, and the three of them clung to each other, sobbing.

Aaron gently closed the door behind them and stood to the side. Alex was glad he stayed. They hadn't left each other's sight since she'd escaped the fog, and the idea of leaving him, even for a minute, terrified her.

After composing themselves, Edith and Jessica prepared a bath for Alex. She clung to Aaron when he tried to go, but he promised to come back the moment she was cleaned up. She trembled as she reluctantly let him go.

Alex gave Jessica permission to burn the clothes she'd been wearing when she came home. In the months at her uncle's, Alex's body had changed as much as her powers. She was a ghost of her old self. Her strength had left her, and by not eating the fish or gruel, she'd allowed herself to waste away. Her hair had become matted, and her eyes hollow and sunken.

"What happened to your back?" Edith asked.

Alex glanced in a mirror and was shocked to see massive red burn marks. The looks of concern on Jessica and Edith's faces intensified when they helped her out of the bath. Their eyes darted from one bruise to the next and to all her scars. It made her feel self-conscious, so when they dressed her and brushed her hair, Alex insisted on hearing about how Michael had proposed and gushed about how lovely Jessica's ring was.

Edith picked Aaron's favorite red dress, and Jessica managed to get it to fit on Alex. But neither could hide their concerned looks after they did the dress up. Jessica placed her crown on her, and Alex looked in the mirror.

Weak. Thinned hair. Too pale skin. Bruises everywhere with more coming in. Scars I can't remember receiving. Alex rubbed the mark on her forearm, sighed, and turned around to head downstairs.

When she stepped off the stairs into her receiving room, Aaron was waiting for her. He stood between her reading couches with his great-grandmother's ruby ring in his hand as he smiled from ear to ear. Alex's own lips curled into a smile at the sight of him. Her feet didn't make a sound as she crossed the stones to wrap her arms around his neck. Aaron held her more delicately than he ever had but still kissed her with everything in him.

I won't break. I promise. Please don't treat me like I'm broken.

Aaron dropped to one knee and held the ring up. Alex smiled and held her hand out, allowing Aaron to put the ring back on her finger and kiss her hand.

"Our fathers are expecting us in the throne room," he said as he stood.

"Why?"

"Your father intends for us to marry tonight."

"What?" Alex released him and pulled away with wide eyes.

"He needs the assurance that Datten will never leave you."

Alex sighed but accepted Aaron's arm, allowing him to escort her. Edward, Emmerich, and Harold were waiting at the front of the throne room with a kindly-looking older man dressed in a beautiful but simple black robe.

"Alexandria, this is Judge Wilhelm," Edward said. "He married your mother and me in secret. Tonight, he'll marry you and Aaron. I know this isn't what you expected or wanted, but I need to know you'll be protected."

Alex released Aaron's hand. "I'm not rejecting you," she said softly and kissed his cheek. Then she walked up to her father and took his hands in hers. "I'm sorry, but no. I want the wedding my mother never got. I won't get married in secret as if I'm ashamed. Besides, Guinevere deserves a proper wedding."

"Elizabeth—" Edward began.

Alex crossed her arms. "No. I don't need Datten to protect me. I can protect myself."

"Good luck, son," Emmerich said, looking from her to Aaron.

Aaron smiled and shrugged. "I agree with her. My mother deserves a proper wedding, but so do we."

"What about what I need?" Edward asked. "I need to know you're safe and cared for, no matter what happens."

Alex looked from Aaron to Emmerich before stepping to her father. "When I arrived home, you followed Emmerich's every suggestion as if it were law, and now you doubt him and Aaron. Is it their desire to keep me safe you doubt or their ability?"

"Alexandria, I didn't mean it like that."

"You made it clear—my marriage is my choice. I won't give that up because you're scared Datten might go back on their word." Alex stood tall as her mother's ghost appeared at Edward's side. Victoria placed her hand on his shoulder, making him shiver.

"Mother agrees with me." Pausing, Alex looked down at the ring on her hand. She spun it around her finger. "But more importantly, I'm not the same as I was when I left. I want Aaron to have time to make sure he still wants to go through with the wedding. I won't hold it against him if he changes his mind." *I need time to heal before I know what's right for me.*

Aaron sighed, and his shoulders relaxed. He walked up to her, and a soft hand caressed her back before he slid his arms around her waist. "Nothing you did at the castle and nothing you ever do would make me change my mind about marrying you." He kissed her, squeezing her tightly.

A knock echoed in the room, and the door opened to reveal their friends—Stefan, Michael, Megesti, Edith, and Jessica. Edith offered Alex a bouquet.

"I said no," Alex said.

"What?" Edith blurted. Her hand shot to her mouth. Harold smiled at her, making her blush.

"We will celebrate my return," Alex continued, "but we're heirs to two kingdoms, and I want us married properly. Before our people."

"Spoken like a future queen," Harold said.

"Thank you, Your Royal Highness," Alex said.

"Seeing as we've settled our alliance, I request you call me Harold."

"Well then, I request you call me Alex," she said as she turned to Aaron. "I like your Edward."

"I knew you would," Aaron said.

The group headed to the dining hall to enjoy the feast. The kitchens had been cooking it up since the first men came back from the battle. Aaron took Alex's hand and led her to the head table. But having eaten so little for so long, Alex found it hard to take more than a few bites, though the food tasted heavenly.

"Eat something for me. You'll want your strength tonight," he whispered.

Alex blushed as his leg rubbed against hers. As her cheek grew darker, a wicked smile crossed Aaron's face.

After finishing the second course of cheese and bread, Alex and Aaron excused themselves to retire for the evening. They barely made it three steps away from the hall before Alex pulled Aaron to her and kissed him. Alex's heart beat faster as she pressed her lips against his and wrapped her arms tightly around his neck, trying to feel as much of him as possible. His hands gripped her rear, pulling her flush against him, and she whimpered. She wanted to be alone with him and forget everything, even if only for a while.

CHAPTER 43
AARON

Aaron was tired of waiting to be alone with Alex and away from staring eyes. He scooped her up and carried her down the hall toward her suite.

"Aaron," Alex said as she tightened her grip on his neck. "Your room is the other way. Remember, my father made it clear any romantic activity between us was to stay in your room."

"That was *before* you vanished. Your father changed his mind. When you left, he made it clear. He doesn't want to hunt to find you ever again. You're to stay in your suite, and if you insist on sleeping with me, then he expects me to be in there too."

"Scandalous. What will people say?"

"I don't care what people think so long as I know you're safe."

"Aaron, I'm sorry for how I left."

Alex trembled in his arms as her eyes fell. He tightened his grip on her slightly and exhaled. "Already forgiven, but I need you to know I understand if you prefer to be alone, even if I hate the idea of being away from you."

"No. I made myself perfectly clear when you took me to Datten. I expect my husband in my bed every night he is in the same castle as me. I've been away from you enough for a lifetime."

Relief flooded him. The idea of leaving her was enough to make him sick. Alex rested her head on his shoulder as he adjusted his grip and carried her to what would be their room. Randal was on guard outside. He opened the door for them and stepped aside. Aaron kicked the door closed before he gently put Alex down.

"He didn't even give a look! I thought the generals would still frown upon this," Alex said. She playfully grabbed Aaron's tunic and pulled him to her. He took advantage of her closeness and kissed her passionately.

"Before, they would have, but we have tradition on our side."

"Tradition?" Alex asked.

"I led an army for six months to bring you home. It's rare, but in both Warren and Datten's history, when a prince saves his princess, it's expected she gives him her maidenhood even if they aren't married yet."

Alex smacked Aaron's shoulder, her nose pinched and her lips pursed. "That is ridiculous."

I knew you'd say that.

Aaron wrapped his arms around her and brought her back to him. "While I agree with you, for once tradition helps us. You've already brought me to your bed, but tomorrow, everyone will have expected it. So it's unnecessary for us to sneak around."

Alex reached up and kissed Aaron again. Her hand felt hot as it slipped into his, and she led him toward the stairs to their bedroom. When they reached the room, Aaron released her hand, leaned against the bedpost, and watched her. Quietly, she walked around the room and looked at all her things—the books, her bed, her doll.

You look lost.

"What are you thinking?"

Alex paused and turned toward him. "Everything feels strange and foreign. I don't know why."

Aaron strutted toward her, and she swallowed. He reached for her but stopped when her eyes grew larger. *You come to me. Nothing happens in here without you feeling completely safe.* He left his hand extended toward her and waited.

Alex looked at him for what felt like forever. Her cheek moved ever so slightly, and Aaron knew she was biting it, another one of her nervous habits. Finally she exhaled, watching his face as she moved toward him. Her hands slipped around his waist and pulled him to her. He dropped his hands and held her in his arms. Alex kissed him. It started gently, but the need behind it was clear. As Aaron's hands tightened around her, Alex gripped his shirt and pulled him against her. Desperate to hold her tightly, Aaron forced himself to slow down, softening his grip on her.

"Stop it. I'm not so fragile you'll break me," Alex said as she stared up at him, a frown on her lips.

"You look it."

Aaron started to tickle Alex's hips, but as he moved up to her back, she gasped and jerked away. Aaron stilled and watched her with concern.

"Why did you pull away from me? What happened to make my touch spark fear?"

"I—" She closed her mouth and looked down.

I can feel the love and desire coming off you, but you're scared. Why are you afraid of me?

"Is it me? Am I upsetting you? Should I leave?" Aaron stepped away, but Alex's head snapped up, and she grabbed his arm.

"No. Don't leave me. I—It's just—"

Alex clenched her hands and looked away again. Aaron moved toward her. He was slow and careful, worried she might run. She looked like a scared, trapped animal. He held his hands out to her, patiently waiting for her to come back to him. He was always gentle with her, but he needed to be even more gentle.

"What is it, my love?"

Tears started down her cheeks. "I'm not the same as when I left."

CHAPTER 44

ALEX

Alex looked at him, but he stared at her. Despite the battle and the journey, she knew he'd still be perfect. Nothing was different about him, but the long mirror at the side of the room showed her everything was different about her. Her breasts had shrunk along with the rest of her and were barely there. Where there had once been muscles, curves, and beauty, there were now sharp bones jutting through her skin. And the scars. Aaron had his arrow marks and the slice across his stomach, but her back was nothing but scars. There wasn't any part left that was her. And worst of all, she didn't know how many of them happened.

I don't even know who I am anymore. How can you love me when I don't even know who I am? I'm so scared you'll leave when you take off my dress. You're a prince. You deserve perfection, and I'm anything but.

Aaron took her face in his hands. He wiped her tears away with his thumbs, pulled her face to his, and kissed her. He was demanding in his kiss and rougher than he would usually be, but it sent a clear message to her. Alex closed the space and pulled his shirt over his head. She looked at his shoulder and stomach, and he smiled.

"Still there," he said. "I'm still me."

"I'm not," she whispered.

"I would love you no matter what happened, no matter what you look like," Aaron said, pressing his forehead to hers. "I fought to get you back, but I respect you too much to demand you give me what the men in my kingdom would think I'm owed. I'm yours as much as you're mine. I meant what I said. If you need time, you can have it."

"I need you to be my husband tonight. Even if you aren't yet." She closed her eyes and swallowed hard.

I need to feel connected to you. To know you still want me, that I don't disgust you after what I did today. Alex pulled Aaron to her and put his hands on her body, pressing him to grip her harder. Then she took a deep breath and looked at him.

"If I scream tonight, I want it to be because of you and not because I'm having a nightmare of being run through. If I'm exhausted tomorrow, I want it to be because I was up all night with my betrothed and not because I fought a war to get home to you. I'm going to have to learn to live with what happened today—what I did. We both are. But tonight, I need you to make me forget all of it. I need to be here with you. I spent six months thinking of nothing but you, and now I'm home. I get all of you ... I demand all of you."

Aaron pressed his lips to hers. "Then I'm yours. Tonight, tomorrow, and every night I have breath in my lungs."

"Then prove it," Alex whispered.

Aaron's grip on her tightened as he pulled her to him. In seconds, he'd ripped her corset ribbon from her dress, sending it to the floor. Alex trembled and tried to hide it, but Aaron's focus on her made it clear he knew. He ran his hands around her waist down to her tailbone. Alex tried to pull away from him, but he'd locked his hands on her. Alex closed her eyes as he gently turned her around and gasped. She sniffled, knowing he was looking at the mess of scar tissue and bruises on her back.

Please say something, anything. Don't leave.

Softly, he wrapped his arms around her and pulled her mangled back against his chest.

"I love you, imperfections and all. I promise you, one day it'll all be better, and you'll finally be able to stitch a handkerchief."

A laugh burst from Alex, followed by tears as he pulled her green handkerchief out of his pocket and held it out to her. She took it and dried her tears with it as he pressed his lips against her scarred shoulder and then moved his fingers to her neck.

"This is new." Gently, he traced the mark there.

"It's my Heart line mark."

"I love it." Aaron kissed her neck, making her moan softly. "Your body is perfect to me because it's yours. It shows your strength and your power, both of which helped you survive to come back to me."

"I don't know what happened to my back. The scars ... I think they whipped me, but I don't remember it."

"When you're ready, we'll talk about each scar and everything that happened there."

"Thank you. I need some time. There are parts I don't remember because Gryphon took some memories from me."

"He did what?" Aaron asked.

"He told me this morning to make me angry at him. I don't know how many memories or why, but I know he took part of the time there from me ... Maybe it's for the best."

"More likely he did it to hide something."

"Aaron, he helped me there. I can't have you hating him."

"It's hard. He enjoyed taunting me at every opportunity.

But you're home, so none of that matters because you have your family books. I'm sure there is a spell in there to get your memory back. After you're settled, you and Megesti can find it, and you'll remember everything and move on from it."

"All right. They can't be worse than slaying my uncle."

Alex rubbed the mark on her forearm as Moorloc's lifeless body flashed across her mind. *After what I did, am I even worthy of love, of happiness, of you?*

Alex shook the memory from her head and leaned in to kiss Aaron, but he scooped her up and carried her to the bed. As soon as he sat her down, Alex moved to Aaron's pants, deftly untying them with her eyes still locked onto his. After she'd removed them, she looked down and gulped. *I forgot how big it is.*

"I don't want you to be gentle," she murmured. "I want to feel it tomorrow so I don't have to feel other things." She looked up at him, her fingers tracing circles on his thigh.

Edging her further into the bed, Aaron nuzzled her neck. "I have no intention of having you only once tonight. The first time, I'll be gentle and behave myself in the manner befitting the betrothed of the Crown Princess of Warren. If after that you want me to allow the battle-hardened Prince of Datten into your bed ... Well, I can't be held responsible for what *he* does to you."

Alex raised herself on her elbows and watched him. *Your perfect blue eyes. Those have been in my dreams every night since I left.* Before she could think, he leaned down and kissed her softly. Aaron let her control the kiss, and she pulled him down on her. He draped himself across her body and playfully pulled on her bottom lip. She gasped and sucked in her breath when his fingers found their way between her spread legs. He barely touched her and already she was losing all sense and focus.

I'm safe. You love me. We're going to be okay.

Heat flooded her. Alex nudged her hips against Aaron's hand, and he understood what she wanted. He kissed her vigorously before moving to her neck. A loud moan escaped her lips when he softly bit her skin. His movements were clumsier than the last time, and Alex suspected he was trying to avoid her many bruises, but he knew the spot on her neck that mattered the most. Aaron had always been a master of finding it, even in the most embarrassing moments. When he found it and kissed it, Alex wove her hands through his hair and her body trembled.

"Aaron, please," she whimpered, begging for him. Aaron stilled and looked carefully at her face. When she smiled and nodded, he kissed her mouth, and he let her wrap her legs around him, bringing him into her.

Her body wanted him, needed him, but her mind couldn't focus. The horrors of the last two days flowed into her vision, and nothing she did would stop them.

Going slowly, Aaron thrust his hips into Alex's. With each movement, her body stretched to cling to him as tightly as on the night she'd given herself to him. He sighed softly when she gripped him.

Alex tried to focus on him, on them, on everything, but Alex tensed beneath Aaron when the pain in her back hit her the same moment as Gryphon's face moved across her mind.

Immediately, he froze. "Alex? Did I hurt you?"

Her breath sped up as she desperately shook her head to get rid of the memories.

"I can't. Aaron, I can't."

Aaron pulled back as she started to cry. He stumbled off the bed, pulled on his pants, and cautiously climbed back in beside her. Fighting the fears that were raging through her, Alex reached for him.

Please don't hate me for this. I want you, I really do, and I can't stop them. I can't stop everything from coming forward all at once.

Aaron took her hand and gently ran his hand along her arm.

"I'm sorry, I thought I could—I want to, I really do, but I can't. I can't stop seeing everything."

Aaron held his arms out to her, and she immediately fell into them, curling up against him.

"You have nothing to be sorry for. You tell me what you need."

"I don't want space. I want you here, but I ..."

"Tell me what you need, and I'll do it."

"I want you here. Holding me. I don't want to be alone." Alex looked up at him.

Aaron kissed her forehead and grabbed the blanket to wrap them both. "Then holding you is what I'll do."

"You aren't upset?"

"Why would I be upset? I'm yours for the rest of our lives. I'll wait as long as it takes for you to be ready—a day, a month, a year—it doesn't matter to me. I need to know you're safe, and if I'm allowed to hold you all night, then I'm more than satisfied."

Alex exhaled slowly and snuggled against Aaron. He held her close, and she gripped him to make sure he wouldn't leave.

"May I kiss you?" Aaron whispered his request into Alex's ear as he nuzzled as close to her as possible. The smell of pine and a forest morning threatened to overwhelm her.

"Yes, please." Alex smiled and moved her mouth to his.

CHAPTER 45

ALEX

Alex woke with a stark shaft of sunlight on her face. Soft blankets bound her limbs, and another body pressed against her naked lower half. She panicked, kicked, and screamed, trying to bolt and flee. Before she could escape, arms gripped her middle to keep her in the bed. Pine and dew hit her nose at the moment gentle kisses touched her shoulder and moved up to that one spot on her neck with precision. Alex moaned softly despite herself and turned to Aaron.

Aaron pressed his forehead to hers and whispered, "Morning, my love. You're in Warren, and you're safe."

When she smiled back, his smile took up his entire face.

"I'm not ready to get up yet," he said. "I want to spend my day curled up with you safe in my arms."

Alex sighed, her breath returning to normal. She snuggled into Aaron's arms as he pulled her back under the blankets. He tucked her hair behind her ear and kissed her softly.

She traced the arrow scar on his shoulder. "I missed you so much it hurt."

"I missed you so much I lost my mind," Aaron said. He

squeezed her tightly, sending warmth through her. "Did you read my journal?"

"Every day. I'm not sorry Gryphon stole it," Alex said.

"I read yours."

Alex sat up. "You have my journal?"

Aaron nodded. "Gryphon gave it to me. I understand now why pages were missing."

"He ripped out pages?"

"Several days' worth. Clearly, a lot of things happened he didn't want you to remember."

Alex opened her mouth to reply when a knock sounded on the stairs.

"Are you decent?" Michael's voice echoed up before he appeared on the stairs. "Your ladies have drawn you *another* bath. Apparently, you'll need another five or six baths before you smell like a princess again."

Alex groaned and pulled the blanket over herself, just then realizing she was completely naked.

"No one said being a princess would be easy," Aaron said. He slid out of bed and retrieved his shirt from the corner of the room where Alex had thrown it the night before.

Peeking out of the blanket, Alex said, "Aaron will need clothes."

"I've fetched Aaron's clothes." Michael held up the pile, and Aaron took them.

"Thank you, Michael. You can let the ladies know she'll be right down," Aaron said. Michael nodded and headed back down the stairs.

"So much for a quiet morning." Alex held her blanket across her breasts and leaned over to kiss Aaron.

"We have a lifetime of quiet mornings and loud nights ahead of us. You should get cleaned up and start things right with your ladies. I expect everyone will be wanting to catch up with you."

Alex whimpered and pulled the blanket over her head.

"I know you want to hide, but the people need to see you're back. Come out for a little. When it becomes too much, you can tuck your hair behind your ear, and we'll go for a ride. Deal?"

Alex shook her head.

"What?"

"If riding is still too much, will you bring me back here? We can read in bed, or you kiss me until I forget everything again."

A mischievous grin filled Aaron's face. "That I'll *always* agree to."

Alex dragged herself out of bed, threw on Aaron's second shirt, and hurried downstairs. Jessica and Edith both hugged her tightly before they forced her into the bath again. This time, both ladies insisted on staying and scrubbed her so long Alex had to reheat the water twice. Not until they deemed her clean was she allowed out of the bath. As they dressed her, she learned even her favorite green dress hung loosely on her.

Once Alex was ready, they brought her back to her receiving room where Aaron was waiting. Jessica and Edith asked her to come to the port.

I don't want to be around all those people.

Before she could reply, Stefan and Michael arrived, suggesting she come for a training round, something Alex was even less ready for. She knew they all meant well, but after months of being barely spoken to, all their love and attention was overwhelming.

Still smiling, she crept away. Michael noticed her expression, and she knew he could tell she was panicking. He stopped talking, stepping back to give her space, but neither Stefan nor the ladies noticed.

She looked at Aaron and tucked her hair behind her ear. He

nodded, and she cracked herself to the stable to get away from everyone. She leaned against one of the large beams to catch her breath.

"Your Highness?"

Alex looked up at him and froze. "Cameron."

Cameron bowed to her. "Welcome home."

"Thank you."

"You're hiding, aren't you?" Cameron asked as he hoisted up several feeding bags. Alex nodded and stepped aside so he could slip past her.

"Flash is down here."

Alex followed him to her horse. As soon as she found Flash, she couldn't help but smile. Cameron handed her a carrot, and she pet Flash while Cameron fed the other horses. Flash wouldn't stop nuzzling her, and Alex was content to stand silently and stroke him.

"I'm sorry about how we ended things. I didn't mean to hurt you," Alex said.

"I already forgave you. I blame Aaron and myself for how things ended. Anytime we talked, if Aaron came up, your face changed. I should have realized Aaron was the right choice for you," Cameron said.

"You believe that?" Alex turned to face Cameron, and he came up and took her hand in his.

"I do. None of your other suitors could have done what he did. I wouldn't have been able to drag a cavalry to Betruger Castle and convince the king to help us, let alone bring that army to the castle. I went along but only to keep the horses running."

"Horses are important."

"I know. No matter how things went down, you're still the Princess of Warren, and that makes you *my* princess. You'll forever have my loyalty, Alexandria. Though I'm never going to listen to Aaron."

"Why?"

Cameron laughed. "I only have to listen to Aaron in Datten."

"Did you know he had that side to him?" Alex asked.

Cameron went silent, pursing his lips. "Are you referring to what happened with Kruft?"

"Yes. I didn't think he had that in him," Alex said.

"I do when my temper gets triggered," Aaron said from the entrance of the stable. "Cameron."

Alex noticed Cameron took a step away from her.

"While rarely seen, your temper does damage. I didn't mean to overstep. We were talking," he said.

"Cameron, don't," Aaron said. "You're still a Baron of Warren—and one day, you will be an earl. You're going to be on Alex's council one day. Even if you outright plan to ignore me, I don't intend to control who her friends are, even if it's the Datten way."

Cameron grinned at Aaron. "You say that because our princess won't let you control her."

"True," Alex said, crossing her arms. She tried to smile at Aaron, but the weight of the previous day was hitting her. The slight tilt of his head made it clear he noticed her exhaustion.

"Apologies. We're going to have to skip the ride. Our fathers have asked that we deliver my mother from Datten. Apparently, she is livid at being left out of the dinner last night and wants to be here as soon as possible for the wedding tomorrow."

"Wedding?" Cameron's shock made Alex smirk.

"Lady Jessica and Sir Michael are getting married tomorrow," Alex said. "They wanted a simple wedding, and since the ladies were both here, they could prepare everything. My father agreed to pay for the entire thing because of the ties the Wafners have to Warren and me."

"And *my* father wouldn't be left out," Aaron added. "Not when the Wafner family is so important to Datten."

Cameron nodded to Alex. "You should go then. My aunt does not like to be kept waiting. I'll see to Flash personally."

She smiled at Aaron, and he took her hand and kissed it gently before she cracked them away to Datten.

CHAPTER 46
ALEX

The sunlight hit the windows, lighting the entire room with a sea of colors. Alex was in the back of the ceremonial hall trying to calm a nervous Jerome. Edith was busy straightening Jessica's beautiful wedding dress. Alex and Edith were dressed in simple golden gowns from Datten. Jessica was so excited she could barely contain herself. Alex peeked down the aisle. Michael looked so nervous he might pass out. Aaron and Stefan were trying to get him to sit down and drink something.

"I can't tell who's more nervous, your father or your husband-to-be!" Alex laughed.

Jessica peeked into the hall. "He looks nervous. Would you—"

Alex strutted up the aisle toward Michael. "Shooo." She waved Aaron and Stefan away and pulled Michael up. She turned him to face the back of the hall. "See that door? Jerome is trying to hold himself together, but your bride is the happiest I've ever seen her. Whatever goes wrong, it doesn't

411

matter. She can't wait to become your wife and spend her life at your side."

Michael beamed and hugged Alex. "Thank you." He took a deep breath. "I'm ready."

Alex winked at Stefan and Aaron and hurried back down the aisle, pausing long enough to shush Harold, who was laughing at Michael from the second row. A minute later, the musicians began. King Emmerich escorted Queen Guinevere down the aisle, and they sat on the bride's side. King Edward followed them, escorting Alex and Edith. Edith joined Harold and her father in the second row, and Alex and Edward took their places at the front on the right. The music changed, and the doors were reopened by Caleb and Julius. Lady Jessica and Jerome stepped in to make their entrance.

Her dress was exquisite. Queen Guinevere had it custom made in Datten as soon as Jessica had announced the engagement. It was simple but elegant—a classic Datten fitted silhouette with a beautiful long train and red and gold lace around the waist and edges to signify the colors of her home kingdom. It was identical to the dress Jessica's mother had worn when she married Jerome. Beaming, she made her way up the aisle to Michael.

Judge Wilhelm waited at the front. When Jerome arrived and gave Jessica's hand to Michael, the judge began the ceremony.

❧❧❧ ❧❧❧

AFTER THE WEDDING, they held a grand feast in the castle. Alex had insisted on holding it in the castle's royal hall as her and Aaron's gift to the new couple. Everyone ate and drank and enjoyed themselves, but the two newlyweds barely noticed.

They were too busy watching each other and being completely in love.

Alex smiled, watching her friends so happy together. She stood with her back pressed against the wall. The sheer number of people here made her nervous. For once, she'd wanted to wear one of her blue dresses to help her hide in the crowd of people, but Jessica had insisted on gold. Suddenly, a pair of strong arms slid around her waist from the side and squeezed tightly.

"Are you doing all right? We can leave if it's too much," said Aaron.

"No, I want to be here for them. It's their special day, and they want it to be full of family and friends. Whose idea was it to give Michael the Wafner name?"

"I wish I could take credit for that, but it was Jerome's. I made Michael my second for the trip, and he stayed by my side the entire time. He has the heart of a Wafner and deserved it." Aaron's chin rubbed against Alex's bare neck and collarbone. "Look over there."

Alex turned and spotted Harold talking to Edith and Julius. For once, the boisterous lady looked shy. When Harold held out his hand, Edith took it, giving Julius her glass. Alex smiled as Harold led Edith to the dance floor.

"Looks like we might have another wedding in our future," Aaron teased as they watched the pair dance.

"Will you gift Edith a gold tea set too?"

Aaron smirked and kissed Alex's cheek. "She told you about that?"

"She did. Apparently, her sisters loved them."

"How would you feel about Harold and Edith together? Betruger men worship their wives."

"I'd be happy with that. Your Edward with my lady's maid."

"And on the other side, your part-guard best friend and your other lady's maid. I don't think we could have asked for a better pair," Aaron said.

"Even better—the sister of my head guard."

Aaron laughed. "And my general's daughter. Did you like your father's surprise?"

"I did. I can't believe he had Verlassen Castle fixed up while we were gone."

"He wanted you to have a home for us to go to. Somewhere quiet where you can hide and adjust to life as a princess at your own pace. Someplace to call our own for the time being."

Alex giggled and covered her mouth.

"What?"

"I think he doesn't want us in the bedroom next to his."

Aaron blushed as he kissed her. "It isn't my fault you're loud."

"Sometimes it is," Alex said. She bit her lower lip and gazed up at Aaron.

Aaron pulled Alex to him. "In nine months, it'll be our turn. Royal weddings take so long to set up."

"It's fine. I'd marry you a hundred times if your mother asked us to."

"Don't give her any ideas!" Aaron laughed. "I still can't believe you wouldn't give in to your father's request to have us married already."

"Your mother deserves a proper wedding from us. It's the only one she'll get. Two, technically. Besides, I want to be healthy for our wedding, not this diluted version of myself," Alex said.

Aaron squeezed her tightly. "I love every version of you."

"I know. But I want to feel like myself on my wedding day." She kissed Aaron and let him pull her onto the dance floor to join their friends.

EPILOGUE
GRYPHON

Gryphon slammed the book shut.

"High Ares! Another dead end." He leaned back in the chair and popped his neck before rubbing the back of it with his hand. He hoisted the massive ancient text and carried it past two rows of bookcases that went from the floor practically to the ceiling. He reshelved the book and walked to the next row to peruse the stacks. The Head's library was the largest in the Forbidden Lands, probably in all of Torian as well. It was overflowing with books and journals from the very gods and sorcerers who founded the lines in addition to previous Heads, titans, and exceptionally gifted sorcerers. A loud, animalistic growl erupted from his chest.

"Millennia of knowledge from every line and not one mention of a sorcerer's eyes flashing black." He smacked his hand into the books on the shelf before him, sending them flying to the floor. He was losing control of his frustration as it turned into fiery anger. He had to get out of the library. While all the books were enchanted to be protected from the powers of every line, his mother would be furious at the mess his explosive temper would leave.

I don't know why she gets so angry at me for my temper. It's from my maternal line. I got Ares from her and my hexa, Eris.

He sidestepped the books on the floor and headed to the opposite side of the library. The other side housed the Head's laboratory where there were shelves upon shelves of plants, herbs, powders, and potions. They even had the last few dragon ingredients left in the world: a handful of scales, two teeth, a vial of tears, and a single dragon's heart flower—the rarest and most prized plant in all the Forbidden Lands. At the end of the shelves was an enormous fireplace large enough to boil three cauldrons at the same time.

The final wall was covered in weapons—swords, whips, bows, and a few maces. Most of them were forged from red steel. In the past, they'd been used to punish those who stepped out of line or offended the Head. Now, they rested, unused. Few had dared to question Garrick, a sixth-generation Head. His father preferred a more public form of brutality, often slaughtering the entire family of those who stepped out of line. Once, he'd executed his closest friend for merely questioning him in front of the other titans. No one had ever questioned him again.

Between the book aisles and the fireplace sat a massive table that was a tree grown into the shape of a table. Those with exceptional Celtic powers were called upon to grow and shrink it as the Head needed. The table served both as a reading desk for the library and as a workstation for the lab. Gryphon grabbed his royal blue robe off the end of the table where he'd abandoned it after he arrived. Since he'd left the human lands, he'd taken to wearing his blue robe, which bore the mark of Mystics. Whenever he looked at his orange robe, he couldn't help but think of Alexandria.

Thinking of her hurts, and I won't risk my parents finding out about her.

The door opened, and familiar footsteps padded toward him. "Hello, Lynx," he said without turning around.

"I thought I'd find you here. You've practically lived here for the last three months."

He turned to face the gorgeous, curvy sorceress before him. Lynx's dirty blonde hair and sandy skin sparkled in the firelight, but her rich brown eyes threatened to penetrate his defenses. Like Birch, she possessed the unique ability to see through his lies. She even claimed she could smell his deceptions. Her marks were an outline of a fox head and a leaf: Tiere and Celtics. Tiere sorcerers were gifted with the best qualities of the animal world in addition to being able to communicate with them.

"I enjoy research," Gryphon grumbled.

"Not *this* much," Lynx said.

"Why are you here?"

"I haven't seen you in some time, so I came to the court to visit you."

"Which means Birch sent you to find out what was going on."

"Of course." Lynx smiled disarmingly and looped her arm through Gryphon's. "You might not really be my little brother, but you're the closest I have, so talk."

But before Gryphon could say anything, a burn shot through their marks.

"We'll talk after the summoning," Gryphon said and cracked them into the throne room.

His father's throne room was circular. In the center sat a dais with two large thrones, and leading from them were ten long rugs. Each rug was the color of one of the ten lines and led to a door made of solid stone. Each door was a different type of stone and had a line mark ornately carved into it. If one opened a door, it would lead to the territory of the line depicted on the door.

The Head's castle was built in the exact center of all ten territories. Doors on the outside of the castle took sorcerers directly to the throne room, ensuring they would never unintentionally enter the other parts of the castle. On the rare occasion someone would be invited into the private areas, an entrance would appear, and they could enter the Head's private abode, the part that should have been home but felt more like a prison to Gryphon.

Portraits of the previous Heads lined the walls. Only one painting contained a sorceress—the generation where the Heart and Head, Tabitha and Grindal, ruled together.

Gryphon looked around. Today, the room was more crowded than normal. That usually meant his father was upset about something, so people were hoping for a show. Gryphon raised an eyebrow at Lynx, but she shrugged. She'd covered her simple dress with a formal dark green robe, signifying her status as Titan of Tiere, the position his mother had given up to bond with his father.

Gryphon was happy Lynx had been made titan. She and Birch were the only titans with the ability to think for themselves rather than blindly obeying his father. But Gryphon also knew it was their connection to him, his mother, and his hexa that kept them somewhat safe from Garrick's temper.

Lynx and Gryphon stayed behind the older sorcerers as one of his father's guards cracked into the room and approached the throne with a hooded figure.

Garrick sat on his throne and, as usual, appeared disinterested. He was tall and muscular with the same obsidian hair as Gryphon, but his streak was gray. His marks, a flame and a moon, sat low on his neck, and his gold eyes glowed like flames as he cocked his head to look at the hooded man before him. The guard shoved him hard enough that he stumbled and landed on his knees, sending his hood back and revealing his face.

Lygari! Sweat poured down Gryphon's back as he cursed under his breath.

Lynx grabbed his hand. "What is it? Do you know him?"

Gryphon glanced at her wide-eyed before he shifted his gaze to his father.

"Who is this treacherous sorcerer, and why is he in my throne room?" Garrick stood and stalked toward Lygari. The Head looked over the scrawny Merlin sorcerer. "What is your name? Where are your marks? From whom are you descended?"

The sorcerers around Gryphon snickered and whispered to each other. Lygari trembled in fear as he looked up at the Head.

"Speak!" Garrick roared.

If he loses his temper, my father might kill him before he talks. Then he'd take the secret of Alex's location with him.

Lygari shook violently as he stood and opened his mouth. "Lygari, son of Moorloc, son of Hermes, son of—"

"Merlin," Garrick finished.

"He lies! The descendants of Merlin vanished nearly a century ago. They're lost."

Lynx and Gryphon turned to see who had shouted, but they couldn't see over all the sorcerers.

"Silence!" Garrick ordered. "Lost does not mean dead."

Gryphon swallowed while his father glared at Lygari. The room became silent as a tomb as the current Head eyed his prey, arms crossed.

"Based on your coloring, you're clearly Moorloc's son—so what are you exactly? Half? What brings a sad, weak half sorcerer here?"

"I bring you the location of the Heart ..." he started. Immediately, a murmur went through the crowd, and he had to raise his voice to be heard. "The location of the Heart in exchange for permission to remain in the Forbidden Lands!"

"There isn't a Heart this generation," yelled a voice from the crowd.

"We would have sensed him," another shouted.

Lord Garrick laughed, yanking Lygari's arm up and revealing the mark of three *x*'s. "You bear the traitor's mark. Why would I believe you?"

"Kill him," Gryphon shouted, and Lynx looked at him, horrified.

"I have the memories to prove I know the Heart," Lygari said.

"Then tell us your tale, and I'll decide if you're worth sparing," Garrick said as he sat back on his throne.

"My father was Moorloc. He fled with his twin brother, Merlock, and their sister, Victoria. My aunt was killed twelve years ago by mortals."

Gryphon noticed his father's hands grip the throne tighter at the mention of Alex's mother.

"My cousin serves the King of Datten. My father and uncle both died the day I escaped. My uncle sacrificed himself for my cousin—Victoria's daughter. She murdered my father."

"So your cousin is the Heart? If he is, then why does he serve mortals?"

"No, my king. My cousin Alexandria is the Heart. She is half mortal and the Crown Princess of Warren."

"My son won't fear half sorceresses." Garrick laughed.

"She's a daughter of Merlin."

"That means nothing!" Garrick drummed his fingers on his throne. "Kill him!"

The guard moved, but Lygari threw his arms up, begging for mercy.

"No! Merlock took her place in the hereafter to fulfill his oath to Victoria. Alexandria carries the powers of all of them—of Hermes, of Merlin, and of Cassandra."

Garrick froze. He stood and stormed toward Lygari. Gryphon grimaced at Lynx before he moved toward the center of the crowd.

"The Heart is a child of Merlin, a daughter of Cassandra, and a Returned One?"

"Yes, my king. Her mother was the most powerful of our line and—"

"Do not speak to me of Victoria!" Garrick bellowed, and Lygari trembled.

"The girl ... she's been trained. A sorcerer named Gryphon helped her. He protected her from my father."

Gryphon cursed under his breath. He clenched his fists at his side and swallowed hard before masking his terror with the cocky grin he was known for.

Garrick's eyes flashed blue. "Khoran! Gryphon!" Garrick roared, coming down the last few stairs.

A tall, gangly sorcerous in a smoky gray titan robe moved slowly through the crowd as it parted. Their ghostly pale neck bore the glowing mark of a grave, and they rubbed their hands together as they came toward Garrick with their head bowed low.

"What wish you of me, my Head?" Khoran asked.

"Does this sorcerer speak the truth? Did a sorcerer sacrifice himself for the last daughter of Cassandra?"

"Yes."

"Why was I not informed?"

"My Head, I didn't wish to bother you with all the trivial things in the underworld."

"Gryphon, what do you know about this? Is what this traitor says true?" Garrick hollered.

Gryphon stepped out from the crowd he'd been hiding in. Lynx's hand brushed his arm to stop him, but he shook her off. The surrounding sorcerers backed away from him. Garrick's wrath at Gryphon was known to make him lash out at others.

"You!" Lygari shouted, pointing to Gryphon. "You're the one who helped her—helped free her from my father's grasp!"

Garrick whipped around to face his son, eyes ablaze. "So that is where you kept vanishing to."

An older sorceress in an orange robe stepped from the crowd near Garrick. Her gray hair hung loosely on her shoulders. He crossed his arms and stared back at his hexa. Nothing he said or did would calm Eris's temper at this point, and he'd learned ages ago to accept his punishment where she was concerned. Her eyes flashed orange as she glared at him in disappointment and rage.

"Show me her face." Garrick rushed toward Lygari and slammed his palm onto the young sorcerer's forehead. Lygari winced, and a ghostly image of Alex appeared in the room, making the sorcerers gasp.

"That is her, my Head," Khoran said, shifting Gryphon's focus off of Alex's image. "Her soul was sent back twice. Once when she was young and again as we accepted Merlock in her place. Merlock performed the transference spell, and as she is the last of her line, her ancestors transferred the power of her lines to her."

Garrick was incredulous. "Returned twice? Which ancestors?"

Khoran swallowed. "All of them. Every sorcerer and sorceress in her lineage transferred their power to her."

Garrick looked at his son. "Gryphon, what did you do?"

"Fulfilling my destiny, just not the one you wanted for me."

"What of the traitor?" the guard asked.

Garrick glanced at Lygari. "Lock him up until I make my decision. I may find some use for him. And you ..." His eyes flashed blue as he snarled at Gryphon.

Eris cleared her throat, and Garrick turned. She leaned toward him and whispered. Gryphon strained to hear, but the room was too loud with the excited chatter from the other sorcerers.

"We will discuss this in private with your mother in attendance," his hexa said, crossing her arms over her robe before she cracked away.

Lynx caught his attention. She shook her head at him with fear on her face, but Gryphon waved and cracked to the lab. When he arrived, his mother was there arguing with his hexa about the prophecy of a green-eyed witch destroying the Ares line.

A sharp pain erupted in his head, and everything went black.

Keep going for a sneak peek at book 3, The Heir Rises, now available for pre-order.

Sign up for Alice's newsletter now to get access to extra scenes and character interviews, along with a FREE ebook of the series prequel, The Spare who Became the Heir and Other Stories: The Early Adventures of the Head, the Heart, and the Heir

NEED MORE OF TORIAN?

If you enjoyed the book be sure to leave a review since they are a huge help to indie authors like me! They can even just be a few words that you enjoyed the book!

Join the Facebook Fan group to engage with other fans and get fun updates from Alice!

Sign up for the monthly newsletter!

Support Alice on Patreon and get early or exclusive access to things.

TORIAN TIMELINE

Sorcerers Arrive	No one Knows
Founding of Datten	year 0
Founding of Warren	50
Founding of six Southern Kingdoms	50-100
Merlock & Victoria arrive in Datten	1469
Megesti is born	1483
Arthur of Warren is born	1484
Gryphon is born	1488
Emmerich of Datten is born	1503
Edward of Warren is born	1510
King Emmerich is crowned King of Datten	1516
Prince Daniel of Datten is born	1522
Prince Aaron of Datten is born	1530
Princess Elizabeth of Warren (Alex) is born	1533
Princess Elizabeth vanishes	
Princess Victoria is murdered	
Prince Daniel is killed	1538
Princess Alex returns to Warren	1552

KINGDOMS
DATTEN

Motto: Honor above All

Royal Family
King Emmerich (1503–)
Queen Guinevere (1504–)
Dead Prince Daniel (1521–1538)
Prince Aaron (1530–)

House of Wafner
Jerome (General of Datten) and dead Lady Gwendalin
Seven children: Patrick (Stefan), Jessica, dead Ryan, Arthur, Samuel, Olivia, and David

House of Merlock
Merlock: royal sorcerer and king's advisor
Megesti: sorcerer apprentice and Merlock's son

DATTEN

THE FIRST KING
OF DATTEN

THE FIRST QUEEN
OF DATTEN

PRINCE DANIEL
OF WARREN

PRINCESS ELFRIEDA

32 Generations

KING DANIEL

KING ALARIC

EMMERICH

GUINEVERE

BERNHARD
STROBEL

ELFRIEDA
BISHOP

CAMERON

DANIEL
First born

AARON
Second born

KINGDOMS
WARREN

PROSPERITY THROUGH COURAGE

Motto: Prosperity through Courage

Royal Family
King Edward (1509–)
Dead Princess Victoria (1451–1538)
Princess Elizabeth aka Alex (1533–)

House of Nial
Randal (General of Warren) and Lady Judith
Three daughters: Abigail, Diana, and Edith

House of Bishop
Matthew (retired general) and Lady Lillian
Three sons: Marco, Aiden, and Julius

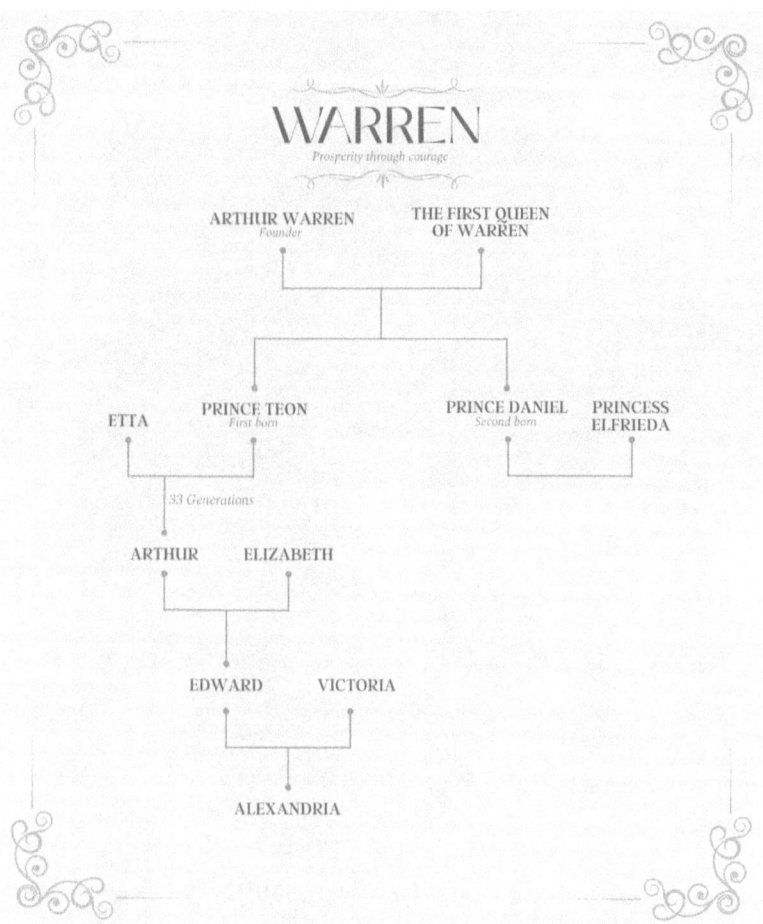

KINGDOMS

BETRUGER

LEGACY NEVER DIES

ALICE HANOV

Motto: Legacy Never Dies

Royal Family
King Harold (1525–)

House of Macht
Bruno (Head Guard of Betruger)

SORCERERS OF TORIAN

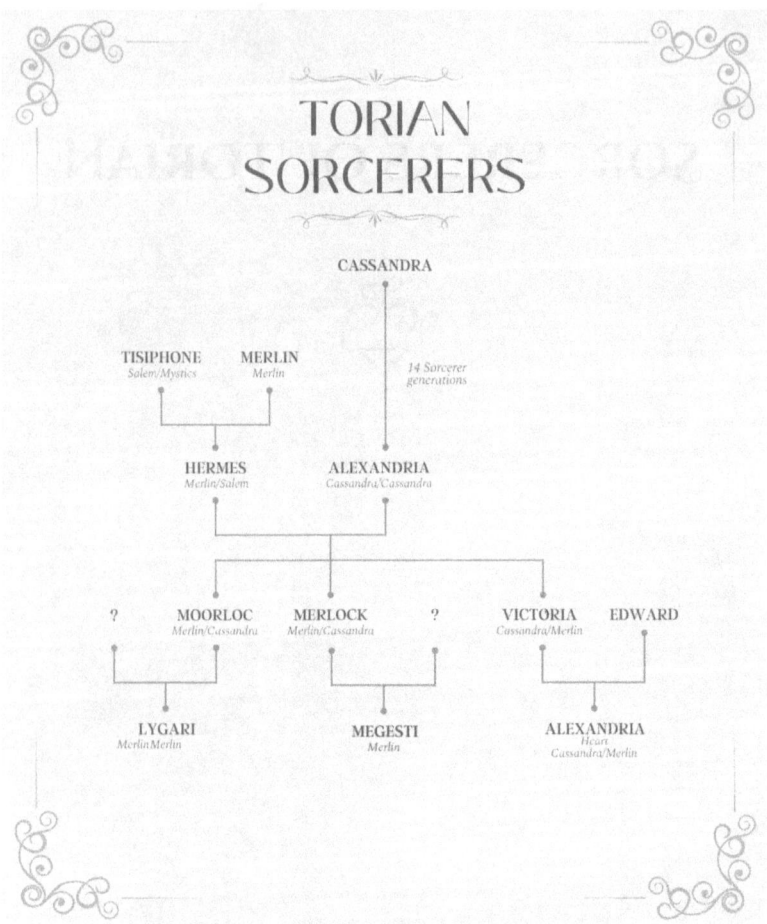

TORIAN SORCERERS

CASSANDRA

TISIPHONE
Salem/Mystics

MERLIN
Merlin

14 Sorcerer generations

HERMES
Merlin/Salem

ALEXANDRIA
Cassandra/Cassandra

?

MOORLOC
Merlin/Cassandra

MERLOCK
Merlin/Cassandra

?

VICTORIA
Cassandra/Merlin

EDWARD

LYGARI
Merlin/Merlin

MEGESTI
Merlin

ALEXANDRIA
Heart
Cassandra/Merlin

ARES

- orange
- chaos and violence

CASSANDRA

- gold
- healing and premonitions

CELTICS

- light green
- plants and peace

HADES

- grey
- death related

MERLIN

- violet
- varies

MIRE

- brown
- earth powers

MYSTICS

- royal blue
- mind control

POSEIDON

- dark blue
- water and weather

SALEM

- maroon
- fire and explosions

TIERE

- dark green
- animal powers

HEAD

- one of two strongest born in a generation
- logic ruled

HEART

- other strongest born in a generation
- emotional ruled

PRONUNCIATION GUIDE

Ares: Air-ease
Bernhard: Burn-hart
Betruger: Beh-true-grrrr
Cassandra: Cas-an-draw
Celtic: Kel-tick
Datten: Day-ten
Eris: Air-iss
Ferflucs: Fair-flooks
Garrick: Gair-ick
Hades: Hay-dees
Hexa: Hex-ah
Hexen: Hex-en
Imelda: Im-elle-da
Lygari: Le-garh-ee
Kharon: Care-on
Kirsh: Keersh
Kruft: Krufft
Macht: Maakht
Merlin: Mer-lin

Merlock: Mer-lock
Mire: Mirr-ah
Moorloc: More-lock
Mystics: Myst-ics
Nial: Nai-uhl
Ogre: O-grah
Oreean: Or-ian
Poseidon: Poe-sigh-done
Rassgat: Ras-gat
Reinhilde: Rine-hill-da
Salem: Say-lem
Tiere: Teer-rah
Torian: Tore-ian
Warren: War-en

GLOSSARY

Betrayer: term used for a sorcerer who tries to kill or severely wound their own family. Appears as three *x*'s stacked on top of each other on the left inner forearm.

Bond marks: a mark that a mated pair of sorcerers share. Each is unique, made up of their line marks, and can appear on the back of either shoulder or neck.

Hexa: sorcerer grandmother.

Hexen: sorcerer grandfather.

Line marks: images used to show the ten sorcerer lines.

Magician: insult that implies a person has no power as all human "magicians" were frauds.

Pearls: magical spheres that show the past (clear), present (white), and future (black).

Returned one: a sorcerer who dies but is brought back.

Sorcerer line: also known as a line, this is the legacy of sorcerers born from a founding sorcerer. For example, the line of Merlin includes all Merlin sorcerers born from him with Merlin powers.

Sorcerer awakening: a time in a sorcerer's life when they go through puberty and subsequently receive their powers and learn which line they are.

Sorcerer: sorcerer who identifies as male.

Sorceress: sorcerer who identifies as female.

Sorcerous: sorcerer who identifies as neither male nor female, nonbinary.

Titan: strongest sorcerer of a particular line.

Usurper: a special sorcerer born every two or three generations who can borrow or siphon the power of sorcerers around them. Only one can ever be alive at a time.

Witch: insult that implies a person has no power as all human "witches" were frauds.

The Spare Who Became the Heir and Other Stories
The Head, the Heart, and the Heir
Broken Sons
The Heir Rises
The Last True Heirs
Book 5 - coming late 2024
Book 6 - coming 2025
Book 7 - coming 2025

Extended Omnibus Kickstarter
Volume 1 - May 2024
Volume 2 - February 2025
Volume 3 - November 2025

A NOTE FROM THE AUTHOR

When I started writing this series, I was intending to write a YA epic fantasy, but my characters had other ideas.

The themes and tropes that are developing as the story carries on, especially book 3 and on are of a much more adult level than originally expected. So in order to be true to the characters and meet reader expectations I'm aging everyone up 2 years.

So if you read this before March 15, 2024 the characters would have been younger than they are in this edition. A detailed breakdown is on my website if you need to visually see what happened.

Thank you for your understanding.

Alice

ACKNOWLEDGMENTS

This book has been another journey for me, and I am so happy to have had all these amazing people along for the adventure!

Once again, I thank my husband, Steve, and our children, Lillian, Katrina, and Zack. I follow my dream because of them, and some days they believe in me more than I do.

To my mom, Elke, and stepdad, Al, I want to say thank you for letting me be as weird and crazy as I wanted to be throughout high school and teaching me that being different is great. Also, thanks for letting me hang out with my friends so much that their craziness rubbed off on me even more.

To my Oma Elfrieda in Germany, thank you for giving me a typewriter when I visited in the summer when I was seven. You allowed me to write all the stories in my head and helped to start me on this journey.

To my amazing online BookTok and Bookstagram friends, thank you for bringing a smile to my face and giving me a safe place to vent and talk books and cry when needed.

To my fantastic author friends I found online, you are shining lights in my dark days. You understand the pain and loneliness that comes with writing and also laugh and share stories about the craziest things we have had to Google! Nikki, Tiffany, Amanda, Sonja, Penelope, Ruby, Rosalyn, Laura, Bekah, Jillian, Lynn, and countless more—you all make writing so much more enjoyable!

I also want to thank my ARC readers and my street team for

taking a chance on my first book and helping to get my book out there! I hope you'll be back for this one!

Along with the beta team, I want to thank my alpha readers, Andrea Hernandez and Christine Hutton. Thank you for your enthusiasm, encouragement, and your love for my characters, my world, and my story.

Thank you to my brilliant artists who helped my line marks and characters come to life! Casey (of RallyBirdBrand), your work is fantastic, and your series and sorcerer marks are just perfect! I love that I got to use them as chapter headings too. Hoang Tejieng, your renderings of my characters helped bring them to life for me, and I love having them around me to help inspire me.

To my author critique group, Stephanie Joyce and Amanda Terry Hamm, you two understand me in a way that is shocking, and despite my crazy energetic antics, you stick around. I appreciate you more than I could ever say, so instead I will continue to mail you random bookmarks, chocolate, and other randomness, because together we WILL conquer the world.

To my photographer, Brittany Nosal, I have never had so much fun on a photo shoot, and I cannot thank you enough for helping bring the true me out in my photos. You gave me photos that are professional enough for my work but still have a whimsical air about them.

I also want to take a moment to thank the team of Intrepid Literary (same company but fancy new name).

Lauren, you are the most enthusiastic boss I have ever met, and I love it. Every time we have a meeting, I'm so excited and it just makes my day. Thank you for being so amazing and helping me achieve my dream but also for having the same energy and excitement for my books as I do.

Shannon and Brooke, you two are so amazing. I can't thank you enough for helping keep all my work on track and making sure we don't miss anything! I did scheduling for fifteen years, so I know how hard it is to juggle all this. You are MARVELS!

Sam, my amazing developmental editor! You made me love editing and editors in a way I never thought would be possible! Thank you for being as in love with my world as I am and for always pushing me to improve my story.

Jackie, you are just as amazing at line edits as you were in grammar fixes on book one. Thank you for taking on the challenge of line editing my book and being so careful about my feelings, even when I didn't mind if you roughed up my book a bit.

Ariane, I can't thank you enough for keeping my book in line with the previous and being so patient with my terrible use of commas. They are like sprinkles—you can't have too many, unless you want to have proper English.

To my cover designers, Alan and Ian, I cannot thank you enough for my gorgeous cover! Thank you for working with me and helping this cover fit with the first but not take away from what will be my proper series covers!

S. E., you are not just my Senior Editor but my Super Editor. Thank you for being part of this amazing milestone and helping me sort out things when it got to be too much!

LAST, THANK YOU, MY READERS. WITHOUT YOU, I WOULDN'T BE ABLE TO DO THIS. SO THANK YOU!

About the Author

Photo by Brittany Jean Photography

Alice Hanov was born in Germany and then raised on Pelee Island in the middle of one of the Great Lakes, spending her days imagining grand adventures in the woods around the island. She has never stopped writing and has a degree in rhetoric and professional writing from the University of Waterloo. Alice lives in Ontario with her hubby and three kids, various pets, and many, many books.

You can visit her online at alicehanov.com.

Read on for a sneak peek of

THE HEIR RISES

by

Alice Hanov

The third instalment
in *The Head, the Heart, and the Heir* series

**Gryphon
Press**

ALEX

Blood, sweat, and death. Alex closed her emerald green eyes and inhaled deeply, hoping to replace the stench that memory always brought. The details of the battle they'd survived—the one that had brought her home—haunted her even now. Moorloc's bloodied face flashed in her mind, and the betrayer's mark on her arm burned even as the cool summer night air kissed her skin.

She smelled earth, pine, and flowers—the comforting smells of summer in Torian's Dark Forest.

Alex opened her magic well and her eyes, ready for her training.

It took her a moment to adjust to the darkness in the clearing where Stefan and Michael had left her. Once she did, she realized she was near her castle.

Didn't even bother to go beyond walking distance? Either you aren't expecting me to put up a proper fight, or you don't want to hobble back when I'm through with you.

She smiled mischievously and tossed her chestnut brown braid over her shoulder. She listened for her attackers, but all she heard was the wind blowing through the trees. As a cloud blocking the moon moved on, the clearing lit up, and for the briefest moment, a glimmer flashed across the grass.

Found you!

Straightening her back and core, Alex twisted her hips and thrust her arms straight out. Soundlessly, vines slithered away from her toward the surrounding trees and returned with a chest plate. A loud bang resounded behind her. She feigned turning toward it and then pivoted in the opposite direction in time to see a blast of fire coming her way.

Flames raced across the ground, encircled her, and erupted upward. As they crackled around her, Alex turned toward the forest where the attacking sorcerer was grinning at her.

"Nice job, Megesti," she shouted. "Our practice is paying off."

Water, wind, or earth? Which will keep you down? Before she could decide, an arrow flew past her hip.

Michael.

Alex dropped her hands and flicked her fingers, drawing water from the air to douse the surrounding flames. A second arrow flew past. Her entire body illuminated with gold light as she turned toward the archer.

"*Ferflucs!*"

Stefan coughed, a trick Alex knew he'd use to mask his laughter. Since she'd returned home, her temper rarely set things on fire. Instead, it made her glow gold like a torch in the halls. It was dangerous for her to glow every time she got angry, so, as her faithful friends and protectors, Stefan and Michael were helping her manage her temper and Megesti was helping her try various remedies from their family journals to keep her from glowing.

Megesti. Despite having become the Titan of Merlin eight months ago when they freed Alex from Moorloc, Megesti hadn't once glowed violet. As much as it annoyed her, Alex understood that at sixty-eight, Megesti had more experience; he controlled his powers. Alex's powers still controlled her.

Around them, the woods came to life as the night animals began their evening routines. A fox cried, sending its prey scattering, while an owl welcomed the night with its questioning *who*. The sounds would serve as a convenient distraction.

Alex was ready for Michael's next arrow. She threw her arms up, and her wind sent his arrow off course. She squatted and brushed the grass with her fingers so the scorched earth became lush and green again. Scanning the tree line, she'd figured out where Michael and Megesti were, but Stefan was still hidden. He was always good at staying out of her line of sight.

Alex sent a breeze through the trees in different directions until the smell of musk hit her.

Got you.

She lowered herself to the ground, and all at once, the three of them attacked. They'd realized she'd found them and thwarted her attempt to grab them with vines. Michael shot another arrow, but Alex deflected it with the same wind she used to send Megesti's next blast back at him. She followed the wind with water, dousing the flames that grabbed Megesti's cloak. She spun and found Stefan behind her with his sword out.

Alex knew he'd wait for her to draw hers. Wiggling her fingers over the hilt, she focused on the blade Aaron had picked out for her from Datten's collection. It had belonged to Emmerich before he'd become King of Datten, a fact he delighted in telling her anytime she wore it around him.

She unsheathed her blade, gripped the hilt with both hands, and stared at Stefan. Her golden glow illuminated his pale face and fiery hair. He stalked toward her with an intense smile, his brows drawn together.

"Brothers." Alex shook her head as she stepped back to circle him.

Behind her, Michael laughed, and Stefan's smile grew larger.

He enjoys beating me, but he won't today!

Alex and Stefan circled one another until she was ready. She opened her well again, and her soft glow became a blinding light. Stefan groaned and shielded his eyes, and Alex leaped into action. She charged him and smashed her blade into his. Stefan's grip was stronger than hers, having been built for battle, so even one-handed, he didn't drop the sword. So Alex dealt the low blow Michael had taught her. She kicked him in the knee, and he cried out. His sword landed in the grass with a dull thud.

"I surrender," Stefan said, holding his hand up.

Alex's chest heaved. It was rare she won, so Stefan giving in so easily surprised her, but then a vine grabbed her ankle, and she slammed into the ground, the wind knocked out of her.

"You forgot about us," Michael said, walking over with Megesti.

Her sword lay in the grass, just out of reach. Michael looked down at her, and his messy black hair almost covered his blue eyes. He drew his bow and aimed at her chest. Lowering the flat arrowhead, he gently tapped her forehead.

"We win tonight."

Alex groaned and covered her face with her arms.

"Don't be discouraged, Alex. You did great," Stefan said as he stood. He held out his hand, and when Alex took it, he pulled her off the ground with a single tug.

"That wasn't great. I should be better." *Stronger, faster, more … me.*

Michael dropped his hand to her shoulder, and Alex felt her golden glow fade as a feeling of safety filled her.

"They starved and tortured you for six months. You've only been home eight." Michael's tone was curt but soft. "Your father's physician made it clear—*at least* two to three months of healing for every month you were there. Stop being so hard on yourself."

"It took you years to learn your fighting skills the first time," Stefan said, slipping his arm around her. "Why do you expect yourself to master these new skills so quickly?"

Alex looked at each of them. "Because I won't be that vulnerable again."

"You won't have to," Megesti said. "Our uncle is dead, and we have the family journals now. We'll keep learning to wield our powers, and you'll get better. Little by little."

Alex sighed. *I know you mean well, Megesti, but it's not the same learning alone. It's harder and takes longer. I wish Gryphon were here.*

"All right, I think it's time to head back for bed," Stefan said, ushering her toward home.

Alex crossed her arms as they headed across the clearing.

Verlassen Castle wasn't huge, but it was the perfect place for Alex to hide from everything while sorting out her powers and dealing with the aftermath of her time at Moorloc's castle. Upon her return, she'd tried to stay in Warren, but there were ... mishaps. Too many people watching her while she struggled to adjust to life outside Moorloc's control. While she'd been gone, her father, King Edward, had the royal builders repair her mother's castle and even made a few additions. Now, it was as beautiful as it had been all those years ago. Her father had suggested she come here, and for the past eight months, this had been her home.

The builders kept the tree that had broken through the hall

alive, and it now grew in the small courtyard. The broken ceilings were all fixed, and they'd remade the library shelves. It was everything Alex ever could have dreamed of. However, besides new bedding and cushions in her favorite color, her mother's room was unchanged. The predominant colors of Warren were silver and blue, but there was a lesser used green, and Edward had proclaimed that since Alex hated blue, everything given to the crown princess must be Warren green.

The large hall was her second favorite room. There was no evidence of the vortex that had almost cost Stefan and Aaron their lives. That history was long ago, and all of that damage was now erased. The walls were covered in paintings, new and old. Those depicting Moorloc had been destroyed. Her favorite painting had been gifted by Aaron's mother, Guinevere; it was Datten's copy of the last painting made of Alex with her parents before her mother died. Seeing it made Alex smile and reminded her how fiercely her mother loved her. Aaron's favorite part of the painting was how regal her parents looked while Alex's expression was the scowl of a furious little girl who hated the blue dress they had forced her into.

They crossed the moat to the castle, and Alex stopped at the main doors. "I'm going to check on Flash. You three head inside."

Stefan said, "I'll have your food sent to your room."

"I'm fine, Stefan."

"I'm still having food sent. You're supposed to eat a little all throughout the day since you can't handle full meals."

Alex stuck her tongue out at him. She'd never admit it, but having Stefan and Michael fuss over her was nice and felt like home.

She walked around the perimeter to the small stable attached to the castle. Edward had extended the moat and kept most of the horses in stables on the other side. Flash,

Thunder, Elm, and a handful of other guard horses were kept nearer the castle. There was a door that connected the castle to the stable, but Alex took the longer outside route and nodded at Julius, who was making rounds. When she arrived, she slipped silently through the small side door used by her stable master.

Aaron was standing between Flash's and Thunder's stalls, holding a carrot out to each of them. His golden hair sparked against his pinkish skin. No matter how much time he spent outside, he never tanned. Alex snuck up behind him, wrapped her arms around his waist, and kissed his back.

"Hello, my love," Aaron said.

"What are you doing hiding in the stables?"

"Waiting for your training to end. I was hoping you'd be up for a night ride. We've both been so busy this week, the only time we spend together is in our bed sleeping or doing other things."

"You mean *my* bed. Your room is on the second floor."

Aaron chuckled and turned around. He cupped Alex's face and kissed her. The scent of pine, dew, and hay nearly overwhelmed her. Gripping his hips, she pulled him closer to deepen their kiss.

"I may have my own room in your castle, but I haven't spent a single night in it since we moved here, and you know it," he teased.

"Are you finished in here?" Alex asked, reaching out to stroke Flash.

"Almost. How was training?"

She groaned.

"Lost again, I see."

Glaring, she reached out to pinch Aaron.

He laughed and hugged her. "I know you're frustrated with your lack of control, but you'll get it back."

"Some days I have full control, and on others, it feels as if my powers are a pot boiling over with a clattering lid."

Aaron caressed her arm. "How did the last memory spell go?"

"Other than sneezing blue pebbles out of my nose? Nothing. Have I said anything new in my sleep?"

He huffed and rubbed the back of his neck. "Same as the last eight months. You cry for help and call his name."

Alex wrapped her arms around Aaron. "What if I can't get them back? Will you be able to live with it?"

His blue eyes sparkled like the sea as he looked down at her. "I'd learn to."

That isn't reassuring. "*Ferflucs!*" she grumbled.

"Now who has the temper?"

"Still you. I'm going to go to the lab and try one of those last spells I found."

"Want company?" Aaron winked as she stepped away.

Alex giggled. "You're a distraction, not help."

"It's not my fault I'm so handsome." Aaron kissed her cheek. "Go to the lab. I'll finish here and go to our room. Come up when you're done."

Alex cracked herself out of the stable and into her lab in the bowels of the castle. The fireplace and torches roared to life as soon as she arrived. She removed her sword and tossed it to the side, cracking it at the same time so that it landed on the table in her bedroom.

Why can I only control useless things? Alex glanced at a decimated chair in the corner, the latest victim of her uncontrolled power. Shaking her fear away, she snatched her notes from the desk and flipped through the last few pages.

"Only one more book to try." *A few more chances to get my memories back.*

She went to the bookshelves, and an icy chill hit her. She

looked up and saw Daniel, the ghost of Aaron's brother, staring at her with a frown and crossed arms.

"Don't look at me like that. I know you don't want me to get the memories back, but Aaron and I decided. You don't get a vote."

Daniel stepped aside. She undid her braid, scratched her head, and put her hair back up in a bun her lady's maid, Jessica, would be ashamed of. Scanning the books, she found the last one she needed to review.

"Then tell him the truth," Daniel said.

"It doesn't matter if I'm scared of what I'll learn. We agreed."

After she'd become a Returned One for a second time, Alex found she could hear ghosts in addition to seeing them—but only if she focused. Whenever she did, it quickly drained her, but Daniel was the exception.

She grabbed a book written by Merlin, her great-grandfather and the founder of the Merlin line. All the sorcerer lines had at least seventeen generations of sorcerers, all except the newest line of Merlin. He'd only had one son, Hermes, and that sorcerer only had three children: Moorloc, Merlock, and Victoria. The remaining children of her generation were the last of the line. Megesti and Alex were using these ancestral journals to help them with their powers, but no one knew where her cousin Lygari was. They hadn't heard any news of him since she'd accidentally banished him during the battle at Moorloc's castle.

She plopped the book down and rested her elbows on the table. There had to be another spell she could try. She flipped through the pages, but the closest she could find was a spell that could return lost things. She sighed and collected the needed herbs from the shelf behind her. Once everything was on the table, she filled a cauldron with water and swung it over the fire.

It took her a few hours to grind the herbs, mix the ingredients, and wait for the mixture to heat. Once it bubbled, the potion turned a swampy green and smelled of compost.

At this point, the spell required she add an element of what she wanted to bring back.

What do you add to bring back memories? She watched it bubble while she pondered and then pricked her finger, hoping her blood would help her remember where her scars had come from. The potion swallowed up the drops and turned bloodred. It smelled grotesque.

Alex lowered a jar into the cauldron and lifted it out full of the burning hot concoction. She wrapped her hands around it and used her Poseidon powers to cool the potion.

Icy wind hit her, and she spun around, expecting to see Daniel, but it wasn't. Startled, Alex dropped the jar, and it shattered, sending glass and thick red potion all over. Her heart pounded.

Her mother pointed at the cauldron and scowled. Then she sighed, and her shoulders dropped. She floated toward Alex and shook her head gently.

Alex swallowed. "*What?* You don't want me to get my memories back?"

Victoria stoically stared at her.

"Why? What happened that you don't want me to remember?"

Victoria frowned but stayed silent.

"I can hear you now, so stop being cryptic."

Alex's cheeks grew cold when her mother reached out and caressed her face. Ice prickled her forehead as Victoria softly kissed Alex and vanished.

She looked from the empty space where her mother had

been to the bubbling potion. "I want the truth. No more forgotten memories."

She grabbed a new jar, scooped the potion into it, and chilled it slightly. When she sniffed the brew, she had to turn her head away to avoid gagging. It smelled worse cold, worse than the dirty stables on a hot summer's day. She shuddered, plugged her nose, and chugged the entire jar of the foul concoction.

It tasted even worse than it smelled. Alex retched. The jar fell from her fingers and smashed on the floor, and she rushed to a bucket in the corner to throw up. Only a little of the potion came up. It was as though it had coated her insides. She rested her back against the wall and wiped her mouth when she heard the sound of a whip cracking.

She stumbled to her feet and rushed into the hallway. The torches roared to life, but no one was there. She climbed the stairs to the main hall and found it, too, was deserted. She ran through every part of the main floor, but she found nothing out of the ordinary.

The hair on her neck stood on end as she returned to the still empty hall.

Crack.

She turned and ran so fast she slipped on the smooth stones outside the library. She rushed through to her bedroom's secret door.

What is wrong with me? I must be hearing things. With her hand on the book that opened it, she covered her mouth and struggled to calm herself.

Finally feeling safe, Alex pulled the book, and her door opened. The fireplace was still glowing, providing a bit of light. Aaron was sound asleep, and her sword rested on the table with their matching crowns.

She draped her wet, potion-splattered clothes on the toy

chest she'd brought from her suite in Warren and put on her nightdress. She lifted the soft green quilt and slipped into bed. Before she could worry any more, Aaron rolled over and embraced her. Alex snuggled into him, inhaling the relaxing scent of pine and letting his warmth lull her to sleep.

GRYPHON

The ground was damp and freezing. Everything about the dungeon cell was wet.

Ares! I hate being wet.

Gryphon sat up and cracked his neck. His side and ribs throbbed from the beating Phobos had administered. This was a cell designed for Ares and Mystics sorcerers. Clearly, his hexa had planned this and put him in a cell between the Ares and Mystics wing and the Salem wing. Even if he hadn't been restrained, the dampness meant he couldn't use his fire powers to escape.

He'd been locked in the dungeon for a month now with a red steel bracelet on each wrist. It didn't surprise him they'd gone to these extremes. Usually, a punishment from his parents meant not leaving the castle, but this time, the Heart was involved. After Lygari arrived and ratted him out, his parents, Garrick and Imelda, had locked him in his bedroom and starved him for a week before they questioned him about how he'd found her. He pretended to give in, but he only confessed to helping her. After that, Garrick ordered his son to stay away from the mortal world and not to go near Alex, and Gryphon agreed. Then, the first chance he'd had, he cracked to her.

She was by that old little castle that had Victoria's magical essence all over it. He'd discovered her and Megesti in the nearby forest. They'd been holding a book and working together to learn a Salem spell. When it got out of control, Alex conjured water to put it out. They clearly weren't discouraged and kept trying over and over.

Alex was still malnourished, but with a book in her hand and Megesti at her side, she seemed happy. He'd watched them for hours until her cheeks grew pink from exertion. Satisfied that she was safe and content, he'd returned home without wanting to interfere in her life any more than he already had. That's when his father's sycophant, Phobos, caught him, resulting in his new accommodations.

After learning his son had helped Alexandria, Garrick had been furious in front of the other sorcerers, but since being locked down here, Gryphon learned he'd played right into their hands. His family had plans for Alexandria. Eris, his mother's mother—his maternal hexa—was a proud Ares sorceress, and she had suspected the sorceress Heart would appear in his generation. She was desperate to get Alex bonded to him so they could create the next sorcerer generation while she was still alive. Eris told of an old Ares legend about an Ares and Cassandra coming together to make the most powerful sorcerer who would ever live. Gryphon had read all the Ares books in their library and never found this legend, but clearly his hexa's premonition had been correct.

It seemed his family had known where the Heart was all along, but they had repeatedly failed to retrieve her, enraging his hexa to no end. Nevertheless, she claimed to have played a successful role in their plot but wouldn't say more. Garrick had attempted to retrieve Victoria when she was pregnant with Alex, but he'd failed because Victoria had fallen in love with Edward by then. Imelda had been sent to find Alex as a child, but she'd also failed since Alex was so well hidden because of her magical necklace. Thus, the job fell to an unwitting Gryphon. By answering Alex's call for help, he'd accidentally played right into their hands. Thanks to Lygari's big mouth, they knew about Aaron, how powerful Alex was, and her mother's castle.

Gryphon had tried everything to keep from revealing her weaknesses, but his father was still the most powerful Mystics sorcerer alive, and once the bracelets were on, he could force himself into Gryphon's mind. He fought back—which made the process excruciatingly painful—and he'd managed to keep a few things from his father, namely Alex's beloved brothers and ladies. When he'd failed to extract the information he wanted, Garrick locked Gryphon in the dungeon, hoping it would get him to talk. But Gryphon would rather die than help them hurt Alex.

Footsteps echoed in the hallway outside of his cell. He knew it was his parents before they even reached the door.

"Have you come to your senses, Gryphon?" Imelda asked. His mother was a voluptuous woman with pink skin, strawberry blonde hair, and blue eyes. Gryphon had towered over her by the time he was thirteen. She wore the Tiere titan cloak even though she'd given up her title to marry his father and become the mother of the next Head. Gryphon found it laughable, considering how little work she'd done raising him. She'd left the hard work to her adopted sister, Birch.

As usual, Imelda had her sleeves rolled up to her elbows, a habit she developed as a young sorceress to keep her cloak clean while working with animals. It also showed off the scar that ran down her left forearm. She'd never told him where it came from.

Glaring, Garrick didn't speak. It only took one glance to see Gryphon was his son, a fact that Gryphon himself loathed. His two-colored black hair came from his father; except Gryphon had a streak of blond through his black hair, an inheritance from his mother, and his father's streak was gray. They had the same bronze complexion, and their eyes were the same gold color.

"And just what am I to come to my senses about, Mother?"

Imelda sighed and placed her hands on her hips. "You know why you're down here. We're finished playing games with you. The Heart is dangerously powerful for her age. She needs our help to learn to control her powers before she hurts herself. We need you to convince her to come to us. It would be better for everyone if she came willingly."

Gryphon scoffed. "Meaning you can't force her to come here, so you need me to manipulate her. Why is that, Mother? Afraid you'll fail again?"

"Catch your tongue, or you'll regret it," Garrick snapped. He was in a foul mood, but Gryphon didn't care. He knew his family too well. They were up to something, and he'd never agree to be part of whatever plan they had to hurt Alex.

"Take off my bracelets, and we'll see if you can make me regret it."

"We're giving you one last chance to come to your senses," said Garrick. "One last opportunity to help us bring *your* Heart home. I lost my Cassandra to a mortal. Are you willing to lose yours too?" His father spoke with the same haughty smugness Gryphon had used when he talked to Aaron and Alex's mortal friends.

"Nature rarely gives sorcerers a bond with the same depth as that which occurs between a Head and Heart," Imelda said.

"You can't ignore it, and you can't possibly want to wait for that mortal mutt who has her now to grow old and die. Ares sorcerers take what they want."

"I'm well aware of what Ares sorcerers do, Mother."

Someone else answered, saying, "I hardly believe that, youngling."

They all turned to find his hexa standing in the doorway. Eris's once powerful body had withered with age. Her skeletal physique made her appear weak, a dangerous assumption that she would use against anyone foolish enough to underestimate her. Despite being nearly three hundred years old, Eris stepped proudly into the room, never once taking her eyes off Gryphon. One eye was gold, and the other was blue. Most lines loved having their hexa or hexen alive to teach the younger sorcerers —but they didn't have the Ares violence and craving for power. Eris shuffled toward him and grabbed his face between her bony fingers.

"Remind me again what your dominant power is, Gryphon."

"Ares."

"Do you consider yourself worthy of that title? You let that mortal boy leave with *your sorceress*. You should have killed him the moment you laid eyes on him and taken your Heart. Are you aware of how our bonds work?"

"Of course I am." Gryphon tore himself from her grasp. "We can lock a nature bond several ways, but the fastest is by establishing a connection."

"And how does a sorceress connect?" Eris asked.

Gryphon looked at the dirt floor. He wouldn't give them the satisfaction of answering.

"With intercourse," Garrick answered. "All you had to do was take her once, and she'd be yours. Even if the mortal part of her still wanted that simpleton, the sorceress part would know better."

"That isn't how I'm going to win her. Alex deserves better."

"Alex? You call the Heart by a nickname? Perhaps you didn't fail as much as we thought." His mother smirked at him as she crossed her arms and cocked her head to the side. "Tell us more about *Alex*."

"No." Gryphon slunk back, his throbbing ribs reminding him of Phobos's beating the night before. Phobos wasn't with them, which meant they weren't planning physical abuse this time. His parents wouldn't bother getting their own hands dirty.

"Darling, you thought that was a request?" Imelda grinned at him as his father stepped forward, his hands extended.

Garrick gripped Gryphon's temples, and a sharp pain bored into his head to find the secrets he'd kept from them. Gryphon used all his Mystics powers to fight back against his father, sending dreams, useless information, and outright lies into the mix of memories his father was hunting through.

Gryphon's head was on fire as he fought the red steel on his wrist, but his powers were draining quickly. Just when he felt he couldn't hold out any longer, alarm bells echoed in the hallway.

"What now?" Eris snapped.

Garrick released Gryphon and turned. "Your useless sister is in my library. No doubt trying to steal more of her father's books."

"Leave Birch alone." Gryphon lunged for his father, but the red steel had weakened him so much that all his father had to do was grab his shoulder. Garrick's hand seared through his tunic and skin, and the stench of burning flesh wafted in the air before his father slammed him to the ground. Gryphon had to fight back tears.

"Leave him," Eris said. "We'll deal with Birch and come back. It's not as though he can go anywhere."

The three sorcerers cracked away, leaving Gryphon alone in his cell. He closed his eyes and tried to summon his Salem power to extinguish the burning in his shoulder. Soon, he heard a key unlock his door. He looked up and saw two figures in gray cloaks.

"Kharon?" he asked.

The first sorcerous dropped their hood, revealing black hair, blue eyes, ghostly pale skin, and a kind smile. "Who else could sneak by unnoticed? No one ever pays attention to Hades sorcerers," Kharon said.

"Considering your robes match the stone walls, I'm not surprised," Lynx said, pulling off her own hood. Even in the dull light, her gold hair sparkled against her tan skin, though her brown eyes were full of fear as she looked Gryphon over.

"What are you doing here?" he asked.

"Isn't it obvious? We're breaking you out," Lynx whispered.

"Birch went to the library to distract your parents and hexa," Kharon said.

"Give me your wrists," Lynx said.

Gryphon held up his hands. Lynx took them in hers and yipped and snarled at the bracelets.

"Of course Mother used wolf magic," Gryphon groaned as the bracelets fell off.

"Did you expect her to *not* use her Tiere powers to bind you? Do you know her at all?" Lynx asked, shaking her head as Kharon helped Gryphon to his feet.

"Can you crack?" Kharon asked as they slid their arm around Gryphon's shoulders. Lynx supported him from the other side.

"I don't think so. I used up everything I had left to keep my father from finding out anything more about Alex."

Kharon and Lynx nodded to each other and cracked them all to the worn stone path that led to Birch's cottage. A moment later, Birch appeared behind them.

"That was an adventure. I got two books this time!"

"You actually stole books?" Lynx asked.

"Naturally. Can't have them thinking I had anything to do with this escape. Now, bring him inside so I can look him over. I suspect he's starving."

"And he was roughed up," Lynx added. "Phobos was in too good of a mood this week."

They had to turn sideways to navigate the narrow path. A menagerie of plants had taken over the yard around Birch's tiny cottage. Once inside, Kharon brought Gryphon to the couch, and the friendly little birds that lived there chirped and rushed to him, sitting on his head and shoulders. Birch handed Gryphon a large mug of foul-smelling liquid. He groaned.

"Drink it," she said. "Your mother and hexa haven't found my new home in decades. If you want to hide here and be safe, we need you hidden from Mystics and kin." She paused. "I added apple blossoms!"

Gryphon sighed and chugged the entire thing as Lynx hurried back from the kitchen with a mug of water.

"Do you have anything for his wrists?" Kharon asked Birch.

Birch grabbed Gryphon's hand and gasped when she saw that the skin where the bracelet had been was completely raw and blistered. "Your parents put you in a red steel bracelet?"

Gryphon nodded and showed her his other wrist. Birch went pale as she bit her bottom lip. He knew that look well; she was trying not to cry. She hadn't let go yet, and he gripped her hand as she hiccuped.

"Thank you … for getting me out," he said. "All of you. I know you risked everything, and I have no way to repay you."

"Don't mention it," Kharon said. "No one will ever suspect I was involved. Hades sorcerers are boring."

Lynx sat beside him and gently took his free hand in hers. "You'd have gotten out eventually, and they would have accused Birch and me of helping you escape, even if you did it on your own. At least this way I'm actually guilty of it, and I can sleep at night knowing I didn't leave you to rot down there."

Birch tossed Lynx a tin of ointment. When she opened it, both Lynx and Gryphon wrinkled their noses and turned away. The overpowering scent of peppermint stung their eyes.

"Put some on his shoulder too," Birch said. "I can smell the burn from here."

Gryphon removed his shirt, and Lynx sighed as she rubbed the ointment into the blistering red handprint that had been burned into him.

After the ointment soaked in, Birch handed him a drink.

He raised his eyebrows. "Another?"

"For sleeping. I'm no Cassandra, so you're going to have to heal the old-fashioned way—with rest."

Gryphon plugged his nose and chugged the potion. As he handed the mug back to Birch, he could already feel it kicking in.

"Rest up, Gryphon." Lynx's voice became softer and more distant as it vanished into silence. "You're safe now."

If you love the series and want to grab a signed copy or some official merch, check out The Head, the Heart, and the Heir store at AliceHanov.com.

www.ingramcontent.com/pod-product-compliance
Lightning Source LLC
Chambersburg PA
CBHW050844210726
48290CB00004B/1074